Dark Passages

Pomegranate Press, Ltd.
NEW YORK | LOS ANGELES

This book is a work of fiction. Any use of real names, places or events is done in a wholly fictitious manner and not to be taken literally. The story is written with more than a passing nod to both the 1960s television series *Dark Shadows* and the New York Playboy Club, but the characters and events in this novel are completely imaginary and not to be ascribed to any real people, living or deceased. Any resemblance to real people or events is entirely a matter of coincidence.

Printed in the United States of America
First Edition: July 2011
10 9 8 7 6 5 4 3 2 1

Library of Congress Control Number: 2011920364

ISBN: 978-0-938817-83-3
Pomegranate Press, Ltd.
PO Box 17217
Beverly Hills, CA 90209

www.kathrynleighscott.com
www.pompress.com

Book design: Cheryl Carrington

Front cover design: Nicholas Evans

For Geoff, as always.

Special thanks to my agent, Cynthia Manson, for her unfailing support and encouragement. Also, my sincere thanks to Eric Wallace, Cheryl Carrington, Jonathan Frid, Susan Sullivan, Brian Kellow, Nicholas Evans, Jo-an Jenkins, Bridget Hedison, Rob Larsen, Laurie Drake, Robert Masello, Ben Martin, Heather Cameron, David Ouimet, Mark Dawidziak, Harry Hennig, Tom Kringstad, Barbara Kringstad, and my good friends in Stony Creek, Hannah and Joel Baldwin. To all my *Dark Shadows* and "Bunny" friends, I hope you get a kick out of my wild imaginings.

Author's Note

I've written *Dark Passages* with an affectionate nod to both the New York Playboy Club, where I worked as a Bunny, and *Dark Shadows,* the '60s soap opera in which I played Josette DuPrés, the doomed fiancée of vampire Barnabas Collins. In *The Bunny Years* and my books about *Dark Shadows*, I've told the story of what really happened all those years ago when I turned in my Bunny ears and joined a small company of actors to create the world of *Dark Shadows.* Now I'm satisfying my itch to write a novel about that time, that world—combining elements of horror and fantasy to tell a story about a vampire, a witch and unrequited love.

—Kathryn Leigh Scott

Prologue

I call myself Meg Harrison, although that's not the name I was given at birth. And there is no name for what I am, other than "vampire," although that hardly defines who I am. I'm certainly not the creature portrayed in folklore, a dead person rising each night from the grave to suck blood from the living for sustenance. Nor am I a craven creature who preys on other people, hunting them to satisfy my own malevolent desires. I am a living, organically developing, non-human being inhabiting the world of humans. I function like most of my contemporaries, and have no knowledge of a past life as an undead creature. But while my essential composition and appearance is that of an ordinary human, I am on the most fundamental level, non-human.

My mother, Ruth, who passed her gift to me, provided little guidance. So far, my path has been one of self-discovery, learning that I am of a breed born of vampiric mothers into human families and utilizing human bodies. My own body is standard issue Northern European Caucasian of a late-blooming variety. Discovering my gifts and learning to harness them has been an arduous pursuit, and one I cannot abandon.

My mortal life will soon depend on my mastery of these vampiric powers.

Growing up, I wasn't much to look at—an end-of-the-gym-line runt, with crooked teeth and pudgy cheeks. Adolescence was no picnic. My sharpened senses, especially hearing, made me privy to every whispered mean-girl barb. I retaliated, of course—lunch passes and eyeglasses went missing, muddy puddles inexplicably oozed over brand-new shoes—but I usually felt bad afterward, a notably human response.

Marilyn, whom I've known since kindergarten, befriended me early on as a lost cause. She claims she can never figure me out, and that's good. Occasionally I freak her out, just for fun. Crossing the cornfield to Twin Lakes Elementary one morning, Marilyn got hysterical when we came across a rabbit struggling to free its hind leg from a trap. While Marilyn raced around looking for something to pry apart the sharp metal jaws, I knelt in the dirt and pressed my lips to the warm blood oozing through the rabbit fur. It was found blood, practically road kill. Waste not, want not, I thought, as I lapped up bunny blood while my fingers snapped the spring loose on the trap.

"What are you doing down there?" Marilyn shrieked. I brushed blood from my lips on the rabbit's fur before holding the limp animal up for her to see. "You didn't give it mouth-to-mouth, did you?"

"Of course not, it must have kicked me," I said, looking into her horrified eyes. "It was just hard to see the little thingy down there that pops the spring."

"Put it down! Get rid of it! You've got icky blood all over you!"

Marilyn, who had been so concerned about saving the rabbit, screamed that I'd pick up a disease just touching it. In fact, I'd sucked up an ounce of pure unrefined fuel. The rabbit could spare the blood, and I'd spared its life, so I saw it as an even trade.

Tanked up, I later knocked a softball over the treetops during gym class (hard to explain that one!) and practically steamed up the pool swimming laps after school. Inscrutability is my best cover, but outright lying works well, too. Besides I wouldn't want to offend Marilyn's sensibilities by mentioning that I'm a vampire. The knowledge wouldn't frighten her so much as provide her with another righteous challenge to meet head on. She would make a futile attempt to cure me "for your own good" because Marilyn always thinks she knows best.

But I was born this way and cannot change. The essence of my being is so powerful, that whether I ever acknowledged my true nature consciously or not, the elements that form me control me. I cannot be deprogrammed, despite Marilyn's best efforts. I am what I am.

Daylight, contrary to popular vampire lore, has never been an issue, incineration by sunlight never a concern for me. I'm nocturnal by preference, but I've grown up on a working farm, where the ability to function during daylight hours is mandatory. Sunlight has also proven to be an energy source, though not a means of getting a tan. My skin does not turn brown any more than it burns, but the sun's rays do produce a fine, pale down on my face and body that probably serves to protect non-humans like me from the harmful nature of the sun's rays, such as sparking immolation.

Being vampiric, I have a pronounced craving for blood, but counter it with an acquired ability to deny myself as a means of controlling the powerful energy it unleashes. I do not become ill when I go without blood, but neither do I function at full capacity. On a human level, I appear normal. I do not have fangs, although when I lost my baby teeth at age six, pronounced incisors that conceal feeding tubes grew in their place. Needless to say, my mother never took me to a doctor or dentist. Frankly there's no need, since my teeth do not decay and broken bones heal almost immediately.

My empathy with the dead is my greatest gift. It is the dead and recently departed who seek me out, humans who willingly submit themselves to my ability to manipulate and influence events. My need is sufficient to summon them. Grandpa Egstrom was the first to appear to me. He was a bantamweight former prizefighter and volunteer fireman, who died around the time my kid brother Eddie was born. I couldn't imagine life without Grandpa Egstrom, who had built a cabinet for my chemistry set and hand-carved toy ducks and whistles. One morning shortly after he died, I sneaked up into one of the apple trees and saw Grandpa Egstrom sitting in the crook of a branch just above me.

"I was just thinking about you," I said, somehow not that surprised to see him up there. He was wearing the faded red plaid shirt with rolled-up sleeves that showed off his bulging biceps. A bristly fringe of white hair formed a half-moon around a bald pate as shiny and rosy as his cheeks. He still smelled of Old Briar pipe tobacco and Luden's cherry cough drops. "I missed you."

He smiled. "I know. I was kind'a waitin' for you to call me."

"I called you? How did I do that?"

"That's not something I would know," he said, "but I'm glad to be here. Anything you need?"

"Just to see you again." But then an apple appeared in my hand, the pink-tinged green apple I'd wanted that had been beyond my reach. My ears were ringing as I rolled the apple in my hand. "How'd you do that, Grandpa?"

"You did it." He shook his head. "Ruthie ought'a talk to you about more'n birds and bees. This is stuff I don't know a thing about, but your grandma did. So does Ruthie."

"So I'm not adopted?"

"No such luck," he smiled. "You'll just have to figure it all out. That's what Ruthie had to do. And you're just the same as her."

My mother would have been an altogether different person had her mother survived childbirth and been able to give her daughter the instruction she required to use her inherited gifts. By the same token, if my mother hadn't strived so hard to pass as a normal human being, she would have instructed me more generously. I could have used a few pointers on such topics as blood and communing with the dead. But, like my mother, I grew up an autodidact in the use of my powers.

I'm therefore isolated by my awareness of what I am: essentially a loner, although I seldom feel lonely. I'm good at keeping things to myself, separating who I am from what I am. My imagination serves me well, play-acting to pass for normal. It's hardly surprising that I usually got leads in school plays. How could I not be drawn to acting as my chosen career? With my heart set on becoming an actor, New York was the place to go as soon as I could break free of Twin Lakes, Minnesota. Nothing was going to hold me back.

Sex is not something I can adequately address because I'm presently a virgin. By choice. Despite my urges, I managed to control the impulse to go all the way with Eric, my sort-of high school boyfriend. We met working part-time at the Red Owl supermarket, he as a box boy and me on checkout, wearing a tomato-red rayon uniform with a googly-eyed owl over the breast pocket. Eric, who'd got his civilian pilot's license at age sixteen and spent a summer rebuilding an old 1946 Taylorcraft he'd bought at a farm auction, wanted nothing more than to join the Air Force.

We both feared that "going all the way" could lead to a dreaded outcome: chained to each other and the town of Twin Lakes unto eternity. This lore became fact when our Twin Lakes Homecoming Queen and the captain of our championship football team headed to Iowa after the big game to get married. Bonnie, already three months' pregnant, did not return to school. Roy turned down a university athletic scholarship to take a job at his dad's filling station. Eric is human, but so am I in this regard: we both viewed this turn of events as a cautionary tale, a car wreck with no survivors.

And, should I get knocked up, there's the added concern of bringing another vampire into the world. Would I rear a vampire better than my mother? I couldn't say. Besides, the one thing my mother was at pains to tell me is that childbirth for the likes of us could be lethal. "You could be the end of the line," she said, looking surprisingly hopeful at the thought.

Against all odds, in high school I started blossoming into something decent to look at. By age eighteen I was in full bloom. I was tall and lithe like my mother, and had her violet eyes, pale skin and thick chestnut-colored hair. This miracle did not go unnoticed in town, and I was pressed into service as a Miss Twin Lakes contestant in the 1962 Corn Husker Festival. Wearing my white satin strapless prom dress with the bouffant tulle skirt, I won the crown. No one was more surprised than me, except perhaps Marilyn, who said she'd never been so shocked in her entire life.

Still wearing my queenly regalia and rhinestone crown, I went for a spin with Eric in his newly refurbished single-engine, fixed wing Taylorcraft so we could survey my kingdom, pop. 6,790. The sheer pleasure of watching Eric at the controls of his airplane was reason enough to enjoy the ride. The view was nothing new for me. Perhaps the gift I most treasured was my ability to leave my body and soar high in the sky at a speed that could far out-distance Eric's Taylorcraft. I could also hover above a crowd, or the town of Twin Lakes, which provided me with a perspective not available to a human. Gliding on my own high above the fields, I could hear the sounds of scuttling insects and chirping birds, instead of the muffled thrumming of the Taylorcraft's four-cylinder engine. Flying his airplane gave Eric his own aerial view, and I shared his joy.

But skimming over a golden wheat field late in the afternoon, a huge buzzard smashed into the wooden propeller, shattering a blade. In the instant the bird struck, its raptor eyes locked on mine, emanating such hatred and spite that I gasped with fright. My hands flew up to shield myself.

"Easy, it's okay," Eric said, his voice calm.

Suddenly, as the blade splintered and broke away, the buzzard vanished, with no sign of flying guts and feathers. The engine rumbled, vibrating hideously. I was afraid it would break loose from its mountings. I glanced at Eric. His face was pale but betrayed no panic as he pulled back the throttle and cut power. "We're fine. Stay cool."

"The boy's right," Grandpa Egstrom said. He was perched on one of the cloth-covered wings, looking contented. "This plane's made to glide, if you know what you're doing. You just enjoy the view."

And I did. With Eric gently feathering the controls, we glided over a stand of birch trees, sailed across my dad's cornfields and landed smoothly on the packed earth behind our barn.

"Gotcha home in one piece," Eric said, his brow glistening with sweat. His hands remained gripped to the yoke as he spoke, his knuckles bone white. My heart rocketed. I leaned over and kissed him, feeling rapture I hadn't experienced before. He hadn't needed my help. And he was human!

"You want to have supper at our place?" I asked, fluffing the tulle of my prom dress.

Eric and I left town at about the same time, heading in opposite directions. "You're letting him slip away," Marilyn warned me. "Some other girl's going to grab him. He looks enough like Troy Donahue to be his twin."

But that wasn't our deal. We needed to go our separate ways. The only one I wanted to take with me to New York was Grandpa

Egstrom. I found him up in the apple tree shortly before I headed for the airport.

"Sorry, gal. I'm staying put. The big city isn't for me."

"But I'll be alone."

"Not for long. Besides, you're eighteen. You can handle yourself. Just keep an eye out for that damn buzzard—whatever shape it takes."

One

Until my acting career took off I managed to keep myself fed and sheltered by working as a Bunny in the New York Playboy Club—or, as my kid brother, Eddie, back in Twin Lakes had smirked, "walking around half-naked serving highballs."

I'd been in New York for a little over eight months, arriving just in time for the Cuban Missile Crisis. On that chilly morning in late October, 1962, I'd skipped past the front-page doomsday news to check the help-wanted listings for a bread-and-butter job that wouldn't interfere with auditions and acting class. An ad announcing tryouts for Playboy Bunny jobs caught my eye: Girls! Step Into the Spotlight! Be A Playboy Bunny! Earn Several Hundred Dollars A Week!

Pictured in the ad was a pretty brunette, breasts overflowing in what appeared to be a one-piece bathing suit, wearing rabbit ears on her head and smiling winsomely. Since winning the Miss Twin Lakes crown that summer, I knew I could deliver winsome, if not cleavage. As further enticement, the small print stated: No Waitressing Experience Required.

I gulped my coffee, grabbed my dance leotard and raced from the Rehearsal Club, a boarding house for aspiring actresses (Carol Burnett was a famous alumna), to the Playboy Club just off Fifth Avenue. If I got the job, I could afford an apartment of my own, acting classes and maybe even a new winter coat. Besides, working nights suited me better than a daytime job as an office temp.

I caught my breath at a traffic light on Sixth Avenue and scanned the headlines at a newsstand. MISSILES POISED. JFK, KHRUSCHEV IN CUBAN DEADLOCK. WARHEADS AIMED AT NYC. Around me people hurried by with their heads down. Fidel Castro and President John F. Kennedy were playing a terrifying game of chicken with nuclear weapons. It seemed Russian-made missiles in Cuba were poised to annihilate the city I'd come to love within a matter of days and with it, all my girlhood dreams.

It had taken me no time to realize New York held every allure imaginable for a vampiric creature. Most appealing was the anonymity of the big city. No one paid attention to anyone else. Without being entirely reckless, I could let my guard down in ways I'd never been able to in Twin Lakes.

I basked in the brisk night air of Central Park my first night in town, feasting on the first burst of blood from a fresh-killed pheasant, leaving the carrion to the coyote that hunted it. Fueled and feeling frisky in the silvery moonlight, I swam among the swans in the pond and scrambled through brambles in search of voles. Sour-smelling humans, curled on benches and hunkered inside cardboard cartons under bridges, saw me as a flickering shadow if they saw me at all. At dawn I sat on cold, hard rock nursing a monumental headache. I surveyed my scrapes and scratches, waiting for them to heal, knowing I'd overindulged. I learned to practice some moderation after that, but still spent nights on the town, exploring. This couldn't come to an end so soon!

I glanced up at the sullen sky, trying to imagine what a missile would look like screaming through the thick blanket of cloud. I quickly figured out I was as close to Ground Zero as I could be, without actually sitting in the Palm Court of the Plaza Hotel. Images of Nagasaki came to mind. What would happen if a warhead fell? Would there be any warning? However powerful my gifts, I knew I was no match for it. The light changed and I shot across the street, racing toward the very crossroads of Manhattan.

Ahead, I could already see the long line of Bunny hopefuls stretching around the corner of 59th Street and Fifth Avenue. Would I get a Bunny job before the End of the World?

Breathless, I took my place in the queue, my eyes trained on the curved brass staircase gleaming through the plate glass window of the Playboy Club, then shut my mind to whatever calamity might plummet through the cement-gray skies overhead. I somehow knew the crisis would pass. Instead of a missile, the sun would pierce the cloud cover, and I would get a Bunny job.

The opening of the new Playboy Club was stalled by key club and liquor license woes, but during the interim we earned minimum wage while in Bunny training. Day after day, clad in tight-fitting satin costumes, we marched around in our stiletto heels in a kind of boot camp learning the signature moves. The famous Bunny Dip (knees together, back arched away from the keyholder while serving drinks); Bunny Perch (knees together, back straight, sitting on the edge of a railing or chair arm); Bunny Stance (model pose) and High-Carry (fully loaded ten-pound tray carried on one hand at least shoulder high while maneuvering through a crowded room—not for the faint-hearted or weak-limbed) were all designed to flatter a silhouette encased in satin corsetry. Needless to say, the High Carry was a piece of cake for me.

For added value, these poses also served to keep breasts from popping out of strapless overstuffed cups and maintain a proprietary distance from any keyholder with a yen to grope a Bunny. We were warned that the fluffy cottontails we wore on our rear ends practically invited pawing. If a keyholder succumbed to the temptation, we were instructed to say, "Sir, please don't touch a Bunny." If that didn't work, one could always dump a tray full of drinks in the offender's lap. My own specialty with an irksome Club member was to heat up his key to branding-iron intensity that either scorched his suit or left its mark on his hind quarters.

By the time the Club opened in early December, I'd also got to know the other young cocktail Bunnies. We were a mixed bag; every size, shape and hue. Noni, a Jamaican folk singer with a husky voice and caramel-colored skin, had grown up in Newark public housing. Allie, an Upper East Side Chapin graduate, was a lithe sophisticate, who quickly became our Media Bunny. She'd already appeared on *What's My Line* and the *Garry Moore Show* to promote the Club. Gloria was a bubbly, pneumatic blonde from Staten Island, who loved to party. Elke, an East German refugee with a toddler named Elle, had escaped Berlin only days before the Wall went up. She'd married a G.I. and become pregnant, only to lose her husband in a deadly Jeep accident months before Elle was born.

The leader of our pack was Savannah, a gangly Wyoming prairie girl, who was allowed to park her motorcycle inside the employee entrance. When I first got to know Savannah at the Club, she was renting a couple of floors above a grimy shop front in a crummy area of Manhattan's meatpacking district near the Hudson River. The sagging four-story brick and clapboard structure huddled on the corner of a cobblestone street in a neighborhood of dilapidated warehouses and stinking refuse.

The place had belonged to a folksinger Savannah met in a coffeehouse. She went home with him, ended up moving in and then stayed on when he left to go on the road. Eventually he sent a postcard from Northern California telling her he was moving to Mendocino. Savannah immediately tracked down the owner and, with her Playboy earnings, bought the whole building. At first she rented out the ground floor shop to a restaurant supply outfit and made ends meet by renting rooms to other Bunnies. Among the first to move in were Elke and her baby.

The structure, already a century old when Savannah moved in, turned out to be a real find. It was a nook and cranny sort of place with fireplaces in every room and odd built-ins cobbled together from mismatched materials, all with a satiny patina of age. I'd jumped at Savannah's offer to move in. Everyone chipped in for groceries. Meals were family style and we all pitched in. Savannah was Mother Earth incarnate, and we always seemed to awaken to the smell of baking bread and bowls of homemade granola.

But once under Savannah's roof, I soon realized I was being scrutinized far more than was comfortable or safe for me. New to New York and unused to living among non-family mortals, I hadn't bothered to conceal some of my customary predilections.

My irregular eating habits and nocturnal prowling drove Savannah crazy. She wondered why my bed wasn't slept in some nights, and how I managed to remove a hot teakettle from the stove bare-handed without getting burned. If Elke, Noni and Allie, who were all living with Savannah at the time, caught me doing something peculiar, I could pass it off with some excuse. I had dozens of explanations on tap but none that worked with Savannah.

Not that she wasn't odd in her own way. Savannah liked guns and was a crack shot. She had grown up around firearms in Wyoming and I think saw herself as some sort of High Plains sheriff. When shots rang out late at night, it was Savannah ("just target practice") wiping out rats ("Some so big you could saddle 'em") that swarmed around the bins in the narrow side alley. She also managed to terrorize the smelly bums that occupied the desolate street corner near her house, who warmed themselves throughout the night with fires they lit in refuse bins.

In her twin roles as Mother Earth Incarnate and High Plains Sheriff, Savannah would walk to the corner offering leftovers from our dinner in exchange for assurances the men would clean up litter and not sleep on her doorstep. I accompanied her on a few occasions and witnessed their timidity in her presence. They'd seen her pop off rats. I'm sure they figured she was always packing heat.

But unless I could curb my own wayward habits, I knew I couldn't room with Savannah for long. One Saturday night, with a full moon blooming in a black velvet sky, I took a midnight roam through Central Park, feasting on squirrel before returning to Savannah's house. The other Bunnies rooming there were all in bed. I went up to the rooftop and perched on the chimney to count stars.

Within minutes I heard Savannah opening the spring-latch door. Damn! I didn't want to be found and have to account for myself yet again. I chose a quick escape option.

Instantly I transformed myself into an owl, a shape I'm practiced in, but is no more inner-urban-appropriate for a New York rooftop than a rabbit, fox or wolf. I should've done squirrel, but it was too late. I perched on the chimney edge, my wristwatch safeguarded in a talon. Without it, I could not transform back. I could only hope Savannah wouldn't see me. With my dull plumage and rigid stillness, there was a good chance she wouldn't. I watched, unblinking, as she emerged from the stairway onto the roof, a bottle of beer in her hand.

"Meg? Meg, where are you? I know you're up here. I want to talk."

I hadn't counted on that. If she'd heard or seen me go to the rooftop, I'd have to eventually explain why I couldn't be found. I watched her peer over the edge of the crumbling crown of masonry surrounding the rooftop, then walk through the long shadows cast by the vents and tall water barrel searching for me. In huntress mode, Savannah stood stock still, her head slowly rotating until her eyes settled on me, an owl perched on the chimney.

"Where did you come from?" She spoke calmly, her voice quiet as a whisper. "What a beauty! And look, you've got yourself a shiny little prize."

My wristwatch, glinting in the moonlight, had caught Savannah's eye. Slowly she set the beer bottle on top of a vent and assumed a wide stance even as she reached inside her waistband. I knew what was coming. If I'd turned myself into a rat (a transformation I find truly repellent), I'd be a goner in a flash. The downside of transforming is that one is vulnerable to harm, even death, while inhabiting a shape. I dug my talon into the brick, securing the watch, my only means of regaining my own identity. I needed to fly, disappear, transform —but in that flash of hesitation, I found myself looking, unblinking, into the muzzle of Savannah's gun. She held me in her sights, her aim precise. Then, with doom as certain as Savannah's need for target practice, she lifted the gun and swung it away.

"Not you, little owl," she whispered, and turned back to the edge of the rooftop, aiming down into the back alley at the bins.

The bums were used to this. I wasn't. And I didn't enjoy being a target. Even as she fired her first shot at a rat, I'd already transformed and tumbled down the backside of the chimney. I scrambled to my feet and brushed myself off.

"Meg? Is that you? What're you doing back there?"

"Hi, Savannah," I said, emerging from the shadow of the chimney. "What're you doing up here?"

"Looking for you. Didn't you hear me?"

"Nope, not until you started shooting. Say, did you see that owl? What a beauty. Got another beer?"

It was a close call, close enough that I decided to find my own digs. Within a week I'd moved into my beloved Gramercy Park studio apartment. I still loved visiting my Bunny friends at Savannah's house, but signing the lease made me feel like a bona fide New Yorker. I had a job, an apartment of my own and I could do as I pleased.

I was happy when word got around my old home town that I was working as a Bunny, even though more than one of my former classmates had asked my brother, "What month is she?" The ignorance in Twin Lakes was stupefying. Didn't anyone know the difference between a Bunny and a Playmate? Serving food and drink in a Bunny costume was one thing; posing starkers in the magazine with a staple through my belly button quite another.

While I enjoyed the notoriety back home, in New York no one outside the Club knew about my secret life as a Bunny, any more than anyone knew about my status as a non-human. The Playboy job held a certain cachet in some circles, but it hadn't taken me long to learn that once someone knew you worked as a Bunny, a veil fell. It was death for a serious actress, definitely the wrong signal to send if you wanted a role, not a date. Therefore, out of practical necessity, my bread-and-butter job and my aspirations for a theatrical career occupied two separate worlds —but then, I was used to keeping certain aspects of my life secret.

Even Wesley Truscott, my agent, didn't know I worked as a Bunny. He was a somewhat fatherly figure—although my own father wouldn't have been caught dead wearing a paisley cravat and clear varnish on his fingernails. An appropriate occasion never arose when I felt I could tell my agent I worked as Bunny Meg on the 5 P.M. cocktail shift, not even the day he called late in the afternoon with an audition for a new soap opera.

"The call just came in, kiddo," he said. "Put on your track shoes and run!"

In pouring rain, a taxi hauled me through cross-town traffic to a studio near Tenth Avenue, in an area known as Hell's Kitchen. Wesley had said the role was that of a governess, supposedly the lead character in a soap called *Dark Passages*. I signed my name on a call sheet and picked up three pages of script sides. At least a dozen other actresses were ahead of me, with more arriving in the crowded holding pen every minute. I tensed, knowing I'd be late for work at the Club.

At last my turn came. As I jumped up, my stocking got snagged on a screw in the chair. My heart caved in as a run zippered down my leg—but I couldn't get it to zipper up again! What was wrong? It should have been a snap reversing a mishap as basic as a run in my stocking. I glanced around the room, looking for an energy source capable of crippling my own. Some force was blocking me, but I couldn't identify its origin, certainly not in the faces of the other actresses who looked my way. Panicked, I bolted into the audition room, moving as fast as humanly normal, hoping nothing would cause me to trip. I lunged for a straight-back chair and stood frozen, one leg wound behind the other to hide my ruined stocking. I could not make myself sit down. My hand was fastened to the back of the chair in a death grip.

DeeDee Snyder, a plump, sweet-faced casting director I'd met on a go-see some weeks earlier, looked at me uncertainly. "It's up to you," she said. "You can stand if you'd like." She then introduced the director, Doris Franklin, a short, tough-looking woman in a tweed and leather jerkin ensemble, and Horace Milton, a bleak-eyed writer, straddling the arm of a couch. The producer, Paul Abbott, a hulk of a man with a lion-sized head and shoulders, sat scowling behind a desk.

Doris Franklin stared at me, unsmiling. "Any questions?" I shook my head. "Then go ahead whenever you're ready."

DeeDee Snyder read the first line and I jumped in, rushing through the words, my voice crackling with nerves. In what seemed like seconds, the scene was over. The director looked at me a moment, glanced at the two men, and then said, "Thank you very much." I nodded and fled the room.

I would gladly have renounced every vampiric gift I possessed to buy back that audition. I stopped in the hallway, halfway to the elevator, about to do the unthinkable—the thing every acting teacher, agent and casting director warns not to do—go back and ask to read again. But I was too weak and shaky. Besides, I was already late for work.

I'd just punched the elevator button when DeeDee Snyder hurried down the hall waving a script. "Wait! They want you back tomorrow morning for a camera test. Eight o'clock. Get here a bit early, okay?"

"Yes, of course, fine," I said, taking the script. In a flash everything that had felt so wrong about my audition seemed exactly right.

Unsure. Vulnerable. A governess with a torn stocking, for God's sake! Whatever energy force I'd thought was working against me, had worked for me! The elevator doors opened. Another actress, shaking a mass of blonde hair loose from the hood of her wet raincoat, stepped into the elevator as I got out.

"It's pouring," she said, as she brushed past me. "Good luck finding a cab."

"Thanks. Good luck to you." I galloped onto the street and managed to catch a Checker cab during the rush hour downpour. I jumped in, stamped my feet a few times to shake rainwater off my good shoes and told the cabbie, "Fifth Avenue at 59th. Please hurry!"

I looked at my watch and my heart sank. I was already late for the cocktail shift in the Playmate Bar. I didn't relish having to face the Bunny Mother's wrath. To make matters worse, I'd recently been promoted to Training Bunny and assigned Bunny Cheri to supervise on the floor. There were quite a number of Bunnies attending college, but no one quite like Cheri, who was brainy, beautiful and never stopped asking questions. She was so curious about everyone and everything, I'd begun to wonder if she was writing a term paper on key clubs. As the cab bumped across town, windshield wipers slap-slapping overtime, I felt my good luck ebbing. The cabbie, heavy-set with a fruity-red boil on his neck, missed every chance to make a light.

With windows steamed up and rainwater sluicing down the windshield, I opened my shoulder bag and set to work. Crouching down in the seat, I stripped off my nylons and put on a pair of black Danskin tights. With the driver veering into one bone-jarring pothole after another, I pressed a compact mirror between my knees and managed to glue on a double spray of false eyelashes. By the time the cab finally pulled up at the Playboy Club, I was in full Bunny makeup.

I rushed into the dressing room, grabbed my costume from the rack and turned to find the Bunny Mother blocking my path. Audrey, who'd been a Playboy centerfold in the late fifties, was still single at thirty-one and thoroughly soured on life. Every Bunny in the Club made more in tips than she did on salary, reason enough to despise us.

"Twenty demerits," she snarled, squinting at me through a haze of cigarette smoke. "That's just for tardiness. And you can forget about being a Training Bunny. I'm docking you another twenty demerits for leaving poor Cheri in the lurch." Poor Cheri? She'd revel in my demotion. I'd have to win "Bunny of the Week" two weeks running to recoup. At the rate I was going that didn't seem likely.

"I'll work extra shifts, Audrey, I promise."

"Damn bet you will. Now get your tail on the floor. Pronto!"

I charged down the hall to my locker, stripped and zipped in record time, tucking my meager breasts over wads of balled-up sweat socks in the 34-D cups of my Bunny costume. In five seconds flat, I'd flung a hairpiece on my head, clamped satin ears on top and scrambled for the elevator while still attaching my bowtie and cufflinks.

As luck would have it, Garrison Schuyler Haddock had arrived at the Club early and was waiting for me. Savannah had been covering my station, but Haddie, as he liked to be called, refused to order his Champagne cocktail from anyone but me.

"You okay?" Savannah asked, handing me several tabs. "What happened?"

I glimpsed Cheri hovering at her shoulder. "Just, you know, traffic."

"If you need help catching up—" Cheri said, looking entirely too eager.

"Thanks, I'm fine," I said. "Sorry I was late, Cheri."

I buzzed up to Haddie's table near the fireplace, Bunny dipped and went into the routine: "Good evening, sir. I'm your Bunny Meg. May I see your Playboy key, please?" Haddie loved the ritual, so I never skimped even though I knew his key-holder number by heart.

His eyes crinkled. "Sure thing, honey. Whatever you want." A broad smile creased his leathery cheeks as he placed the key in my palm, then folded my fingers around it. "You take good care of it, now." He winked. I winked back.

He liked his Champagne cocktail with two sugar lumps laced in Angostura bitters. I always brought him an extra sugar lump on a napkin. For me, he was money in the bank and entitled to as many sugar lumps with Angostura bitters as he wanted. I couldn't have paid for my acting classes without the extravagant twenty-dollar tip he always left me.

Mr. Haddock, who always came to the Club alone, was a widower in perpetual mourning for his wife, Ruby, an aquatic chorus girl, who had appeared in several Esther Williams MGM extravaganzas.

"You know, you look a lot like my honeypot," he'd always say, as though telling me for the first time. Then he'd hand me the picture he kept in his wallet of Ruby swooshing out of the water in *Million Dollar Mermaid.* "She was tall like you, all legs," he'd say. "Chestnut hair and a hundred-watt smile."

I'd hold the photograph in my hand, remarking on the resemblance, until Haddie eventually reached for it. "Of course, there was only one of her," he'd always say, then tuck the picture back into the fold of his wallet.

But that afternoon, he'd looked up at me and added, "She left my life all too soon. It doesn't get easier." Tears welled and rolled into the parched creases of his face. He didn't brush them away.

"Haddie, I'm so sorry!" I said, smoothing my hand across his shoulder.

Bunnies weren't supposed to touch customers, and it was strictly forbidden for them to touch us. But feeling Haddie's shoulders slump, I'd breached Playboy protocol and sat on the arm of his chair. Worse, I put my tray down to give him a hug, and pressed my cheek against his salt-and-pepper brush cut that smelled of Wildroot Cream Oil.

"Haddie, are you all right? Do you have anyone you can be with? Any family?" He shook his head and wiped his eyes on the handkerchief he pulled from his breast pocket.

Out of the corner of my eye, I could see the Room Director, a mean glower on his Neapolitan mug, advancing in my direction. Cheri, perching prettily on the Piano Bar railing, wasn't missing a thing.

"Look, Haddie," I said, "if you ever want to talk, just call me, okay? Any time."

I quickly jotted my telephone number on the inside of a book of Playboy matches and stuffed it in his pocket. By giving Haddie my phone number, I'd gone from "mingling" to "fraternizing," grounds for immediate dismissal. No amount of good Bunny deeds would get me out of this one if Rocco Bennetti put me on report.

I raced to head him off as fast as my four-inch stilettos would decorously allow. "Sorry, Mr. Bennetti," I said. "His wife died and he's really upset. I wasn't actually sitting with him, just sort of perching, okay? Please?"

"Looked like mingling to me," Rocco said. "You know, some clown from the State Liquor Authority sees a thing like that, we're all out of a job, get me?"

"Absolutely, Mr. Bennetti. It won't happen again."

Bennetti was letting me off with a warning, but it was a close call. I could only hope Cheri wouldn't look for an opportunity to tell the Bunny Mother. I brought Haddie some spareribs from the buffet, and he ordered a second Champagne cocktail.

"It all comes back at you sometimes," he said, saluting me with a raised glass. "Master Sergeant, Company A, 356 Infantry. Came through without a scratch. Demobbed in '46, but that's when the shrapnel hit the fan. Don't know what I would have done without Ruby. Met her when she was touring with the USO. Saved my life. Wish I could've done the same for her."

That's when he reached in his pocket and gave me the camouflage-painted Zippo lighter with the old-fashioned flint and wheel. "The flame won't ever blow out on you, even in a strong wind," he said. "You keep it for good luck. It saw me through D-Day plus-one."

The instant I held it in my hand, the lighter became my lucky charm. If the worn Zippo had seen Garrison Schuyler Haddock through the horrors of the Normandy Invasion (surely he hadn't stopped on the beach to light up a Camel?), I was willing to invest faith in its power to see me through whatever blew my way—that is, anything my own special powers didn't cover. I was not deterred by the knowledge that since surviving the Normandy landing, Haddie, whom I'd only known for a few months, seemed to have weathered more than his fair share of misfortune. Losing Ruby was the cruelest blow, but he'd even pulled through that. I wrapped my fingers around the lighter and felt it grow warm in my palm.

"You take good care of it, Meg. It'll see you through like it did me."

By the time Haddie got up to leave, shortly before my shift was over, he seemed fine again. Yet a gloom descended on me and I knew something was very wrong. "You're sure you don't want to keep your lighter, Haddie? No need to give it to me now."

I tried to drop it back in his jacket pocket, but he held his hand over the flap. He shook his head slowly. His eyes looked tired. "It's yours, Meg."

"Thanks, Haddie." I put my hand on his sleeve, feeling a cold dread as I did so. "Wait a bit and I can walk you home. Just meet me up the street."

Bunnies weren't allowed to meet anyone within a three-block radius of the Club, but Haddie knew where to wait for me.

"No need," he said. "Be good and take care of yourself."

"Call me if you need to," I whispered. "I mean it, just call."

I watched Haddie walk slowly down the spiral stairs past the piano bar to the hatcheck, his shoulders slumping more with each footfall. Elke was on Door Bunny duty that night and left her perch to help him on with his coat. He slipped her a folded bill. I knew it was one of the twenties he kept in his pocket for Bunny tips. They talked for a moment before he stepped out into the chill rain.

I pulled the roll of cash tips from my cleavage and wrapped the bills around Haddie's lighter, then tucked it all back between my breasts for safekeeping.

Two

Two detectives from the 16th Precinct rapped on my door shortly after 7 A.M. to tell me that Mr. Haddock was dead. He'd fallen from the bedroom window of his 11th-floor apartment, they told me. His body had been found at dawn by a neighbor walking her dog.

"Sorry to break it to you like this, sweetheart." A beefy detective, who didn't look a bit sorry, sucked his teeth and said, "We found your name and phone number inside a Playboy Club matchbook that was in his hand when—you get the picture, right, kid? So when did you last see him?"

"Last night, at the Club," I said, hanging on to the doorknob with both hands. *Haddie? Dead?* I could barely breathe.

"You mind if we come in, have a word with you?"

I stepped aside. The two men, stinking of cigarettes and a long night in overcoats, squeezed into the narrow foyer of my studio apartment.

"You want some coffee?"

"Sure thing. You up early or just getting in?" the one doing all the talking asked. His voice was flat, his insinuation clear.

"I was getting ready for an audition. I have a camera test this morning."

"Yeah? I thought you were a Playboy Bunny."

"I am. I work at the Club, but I'm an actress. Look, if you have to talk with anyone at Playboy, could you please not mention the bit about Mr. Haddock having my phone number? Please?"

The skinny, younger detective not doing the talking pulled a notebook and pencil from his coat pocket. My heart bumped down a flight of stairs. I regretted offering coffee. I was sorry I opened the door. I could see the tabloid headlines. BUNNY CALL GIRL INVOLVED IN GEEZER DEATH. I would lose my job and the Club would lose its liquor license, bringing down the entire Playboy empire. Worse, I'd miss my camera test.

"Please," I pleaded. I was on the verge of tears and didn't want puffy eyes for my camera audition. "I'll tell you all I know about Mr. Haddock, just please don't go to the Club with this!"

"Just doing our job, kid."

"You don't think that he—" I couldn't make myself say the word.

"Jumped? Now why would he do that?"

"He was depressed about his wife, that's all. She died and he was all alone. I told him he could call me. To talk."

"Yeah? And did he?"

"No! I wish he had!"

"We can get phone records, you know. So his wife died when?"

"I don't know. Maybe seven, eight years ago."

"And he was still depressed?" The beefy one heaved a sigh. "So he was lonely and called and you went over there?"

"Of course not! If I had, I would've made sure he didn't fall!"

None of this was sounding good. Worse, I'd carelessly left my roll of cash tips with Haddie's lighter on the kitchen table. I'd been too tired when I got home to count the bills and put them safely in a drawer. What would these detectives make of seeing a wad of money lying around, especially if they discovered the lighter had been Haddie's? I had to get them out of my apartment and make it to the studio on time.

"Look, he was a nice old guy. He left the Club and I didn't see him again," I said, focusing my energy on their overcoats. "I came straight home after my shift."

A thick sheen of sweat surfaced on their faces. The beefy one, his cheeks slick and red, fumbled with the buttons on his coat, pulling it open. "You keep it awful hot in here, kid."

"Really? I was going to turn up the heat," I said, hugging my arms and shivering.

The detectives exchanged looks, sweat dripping off their chins and soaking through their shirts. A sickening fug of scorched, unwashed flesh clouded the air around them. The skinny one shook drops of moisture off his notebook and fanned himself.

"Okay," the heavyset detective said, mopping his face with a sodden handkerchief. "Nothing we can't check out. We know where to find you."

He opened the door and they left, taking the putrid stench of sweat with them. With shaking hands I double-locked the door and pulled the chain.

Poor Haddie. If I'd been focusing properly I could have prevented his death. But it was clear to me what was wrong. I was functioning nowhere near capacity, and it was my own fault. After a few too many nights on the town, I'd reverted to my Twin Lakes regimen. I had decided that if I was going to be a serious actress and prove I had the talent on my own to compete on the level of humans, I had to deny my vampiric nature. To feed on the blood I craved meant enabling my supernatural powers. Juiced on fresh blood, it was almost impossible not to take advantage of superhuman strengths and abilities. That's not how I wanted to win a role.

But denial had taken its toll. I was in a weakened state. Even the slight exertion it took to turn the detectives into human furnaces had left me drained. A simple act like that should have been easy, but had required all my energy to pull off. I'd actually begun to require sleep at night. My calves ached from wearing four-inch stiletto heels at the Playboy Club, and I could barely hold my tray aloft by the end of my shift. I'd allowed my nerves to get the best of me at the audition. My stomach had taken an elevator ride just hearing my name called to go in to read for the role. Signs of my blood deficiency should have been obvious to me.

How else could I account for snagging my stocking—and then not being able to repair it instantly! I also had the nagging suspicion that some other force had been present countering my own basic, human-level energy. Friend or foe, I should have been able to identify the source.

It had been weeks since I'd last tanked up. My energy reserves were dangerously depleted. For a while I'd been binging on steak tartare at Brasserie, normally low-grade fuel but not in the quantities

I'd been consuming night after night. I'd also regularly breezed through Central Park on my way home from the Club, consuming tangy sparrow blood and the nutty-flavored squirrel blood I'd come to like. My mother would have been appalled had she known about my indulgence.

Meat, when she occasionally ate it, could never be cooked well enough for Ruth, who avoided blood at all costs. "Farm folk always eat their meat well done," she'd tell us, serving up her charred pork chops and desiccated meatloaf.

I didn't know meat could be pliable, let alone pink, until I was in high school. Homegrown vegetables were the staple of our diet. My dad grew corn, cabbage, tomatoes, rutabaga, beets, lettuce, potatoes, peppers, boiler and green onions, three kinds of squash, three kinds of beans, crabapples, rhubarb and muskmelons that he took to market three mornings a week to sell to restaurants and grocery stores.

We also had fresh eggs, but no poultry was ever killed on our farm. The chickens we ate, roasted to a crisp, were home-grown but came back to us dressed and oven-ready through an arrangement with a neighboring farmer. Mother took denial to extremes to prove she could be just as human as anyone else, but it left her listless. Now I was emulating her, to my own detriment.

I only once saw my mother resort to blood lust. That was to aid my father, Orville, a tall, rugged human with broad shoulders, who wore overalls six days a week and spent most of his time in the fields. One Saturday morning in early spring, my dad was plowing the fields in the meadow near the house while mother and I were setting out trays of cabbage seedlings from the cold frames. We both happened to look up to see my dad swing the wheels of the old Allis Chalmers around the end of the field to begin another furrow. He was steering the tractor with one hand, as always, and leaning over to check the placement of the plow.

Suddenly my mother gasped and started running toward the meadow. My insides churned and I started running after her. Moments later, the tractor lurched forward as the right wheel struck rock and slewed sideways. My dad jounced in his seat, lost his balance and fell backward off the tractor.

I stopped in my tracks, screaming, but my mother kept running, her feet flying across the field to reach my dad. The tractor leaned precariously, its wheel spinning in the furrow, spewing dirt as it ground deeper into the earth.

I ran even faster, racing toward the tipping tractor. I clambered up the far side, gripped the steering wheel and punched my hand against the choke. I don't even know how I knew to do that, but the motor shuddered and jolted to a stop. The wheel, jammed against a deep boulder, rocked back and eased into the earth. I held on to the steering wheel with both hands, my eyes clamped shut, fearful of what I would see when I looked back at my dad.

Slowly I turned my head and opened my eyes—but what I saw stopped my breath. My father lay cradled in my mother's arms, her head bent low over his bloody upper torso. As I watched, she lifted her face and looked up at me with glittering eyes, her mouth dripping blood from the bone-deep gash in my father's shoulder.

"Look away! Go!" Her voice was a snarl, deep and guttural. "Go!"

I jumped down from the tractor and sped toward the neighbor's house on the far side of the meadow, knowing that's what my mother meant me to do. But as I ran, the image of my mother's bloody face and burning eyes seared my brain, branding itself forever in my memory.

At the edge of the field, I turned back and saw my mother on her feet, striding across the meadow toward our farmhouse carrying my father in her arms as though he weighed no more than a small child. She must have sensed me watching. She spun around and glared at me with a face so fierce I jumped with fright. She'd torn my father's work shirt and bound his head and arm. There was no sign of blood on her face.

My father healed quickly, faster than anyone could have expected. Meanwhile, my mother, with newfound energy, seemed to thrive on hard work and long hours, appearing more robust than I had ever seen her. I'd awaken in the morning, smelling fresh bread, and find her in the kitchen, humming to herself, her long, wavy hair loose on her shoulders. She and my father seemed happier together, too, laughing and teasing each other.

Over time, my mother settled back into her normal routine, with her hair twisted into a tight bun and a sour look on her face. My dad started working the fields again. The only new thing that happened is that the following winter my baby brother Eddie was born.

Yet the fearful image of mother's bloodied face and glittering eyes, my father cradled in her arms, was locked in my memory. The only mention she made of carrying my father across the field was to say, "In times like that, you don't know your own strength. You get a rush of adrenaline—there's no limit to what the body can do." But I knew it was the rush of blood that accounted for that fearsome energy.

Still, I was determined to deny myself the advantage a surge of fresh blood would give me. I couldn't give in, even with my first camera test hanging in the balance. I slipped Haddie's Zippo lighter in my pocket before leaving my apartment for the studio. There was no reason not to put my faith in plain old luck.

When I arrived at the studio I was still shaken from hearing about Haddie, but then had another shock. Brian, one of the Playboy bartenders, who was also an actor, was sitting in one of the makeup chairs. The last thing in the world I wanted anyone at the audition to know is that I worked as a Bunny.

Brian looked as startled to see me as I was to find him there. "Hey, is this you?" he asked, holding up the call sheet. "Morgana Harriott?"

"Surprise," I said. "It's my stage name. But you can call me Meg."

"Yeah? Well, looks like we're testing together, Meg," Brian said. "I guess you wanted to leave the floor early last night so you could study the script. You shoulda said so."

"Not at all," I said, looking at his reflection in the makeup mirror. He'd clearly slathered on Man Tan that morning and looked like a burnished orange. "Maybe we can run some lines later."

"Sure thing. Say, Rocco told me he caught you flirting with your sugar daddy again last night. You better watch it."

The makeup woman caught my eye. She was taking it all in.

"Bennetti's got it all wrong as usual," I said quickly, relieved he didn't seem to know yet about Haddie's death. "Look, as soon as I'm out of makeup, let's go over the scene, okay? I'll wait outside."

Before Brian could say another damaging word, I slipped out of the makeup room and hovered in the hallway near the studio's entrance foyer. A flickering gray image on a television monitor caught my eye. A news reporter was standing with a microphone outside the canopied entrance of an East Side high rise. I moved closer to the monitor when I heard, ". . . body was found in the courtyard." The reporter edged toward a middle-aged, doughy-faced woman caught without makeup, wearing a cotton shift I'm sure she never dreamed an audience of early-rising, news-hungry New Yorkers would ever see her in. I guessed she was also wearing scruffy slippers and not much in the way of underwear.

"Morning walkies," she told the reporter, hugging a trembling dachshund between her breasts, that's how she and Fritzie came across the body. "I always used to see Mr. Haddock sitting on the window sill up there, looking out. I just knew it'd come to a bad end," she whimpered.

She looked like she was going to be sick. I felt sick, too, knowing I could have somehow prevented his death. I turned away just in time to see Brian loping down the hallway toward me.

I cut him off at the pass and pulled him into one of the dressing rooms, safely out of earshot of the hair and makeup staff and nowhere near the TV monitor.

"You better get your butt into a makeup chair," Brian said. "They're looking for you."

"Righto. Listen, I was thinking, no need to mention the Club to anyone here, okay? Not that there's anything to be ashamed of," I assured him. After all, he worked at Playboy, too.

"Sure, kid." He slung an arm around my shoulders, something he wasn't allowed to do at the Club. "But I betcha we're both gonna get cast and then, hey! Who cares?"

I knew Brian was the sensitive sort. He was Welsh. When in his cups and feeling especially morose about his non-happening show biz career, he'd quote passages of Dylan Thomas while pouring Rob Roys and Manhattans. Sometimes I'd catch him in the coatroom in front of a mirror practicing quick draws, cocking an imaginary Colt, in case Hollywood called. How he kept his job at the Club was beyond me, except that management liked it when his girlfriend, a veteran musical comedy star, showed up after her curtain went down and held forth in the Club's Piano Bar.

I hurried down the hall to the makeup room and climbed into a chair. That's when I learned that I was set to camera test with two actors that morning. The other was Michael Halliday, a legendary drunk. During my first week in New York, I'd been lucky enough to cadge a freebie student ticket to one of the last performances of a Central Park production of *Othello*, in which he played Iago. I was enthralled until I realized that Iago and Othello were both plastered and exchanging each other's speeches.

Brian and Michael had both shown up sober for the camera test, perhaps because it was early in the morning. They knew each other from AA and the Actor's Studio, as it turned out. After our audition they invited me to tag along for breakfast at Joe Allen. I jumped at the chance. It was the hallowed hangout of working actors, a club I was eager to join. At least I had an agent, thanks to a non-paying role in a playwright's workshop production. I'd also done a shampoo commercial, my one on-camera job.

I hadn't had time to think about Haddie's death until I found myself sitting on a bar stool in Joe Allen between two actors talking baseball. While one ordered seltzer and the other black coffee, I'd opted for a grasshopper. It wasn't even noon yet. I don't know why I ordered a drink in the first place, let alone a grasshopper. I'd eaten nothing and my stomach was soured on too many adrenaline rushes. If I'd had any sense, I would have ordered a bloody Mary, something morning-appropriate with a little vegetable nourishment.

While the guys talked baseball, I sipped my grasshopper. It was doing its job, taking the edge off my nerves. I swirled my drink, swishing the foam clinging to the sides of the glass. "Bottom's up," I said, raising my glass.

"You really drinking that stuff?" Michael asked.

"It's nothing but creamed mouthwash," Brian said, sipping his seltzer.

"Hm, good," I said, taking a big gulp, licking my lips and holding up the glass. "And so good for you!"

"Cute," Michael said. "You could sell anything with a kisser like yours."

As quick as that I started falling for him. While the guys went back to talking baseball, I licked up the remains of the grasshopper and indulged my freshly minted fantasy. Looking at the two of them reflected in the oak-framed mirror behind the bar, there was no question which one I wanted to have get the role. Both were tall and actor-handsome, but I liked Michael's dark, craggy features more than Brian's sleek, blonde look. I leaned slightly to my right, brushing against Michael's shirt, picturing the two of us on camera together, my own long, straight dark hair next to Michael's thick, wavy hair.

That's when I glimpsed the bartender wince and put down the lemon he'd been peeling. He jammed his hand in his mouth, sucking on the web of skin between his thumb and index finger. I could taste the blood in his mouth from his cut hand and felt sick with thirst. I stretched out my hand, reaching for the lemon rind on which a few smeared drops of blood glistened. The fruit was almost within my grasp when the bartender swiped it into the waste bin. I let out a small cry, my body almost shaking with want.

"Here, you're not getting sick are you?" Michael asked. "I don't want you falling off the stool."

"Sorry," I said, sitting up straight again and gripping the bar.

"Nothing worse than a sick drunk," Brian said. "A woman shouldn't drink if she can't hold it."

"I'm fine," I said. Actually I'd begun feeling queasy. Looking into the mirror, I saw that my eyes looked a bit dopey.

"Did you eat anything?" Michael asked. "You gals starve yourselves trying to keep skinny."

"Really, I'm fine." I was starting to feel a lot less fine. I slid off the stool and stood for a moment steadying myself. "S'cuse me. I'll be right back."

As I weaved my way to the ladies' room, I heard Michael tell the bartender, "Better bring her some eggs. She's gonna upchuck whatever's in her now."

Minutes later I gripped the sink in the ladies' room and stared hard at myself in the mirror. Why didn't Haddie call me last night? If only I'd had a chance to talk with him. If only he'd called.

My eyes couldn't focus through the sheen of tears. I considered splashing water on my face, but with all the camera makeup I was afraid I'd end up looking like a mud pie. Besides I didn't dare let go of the sink. With one hand I wet a paper towel and dabbed at the mascara streaking my cheeks. My mind swirled and I felt sick again. I reached into my pocket and wrapped my fingers around Haddie's lighter, feeling lightheaded.

"Forgive me, Haddie," I whispered. I felt a shushing sound in my ears and hoped I wouldn't faint.

I took a few deep breaths before going back to the bar. Brian and Michael were still talking baseball. I tried not to look at the plate of fried eggs as I left some crumpled bills on the bar. The bartender nodded his thanks and picked up the money, a flesh colored bandaid visible on his hand. What a waste.

I made my way home by subway, feeling miserable. Had I wrecked my chances at getting my first real acting job over some stupid bargain with myself over blood? I'd gone cold turkey instead of weaning myself. Just a taste would have made all the difference, but I'd been too pig-headed to give in. I kicked myself the whole way back to my apartment, certain my career was over before it had begun.

I no more than got my key out of the lock before my phone started to ring. I made a mad dash, praying it was Wesley Truscott calling to tell me that I'd got a role in *Dark Passages*. It was. I think I went into shock. My ears started ringing and I barely heard the rest of what he said. I only knew with certainty that my good fortune was entirely due to Haddie's lighter.

Once I was off the phone, I flopped on my bed and cried my eyes out. I was sad about Haddie, and scared, too. Everything was out of control. My worlds had collided catastrophically, like Mars careening into Earth. But I was determined not to give in. I'd got my very first acting job on my own merits without consuming even a sip of blood.

Three

It wasn't until Wesley Truscott treated me to lunch at Howard Johnson's on 46th and Broadway that the reality of my new job really sank in. I hadn't got the lead role of Elizabeth, the governess in *Dark Passages*. The part had gone to Rebecca Daly, whoever she was. Instead, I'd been cast as Margie, the waitress in a roadhouse diner. I imagined the uniform I'd have to wear, probably stiff cotton with a hanky in the breast pocket.

"You're working, Morgana. You've got a job. That's the way to look at it. After all, there are no small roles. Only small actors." I winced, hating to be on the receiving end of sentiment I suspected Wesley Truscott didn't believe any more than I did.

Nevertheless, I was thrilled to be a working actress. I would be going to a studio every day, getting paid to act. I wouldn't have to go to cattle calls. I could call myself an actress and not blush. I could buy myself a really nice cocktail dress. I could quit my Bunny job.

"Just two things, my dear. Are you sure you want to keep calling yourself Morgana Harriott? There's nothing wrong with the name Meg Harrison, you know. Now's the time to decide. It'll be hard to change your name back again once they do the credits. Think about it."

"But I really see myself as Morgana. It's just so classy . . . and Meg is . . ."

"Just think about it, okay? Also, do you need any, uh, funds to tide you over?"

"Oh, no, Mr. Truscott. I can manage. I've still got some savings from the shampoo ad."

"Call me Wesley," he said, looking at me over the gold-framed bifocals tipped on his nose. "You're a good girl, Morgana. A penny saved is a penny earned, especially for a young actor. This is just the beginning and you have to expect lean times ahead." He dipped his fork into his cottage cheese and shook his head. "You have no idea how many foolish young actresses rush out to buy party dresses with their first paychecks."

I nodded in agreement. This was not the time to mention the Playboy Club, or my desire for a slinky black sheath. "Uh, Wesley, how much do I actually get paid?"

"Well, my dear, we have you on a three-year contract. You're guaranteed three shows a week on a thirteen-week cycle, with a pickup option. You'll get two-fifty for the first show, but on a sliding scale per week depending on how many half-hours you do. It tops out at nine-fifty if you work Monday through Friday. That's not likely to happen, of course, unless your storyline gets really hot."

"Wait a minute. You're telling me I get two-hundred and fifty dollars to do one show?"

"I'm afraid so," Wesley said, tapping his lips with a paper napkin. "But that's only for the first show. You get less for each subsequent show you do that week, but they insisted on this sliding scale. Nothing I could do. It's your first soap so we didn't have a lot of leeway. But here's the good news—"

"Two-hundred and fifty!" My brain was still trying to grasp the fact I would be earning more in one day than I did working five afternoons on the cocktail shift at the Playboy Club—and no girl I knew earned more than a Bunny! In fact, that was much more than my mother earned in two weeks working her new job at J.C. Penny. My rent was only fifty-nine dollars a month for a studio apartment in Gramercy Park. My God, I was rich! I could take singing lessons. I could sign up for classes with Uta Hagen and Sandy Meisner. I could buy shoes and a matching handbag. I could—

"Did you hear what I said, Morgana? You will be working with one of the great Hollywood legends of all time. Moira Shaw. *Moira Shaw*," he repeated for emphasis. "No one of her caliber has ever worked daytime before. It's unheard of. Quite the coup." Wesley Truscott's little cookie duster mustache quivered with emotion and his eyes grew moist. "Moira Shaw."

"I think I used to see her on *Midday Matinee* back home growing up," I said. "I remember her in all those movies with maids and butlers."

"And the stage, my dear. She was heaven on stage."

"So when do I start?"

"You have a table read this Friday. Beginning Monday you'll have a full week of rehearsals for the first five on-air episodes you'll do the following week. After that, you do a complete half hour show each day."

I stared at him blankly. "And it's live, right? What time of day? I'd like to tell my folks so they can watch."

"Well, not exactly live, but don't worry about all this now, Morgana. You'll be sent scripts and a schedule with everything you need to know." He patted my hand. "I must say, I do envy you," he said, picking up the check. I knew he was still thinking about Moira Shaw.

I was thinking it was time to call my folks. I decided to walk home and save the subway token. I had bigger and better things to spend my money on. Besides, I'd have to take the subway later to work the cocktail shift at the Club. If I timed it right, I could make a trunk call on my home phone and save the person-to-person charges. I wanted to talk to both of my parents at the same time.

Strategy: Always provide an item of good news to blunt bad news. As in, "Hey, guess what? I got a job—and, by the way, I've changed my name."

This has worked in the past. When I left home (taking a cheap milk flight that stopped in both Detroit and Pittsburgh before arriving at New York's Idlewild), I packed a bottle of Scotch whiskey in my flight bag. My parents did not discover the bottle missing from the cupboard over the sink until nearly two months later. I'd taken the whiskey knowing they would never use it. The Scotch had been bought in a duty-free shop by visiting cousins who didn't know my parents well. My folks drank Canadian rye. I, on the other hand, knew from ads in magazines that sophisticated people in urban areas drank Scotch. The first thing I did after moving into my apartment was to arrange the bottle of J&B Scotch on a tray with two small cut-glass tumblers and place it on the counter of the kitchenette. The tall, green bottle with the bright yellow label looked so cheerful in my black and white-tiled kitchen. I knew I was meant to have it.

By the time my parents discovered my theft, I was full of good news about my terrific rent-controlled apartment.

Parents will fool you, though. There was silence after I told them about getting the soap opera. Finally my mother said, "You're sure about this? I've never heard of that show."

"It's new, Mom. I start day after tomorrow." I wasn't going to mention how much I'd be earning because I didn't want to hurt their feelings. How could a daughter flouncing around on TV earn more than her father working the fields on his own farm?

"Does this mean you'll be quitting your Bunny job?" my mother asked. "Because I wouldn't do that if I were you. These shows come and go. You don't want to be left without."

"Good idea. And, oh, before I forget—I figured I better take on a stage name. I was thinking of something like—oh, I don't know, Morgana Harriott. Cute, huh? What do you think?"

More silence. I could hear my father breathing on the extension line. Then my mother spoke. "Didn't you already change your last name to Harrison? What's wrong with calling yourself Margaret Blatch? Why do you need a stage name?"

Why indeed? How to explain to your parents, Orville and Ruth Blatch, that the family name sounds like a brick dropped from a great height? "Oh, I don't know. Everyone does it. Harrison was okay . . . but Harriott sounds even better."

"Not out here. The Blatch name has been around a long time. Good people have been known by the name Blatch. You're not ashamed of us, are you?"

Guilt. Shame. "Look, it's not legal or anything. If you're really that upset I can go back to being Margaret Blatch— maybe."

"Nevermind. I kind'a think we were expecting something like this."

Imagine if I'd told them about Haddie? They certainly wouldn't have been expecting something like that! Some things just shouldn't be mentioned to parents, like cops showing up on the doorstep at dawn.

My next trunk call was to Marilyn. I couldn't resist telling her my good news. She hadn't been at all encouraging when I'd told her I wanted to go to New York to be an actress and experience big-city glamour and excitement.

"You'd be much better off staying here and getting a teaching certificate," she'd said. "Besides, you can find all kinds of excitement right here in Twin Lakes, if you look for it!"

To say nothing of glamour, I thought.

On my first trip back home from New York after I started work at the Club, Marilyn invited me to visit her sorority house near the University of Minnesota campus because, she said, otherwise the girls were unlikely to ever meet a Playboy Bunny. I packed up handfuls of swizzle sticks from the Club as souvenirs, and brought along my Bunny manual. Marilyn had instructed me to dress as *Vogue*-chic as possible for the sorority tea she organized. I obliged by wearing a sleek red sheath, matching high heels and a beehive hairdo. The effect of wearing this getup in the common room of Delta Gamma amidst a sea of Peter Pan collars and *Town & Country* plaids, was to be referred to by one and all entirely in the third person as though I were a department store mannequin.

"She's wearing false eyelashes, I'm just sure of it." (I was.)

"She's wearing the pointiest-toed high heels I've ever seen!" (I was, indeed.)

I was asked to demonstrate a Bunny Dip, and confirmed that Warren Beatty was in the Club almost every night. (At least that's what I'd heard, though I personally never laid eyes on him.) Everyone was impressed when I revealed how much I earned in tips, even Marilyn. "Now don't go getting any ideas!" she chided. One or two of her sorority sisters were clearly getting ideas.

Marilyn took inordinate pleasure in telling everyone what a "mouse" I'd been growing up. "You wouldn't believe it to see her now." She then produced several particularly cruel snapshots from her scrapbook. The worst of the lot was taken at Swallow Lake when I was thirteen, and still woefully underdeveloped. I'm standing on the shore squinting at the camera, my beanpole legs attached to an entirely shapeless body wearing a limp one-piece. My skinny arms are holding a huge inner tube above my head. I look like a spider carrying a doughnut. Marilyn made sure this picture made the rounds very slowly as she repeatedly said, "And just look at her now. It's a miracle, really."

Marilyn also flashed a photograph of my being crowned Miss Twin Lakes so her sorority sisters could mark this transitional period from mouse to Playboy Bunny.

After the tea, during a walk on campus, Marilyn asked me how I could possibly be happy living in New York. "God, kid, don't you feel out of it there?"

That comment still rankled. My fingers shook as I dialed the number of the sorority house. I was lucky and reached her just as she was finishing lunch. I blurted out my news.

"So now you're a big movie star, is that it?" she asked. I could hear her chewing.

"Just an afternoon soap opera, but it's a start," I modestly replied. "Of course I'll be working with Moira Shaw."

"Who?"

"Moira Shaw, for God's sake. She's a Hollywood legend. Anyway, I've decided to take a stage name. Not that there's anything wrong with the name Blatch, but I thought something more lyrical. I don't know, something like Morgana Harriott, maybe."

"Are you kidding me?" Marilyn shrieked with laughter. "I'm s'posed to call you Morgana now? That's the funniest thing I ever heard."

I let Marilyn laugh. There was no point in telling her that Cary Grant's real name was Archie Leach. That Tony Curtis was Bernie Schwartz. For that matter, was Moira Shaw always *Moira Shaw*?

On my way to the Club to work the cocktail shift, I decided not to mention my acting job to the Bunny Mother. My own mother just might be right and it was probably prudent to wait and see if the soap opera lasted.

A notice posted next to the work schedule in the Bunny dressing room invited "Playboy personnel" to a graveside service for Garrison Schuyler Haddock at 2 P.M. at the Sleepy Hollow Cemetery in Tarrytown, New York, the following day. Most of the Bunnies who knew

Haddie were scheduled to work either the lunch or cocktail shifts, including me. But I couldn't let Haddie down. I managed to find a replacement so I could attend his funeral.

When I woke up to the steady drumbeat of rain on my windowsill, I decided to allow plenty of time for the train trip to Tarrytown. By mid-morning, I'd packed some sandwiches, pulled on my rubber boots and hurried to catch the subway to Grand Central Station. The Hudson Line took me to Tarrytown's gray stone Philipes Manor train station in a little more than an hour. I got directions at a ticket window and walked the half-mile to the gates at the cemetery entrance. The rain had let up, but a fine mist hung in the air.

A sweet-faced, quiet-spoken matron in reception gave me a map of the grounds and marked the location of Haddie's graveside service. She also handed me a printout of Washington Irving's *The Legend of Sleepy Hollow*. I'd read the story of Ichabod Crane and the Headless Horseman in school. Since I was early for Haddie's funeral, I decided to visit some of the places of interest in the old section of the cemetery marked on the map.

For the most part I stayed on the gravel path, but occasionally walked on the spongy grass to inspect old headstones, many dating to the late 1700s. A dark-haired woman, wearing a pale blue coat, was walking a small white dog just ahead of me. I found myself following her as she strolled among the gravesites, but never managed to catch up to her. I wondered if she was attending Haddie's funeral, too, since we seemed to be heading in the same direction.

I was glad I'd brought sandwiches. I couldn't imagine there would be a reception following Haddie's service. Back home in Twin Lakes, Pastor Odegaard and pallbearers carrying the casket would lead the way to the interment in the cemetery next to the church. Then everyone would make a beeline for the steamy warm church basement where casseroles (known generically as "hot dish"), containing every conceivable combination of tuna, mushroom soup or ground meat with various species of egg noodles and crunchy toppings, would be displayed on an oilcloth-covered trestle table. Backing them up would be a rainbow of Jell-O molds, most containing canned fruit cocktail and marshmallows. Sugar cookies and little squares of frosted white sheet cake would be displayed on a separate table next to a coffee urn. Normally a funeral lasted the better part of the day, and quite a lot of thought went into choosing the music and scripture. None of this looked likely with Haddie's funeral.

Haddie would already be in a closed casket, of course. There would be no reviewal (an odd term, when you think of it, but that's what we called it back home) prior to the service. That was fine with me. I wouldn't have expected an open casket anyway, under the circumstances.

Up ahead, the brunette and her white dog rounded a curve and disappeared from view behind a small stand of trees. I cut across a grassy knoll and walked into the wooded area, and stood for a moment under the leafy canopy of a maple tree, breathing in the sweet, earthy dampness.

The woman in the blue coat had reappeared, standing near a mass of rock at the edge of the maple grove, her white dog dancing excitedly at her feet. She glanced over her shoulder, seeming to sense my presence in the hush of the woods. I didn't recognize her, although she looked oddly familiar. She made no sign that she knew me, but turned, tugging gently on the dog's lead, and walked toward a gravel path.

The smooth rock, protected from the faint drizzle by the overhang of tree branches, looked like a good place to rest and eat my tomato sandwiches. But as I moved toward the gray stone, glittering with specks of mica, something brownish red started trickling down a crevice. At once I saw the source, a squirrel in its last throes lying on top of the rock, blood oozing from its chest.

Before I could stop myself, I was at the rock with my lips pressed to the wound, feeding on the rich, warm blood, the best I'd ever tasted. From the first sip, my senses electrified. I could hear insects scuttling under the rock, smell the scent of birds in the trees overhead. I fed greedily, stopping only when the squirrel was drained. I wiped my lips clean. Energy surged through me, and I looked around with crystal-sharp vision.

Through the trees I saw a hearse glide slowly up the drive toward a mound of freshly dug earth and knew it was Haddie's gravesite.

I moved so quickly, I was at the hearse before it had come to a complete stop. The driver turned his head, surprised to see me, and rolled down the window.

"You with the Haddock party?" he asked. "The others are right behind me." He climbed out and went to the rear of the hearse to open the doors. "Good thing the rain stopped, right?"

"Right," I said, looking at the casket.

Whatever remained of Haddie was in there. I stood transfixed as the driver trudged over to inspect the gravesite. I'd had little time to reflect on Haddie in the days since his death. Such a lot had happened, most of it good. The police hadn't been in touch again, possibly to avoid the sauna they'd experienced the first time. There had been no mention of my name in the newspapers in connection with Haddie's death, which had been ruled accidental.

The casket was bare except for a small spray of wilting mums. Why hadn't I thought to provide flowers for Haddie? He'd been so generous to us. I'd even got an acting job, thanks to his Zippo lighter. I was consumed with regret, wishing with all my heart that I'd arranged for a bouquet.

Another car purred to a stop behind me. I glanced over my shoulder and saw a man at the wheel with two people in the back seat. I realized I would have only a moment on my own to whisper a private farewell to Haddie.

I turned back to the casket, astonished to see it covered in a lush blanket of spring flowers. The sweet, moist fragrance of lilac, peony, lily, iris, snapdragon, sweetpea and roses of every hue perfumed the air. I breathed deeply, then leaned close to the casket, clutching Haddie's Zippo lighter tightly in my pocket.

"I got an acting job, Haddie. On television! I wish you could be here to watch me," I slipped my hand among the flowers on the casket and whispered. "I'll miss you. Find peace. And Ruby."

"That wasn't my mother," a voice said. I turned and looked into the eyes of a man, who could have been Haddie. "Ruby was my stepmother."

"I know," I said. "He used to show me her picture."

"My mother died in a car crash close to home while he was fighting a war on the beaches of Normandy. Ironic, isn't it? "

"Sad, I'd say. I'm so sorry. It must have been hard for you and your father."

"Well, he picked up with Ruby. She's buried right over there. I'm Lloyd Haddock. And you're . . . ?"

"Morgana Harriott. I'm an actress. But Mr. Haddock knew me as Meg."

"One of the Bunnies, I suppose. My wife and I figured there'd be quite a few more of you here. And some of the Copacabana girls."

"The Copa girls?" So Haddie would go to the Copa after cocktails at the Playboy Club? It figured. The Copacabana nightclub was on 60th Street between Fifth and Madison, right around the corner from the Playboy Club. It wasn't as though Haddie was two-timing us, but it felt like it.

"I doubt they'll turn up," I said, feeling a bit huffy. "They need a lot of time to get into their feathers for the first show. And the Bunnies are working either the lunch or cocktail shift, so no one else could make it. I got time off."

He nodded, looking a bit resigned. "Well, glad you made it at least." Haddie's son was good-looking, in an antiseptic Sears-Roebuck catalog sort of way. He had Haddie's facial features and height, but he was less angular, more robust. "My dad loved the ladies, though. He'd be disappointed."

A plump, tired-looking woman with a frizzy perm appeared next to Lloyd. "Hi, there. I'm Lloyd's wife, Eileen." Her eyes popped as she took in the mass of flowers covering the casket. "Where in the world did that come from?" she gasped.

"The Bunnies," I said. "We chipped in for Haddie."

"Tips must be good," she sniffed. "You must've cleared out a greenhouse. Anyway, looks like we're it. We should probably get on with this, right Lloyd? Tell the man from the mortuary to get a move on."

A slight man with a shock of white hair, who had driven the car carrying Lloyd and Eileen Haddock, joined us. He introduced himself to me as Mr. Sloan. He and the driver of the hearse had been conferring, and both looked unhappy. "I'm sorry about the delay," Mr. Sloan said. "We were supposed to have some assistance graveside, but they appear to be shorthanded today. In any case, perhaps the bad weather has delayed some people, so it wouldn't hurt to wait a bit."

"Nope, we're all here," Eileen said. "Let's get a move on, okay?"

"But there was a woman with a dog," I said. "She seemed to be heading here, too."

"Hardly," Sloan said. "No dogs allowed. She wouldn't have been allowed to bring a dog onto the grounds."

"Well, we can't just stand around," Eileen said. "It's going to pour any minute." We all looked up at heavy rain clouds that looked close to bursting. Eileen poked Lloyd on the arm. "I don't know why your father couldn't have been buried in Scranton next to your mother instead of in this godforsaken place. Anyway, can't we just haul his casket over there on our own?"

"I don't see how," Lloyd said. "Really, Eileen, it's not how things are done."

"Look," she said, with thunder in her voice, "we still have to finish emptying Pop's apartment when we're done here."

She sighed heavily and turned her back on Lloyd to address Sloan, the driver and me, speaking slowly and deliberately so we'd be sure to understand. "We need to get my father-in-law buried. *Now!* The kids are alone in Scranton with my mother and we've got to get back home. So let's just do this, okay? *Now!*"

Not a problem, I thought. I could do it on my own, but not with an audience. Eileen was actually tapping her foot, as though that might spur us on.

I glanced up the drive and saw the dark-haired woman with the dog watching us. I knew better than to draw Sloan's attention to her. I suspected no one other than me could actually see her. I also figured she had probably provided me with the squirrel blood—and probably the lavish floral tribute for Haddie, as well. But why? Foe or benefactress? I couldn't be sure, but my body throbbed with energy, all of it directed toward releasing Haddie from this earthly horror. How could he possibly have allowed Eileen to call him "Pops"?

"Maybe we could get a start," I said. "If we all pitched in, we could probably get the casket to the grave."

"Yes, with all hands on board we could probably manage," Sloan agreed, then caught his first glimpse of the flowers blanketing the casket. "Excuse me, but does anyone know where —"

"Bunnies," Eileen muttered. "A lot of Bunnies, a lot of flowers." Her hand was already gripping a handle. "Lloyd, grab the other end. C'mon, everyone, let's go!"

With Eileen already tugging the casket, we all jumped to help. With my superior strength, I supported the bulk of the weight, with no one the wiser. In no time we'd lugged the casket graveside. Sloan launched into an abbreviated service that would have deeply offended Pastor Odegaard.

Sloan had barely concluded his brief remarks when thunder and lightning rent the skies, producing a torrential downpour. Eileen and Lloyd raced for the car, with Sloan on their heels. The driver of the hearse grabbed my arm, but I shook him off. Moments later, I was left standing at the graveside, soaked to the skin and glad to be by myself.

I lowered the casket into the grave on my own. Covering it with earth and fragrant flowers filled me with joy. It was the last, best thing I could do for Haddie—except maybe handing him a Champagne cocktail with extra Angostura-drenched sugar cubes. I hoped he'd already hooked up with Ruby. I smoothed the last bit of muddy earth on the mound and stood up to let the pounding rain wash me clean. I then headed for the train station.

On the knoll above the gravesite, I turned back for a last look. The shapely brunette with the white dog was tending a flower garden that had miraculously appeared on Haddie's grave. She glanced up, but gave no sign of greeting. I hoped it was Ruby welcoming her hubby home at last.

I continued on to the Philipes Manor station. At least I had my damp tomato sandwiches to eat on the way back into Manhattan since no one had thought to provide hot dish and sheet cake.

Four

Moira Shaw arrived by taxi carrying a small Tiffany shopping bag. I was stepping off a bus half a block away, but recognized her immediately. Even if I hadn't known it was Moira Shaw entering the studio, I would have taken her for someone important. She was wearing a pale pink suit and large blue-lens sunglasses with a silk scarf loosely tied to her handbag. I was wearing a slim skirt, twin set and flats, but as I walked toward the studio entrance, I affected Moira's gliding slouch. It slowed me down considerably. I reminded myself that Moira was old, certainly my mother's age.

I followed the signs directing me to the rehearsal studio on the second floor. A clamor of voices led me down a wide hallway. I stopped on the threshold of a cavernous room and spotted Michael Halliday, wearing blue jeans and moccasins. He was pouring coffee and bringing it to Moira Shaw, who was already seated in a folding chair near a window.

As I scanned the assemblage, my mouth went dry. My kneecaps unhinged and I was afraid my feet wouldn't work. I was too scared to move. I tried to reason with myself. After all, I'd been hired! I was supposed to be here! But a little voice said, what if it was all a mistake? They hired the wrong girl! My eyes roamed the room looking for some sign of welcome.

In one corner of the room, Doris Franklin, Horace Milton and Paul Abbott huddled together poring over the script. A man in a dress shirt and slacks conferred briefly with Doris, then went back to laying yellow tape in long stretches on the linoleum floor. Assisting him, with a stopwatch on a cord around her neck and a tape measure in her hands, was a bulky young woman with a Dutch boy haircut.

The actors were gathered around a table in the far corner that held a coffee urn and bakery boxes overflowing with pastries. Preening and posing, they flitted around the room, their burbling voices rising and falling. If I could will myself to move, I knew that's where I should be.

I recognized several of the actors, among them Ginny Blake, the young blonde actress playing Angela, the daughter of Moira Shaw. Next to her, his navy blazer draped across his shoulders, and a hand on his hip to show off his slim torso, was movie-star-handsome Maxwell Faraby, who had been cast as Moira's brother, Shelby. The plump woman devouring a cream bun had to be playing the housekeeper. I figured the portly man with the tweed trilby was most likely playing my father.

A beautiful girl with porcelain skin, her long, dark hair gathered in a ribbon, emerged from the group at the coffee urn and moved toward Moira Shaw—and knelt at her feet! There was only one role she could be playing: the ingénue lead, the governess, whose arrival at the mansion on the hill sets the story in motion—my role!

Envy—pure, white-hot envy—shot through my limbs. I was wearing Capezio flats and a sweater set in the best lamb's wool I could afford, but even at a distance of some twenty feet I knew she was wearing Pappagallos and cashmere. Worse, Michael Halliday's fingertips were lightly touching her glossy dark hair. Not only did this girl have my part, but she seemed to have attracted Michael, as well. A surge of adrenaline unfroze my limbs. I was ready to make my move. Which way? Join the convivial hub at the pastry table or barge straight over to Moira Shaw?

I was momentarily spared the decision by a bump and creak behind me. I turned to find a sandy-haired boy pushing his bike into the rehearsal room. He shoved the kickstand down with his foot and stuck out his hand. "Hi. I'm Daniel Ballard. It's okay to call me Danny."

"Hi, Danny. I'm Morgana Harriott."

"Sounds made up. Is that your real name?"

"It is now. Believe me, it's an improvement."

"I'll take your word for it, Morg." Jamming his hands in his pocket, he glanced around the room. "Looks like a late start. The floor's not taped yet. S'cuse me, I'm gonna find the bathroom."

With more aplomb than any kid I'd ever met, Dan Ballard, the boy playing Maxwell Faraby's son, ducked down the hallway in search of the men's room. But the boy had shown me the way: Just stick your hand out and say your name. I crossed the expanse of pockmarked linoleum and stuck my hand out to the portly man with the tweed hat.

"Hi, I'm Morgana Harriott. I'm playing Margie. You must be my father."

"If that's the case, I must've had one helluva beautiful wife. I'm Ed McNabb." He slipped his arm around my ribs, his hand sliding under my breast, and pulled me towards him. "You're sure a 'purty' lady."

My fingers gripped his hand, prying it loose. Had I been at the Playboy Club, I'd have jammed my stiletto heel into his foot, signaled for a Room Director and dumped Irish coffee in his lap. Instead, unarmed and in so-called friendly territory, I smiled, encased his hand in both of mine and stepped away. "Great to meet you, Ed. I'm really looking forward to working with you."

I dodged toward the safety of the coffee urn. As I was filling a Styrofoam cup, a voice breathed in my ear, "You were probably hoping they were serving grasshoppers and gin fizzes this morning."

I laughed and turned to face Michael. "I learned my lesson. Black coffee until the sun's over the yardarm."

"Then you can't go wrong. I see you got a taste of the letch already. I wouldn't go running lines in his dressing room, if I were you."

"I figured as much." My heart pounded, hoping I'd have lots of lines to run in Michael's dressing room. "Do you know everyone here?"

"Pretty much. C'mon, I'll introduce you to Moira. She's a great old gal. Sorry, didn't mean old," he whispered, moving back toward the window.

I grabbed my coffee and a cheese Danish before following him across the room. As Michael introduced me, I realized too late that my hands were full. I looked with regret at the small, slim hand Moira extended, each finger encircled with precious metal and sparkling stones.

"Sorry!" I said, awkwardly looking around for a place to put down my coffee.

"That's all right, dear," Moira said, her eyes warm and moist, her aura scented with the costly aroma of Chanel N°5 perfume. "I'm so glad you joined us. Have you met this darling girl who's playing Elizabeth, the governess? Rebecca Daly, this is Morgana Harriott."

My eyes met Rebecca's and we both smiled our hellos. In a surprisingly breathy little voice, Rebecca said, "I couldn't help but notice what a great color that is on you. Melon?"

"Peach," I said, still smiling. "Thank you. I really love your flats."

"Thanks. They're okay for work." Just when I figured I had no choice but to hate her, she wrinkled her nose and whispered, "Wow. Scary, huh? I've never worked in front of a camera before. Have you?"

"Not much," I whispered back.

"Well, you two are going to get on just fine," Moira said. "Both of you such pretty young things." Her bracelets jangled as she put her blue-lens sunglasses back on and stroked her neck. "I suppose there's nothing much we can do about the fluorescent lighting in here. I fear we'll all go blind." She cocked her head in Michael's direction. "Shouldn't we be starting? From what I can tell of this script, we've got a lot of work to do."

Moira Shaw rose and looked around. As if on cue, the chattering diminished and everyone began moving toward chairs spaced around a long table. Before beginning her progression, her hand tucked inside Michael's arm, she turned to me and eyed the pastry I'd not yet begun to eat. "I'd lose the sweet roll, my dear. Remember, the figure you have now is the one you'll want to keep for a lifetime."

My eyes dropped to the cheese Danish, a greasy cow pie on the palm of my hand, then looked back to the slim, firm figure of Moira Shaw, her hand holding Michael's, as she took her place at the head of the table. The pastry slithered off my hand into a wastebasket as I made my way toward a chair for the first table read of *Dark Passages*.

Not surprisingly, we'd instinctively seated ourselves according to our relationships in the show. The entire Stanhope family, including Moira, her daughter, Maxwell and his son, occupied one end of the table. Rebecca, Michael and the housekeeper positioned themselves across from them. Ed and I sat next to each other in the middle. The director, producer, stage manager and production assistant arranged themselves around the other end of the table. A knot in my stomach pressed itself against my lungs as I opened the script. A case of lockjaw was coming on. I had to remind myself to breathe.

"All right, let's get started. I think we've all met, but let's make it official. I'm Doris Franklin, your director. This is Paul Abbott, our producer. Horace Milton, our head writer. Nigel Baker is the stage manager, and Donna Cruikshank is serving as our production assistant. You've all had a chance to get acquainted over coffee, but let's go around the table and have each of you introduce yourself. Let's begin with Moira Shaw, who is playing Diana—"

Moira rose slightly from her chair, tipped her glasses up and trilled in perfect pre-war, movie-star diction, "Such a thrill, our first day! And such an adventure into a great unknown! I'm so looking forward to getting to know all of you. Let's have a great time together. Rebecca, dear?" Moira cupped her hand over Rebecca's and patted it. I ached to have my hand patted by Moira Shaw.

We continued around the table, with young Dan warily eyeing Maxwell Faraby, who playfully tousled the boy's hair. Amid giggles and hand flapping, the petite blonde playing Angela introduced herself as Ginny Blake. A flash of harsh sunlight struck her face and I knew instantly that Ginny was probably a good five years older than she'd like any of us to know.

Ed introduced himself—and me! With his hand climbing up my thigh, he affected some strange Scottish brogue and said, "How, I ask, could the likes of me have such a fair lass as Morgana Harriott, here, for a daughter. I'm a lucky old sod!" I dug my thumb into his wrist to stop his progression mid-thigh, and managed to say, "Hi, I'm Morgana. Nice to meet you all."

Rebecca Daly was indeed scared, so petrified that her voice shook when she spoke her name. I took some comfort in that. I stroked Haddie's lighter in my pocket and felt the knot in my stomach dissolve, replaced by a tingle of excitement. I was jealous of Rebecca for getting the lead role, but even as I listened to her wavering voice speak the first lines of the script (the very words I'd read for my audition as the governess) I realized I no longer hankered to play Elizabeth.

I'd spent hours creating Margie's back story, analyzing every aspect of her character and drawing on my own experiences working as a "glorified waitress" at the Playboy Club. I'd carefully annotated every line. My pages were black with notes. When my turn did come to read a scene with Ed McNabb, I only pretended to read from the script. I'd learned my lines as soon as my agent told me I had the job. There was no question I was born to play Margie. I'd invested my very being in her.

The reading over, there was a smattering of applause. "Great job, everyone," Doris Franklin said, her voice sounding anything but celebratory. "Okay, before we take a break, let's make a few cuts. We're way over."

I sat in horror as Doris worked her way through the script, relentlessly crossing out entire speeches, many of them from the scene with my father. I loved those lines! My character was an empty shell without these words. Ed gleefully struck out his own speeches, happy not to have to learn any more words than necessary. I lost three whole speeches in my precious scene with Michael. How could she do this? Was it my imagination, or were most of the cuts made in my scenes? By the time we broke for coffee, I was numb. Did I read that badly? It seemed to me Rebecca and Ginny hadn't lost as many lines. I made a mental note to count them later.

I slunk toward the coffee urn, devastated. Michael intercepted me. "Hey, sweet thing. Don't look so tragic. It's normal, okay?"

"Normal? I've barely got anything left to say."

"Then say what you've got as good as you possibly can. Don't let it get you down. This is just the first day, kid."

On my way back from the ladies' room before a second read-through, I passed the production office adjacent to the rehearsal room. I stopped in my tracks when I heard Doris speak my name.

"Maybe Morgana can act the role, but we've got a problem here. Sorry, Paul, I told you right off the bat that she and Rebecca look too much alike on camera. For me, it doesn't work."

"So what are we supposed to do about it now? Replace her? Trust me, nobody's gonna mix 'em up."

"Everybody's noticed it. Dark hair, for one thing."

"So put her in a wig. Make her a redhead. A blonde. Who cares? Just get her a short wig."

"So who's going to persuade her to lose the false eyelashes?"

"Let her keep 'em. She's a waitress, for God's sake. It cheapens her."

I headed back to the rehearsal room, stomach churning. A wig? I was supposed to smother my hair under a stupid wig? Why me? At least I would get to keep my false eyelashes, which were genuine mink, and anything *but* cheap. I couldn't imagine going out to the deli in the morning without my lashes on. I'd even mastered the Jean Shrimpton look, gluing a fringe on my lower lashes—and there was nothing cheap about The Shrimp, the English model who was on the cover of almost every fashion magazine. What were they thinking?

"I don't know what you're so pissed off about, baby," Ed said when we broke for lunch. "Think of it this way. You wear a wig, you save yourself time in the makeup chair."

For his lunch, he'd brought in a small, straw hamper containing a split of Champagne, a wedge of brie and breast of capon in mustard sauce. So much for any Method acting out of him. He was supposedly playing a starving artist who could barely afford beans on toast. Moira joined him during the lunch break, feasting on crustless finger sandwiches and chicken soup that her housekeeper had packed in the Tiffany shopping bag. Maxwell Faraby parked himself at their table, too, after ordering tuna salad from a deli.

I angled to join Michael for lunch, but he headed off to a restaurant with the director and producer. Rebecca and Ginny, who played most of their scenes together, hurried off to a nearby coffee shop without inviting me to join them. I stood at the window watching young Dan walk down the street to get a hot dog at the stand on the corner. Since I was left to eat on my own, I decided to save the calories and just peel the grapefruit I'd brought from home.

The mystery of where the housekeeper ate her lunch became apparent during afternoon rehearsals. Reeking of whisky fumes, she lurched into the rehearsal hall a half hour late, sat down and almost tumbled off her chair. The stage manager hauled her to her feet and walked her into the hallway.

"The old brown bag lunch," Maxwell whispered, and there were titters all around.

"Poor Maeve," Michael said under his breath. "I should'a seen that one coming. I'll call her sponsor."

During the break, I was sent to the hairdresser to try on wigs, not one of them in a color known to nature. Madge, a stringy woman in her fifties, whose own hair looked like a bird's nest, fussed and fingered, while I stared glumly into the mirror. I knew she was trying her best, but each time she showed me another wig, I shook my head and pulled it off. The rejects piled up. With only two left to try on, I selected a Dutch bob in a reasonable shade of red.

"You're sure now?" Madge had asked. "You want to try some of these others again?" Wanting desperately to please, she picked up a vile mass arranged in some sort of poodle cut. At least the one I selected didn't make me look like someone had plopped a dead pet on my head. Wearing the ginger-colored bob, I went back to the rehearsal room to show the director.

As I walked in, Moira looked up and gasped. "My God, that's Lucille Ball's ghastly color."

"You'll stop traffic, kid," Ed said.

"Quite literally," Maxwell added.

Ginny and Rebecca turned away, covering their mouths with their hands. Close to tears, I whipped the wig off my head and dangled it on my finger. "I don't think this'll work. Maybe I could just wear a pony tail?"

Paul Abbott and Doris Franklin exchanged looks. "You think it looks that bad?" he asked. "Maybe we could just cut her hair. What d'ya say?"

I stopped breathing. First they'd cut my lines; now they were after my hair. Out of the corner of my eye, I could see Ginny and Rebecca watching me, not moving. There was tomb-like silence while everybody stared at my head.

"Shorter's better," Doris said finally. "It's the color, though."

"I could bleach my hair," I said, my voice wobbling. "Or wear the wig, maybe." Anything was better than cutting my hair.

"So maybe we could see more wigs," Doris said. "Madge, round up more wigs before tomorrow. Okay, let's move on. Nigel, set up the next scene, please."

I breathed again, reprieve hanging in the balance. We were set to rehearse the first five shows for a full week before going live on camera the following week. I had time to figure something out. I vowed to do anything to save my own hair, even if it meant wearing a god-awful floor mop on my head.

I looked at Madge hovering in the doorway, a clutch of wigs in her hand. She motioned to me, her eyes anxious. I joined her in the hallway. "Bleach would just ruin your hair in no time, my dear. Don't you want to take another look at these wigs? Maybe try them on at home? I'll put them in a bag for you, okay?"

I nodded. "Thanks, Madge, and don't worry. We'll come up with something." Why was I reassuring her? I watched her scurry down the hall, grateful that at least one person seemed to be on my side.

After rehearsal, I stopped by the Playboy Club to ask the Bunny Mother to reschedule me for weekend shifts only. The way things were going, I was glad I hadn't mentioned my role on the soap to Audrey. There was a chance I wouldn't survive even the first episode. As my mother had so aptly put it, "You don't want to be left without."

As the service elevator stopped briefly on the fourth floor, I spotted Brian Duncan, the actor who'd lost the role to Michael, in the Playroom bar talking to Rocco Bennetti. I waved to them.

Just as the elevator doors closed, Bennetti hollered, "Hey, sorry old man Haddock croaked, kid." I rode the rest of the way up to the Bunny dressing room resisting the temptation to send Bennetti hurtling down the elevator shaft. I forced the thought from my mind for fear I might actually make it happen.

"Great! Get your costume on," the Bunny Mother bellowed, as soon as I walked in the door. "I'll give you twenty merits to fill in tonight. We're short a Bunny in the Playroom."

I reluctantly agreed, so long as I could leave after the first show. I then negotiated with Audrey for a good weekend schedule. It took me all of five minutes to slap on a showgirl's face; another few minutes to zip myself into my Bunny costume with collar, cuffs and ears.

Brian had already been notified that I was the substitute and was waiting for me. "Congratulations, Meg. I gotta hand it to you."

"Thanks. Can you let me out early? I have to be back at rehearsal in the morning."

"Sure thing. Put in a good word for me with the right people, okay? Maybe something else will come up on the show, know what I mean? By the way, puss, you're on stage tonight announcing the talent."

I groaned and picked up the headliner sheet to study. Just what I needed, more lines to learn. Peter Allen and his brother were on again, so at least it would be a good show. Maybe even Peter's girlfriend, Liza Minnelli, would show up.

By ten o'clock I was back in the dressing room pulling my street clothes out of my locker. As I was about to leave the Club, I decided to take my satin Bunny stilettos with me to get them re-heeled, and threw them into my canvas shoulder bag with Madge's wigs. Five minutes later I was heading for the subway at 60th and Fifth, figuring I'd be home in bed well before eleven.

Fifteen minutes and a train-change later I reached my stop and hurried down the street toward my apartment. On impulse, I popped into the deli on the corner. I was feeling weak and should have bought vegetables, but the spinach looked limp, the carrots dry. Instead, I bought a pint of Häagen-Dazs chocolate ice cream, a bag of peanut M&Ms and some red licorice to make up for a missed dinner. I crammed the groceries into the canvas shoulder bag, then peeled a five-dollar bill off my roll of tip money and gave it to the clerk. I stuffed the change and the rest of the crumpled wad of bills back into my leather handbag and set off down the darkened street.

I sensed trouble before it happened—just not soon enough. Less than a block from my apartment, a hand clamped around my neck, jolting me backward. A shudder ran through me. I knew someone had fallen in step behind me when I left the deli. I should've paid attention!

My leg scraped against a railing as strong arms hauled me backward down the stairwell of a brownstone. My hands clung to the shoulder bag, hugging it to my chest as a shadowy, foul-smelling man shoved me against a wall. Cold metal was pressed to my cheek. I could feel the sharp edge of a knife.

"Don't move, bitch. We gonna have some fun." He yanked at the straps of my handbag tangled inside my shoulder bag, trying to wrench it free with one hand, the other pressing the knife near my chin.

"Please," I breathed, straining to pull away from the knife blade. "Just take the money. Take it."

He yanked me back, his mouth at my ear. "I take what I want, bitch!" He slashed the straps of the canvas bag. Wigs, satin shoes and ice cream fell at my feet.

His hand dug into my jacket pocket, grabbing Haddie's lighter. "Whadda we got here?" He flicked the wheel. A flame sputtered and danced in the darkness. "Hey, look'a that," he laughed, waving the lighter back and forth.

The flame wavered, its intensity growing hotter and brighter. I gasped as Haddie's face, ruddy and fierce, materialized in the heart of the glowing flame, his presence filling the grubby, musty cellar.

Terrified, the man cried out, flinging the lighter to the floor. Before he could make another sound, I jammed my elbow into his neck, jerking his head backward. Then I tore back his greasy denim sleeve, biting down hard on his exposed wrist. He dropped the knife, trying to wrest his arm from my jaw. Blood pumped from the artery, filling my mouth with a sour, musky taste. Human blood, almost gagging me with its potency, surged into me.

Still feeding on his wrist, I hurled his body back against the wall and slammed my knee into his groin. He sagged, half-conscious, against me. I bit into his neck, unhinging my jaw to drink deeply from the severed artery. Tremors shook his body as I fed on his blood. A force of energy more powerful than anything I'd ever experienced ripped through my limbs.

I released my mouth from his neck only when his body began to cool and he hung limp in my arms. I breathed in a great lungful of air, and ran my tongue across my swollen lips. Every pulse point in my body throbbed, suffused with heat and energy. I threw back my head, the roar building in my chest escaping my lips in a long sigh.

My attacker was still breathing, but only barely. He looked up at me, eyes glazed with fear. What had I done? Anger, retaliation, whatever made me do it? I was filled with remorse. I hadn't consumed enough of his blood to kill him outright, but I couldn't leave him there to slowly die.

I quickly stuffed the ice cream, wigs, satin shoes and my handbag into the canvas bag and slung it on my shoulder. I retrieved Haddie's lighter from the cracked cement floor and tucked it in my pocket. I then scooped the mugger across my arms and carried him up the steps to the stoop of the brownstone. I'd moved quickly, so fast I'd be perceived as no more than a shadow by the young couple approaching on the street. But this was my neighborhood. I couldn't linger. I couldn't be seen.

I fled, flying down the street, my feet barely touching the pavement. As I reached my building, I heard the scream, knew the mugger had been discovered. I ripped the keys out of my handbag and opened the door of my apartment, flinging my canvas bag onto the floor. I locked the door, pulled the chain, then doubled over with agonizing stomach cramps. Sick, sour human blood curdled in my stomach. My head spinning, I looked at the debris at my feet. Wrecked Bunny shoes, a tangle of wigs. The lid sprung loose from the ice cream carton. M&Ms rolling everywhere. *Fun? Fun?*

Breathless and shaking with nausea, I picked up the shoes and flung them against the wall. They bounced back and I kicked them again, then kicked the ice cream, sending the carton skittering across the floor. I tossed the wigs at the ceiling again and again, watching them fall, red and yellow hairballs flopping onto the floor. *Fun?*

I unsealed the bottle of J&B and splashed whisky into one of the cut-glass tumblers. Leaning against the wall, sipping alcohol to cleanse the poisonous taste in my mouth, I fixated on the hairballs lying at my feet. I hated them, hated the idea of having to wear an old lady wig. I reached into a kitchen drawer for a pair of scissors and stabbed one of the wigs, a blonde bubble cut, and carried it into the bathroom.

For some minutes I stood sipping the tongue-stinging whisky and staring at myself in the mirror over the sink, my eyes hollowed, smudged with mascara. I held the blonde wig, speared on the scissors, next to my own long, dark hair and started to cry. The wig, a mass of straw-colored curls, looked cheap in the harsh light. I threw it in the sink, piled my own hair on top of my head and then yanked the wig on, securing it with hairpins.

I took another sip of whisky, picked up the scissors and began clipping. Tufts of blonde hair fluttered into the sink. I hacked away at the bubbly curls, shaping a boyish, close-cropped shag. Minutes later I put down the scissors and finished off the whisky.

A pulsing warmth like a beating heart throbbed in my jacket pocket. I slipped my hand inside and wrapped my fingers around the lighter, then set it on the edge of the sink. Its camouflage colors winked through the cut-glass tumbler.

"Thank you, Haddie," I breathed. "I needed you."

"Not at all, my dear." Haddie appeared, hovering over my shoulder, a glimmering, ghost-like presence in the mirror. "You've been so kind to me, I'm happy to be of use."

"It's been an awful day. Everything's gone wrong." Tears rolled down my cheeks. "I feel terrible, Haddie. I shouldn't have done that —I'm not used to human blood. I don't think it's good for me. What made me do it?"

"Shhhhhh, you'll feel better soon enough." A gentle touch brushed my cheek, wiping away my tears. "I won't let anything hurt you. But there is a force out there that wants to cause you great harm, something far more dangerous than a street thug. We must be vigilant."

"I'll be careful, I promise." But I was looking in the mirror, only half listening. My eyes stared back at me from a pale, drawn face. I felt like crying again. "Look at me, Haddie! My poor hair!"

"I think you look like a tired, overworked waitress in a roadside diner, my dear. Isn't that the point?" His face creased in a gentle smile. "Just trust yourself. You'll be fine."

"Thank you, Haddie. How are you doing? Did you see Ruby yet?"

"Of course, my dear. But so did you." His smile broadened. "Don't look so surprised. I told her all about you. She was waiting for you at the cemetery."

"With the little dog? So that was Ruby?"

"You bet." He winked. "Still my million-dollar baby."

Five

The script lay open on the kitchen table, but I couldn't look at it one more time. I knew not only my own lines, but everyone's dialogue. I was eager for my first day on camera—and nervous, too.

I'd made peace with the ghastly wig. Wearing it every day for rehearsal had accustomed the cast and crew to seeing me in shorn blonde hair. I also realized the shaggy haircut was affecting my behavior as Margie. I wore my peaked waitress cap at a cocky angle. I'd taken to shoving a stubby pencil above my ear after writing up an order. I affected a careless slouch, and my speech took on an edge, all of it playing into making Margie a gal from the wrong side of the tracks with a chip on her shoulder.

Margie had her own secrets, as I did, and we shared a core of vulnerability. I drew on my experience with the mugger because I could tap into my rage at having to keep silent about it. I told no one at the studio or the Club about the incident because I couldn't reveal what had actually taken place. I still felt revulsion at having fed on the blood of another human being and vowed never to do so again, whatever the provocation. I restricted my diet to human food, more than ever determined to prove I could succeed on my own talents, without resorting to supernatural gifts.

The cast had spent the entire previous week working on just the first three scripts, building characters and relationships. For the first few days we'd worked in the rehearsal room, miming opening doors and climbing steps that were indicated only by strips of yellow tape on the floor. Folding chairs represented couches, beds and my work counter in the diner. On Thursday, after one final morning run-through in the rehearsal room, Doris had announced, "We're as ready as we're ever going to get up here, folks. Let's go down on the floor for camera blocking."

"Oh, goodie, magic time," Maxwell said, executing a little buck-and-wing step, reminding us all yet again of his years as a musical comedy star. "Off we go to see the wizardry. What bliss to sit on a proper divan."

He'd tucked his arm through Moira's and led us in a ragged procession down the stairs. The studio had been off limits to everyone but the production staff while the heavy, permanent sets were loaded in and lights hung. None of the actors had yet seen any of the sets. We were all eager for our first glimpse of the make-believe world of Stanhope.

"Tread carefully, mind the cables," Nigel Baker, our stage manager, called out as he pushed open the bulky door.

A hush fell as we stood for a moment adjusting to the dank gloom and padded silence of the cavernous space that smelled of sawdust, paint resin—and magic. With Nigel in the lead, we groped our way over cables and around a stand of fake shrubbery to the arched Gothic entranceway of the Stanhope mansion. With a flourish, Nigel pushed open the intricately carved front door, revealing the oak-paneled expanse of the grand reception hall with its long refectory table.

Moira, first to cross the threshold, cried out, "Home! At last!"

We laughed, but it was tinged with awe. The period décor was magnificent. A curving staircase led to a mezzanine with stained glass windows. A tall grandfather clock stood next to the arched entrance to the drawing room. Danny bounded ahead and let out a shrill whistle.

"Don't do that, you silly boy!" Maxwell said, his voice rising. "You'll bring bad luck on us all!"

"Oh, come on," Danny said. "This isn't the theatah."

"It is our stage, young man." Maxwell's voice boomed so impressively, he repeated himself. "The stage!"

"Well, moving on," Nigel said. "Paint's still wet, so mind the walls."

In the long shadows cast by a dim work light, two prop men were hanging long red velvet drapes against a bank of mullioned windows. A painter touched up the carved handrail on the grand staircase.

The massive oak-paneled drawing room set loomed two stories high, with a fireplace taking up most of one wall. French doors hung with heavy drapery opened onto a stone balcony. Edging my way across a Persian carpet, I peered around at the display of family portraits in heavy gilt frames.

Moira, to the manner born, had already settled herself on the plush brocade couch and was paging through her script. Max and Rebecca perched on the arms of the ornate high-backed wing chairs to run lines. With a pang of disappointment, I realized it was unlikely Margie, the waitress, would ever have occasion to play any tea-and-crumpet scenes in the Stanhope mansion.

I looked around and spied my diner set in a rear corner of the studio, cast in almost total darkness but for a pool of pale work light. My heart throbbed as I edged closer and saw the enamel and chrome soda fountain, glass-domed pie stand and Silex coffee maker. Chrome and red leather stools lined the counter. Red-checkered cloths covered two small tables, with matching curtains at the windows. It was so homey, so real, I felt like I'd known the place my whole life. I picked up a cloth and, with no one in the vicinity watching me, started to wipe down the counter, humming quietly, imagining that this was the lull before the noon rush. I polished up the salt and pepper shakers and set them hugging the toothpick holder and sugar and napkin dispensers.

As I worked away, it came to me why Margie loved her job. She was in charge here, the diner a refuge from her father and his bouts of drinking. More than that, I thought of Ed's hands straying toward my breasts at every opportunity, and shuddered at the thought of Margie's father's hands touching his daughter that way. It was unimaginable in my own experience, but what if Margie had to endure a home life like that? Of course she'd mask her feelings, coming across to others as flip and edgy. I pushed up the sleeves of my sweater and swept the floor with a broom I found leaning against a flat.

Sitting in the pre-dawn stillness of my little kitchen at home, I had imagined myself in a matter of hours being back in the diner set for my first day on camera. I shivered with anticipation, nervous and excited all at once. I forced myself to wait for the first rays of light to peep through the French windows before I showered. I tried to make myself slow down, take my time getting dressed. It was way too early to leave for the studio, but I shoved the script into my shoulder bag and set out anyway. Somehow I had to stop the endless loop of dialogue coursing through my brain.

A bus was pulling up at the stop on the corner. I ran to catch it, amid catcalls and whistles from a construction crew arriving to work at a building site where the Mayflower donut shop had stood. I boarded the bus and slipped into a seat, trying to remember how the street had looked only the week before. Overnight, it seemed, an entire block of stoop-fronted brownstones and small shops had disappeared. I missed the old worn steps and wrought-iron railings as much as the quaint donut shop that reminded me of a coffee shop in Twin Lakes. I hadn't been a New Yorker for more than a week before I'd become nostalgic every time I saw a sagging building boarded up. I wanted nothing to change.

Back in Twin Lakes, nothing ever did. You could count on it. Everything would always remain in exactly the same place, with the fire station next to the post office sounding the noon alarm as it had every day since I could remember. It was a comfort to know the town was there, unchanged, even though I had no desire to return. Besides, it wasn't home I missed. It was Eric, and I wanted him to remain just as I remembered him. Eric was now stationed at an air force base in Northern California. I'd sent him a letter telling him about my role in *Dark Passages*, and got a reply practically by return mail.

> *I'll try to get used to calling you Morgana (how'd you come up with that monicker?) if you can see your way to addressing me as 2nd Lieutenant Eric Tyler. Yahoo, I got my commission. Let me know when your first show is on and I'll make sure to catch it. Hope you won't get too high-hat for me when you become a big TV star! Keep those letters coming. Don't yet know where I'm headed next, but I'll keep you posted. Your guy in the sky, Eric*

I'd followed up with almost daily letters telling him all about rehearsal and the terrible wig I'd been forced to wear. I'd been thinking quite a lot about Eric, surprised he'd been so much on my mind. It didn't sound like he had a girlfriend, but if he did there was no reason why he wouldn't mention her to me in a letter. We hadn't made any promises to each other.

We'd kept in touch, mostly jokey letters and funny postcards. His letters to me were almost better than Eric in person. I could hear his voice and picture him as I remembered him best, standing in the field next to his Taylorcraft, late afternoon sun dappling his freckled face. His name slipped almost soundlessly from my lips. What was wrong with me? Sometimes I would carry on lengthy conversations with him in my head and then, quite unexpectedly, his name would pop out of my mouth—in a breath, an exclamation. Occasionally, I'd been overheard. Young Danny, who overhears everything, looked at me sharply during rehearsal one day. I covered myself by coughing.

The truth is, Eric was always on my mind. When I closed the door to my apartment, I'd hear his name as the latch caught. His name became the cadence to my footsteps as I walked down the street. I'd hear crickets in the night and could swear they were chirping *Er-ic, Er-ic*. I wondered if I was on his mind just as much.

When I got fitted for my Bunny costume, the Bunny Mother had plopped a pair of green satin ears on my head before taking a Polaroid. I posed self-consciously, still not believing that I was among the chosen.

"Let me take another," Audrey had said, "so you can send one home to your mother—if you dare."

Everyone in the fitting room had laughed. I'd taken the curling strip in both hands, watching my image appear in the sticky gray emulsion. My hair was tucked behind my ears with thick bangs brushing my brows. A broad smile showed my dimples. I wasn't much of a glamour-puss. I looked like what I was, a grinning schoolgirl with a pair of satin ears clamped on her head. That's the picture I sent to Eric, enclosed with the Bunny ad torn from a newspaper: STEP INTO THE SPOTLIGHT! BE A STAR!

Eric, in turn, sent me a picture of himself in his flight suit, his hair shorn, standing next to a T-28. He still looked enough like Troy Donahue to be his twin. I'd taped the snapshot to the door of my fridge and wondered when I'd ever see him in person again. At least he'd be able to watch me on television.

As the thought of the television studio crossed my mind, the doors of the bus wheezed shut. I looked out the window and realized buildings were no longer familiar—I'd missed my stop! I'd be late for my first day on camera! I leaped up as the bus began pulling away. "Wait!" I shouted, "I have to get out here!"

The driver looked into his mirror, glaring at me, but the doors shuddered open. I stepped off the bus and stood for a moment, getting my bearings. Today of all days! I hurried toward the studio even though I knew I had plenty of time.

I was still one of the first to arrive in the rehearsal room. The cast congregated around the coffee urn as usual, but the normally languid conversation sounded forced, a little too upbeat. Everyone looked as pumped up as I felt. Our first day on camera was meant to set the pace for the daily schedule, with a blocking rehearsal beginning promptly at 8 A.M. Despite having fully rehearsed the first episode the week before, Doris took us through a run-through of the blocking.

We broke mid-morning and went to our separate dressing rooms to prepare for camera blocking in the studio. I slipped downstairs early to have a few minutes on my own in the diner set. I polished cups, rearranged menus and swept the nooks and crannies of the Stanhope Diner, the place where Margie spent most of her waking hours. I was so wrapped up in my own thoughts that I was startled when bright lights suddenly illuminated my small corner of the studio. Looking up, I saw Nigel and a phalanx of cameras and technicians invading my diner.

"Ready for your close-up, darlin'?" Nigel asked in his chummy cockney accent. "Places, everyone. Anybody seen our lovely Ed?"

"Probably checking out the TelePrompTer," Paul muttered.

I caught his eye. He gave me a stern look and shook his head. "Forget it's even there, okay?"

"The what?" I asked.

"You won't need it," Doris said. "Ed will. Do you mind running lines with him during the break? I'd like to get as clean a run-through as possible before dress rehearsal. We still have to make some cuts."

Cuts? Now? My stomach somersaulted. Ed appeared and, still with his script in hand, we began running through the camera blocking.

The mystery of the TelePrompTer was revealed when I saw our dialogue appear in block letters on a yellow roll of paper moving through a device mounted on each of the three cameras. Ed's eyes flicked past my left ear and I realized he was reading virtually every word off the yellow scroll. I looked over Ed's shoulder and saw my own speeches flowing through the black box. I was instantly mesmerized. I could barely pull my eyes away and stumbled on my next speech. Out of the corner of my eye, I saw Paul glare at me. This new toy was indeed seductive!

It was a strange experience having no eye contact whatsoever with Ed, even when we were directly facing each other, but his shifty look probably worked for his character. The scene we played had to do with my suspicion that my father was getting mixed up in fraudulent dealings with Max's character, Shelby. I got worked up, as I always had in rehearsals, but Doris laid a hand on my shoulder. "Save it for the air show, dear. Nigel, could you mark her here, please? Moving on."

Ed smirked. "Acting our little heart out, are we?" I could already smell the brine of cigarettes and alcohol on his breath. It was barely noon.

I was sent off to makeup before my next scene was blocked. Rebecca was already in the makeup chair. Claude, the burly makeup man, dusted her cheeks with blush.

"Scary, isn't it?" she murmured, an expression she used all too often.

"Scary enough," I said, and squeezed her hand. We had only a brief scene together at the end of the first show, when Elizabeth enters the diner to ask for directions to the Stanhope estate. I offer her a cup of coffee "on the house," and then warn her to watch out because "strange things have been known to happen in the mansion on the hill."

As actors, we had no idea what those "strange things" might be. During rehearsals, Moira had said that she suspected the writers didn't know yet, either. Horace Milton, the head writer on *Dark Passages*, had vanished from our lives after the first read-through.

It wasn't until dress rehearsal that I got my first real attack of nerves. For one thing, the studio was dead quiet for the first time that day. Paul, Doris and the rest of the tech crew were in the control room. Only Nigel, wearing an earphone, remained on set. Even the cameras gliding into place for my opening scene made only the barest whooshing sound on the smooth concrete floor.

As Nigel began the countdown for my opening scene, my hands started to shake. A spoon flew off the saucer I was holding. For one breathless moment I wondered if it was okay to pick it up.

"Sit slowly, rise slowly," Doris had repeatedly reminded us, "or the camera will lose you."

I heaved a sigh and ducked slowly to pick up the spoon before wiping down the counter. The sigh alone calmed me. The scene with Ed went better than it ever had during rehearsal.

Michael gave my shoulders a squeeze after our scene together and brushed his lips against my hair. "You're a pro, baby. Sailing through."

After the dress rehearsal, we all headed up to the rehearsal room for final notes. I was feeling confident until Paul pulled me aside and said, "We're still having a little trouble with that accent of yours, Morgana. It's 'roof,' not 'ruff.' You were doing fine in rehearsal, but you're back to saying 'wuhtrrrr' instead of 'water' again. Maybe it's nerves, but you gotta work on it, okay? We're not in Kansas."

I nodded. Kansas, Minnesota, same difference. Paul had been harping on my Midwestern accent all week. "You sound like you just got off the boat," he'd say.

I thought he was kidding. "Minnesotans don't have an accent," I told him.

"Maybe in Minnesota they don't. Here they do. There's no need to wrestle those vowels. Your O's sound like a cold, north wind," he'd said, in what I considered a terrible New York accent. I'd tried mightily, even working with a tape recorder at home at night.

"Water," I said carefully. "Roof. How's that?"

"Better," he said, in what sounded like "beddah" to me.

At least there were no more cuts. My only notes from Doris were, "You're not going to drop the spoon, right? And take it easy, Morgana. Relax with it now."

As the clock ticked toward three o'clock, Claude and Madge appeared in the doorway. "Okay, last touchups, please," Doris said, picking up her script and note pad. "Good show everyone. We go to air in ten minutes."

There is a show biz adage that a bad dress rehearsal means a good performance. I can only think the opposite must also be true. Cold, paralyzing stage fright seized my entire body the moment I saw the cameras bearing down on me during the commercial break. My scalp constricted, squeezing the blood out of my brain. I went deaf. Stone deaf. I then realized in the silence that Nigel was only mouthing "Five . . . four . . . three . . . two. . . ."

He pointed his finger at me. The red light on Camera Two popped on. Then, not only the spoon, but both the cup and saucer bobbled in my hand, making a terrible clattering sound. Coffee slopped on the counter. My other hand swept up to steady things, and my thumb knocked everything—cup, saucer and spoon—into the sink. I heaved another sigh and began mopping up, for the first time really having something on the counter to clean. I forged on, all of us having been warned not to stop under any circumstances. There would be no second chances, no retakes.

Ed entered early. "Pop!" I said, as though startled by a ghost.

I had nowhere near finished my business behind the counter. Ed tripped and bumped into a table on his way in, which made me feel better.

I offered him coffee, as scripted, "and a—." I couldn't think of the word, so I pointed.

"Muffin? Sure thing," Ed said, actually looking at me for once.

The moment served to restore my equilibrium. We managed to say all the rest of the words in almost the right order, though the scene seemed to play faster than it ever had before. Ed looked sweaty and a bit unsteady at the end. I felt completely short-circuited, as though a bolt of electricity had shot through me.

I stood behind a flat, shaking, trying to calm myself. I breathed, trying to remember how to exhale. I counted my fingers, some twice. I looked at my feet, which appeared to be at least a city block below me.

I'd settled down considerably by the time Michael appeared for our scene together. Nigel gave us the countdown and Michael stepped behind a flat to peer at me through the window of the diner. I looked up and he waved, just as we'd rehearsed. I felt like I was back in real time. The scene played well. Michael quizzed me about my father and warned me he "might be up to no good."

I felt a surge of relief when the cameras swung away. I hadn't screwed up. Michael signaled "thumbs up" and hurried across the studio for his next scene.

I had only the teaser at the end of the show left to do. In that final scene, I pull the shade down on the window, preparing to close the diner, when I see Elizabeth huddled outside. I'm supposed to motion her to the front door. But Rebecca wasn't in place. I pretended I could see her, motioned anyway and then went to open the door. Rebecca stood there, pale and quaking. I grasped her hand and pulled her into the diner. She was clearly terrified. If anything, her fear played well to my warning about the Stanhope family mansion—but she wasn't acting.

When we finished the scene, Nigel said, "Hold it, everyone. Stay in place while we check clearance—"

After a moment, we heard Doris Franklin's voice booming over the loudspeaker, "Thank you all. That's a wrap. Great job!"

Tears rolled down Rebecca's cheeks. She sank against me, pressing her face into the stiff cotton of my waitress uniform. "Scary," she sobbed, holding me tightly. "That was so scary. I don't want to do this anymore. It's too scary!"

"Are you two okay?" Nigel asked, turning to look at us.

"Just happy it's over," I said. "We're fine." I stroked Rebecca's back, feeling her damp cheek against my neck.

"I could weep myself," Nigel said cheerfully. "Good show. Rehearsal in half an hour. Better get changed, ladies."

Rebecca swiped the tears from her face and the two of us hurried out of the studio. As I raced up the stairs to my dressing room, unbuttoning my waitress uniform as I went, I thought of Eric. I'd have to let him know I'd earned my wings, too. As I closed the door to my dressing room, I whispered his name. "Eric," I said aloud, as I stepped out of the waitress uniform. I gave myself a stern look in the mirror. Stop it! Yet his name once again formed on my lips.

I zipped up my skirt, tucked in my shirt and hurried down the hall to the rehearsal room. With a bit of luck, I'd find a letter from Eric in my mailbox when I got home. In any case, once I'd studied my lines for tomorrow's show, I'd write to him. I had so much to tell him.

Six

Although we were doing *Dark Passages* "live," we'd completed ten half-hour episodes before the series debuted on national television. Kinescopes, recordings made by filming the show off a video monitor while we worked live in the studio, were shipped to network affiliates throughout the country for local broadcast. The first episode was scheduled to air as a "teaser" on a Friday afternoon and then replayed the following Monday for the official launch of the series. We had no opportunity to see the episode in advance. We waited nervously to watch the debut on television, knowing the show had been recorded, mistakes and all, with no edits. I feared the worst, especially as the first episode was airing on Friday the 13th.

I squeezed into the crowded Green Room to watch Friday's "teaser" show with the other actors, crew and production staff. Most of the actors were still in costume, having barely finished that day's recorded show. Ed McNabb had managed to wedge himself behind me and attach his hands to my hips.

"So, where's the Champagne?" Ed asked, as the logo appeared on the screen. "Time to uncork it, Paul, you cheapskate producer."

Everyone laughed, including Paul Abbott. He leaned against the doorjamb, arms crossed. "Not until after rehearsal, you lush. I'm not taking a chance."

"Dutch courage, that's all we're asking," Maxwell Farraby drawled, fingering his cravat. "I, for one, am in dire need."

"Hush," Moira said, her voice smokier than usual. "It's too bloody late anyway, *n'est-ce pas*? That's the hell of doing these things, kiddies.

Thank God, we'll see it once and it'll all be over. Enjoy!" Moira's droll delivery earned a smattering of laughter, but everyone's eyes were on the wall monitor watching the opening credits.

The music swelled, eerie and portentous. We all fell silent as Rebecca's voice-over faded in on an establishing shot of the Gothic mansion where she'd been installed as governess. Although weeks earlier I'd watched rehearsals of the initial scene between Rebecca and Moira, seeing it unfold on the television monitor was a revelation. Rebecca, against all odds, was terrific. I watched spellbound as Moira, playing the haughty and elegant Diana, swept down the staircase in a shimmering gown to greet the new governess. Rebecca, as Elizabeth, stood in the doorway, looking meek in a shabby coat. I knew how scared Rebecca had been that first day, yet her terror was hardly evident. She appeared shy and vulnerable—and utterly captivating.

There was no sense that a stage manager was signaling the countdown, or that a boom operator was swinging a microphone within a hair's breadth of a tightly-framed closeup. There were no clunky camera movements, no sign that the actors were struggling to hit marks on the stage floor.

After a commercial break, jukebox music played. My first scene was coming up. I half hid behind Max Farraby's sleeve as the camera swung from the jukebox to me busily wiping down the counter. What? There was no sign of me spilling coffee. The camera must have been on the jukebox when I dropped the cup and saucer—nobody would ever know! I stood watching myself on-screen, taking it all in, trying to remember every detail even as the scene passed in a blur.

The wig looked okay. My acting was passable, particularly when I forgot the word "muffin." I decided that I would always try to make a mistake, do something a little wrong to appear more natural. But why was I hunching my shoulders? Nerves, probably. I made a mental note to watch my posture. My eyes flicked around too much, and my mouth was a little stiff. Nerves, again. But my voice sounded confident, even as I pronounced "water" and "roof" correctly.

"You look good, kitten," Ed whispered in my ear, his thumbs tickling my ribs. His breath was stale with a toxic combination of cigarettes and noontime martini.

"Thanks, Dad." I hugged my arms to my chest, effectively checking his inevitable advance on my breasts, but my mind was on my performance.

The moment the show was over, I raced down the stairs to the pay phone and called Wesley Truscott. All I could think about were the shaky, stiff moments in my performance, the times when I looked unsure of myself. "Was I okay?" I blurted, when he came on the line.

"Of course you were. Take heart, my dear, all you need is experience. You were really quite entrancing, like a young Margaret Sullavan. All the more endearing for little flubs."

I wanted desperately to believe him. Wesley Truscott's words sounded as soothing as Pastor Odegaard's back home, though our preacher wouldn't have used such excessive language. "Good" or "real nice" would have been lavish praise coming from Pastor Odegaard, or anyone else in Twin Lakes.

"This is the beauty of it, Morgana," Wesley went on. "Consider the show a lab. You must experiment. Be brave. Nobody is watching anyway, except housewives and kids. It goes by in a zip. If you make a mistake, who cares? Have some fun with it."

I hung up feeling better, but still doubtful. Have fun? Had he no idea how frightening it was when the little red light went on?

"Don't be so grave," Wesley had said. "Just toss those lines away!"

Okay, I'd try to be more flip. Doris had told me more than once that it wasn't necessary to always stare into the other actor's eyes. "Just pour a cup of coffee, like the guy needs a refill, and move on," she'd told me.

I mounted the stairs and headed for the rehearsal room. Paul had indeed laid on Champagne and sheet cake decorated with the soap's logo. He was proposing a toast as I walked in.

"Here's to all of you, our *Dark Passages* family. Let's hope today's audience spends the weekend talking about the show and that all of America tunes in on Monday. May we prosper and enjoy a long, happy run! Salud!"

"Hear, hear! Congratulations, everyone. Onward and upward!" Doris Franklin chimed in, while deftly removing a glass of Champagne from young Dan's fingers. Moira, ensconced in her usual seat at the head of the rehearsal table, tapped Danny's hand as he reached for another glass.

I caught Michael's eye and he winked. I saw he was drinking coffee. Not so Ed, who was pouring himself another glassful of Champagne and passing the bottle to Max Farraby. I smiled at Michael and raised my glass in a silent toast.

My best scenes were with Michael. He always did something to throw me off, catch me unawares, and it worked to my advantage. In the second episode we'd taped, he'd slipped his arm around my shoulder, giving me a squeeze when he asked about my father. I was so surprised I'd almost dropped the Silex. We hadn't rehearsed the scene with his arm around me, but it seemed so natural that I grinned and leaned into him, one of my few spontaneous moments in the whole show.

I fantasized that the writers would pick up on our chemistry and make Margie and Steve an item. The thought of playing love scenes with Michael left me limp. But I sensed it was not to be. Michael's character was already romantically linked to Elizabeth, Rebecca's role. So far, they'd only brushed lips and held hands, but I ached watching them rehearse. Everyone seemed to think they were hot together, the shy, naïve governess seduced by the "bad guy back in town."

While Eric was always in my thoughts, he was also a world away. I missed him, but still thought of him more as a buddy than a boyfriend. I was around Michael every day. He flirted and teased, and it was little wonder I'd developed a crush on him.

Maybe I was imagining it, but it seemed that Michael had his eye on me, too. If I were to lose my virginity, Michael was my choice. He wasn't married. He didn't seem to have a girlfriend. So how was I supposed to set this up? I'd imagined various scenarios, but none of them panned out.

I'd had a few other crushes since I'd come to New York. I'd briefly fallen for a guy named Vic in my acting class. His dark good looks and edgy James Dean persona were irresistible. I'd finagled doing a scene with him from *Bus Stop*, a William Inge play in which Vic played a cowboy marooned with a blonde siren—both lost souls.

We rehearsed in his place, a fifth-floor, cold-water walkup in the West Village, where he'd installed a full-length panel of mirror on the back of his apartment door. As we ran through the scene, I'd find him checking himself out in the mirror, observing every gesture, altering his inflection and changing his stance. It was distracting, but he was cute.

But then, after rehearsal one afternoon, we went to Café Figaro and shared our dreams. It turned out he really wanted to be a movie star—*really, really* wanted to be a movie star. It didn't take me long to realize he'd chosen the booth we were sitting in because there was a mirror mounted on the back wall. We held hands over our cappuccinos, but I knew he was scrutinizing himself in the mirror over my shoulder, analyzing his every gesture and facial expression. Occasionally he would tip his head and repeat himself as though going for a more advantageous take. The thought of that sort of self-scrutiny in bed was distinctly unappealing, no matter how cute he was.

I'd met Howie, an NYU film student, at a folk concert in Washington Square on a Sunday afternoon. It turned out he wanted me to play a dead body in a vacant lot for an eight-minute short he was filming for class. I obliged, despite a wind-chill factor and the smell of putrid garbage. After spending an hour lying in rubble somewhere near the Holland Tunnel, a pretty blonde showed up and I realized she was his girlfriend. Why didn't she want to play a dead body in his damn movie?

I'd also angled for a date with Josh, the bartender in the Playmate Bar at the Club. We weren't allowed to "fraternize" with other employees, but Josh was cute like Vic, had an Irish accent and the dark good looks I fancied. It turned out he was married with three kids and a pregnant wife, but claimed they had an "understanding." When he passed along this information, I stared hard at him over draft beers at a pub on Second Avenue. All I could see was a train wreck down the track. "But you don't have an understanding with me," I told him, and left.

Losing one's virginity wasn't a careless act, like leaving favorite sunglasses behind in the post office. "Losing it" required an inordinate amount of scouting, planning and organization. It wasn't that guys didn't come on to me—they did. But it was all creepy, flirty, whistles-on-the-street stuff, never a proper date with cocktails and dinner that led to something. I was picky. Not just anyone would do.

There had to be an element of romance or, failing that, some attempt at significance.

Another major factor to consider is that I wasn't at all sure just how different I was from a regular human girl. I certainly passed for normal in most regards. Only a dental exam would reveal the feeding tubes. I had no intention of submitting myself to any sort of physical exam. I'd already had some indications that my pale flesh tone, pulse rate and body temperature weren't quite standard. Eric was always trying to warm my icy hands, and Marilyn would insist I put on a sweater when I had no need of one. But everyone saw I could run fast, swim lengths better than any boy in class and was fearless climbing trees, so my slower pulse rate was put down to that of a good athlete. Besides, I was undeniably healthy because I never got sick, not even when everyone else got measles and mumps.

But sexual intimacy was venturing into the great unknown. My mother had shown no inclination to give me any pointers, and I wasn't about to ask her. It had occurred to me to test drive my sexuality on a complete stranger in case things went terribly wrong. But since I didn't know entirely what was expected, I couldn't predict what particular body function might let me down. A stranger—not someone from acting class or the Club that I would run into again—might be the answer. But I couldn't face offering myself up to someone I didn't know.

Eric, if he weren't on the other side of the continent, would have been a candidate. I somehow knew he'd take whatever happened in stride. If worse came to worst, I could tell him I was a vampire and see what happened. At some point during their courtship, my mother must have confided in my father, and he seemed to handle it. I was in a quandary I couldn't seem to resolve. I'd have to let fate takes its course. But back in my dressing room, with the taste of Champagne still on my lips, it was Eric's name I breathed. Finally, something on my mind that I didn't care to write to Eric about!

I was not in Monday's episode, so I didn't have to stay for the afternoon rehearsal. Instead, once I changed out of Margie's waitress uniform, I caught the crosstown bus to the Playboy Club to don my Bunny costume for the cocktail shift. The irony was not lost on me.

Nor the idea of how much I enjoyed the rhythm of my new life. I was scheduled to do three shows a week, which left me time to take scene study classes with Uta Hagen, jazz dance with Luigi, voice lessons with Sue Seton, and still work Friday and Saturday cocktail shifts at the Playboy Club.

Once *Dark Passages* was on the air, it had been my plan to stop working at the Club. But I walked into the Bunny dressing room that Friday afternoon, signed in, took my costume off the rack, and realized I didn't want to quit. I'd miss my Bunny friends. I'd even miss Audrey!

The Bunny dressing room was an oasis of girly smells—swirling fragrances of hairspray, lotions and powders—and the chatter of female voices. I liked the routine of opening my locker, shedding my daytime clothes and then sitting in front of the bright lights at the makeup table, wearing only my sheer black tights while glamming up with eyeliner and false lashes. With time to spare, I brushed my hair, swept it up into a French twist and pinned on my Bunny ears. *How could I abandon all this?*

Audrey stepped out of her office and bellowed for volunteers to work a private party Sunday afternoon. I raised my hand, along with Noni and Allie. I wasn't working on *Dark Passages* until Monday afternoon's rehearsal for Tuesday's episode. I still hadn't told anyone I was on the show and wondered if someone had watched the teaser episode that afternoon before coming to work. So far no one had mentioned a word about seeing me on television.

I stepped into my costume and bent over, holding my breasts in the cups, so Noni could zip me up. "Hey, guys," she said, "big news!"

I held my breath, waiting to hear that Noni had seen me on *Dark Passages*. I liked the idea of surprising everyone and having them crowd around congratulating me.

"I'm subbing for Savannah tonight because she's got a big date. Guess who?"

"Who?" I asked, disappointed the big news wasn't me.

"Nick Westry, that fireman from the station near the house. He came over last night and asked her out."

"Finally, someone as take charge as she is!" Allie laughed.

"And he's cute. Shy, but cute," Noni said. "She's over the moon."

"Good for her," I said. "Worth taking the night off for."

We all trooped into Audrey's office for final inspection. She always found something wrong. Noni had a snag in her stocking. I'd clipped my cufflinks on backward. It gave Audrey no end of pleasure to send us back to the dressing room to "shape up or else." With seconds to spare before we had to relieve the Lunch Bunnies, Audrey finally gave approval so we could go down for the cocktail shift.

None of my customers mentioned seeing me on *Dark Passages*, either. Of course, it was a daytime show and most people would be at work, but I was still disappointed. I wondered if Eric, my parents or anyone back in Twin Lakes had managed to watch.

Then, as I was serving a party of four at a table in the Living Room, I looked up to see Eric walk into the Club. I froze and almost dropped my tray. He was togged out in his Air Force uniform and buzz cut, talking to Elke, who was on Door Bunny duty.

She directed him toward the spiral stairs. I watched him look around, tall and easy in his uniform, and walk toward the staircase near the piano bar.

I almost waved to him, but caught myself. Instead I sauntered slowly to the piano bar and perched against the railing. It seemed an eternity before he paused halfway up the stairs and saw me. First, the shock of recognition and then a slow grin as he took in his girl-next-door-turned-sex-goddess in a Bunny costume.

"Well, look at you!" he said, not at all bashfully.

"Well, look at you!" I said grinning. "I'd give you a hug, but I'd get fired."

"I'd do more than that and get arrested," he said.

"So, what the heck are you doing here?" I asked, laughing.

"That's a big, dark secret, but let's say I was in the neighborhood and wanted to see my girl. Say, can a guy get a drink here?" He was doing his best Bogart, squint and all.

"Sure can, mister," I said, in my best Bacall. "Follow me."

I settled Eric at the Piano Bar, showed off my Bunny Dip and raced off to the service bar to get him a Tom Collins.

"So, who's the cutie?" Noni asked me. Before long, every Bunny on the floor knew my old boyfriend was in town. They lavished him with attention. He ate it up. There wasn't a sign of the shyness I remembered from school. He'd filled out in the shoulders, grown a little taller (or maybe it was the thick-soled black shoes), and he looked great. I did the Twist on top of the piano, doing a crazy backbend shimmy that defied my breasts to stay in the costume. Eric clapped and whistled, then helped me step back down to the floor, loving every minute of it.

I arranged for Eric to meet me after work in the side entrance of FAO Schwarz, which was, according to the Bunny Manual rules, beyond the regulation three-block radius of the Club. By the time I finished my cocktail shift and stepped out of the employee entrance on 59th Street, it was dark and the air had cooled. I hurried down Fifth Avenue, stuffing my hands in the pockets of my blue jeans, feeling like I'd left all my confidence back in the Bunny dressing room with my ears and cottontail. What would we talk about after all this time apart?

Then I saw Eric in the doorway of the toy store, his eyes scanning the street looking for me. I waved and started to walk faster, skipping and kicking up my heels to attract his attention, but he didn't see me. I broke into a run the last few yards and jumped up, throwing my arms around him.

"Here, Miss!" he said irritably, pulling my arms from his neck. "What do you think you're doing? I'm meeting a Playboy Bunny here!"

"Damn you!" I laughed, and he started tickling me. We were like two puppies off-leash, playfully pawing and pushing each other in the doorway of FAO Schwarz, in front of its vast window display of Hula Hoops and plush animals. Then we kissed. We had kissed before, but not like this. He was new to me, the bulk of his arms, his assurance. Yet the taste of his mouth was so familiar. We kissed for a long time.

"So, do those things come off at night?" he asked, gently running the edge of his thumb across the thicket of my false eyelashes. I shivered and ran my hands up inside the back of his jacket, feeling the hard muscle and the warmth of his body.

"Yup," I said. "I stick 'em on the bedpost overnight, along with my chewing gum." He started to kiss me again, but then we both began laughing.

Hand-in-hand we walked down Fifth Avenue, ducking into doorways along the way to kiss and just hold each other. At Rockefeller Center we turned west, toward Broadway and then cut over to Joe Allen on 46th Street. We sat for a long time, drinking beer with our burgers and chili at a small corner table with a red-checkered cloth and a candle stuck in a bottle, dripping wax. I told him about the morning I'd sat at the bar with the two actors after our camera tests, but didn't mention the grasshopper I'd consumed. It occurred to me that back in Minnesota, Eric and I were both still under the legal drinking age, but didn't mention that, either.

Eric and I caught up on news from the home front. I heard all about his pilot training. He was being sent off to Southeast Asia on a mission to teach guerilla pilots to fly T-28s. I told him about watching our first episode, which he'd missed seeing because he was in flight when it aired. I told him I'd even come around to liking my terrible wig.

"I couldn't bear it if *Dark Passages* got cancelled. I'd be back auditioning again."

"Well, if it doesn't work out, you know you can always go back to Twin Lakes. I hear the Red Owl is hiring. You're one heck of a checkout girl."

I punched him in the shoulder. "You can always get work flying a crop duster, you know."

Afterward, we walked past Sardi's as Marlene Dietrich swept out the door to a waiting car. We stopped for cheesecake at Lindy's, peeked in the windows of Toots Shor's and stood outside the Metropole listening to Gene Krupa play drums.

Eventually, and in no particular rush, we arrived at my small garden apartment near Gramercy Park. We had all the time in the world, and it had always been that way when we were together. I unlocked the door to my apartment and stood back so Eric could enter first.

My pride in my little fifty-nine-dollar-a-month studio was unabashed. The best vantage point of the entire apartment was from just inside the front door. We stood together on the small patch of black and white tiles in the Pullman-style kitchen. The entire apartment consisted of one very large room with tall, built-in bookcases on either side of French doors leading to a garden. A short hallway next to the kitchen led to the bathroom and walk-in closet. A French daybed piled with pillows, a rattan chest that served as a coffee table and a portable phonograph with a stack of LPs constituted my entire inventory of furnishings. I did not own a television set, and I hadn't yet had a single visitor to my apartment. Eric was the first.

"Well, the ceiling is high," he ventured, "too bad you can't turn it on its side."

I laughed, and showed him around the black and white tile bathroom, pointing with pride to the big, old-fashioned bathtub. I gave him a tour of my closet, a space slightly bigger than the kitchen. We then hung up our jackets together, an undertaking so intimate, I could barely breathe.

I put on a Sinatra album while Eric checked out my refrigerator. He had never seen a fridge that small before, or that empty. I had a tomato (puckered with age), two eggs and three bottles of beer. I had not bought the beer for drinking or the eggs for eating. I used both on my hair to give it body, but I didn't mention that to Eric.

"How about a Scotch?" I reached for the bottle I'd relieved my parents of, eager to show off my fancy cut-glass tumblers.

"Beer's fine," Eric said, and popped the caps on two bottles. We settled on the daybed, sipping our beers and listening to Frank sing "In the Wee Small Hours of the Morning."

After a long kiss, Eric pulled my sweater over my head. I lay back against the pillows looking at him in the wash of moonlight spilling through the French doors. I reached up and lay a hand on his chest, my fingers fumbling with his shirt buttons. His hand, warm and gentle, folded over mine and he kissed my fingers. He slipped out of his shirt, then deftly unzipped my blue jeans, his hand brushing across my bare belly.

"Do I have to be careful?" he whispered, kissing my neck.

"No," I said, barely able to breathe. So far, so good. Everything was in working order, as much as I could tell.

"No?" he smiled, "I didn't think so. But you're sure I don't have to use anything?"

I bobbled my head in some sort of response. We kissed again. That Eric knew what he was doing, and I didn't, mattered little. I melted in an unfolding of sensations so achingly intense I longed for him even as I lay in his arms. Eric soon realized it was my first time. For a moment he just held me, then kissed my breasts.

"I'm so glad it's you," I breathed, and kissed his eyes, his lips.

Afterward, in that quiet time when I lay with my head on his chest, he whispered, "You should have told me, you know."

"Who would admit a thing like that?" I laughed.

"Is it what you thought it would be?" he asked. "Are you okay?"

"More than okay," I said. "You're sure I was okay?"

Eric laughed, and we made love again. I'd wanted to ask if he'd found me normal, but it appeared he did.

It dawned on me what he must have been thinking when he saw me at the Club. I was made up like a showgirl, all eyelashes and bright lipstick. I certainly didn't look or behave virginal, especially while shimmying on the piano. I'd been living in New York on my own, working most of that time as a Playboy Bunny. Why wouldn't he think I was on the Pill and having a high old time? Instead, while I looked the part, it was Eric who was experienced. And as far as being careful, that was one thing I didn't have to worry about. My mother had made it clear that pregnancy for our kind was difficult and often lethal.

Eric and I spent the rest of the night talking, holding each other close. Shortly after dawn we went to the corner coffee shop for breakfast, arriving just as they opened the plate glass door. We ordered eggs, and managed to hold hands even as we ate. I couldn't bear to say goodbye, but Eric had to "report back by 0900," he said.

"When will I see you again?"

He shrugged. "It'll be a while. Just write, okay?" He wrote his address on a paper napkin and slid it across the table.

As I stuffed the napkin in my pocket, my fingers brushed Haddie's old camouflage-painted Zippo. I cupped the smooth metal in my palm, feeling its weight and warmth in my hand. Then, my fingers wrapped tightly around the lighter, I reached across the table and handed it to Eric. "Have you got a cigarette on you?"

"Sure," Eric said, pulling a pack of Old Golds from his pocket and offering me one. He flipped the metal lid on Haddie's Zippo and lit my cigarette before lighting his own. "Where'd you get this thing? I've never seen one like it."

"An old friend gave it to me for luck. He told me it wouldn't ever blow out on you, even in a strong wind. Keep it."

"You sure?"

"I'm sure. I don't really smoke, anyway. Just write to me. As often as you can."

Later, I stood on the morning-wet sidewalk watching Eric's taxi drive down the near deserted avenue. His last kiss was still warm and fresh on my lips. How could I ever forget lying naked in Eric's arms? I walked back to my apartment and curled up on the rumpled daybed to write him a letter.

Seven

Beauty is a talent. To my mind, as with any natural talent —a good singing voice, an ability to dance or play the piano—it's up to the lucky recipient of such a gift to make something of it. I was perfectly willing to exploit my own human attributes and talents. I only drew the line at achievement by dint of my supernatural gifts.

But Rebecca, a human whose primary talent was beauty, did little to trade on her singular gift. Her translucent skin required no makeup. Her lashes were lush and dark without mascara, her brows perfectly shaped without plucking. Her thick, dark hair did not require curling, and her lips looked full and glossy with the aid of nothing more than Chapstick. She moved with natural grace, and her whispery voice managed to convey vulnerability, mystery and intimacy all at the same time—despite having never studied any acting techniques. Rebecca did nothing to enhance her advantage or exploit her potential, but reaped benefits anyway.

It was maddening, really, to know how terrified she was to appear on camera and to see that her stage fright did not register on the screen. She was completely natural, her every word and expression entirely believable. Rebecca did not seem to have to work at anything, nor did she show any signs of striving. I came to realize that this was probably her greatest gift, even more enviable than her exceptional beauty.

It was inevitable that Rebecca would move on to bigger and better things—but who could have predicted it would happen so quickly? Only weeks into production on *Dark Passages*, Rebecca was on her way to Hollywood, a network contract in her pocket. Her release from the soap had been negotiated quietly, but word leaked out that she would be off the show well before we were even midway in our first thirteen-week cycle.

"Our little sparrow is flying the nest," Paul Abbott said, making an official announcement before an afternoon rehearsal. "Rebecca is off to Tinsel Town next week to star as a rookie policewoman in a new prime-time drama for this network. I'm sure we all wish her the best."

He gave her a hug and pressed a kiss on her head before hurrying back to his office for a meeting with Doris Franklin.

Although we had an inkling Rebecca would be leaving, the news was still a shock. Ed, Moira, Danny, Michael and I stood awkwardly around the coffee urn looking at Rebecca. She put her hands to her face, her gesture utterly beguiling.

"Well, here's looking at you, kid," Michael said, toasting her with his coffee cup. "I wish it was me heading out there. Man, I could go for some of that sunshine about now."

I looked at him quickly. He'd tossed the words out in his offhand manner, but I knew he was hungrier for a network contract than beach weather. So was I.

"I'd go in a second," Danny said, his voice on the verge of a pubescent crackle. "Aren't you excited?"

"Who knows what's in store," Rebecca shrugged, her voice soft. "My agent told me last week that the network had another project for me. Now I have to move all the way out to California. Alone. It's sort of scary."

"I think it's fabulous," Moira said, smoothing her hand across Rebecca's thin shoulders. "At your age, I, myself, was plucked from a Broadway play and whizzed aboard the Twentieth Century passenger train with a Warner Bros. contract in hand. A week later I was on a Hollywood soundstage with Gary Cooper. It was heaven, my dear. Now this is your break, and I promise you'll never look back."

A look of alarm fluttered across Rebecca's face, rendering her even more appealingly vulnerable. "Oh, dear. Gary Cooper? Is he still alive? I think I'd rather stay here. I'm going to miss you guys."

"Listen to her," Ed boomed. "She thinks we're actually going to be here a week from now. Baby, this show is on its way down the toilet. Finito. Grab your exit ticket while you can, kid."

"No, the cycle's not even half over," I said, trying to check my desperation. "They have to give us a chance. We've only been on the air a couple of weeks."

"Not with our ratings," Danny said, doodling on his script. "My agent said we could fold any day now. That's life. Get used to it."

There was a moment of silence, broken by Ed, his voice unnaturally harsh. "Yeah, listen up to Danny. It's hard to argue with a twelve-year-old who knows the ropes. So what're you gonna do, kid? Throw over show biz for junior high?"

"Hey, easy, Ed," Michael said. "We'll all be looking for work soon enough. Except for Rebecca, here." He slipped his arm around her waist. "Put in a good word for us out there, would ya? I'd fly out any chance I got to do a guest star role with you."

"Well, it'll be back to the stage for me. I long to be on the boards again," Moira said, sagging into a chair at the rehearsal table. "Just hand me a good, meaty role, that's all I ask. I'll supply wardrobe."

My stomach was curdling, and it wasn't coffee souring it. Could it get any worse? I looked at Rebecca, her eyes sad for us. I couldn't hate her. I just wanted what she had: everything easy, everything on a silver platter without even trying for it. Instead I was soon going to be out of my first big acting job, and there was nothing I could do about it. Thank God I'd saved some money and hadn't given up my Bunny job. I sank into a chair next to Moira hoping I could stave off the tears until I got home.

Then Nigel hurried into the rehearsal room and laid a hand on my shoulder. "Morgana, love, the powers that be would like a little word with you."

"Now?" Alarm bells clanged in my head. "Why? What'd I do?"

"The headmaster's not going to flog you, child. Just come along."

"It's Ten Little Indians, Morgana. We're all being picked off, one by one," Moira said gloomily. "I can smell it. Time to pack up the slap and good-luck telegrams."

"Not quite the death knell yet," Nigel said. "Come along, Morgana."

I followed Nigel to the producer's office. "Slap? What does she mean, *slap?*"

"Makeup. In Moira's case, greasepaint. The old dear's been around since the commedia dell'arte. Here you go, smile prettily," Nigel said, opening the door to Paul's office.

I was on the verge of tears as I stepped over the threshold. Paul looked up as I entered, his face grim. Horace Milton, whom I had not seen since the first read-through, sat in an armchair, staring at me blankly. Doris, arms crossed, stopped mid-pace and swung around, looking me up and down.

"Could we see your hair, Morgana? I mean, without the wig?"

"Now? Sure, but it's all mashed up. Let me get my hairbrush."

"No need. Just shake it out."

I pulled out a few hairpins and slid the wig off my head. I quickly ran my fingers through my hair and tried to fluff it up, but I knew it was a kinky mess.

"What do you think, Paul? Horace? Does it work for you?" Doris demanded. The two men leaned forward.

I caught my breath. It dawned on me what they were thinking. Of course, I was being considered as a replacement for Rebecca! I blinked. I smiled. I pressed my hands to my cheeks. I turned my head this way and that way, hoping my hair would swing free and loose like Rebecca's. I felt like twirling.

"Hold it," Paul said. "Could you stop squirming around for a second? I'm just trying to get an idea, here."

"Sure," I said eagerly, standing stiff as a soldier, trying not to breathe.

"Any chance we could see her without the false eyelashes?" Paul asked.

"I'm sure we can manage it," Doris said, stepping directly in front of me. "How about it, Morgana. Would it be much trouble?"

In a flash, my practiced fingers snatched the false lashes from my lids and secured them, like dead cockroaches, in the palm of my hand. They could now see what only my bathroom mirror and I ever saw. Naked eyes.

"Better," Paul said. "Horace? Any comments?"

"Fine, whatever you say. I'm only the writer, what do I know? Who am I to complain? We have Diana, in need of a governess, asking the local waitress to step in. Margie, with barely a high school diploma but a knack for flipping flapjacks, takes the tutoring job, and her hair miraculously grows long and dark. If you think the audience will buy that, go ahead." Horace rolled his eyes and shook his head. "Who's got time for logic?"

"We sure as hell don't," Paul said pointedly. "And we gotta lose the diner set because there's no room for it on the studio floor, so we sure won't be needing a waitress for the next nine weeks of her contract. Look, Morgana, what we have in mind—"

"I know, I know," I said, words rushing out of my mouth. "But how about if Margie just goes home from work one day, takes off her wig and washes her face. You know, like she just wears a wig . . . for work . . . but not, you know—" I faltered, my voice drying up.

Paul looked at me and shook his head. "Not your problem. We'll figure out a way to scrap the wig somehow. Okay, kid, you're the new governess up on the hill. You can thank Doris for this brainstorm."

"Oh, Doris," I said, throwing my arms around her. "I promise it'll work. Oh, wow, thank you!"

As I hugged the director, it came to me that just being in the right place at the right time might be a talent, too. I hadn't really done anything to make this happen, except be there.

I couldn't wait to write Eric about my good news. I'd taken to sending him a letter every other day, although I'd had only two letters from him. He'd written, *Let's call it the Garden Spot, as I'm not allowed to be more specific about our location here, but that's as good a description as any of Southeast Asia.*

At night I curled up with the pillow he'd slept on, picturing Eric in his uniform walking up the stairs to the Piano Bar and seeing me. I replayed the loop over and over, hearing his voice, smelling his warmth, until I fell asleep. In the morning, when I awoke, his name was on my lips. *Eric.*

I'd made a few more trunk calls home, mostly to my folks. I'd also called Marilyn. She said her sorority sisters were watching *Dark Passages* every afternoon, "getting hooked." She mentioned that one or two had even taken to skipping classes so they wouldn't miss the opening credits with the swelling music and waves crashing on a rocky shore.

"I'd be sort of a hero around here if you could autograph one of your scripts and send it." There was a touch of awe in her voice that made me think I might finally be one up on Marilyn.

My parents had taken to having their afternoon coffee while watching the show. "Makes a nice break," my father said. "We've had quite a bit of rain out here lately."

My mother thought I moved my face around too much. "Nobody around here gets that worked up just talking," she told me. "You could stand to settle down a bit and not wave your hands around so much." She also mentioned it had taken quite a lot of explaining to her friends at church and J.C. Penney when they saw I'd changed my name. "Nobody can figure it out," she said. "Nobody around here has ever even heard the name Morgana before. Sounds foreign." There was a long silence. I didn't know what to say.

My brother asked me if the kid playing Danny was "a fruit." I said, "No, of course not." He said someone at school told him most actors were fairies. I said I wasn't surprised to hear that. I also told him Danny was pulling down a couple of hundred bucks a week.

"Yeah? You think I could get a job on your show?" he asked.

"And risk becoming a fruit?" I answered. Frankly, 13-year-old brothers ought to be caged, but that's just my opinion.

The timing never seemed to be right to mention to my family that I'd seen Eric in New York. But I think the real reason I didn't say anything is that I couldn't trust my voice. My mother would've noticed something. It would have led to a conversation I didn't want to have with her.

Over the course of the following week, Stanhope lost its diner, its waitress—and seemingly any connection with the real world in the land of Soap Opera. Only three episodes were required to send Rebecca's character over a cliff in a deadly accident, install Margie as the new governess (with long, dark hair) and introduce an eccentric, thoroughly unexpected visitor to our remote coastal town located somewhere on the Northeastern seaboard. Viewers who had television sets on the blink that week wouldn't have stood a chance of making any sense of things.

But, as Paul Abbott said, "Damn it, who can remember what they ate for supper last week? If the show's interesting, they'll keep tuning in."

Horace Milton, it seemed, had simply tossed several story lines in the air to see which ones might stay aloft. Angela, played by pretty Ginny Blake, had become a portrait subject for my artist father, who was struck by her resemblance to a long-deceased Stanhope ancestor. Ginny was thrilled with the new storyline, as it provided her with scenes in the mansion's attic trying on fancy antique gowns. She also spent considerable time in Ed's dressing room with the door closed running lines with him.

Danny's character Joey had become intrigued by rumors of buried pirate treasure in the caves along the shoreline that were reachable only at low tide. As his governess, Margie was often dispatched at dusk to search for him, which meant I walked in tiresome circles waving a flashlight around a small patch of rock and brambles piled in a corner of the studio. How I missed my diner set!

I'd wondered if love scenes with Michael came with my new role, but the closest we came to romance was an accidental moonlit encounter in the aforementioned brambles on one of my searches for young Joey. Michael, looking handsome and mysterious with the collar of his trench coat turned up, appeared out of the gloom, startling me. I screamed. He put his hands on my shoulders and asked me what I was doing on the cliffs so late at night. After warning me to be careful ("There are strange goings on up here, Margie"), he drifted off into fog, a white mist produced by a prop man aiming a portable hairdryer at a pail of dry ice.

Michael's character, Steve, once the "bad boy back in town," had become some sort of investigator working undercover, seemingly focused on the shady dealings of Shelby Stanhope, Max Farraby's character. While Michael was observed skulking around town, interrogating everyone and looking matinee-idol handsome (even his trench coat was starting to get fan mail), Moira, as Diana, was busily planning a gala costume party inspired by the gowns Angela had found in the attic.

"Just who is invited to this shindig?" Doris asked Paul and Horace, who had taken to attending our afternoon rehearsals. "There are only nine people in this town, including the housekeeper. Doesn't sound like much of a party."

"So we'll hire dress extras and put 'em in masks," Paul said. "Christ, I never know anyone at a party, do you?" We all laughed.

After the harrowing double whammy of learning that our ratings were plummeting, and that Rebecca was being airlifted to the relative safety of prime-time and possible Hollywood stardom, an easy-going, what-the-hell camaraderie had settled in among the cast members.

"If we're going down, we'll go down together and in style," Maxwell Faraby crowed, shuffling his feet in a vaudeville buck-and-wing and sounding not unlike a character he'd once played in the musical *Broadway Bound.*

I'd been given a new wardrobe consisting mostly of plaid skirts (which I begged the wardrobe woman to shorten) and twin sets with detachable white Peter Pan collars. I was forbidden to wear false eyelashes, but at least the blonde wig was history.

Moira was sent out to appear on various talk shows to promote the show. Michael had been featured on the cover of a soap opera magazine as "Hunk of the Month," resulting in a flood of fan mail. "There goes my career," Michael fumed, tossing the magazine on the rehearsal table one morning in case one of us may have missed seeing the photo layout. "No one told me about this beforehand, or I would've told 'em to shove it!"

"Like hell you would, dear boy," Maxwell purred. "You're licking it up. Your sweet little Burberry with the lovely lining is making you a star."

"Boys, boys," Moira said, "believe me, any publicity is good publicity. The public barely knows we exist. Who in the world watches television at three-thirty in the afternoon, except kids and bored housewives? That's where these fan letters are coming from."

And, I might have added, Orville and Ruth Blatch in Twin Lakes, if it's raining and the fields are wet. Also, Marilyn and her sorority sisters.

But Doris had a point. We were still looking for our main storyline and a breakout character that would attract a mass audience tuning in before the *Four O'Clock News.* The betting was on our resident hunk, Michael, who was showing every sign of appealing to romance-hungry housewives.

In fact, Michael was eating up all the attention, striding around the studio with his trench coat flapping open, and leaving his shirt unbuttoned to reveal chest hair. I began to suspect Horace had cooled on the idea of a romance between Steve and the governess to keep Michael's character a desirable, unattainable catch in the eyes of his female fans.

The strangest development, however, was the casting of a tall, craggy-faced English actor in his mid-twenties. Ian Fletcher had appeared briefly in one episode wearing a swashbuckling pirate costume and waving a battered scroll. Young Joey had observed this character walking the cliffs (the miniature bramble set again) and then disappearing into a cave (a black tent affair shrouded in foliage and fog).

"So, who is he?" Doris demanded. "Some partygoer on a scavanger hunt? A pervert? The ghost of Captain Kidd?"

Horace shrugged. "Our mystery man. Maybe he's a murderer, a con artist," Horace said. "Stay tuned. Let's see what happens."

"Steve's got to have something to investigate, right?" Paul said, slapping Michael's shoulder. "Can't have you just prowling the town asking questions forever. A murder might be nice."

"Whatever you want, I'm up for it," Michael said, hunching his shoulders in his Burberry. "Just so you know, Paul, I'm pretty adept at handling firearms."

"Wait a minute," Doris said. "Let's not get carried away here. We've got a problem. Why doesn't Michael see this character lurking up on the cliffs when he's standing only two feet away. You've got Joey spotting him but no one else? That makes this guy a ghost in my book, and only the kid can see him."

"A ghost? Now that's interesting," Paul said, locking eyes with Horace. "So he's a ghost. I'll go along with that."

"Are you nuts?" Moira asked. "What is this, Hallowe'en? You can't just throw a ghost into the show. Nobody'll want to watch except children."

"Just wait and see," Horace said. He waved his fingers like a magician and repeated in a spooky voice, "Just wait and see. Maybe he's a vampire."

"Be still my heart," Moira said. "That's all we need."

I couldn't have agreed more. My own heart stopped stone still. I wasn't breathing. Or rather, I forgot to keep breathing. The first thought that crossed my mind was what would my mother think when she watched the show? A vampire appearing in the plot line? She'd think I had something to do with it. She'd be offended. She would consider it ridicule, and Ruth did not handle ridicule well. I stood motionless as these thoughts flashed through my mind, my ears attuned to every heartbeat in the room, every movement. The atmosphere was thick with tension. Was anyone suddenly looking at me oddly?

I tried not to look at Haddie, who had appeared as a pale specter next to the coffee urn, grinning as though he found all this terribly funny. He hovered virtually shoulder-to-shoulder with Maxwell, who didn't appear to be aware an actual ghost was sharing space with him.

Tempting as it was to have sugar packets dance on the coffee table, or make the vase of gladiolas from the reception desk materialize on the rehearsal table, I refrained from doing so. Pandemonium would have ensued.

"Nonsense, Horace!" Ed sputtered, breaking through the pall of silence. "What are you thinking? Not that Bela Lugosi couldn't use a job, but we'd be a complete laughingstock."

"Hear, hear!" Maxwell said. "A nice serial killer, maybe, for dear Michael to track down. Maybe Michael had his little collar turned up and that's why he didn't see the fellow up there. But no vampires, please."

"Very well," Horace said. "I'll come up with something."

Haddie winked. I winked back. There'd be no vampires in Stanhope.

With all the new developments on *Dark Passages*, Paul Abbott didn't seem to mind too much when I went to his office after rehearsal and asked him to please change my name in the credits.

"I don't really think the name Morgana Harriott suits me. I'd like to go back to my real name," I told him. "Now would be a good time since my character is changing."

"And your hair," Paul said, "to say nothing of your wardrobe and job description. Do we know what your real name is?"

"Meg Harrison," I said.

"That's a relief," Paul said. "Consider it done."

Eight

Ginny Blake announced, "Actually, I'm twenty-two." She arched her right foot on the windowsill of the rehearsal room and began doing her ballet exercises.

I looked at her in some wonder as she stretched her little-girl hand over her head. She looked barely seventeen on camera, the age of Moira's daughter Angela, the character she played, although Ginny was a few years older than me. A petite blonde, stick-thin and given to sudden ecstasies of emotion, Ginny could cry on cue, an actor's gift I envied with all my heart. But she also had an irritating penchant for doing pliés while you were talking to her, her head bobbing up and down, her arms swooping, as though she felt the need to make use of the time you were taking up. Yet, she was a pleasure to work with on camera, entirely focused and thoroughly professional.

Her downside was that she had absolutely no sense of humor. Hyperbole struck her as lying. Irony left her bewildered. Therefore, it came as no surprise when Ginny asked me why I had teased her about hanging out after work with Ed at Flinty's Bar and Grill, our corner watering hole.

My exact words were, "Take it from his daughter, you better watch the old geezer, or he'll make a move on you."

She had responded, "You're not really his daughter, you know. And I really, really like him."

I stood stock-still, not believing my ears. "Just how much do you like him, Ginny?"

"A whole lot," she said, a wistful, faraway look in her eyes. "I'll probably marry him."

"But he's old enough to be your father."

"Actually, he has a son older than me, but they don't get along. Do you really think age matters? Ed says it doesn't."

Age, I thought, would be the least of her problems with Ed. My God, what else was the old fart telling her? She was certainly easy pickings. I'd wondered why Ed had found fewer occasions to insinuate his hands onto my breasts. Her admission provided an explanation. I shuddered to think what the two of them were getting up to once they left Flinty's. Meanwhile, I didn't know Ginny that well, and I was reluctant to go out on a limb in case she actually married the old fool.

"It all depends upon the two people involved," I told her. "You want to run lines?"

We'd begun to have more scenes together since I'd become Joey's governess and moved into the Stanhope mansion on the hill. In preparation for the big costume party, Ginny and I had played several scenes in the attic.

In one episode, I helped her shove a trunk aside, only to discover an oil portrait of a beautiful blonde woman dressed in an eighteenth century gown. Upon seeing the painting, Angela excitedly declared that's how she wanted to dress for the ball, and began rummaging through various trunks in the hope she would find the actual dress.

Meanwhile, the big climax on the previous Friday's episode had been the forensic report on a woman's body, subsequently identified as the gardener's wife, that had washed up on the rocks below the cliffs. Michael, his trench coat belted to look official, had broken the sad news to the members of the Stanhope family.

"It's curious," Michael said, "that those two puncture wounds on her throat are not in keeping with injuries she would have suffered following her fall to the rocks. Clearly these wounds occurred before her fall, and may well have actually caused her death."

"Could a wild animal have attacked her?" Shelby asked. "Surely no human being could have been so heartless. She hadn't an enemy in the world, poor woman."

"Perhaps it was an enemy outside our world of understanding," Michael said, "a highly intelligent, non-human species with an uncontrollable blood lust. You see, her body was found to be almost completely devoid of—"

"What are you saying, man!" Shelby exclaimed. "Be clear about this! You can't mean—!"

"Yes, I fear it's true," Michael intoned. "I've long suspected the caves below the cliffs of Stanhope give refuge to . . . a vampire!"

Cut to commercial, and the cards were on the table. We'd all groaned when we'd first read the script aloud at rehearsal.

"Paul, you promised we wouldn't go in this direction! We'll become the joke of daytime television!" Moira exclaimed. "This is not what I signed on to do. I'm having my agent look into the full implications of this. It's madness! This is nothing more than drive-in movie fodder, completely exploitative."

"I couldn't agree more," Maxwell had said. "How can we hold our heads up? How can one even repeat these silly words without cracking up?"

"One answer comes to mind," Paul said, his voice tight. "Where do you want to work next week? You got another paying job on the back burner?"

"Well, I certainly didn't imply that I was walking out," Maxwell said. "Did anyone hear me say that? I was just voicing artistic expression, that's all."

"I haven't actually instructed my agent yet," Moira said in a small voice. "One prefers to consider all options, of course."

Subsequently, Ian Fletcher, the English actor playing the pirate, made two more brief appearances on the cliffs. Clearly he'd been tapped to become our resident vampire. He was not to play a ghostly apparition after all, as I, too, had bumped into him in one episode. The scene had taken place shortly after sundown while I was once again searching for Joey. A cloak had been added to the pirate regalia, making the outfit look even more eccentric. Ian was classically trained and obviously knew how to work a cape to advantage, but still had no clear idea of his character.

"I feel a bloody fool swanning about in this gear," he whispered to me before the air show. "Surely this vampire dwells somewhere, doing something in his off-hours. I mean, do these creatures ever take a piss?

I ought to be given fangs, I should think. Otherwise, I'm just rushing about like a hermit, who hasn't been informed the War of 1812 is over. I mean, what am I? A vampire or some idiot pirate who's lost his bloody ship?"

I sympathized. "Listen, I'm a waitress-turned-governess who's never given Joey a lesson. The kid is twelve and probably can't spell his name." We laughed.

Ian Fletcher, despite his ready wit, had the look of a cheerless person. He was lean to the point of emaciation. His clothing hung loosely on his lanky frame, which only contributed to his joyless demeanor. His pale, wolfish face was long and narrow with a pointed nose, giving him a haunted look that was oddly attractive. High cheekbones, cragginess around the eyes and a thick head of hair gave him what Moira referred to as "Byronic splendor." She was probably thinking of Tyrone Power again, but it would have to have been Ty Power after a prodigious fast and a year spent nowhere near a beach. Despite his melancholy nature, Ian and I hit it off from the beginning. He was self-deprecating well beyond just being English, which was funny and appealing to me.

We also worked well together, which was apparent from that first scene we played in the rock-and-bramble set when I was searching for young Danny. Ian had appeared out of the mist, like Heathcliff coming across Cathy on the moors, but more of a modern-dress-meet-and-greet-in-a-spooky-setting. In soap opera, one never knows where these encounters may lead, so it's best to play safe and pull out all the stops. Ian and I clocked the full gamut: surprise, fear, confusion, intrigue, fascination and underlying lust in what amounted to a two-minute scene.

Off camera, few of the other cast members spent much time with him. He wasn't anyone's favorite lunch companion. At Flinty's he stood alone at the bar unless I joined him. This stand-offishness added up to a perfect profile for a vampire: forlorn, brooding and a bit creepy. And that was part of the reason the other cast members wanted little to do with him. No one wanted to think Paul Abbott was taking us down *that* road, that we might be embarking on a spooky daytime horror show. Ian didn't want it to happen, either, and that partly accounted for his general gloominess.

Everyone professed to know how vampires should behave, except Ian and me. In my case, it wasn't a discussion I cared to have for fear I would slip up and draw unwanted speculation. No one had caught me out yet, but there were times when I took chances. When I thought no one was looking, I'd occasionally mount the back stairs to the dressing rooms at unnatural speed, listen in on conversations beyond closed doors and take leave of my body to enjoy an aerial view. Kid stuff, but fun. It always amazed me that people were so willing to provide explanations for any odd behavior.

On one of my out-of-body travels in the studio, Ed knocked my inert body in the ribs and said, "Wake up, kid." I quickly regained possession of my body before he could send me reeling out of my chair. "Daydreaming again," he said, waving his hand in front of my eyes. "You were a million miles away."

"No, Ed," I might have responded, "just hovering above the control booth for a moment, checking my makeup on the monitor."

One afternoon I'd shown up at Flinty's bar before anyone else arrived, even though they'd all left the rehearsal room before me. "Good heavens, did you fly up here?" Maxwell asked.

"Took the back stairs to the street," I said. In fact, I'd flown.

The consensus was that vampires perished in sunlight and couldn't be photographed. I figured I was pretty safe on both counts, since I was seen on camera and worked during daylight hours. There was also talk of crosses, silver, garlic, wooden stakes and sleeping in coffins, all of which made me cringe and vow to keep my mouth shut. I just shrugged and claimed never to have heard of Dracula. Perhaps there was a real-life vampire species out there with gleaming needle-sharp fangs, either retractable or permanently fixed like airplane landing gear, but it wasn't my area of expertise. I could speak with some authority on feeding tubes that had puncture and tearing capabilities, but they weren't housed in great white incisors.

The gardener's wife, portrayed by a day player with no dialogue, had only to scream into camera before the commercial break and lie in brambles with her neck exposed to camera after the break. Claude, the makeup man, had fashioned a latex patch in flesh tones that had two holes dabbed with a sticky red substance that could pass for congealing blood. It looked gory enough on the neck of the gardener's wife. We all took turns admiring Claude's handiwork. He proudly told us that he'd poked holes in a veal cutlet with the prongs of a meat fork and used the veal as a mold for the vampire wound.

I examined the latex piece closely and had to admit that feeding tubes could have done the job. How had Claude come up with such an inspired prosthetic? Needless to say, Claude was alone among us in hoping there would be more vampire activity in Stanhope.

I mentioned the vampire story line to Wesley Truscott, who responded, "Whatever works, kiddo. The trick is to keep the show on the air and you employed."

Meanwhile, no one else in Stanhope was attacked by this "savage on the prowl." Paul continued to assure us that "all would be revealed in good time," which we took to mean he was waiting to see the ratings. In the interim, attention focused on the costume ball and another major diversion in the storyline that Horace had come up with.

A mystery woman, masked and speaking only French, would sweep into the party wearing the identical gown Angela had admired in the portrait. Her name: Charmaine du Champs, a long-lost Stanhope cousin with a dark secret. At the stroke of midnight, Diana would instruct us to remove our masks and meet her surprise guest, Mme. du Champs. With all eyes on her, Charmaine would cast a spell on all the party guests by twirling the crystal pendant around her neck. We would then be swept back to the year 1790, each of us reincarnated as another character. Michael Reynolds was to play a dashing highwayman, while Ginny would appear as a music hall performer.

"Time travel courtesy of witches? Now I've heard everything!" Moira snorted. "Space ships and hobgoblins next, I suppose."

"Hang on, my plum. Think of the lovely frocks." Maxwell Faraby was already pointing his toe and imagining himself in satin breeches.

The moment I heard the news that the role of Charmaine du Champs had yet to be cast, I raced to the pay phone to call Reine Seigneur, a French girl in my acting class. We'd done a couple of scenes together, and I really liked her. Unfortunately, her accent was thicker than paté, and she hadn't managed to land an agent.

"Listen," I told her, my hand cupped over the receiver as though imparting army intelligence. "This role is perfect for you. Get over here to the studio as fast as you can and I'll give you a copy of the script. Meanwhile, I'll talk to the producer and try to get you an audition."

One major dividend that came with my promotion to governess (no increase in pay of course) was the considerable cachet of now having the ingénue lead in *Dark Passages*. I'd turned in my uniform and wig for nice sweaters and skirts, but even better, the promotion earned me a new level of respect from the cast and staff. However subtly, Doris, Paul, the crew and cast members all paid more attention to me as Margie the governess than they had when I was a waitress in a diner.

I was on the schedule for more episodes per week, my voice-over introduced each episode and I was no longer peripheral to the major storylines. Both Margie and I grew more confident once my character moved into the Stanhope mansion on the hill. Therefore, I didn't think twice about approaching Paul with a suggestion, and knew he would take me seriously.

I hung up the phone and ran into Paul's office. "Hey, I just read about this new character, and I've got the perfect actress for the role."

"What does she look like? Can she act?"

"She's terrific on both counts. Petite with curly dark hair, and not only can she speak French, but she *is* French! You've just got to see her."

"Sure, why not? We're auditioning people tomorrow morning at the casting director's office. Leave me her name and tell her to be there at ten."

Reine made it to the studio in half an hour, breathless and eager. I gave her the script, the address of the casting director's office and a quick hug. "Be there at ten and wear something low cut. She's supposed to be mysterious—and French! You're perfect casting."

"Oh, you are too wonderful," she said, her eyes sparkling. "Do you really think?"

"I know it," I said, puffed up with certainty.

By noon the following day, there was a message on my answering service from Reine. She thought she'd done well at the audition and was sitting at home waiting to hear. I was on tenterhooks, too. At four o'clock, the cast gathered in the rehearsal room, but the actress playing Charmaine du Champs was still a no-show.

"She'll be a few minutes late, I'm told," Doris said. "I wasn't in on the casting, but I understand she's very good. Don't ask me why everything has to be done at the last minute. We'll start the read-through without her."

Nigel finished distributing scripts for the ensuing four episodes, and we all settled down in our usual places around the table. Ten minutes into our reading, Paul Abbott pushed open the door to the rehearsal room and ushered in a tall, eye-catching blonde, wearing a close-fitting blue suit and high heels. A look of surprise fluttered across her face as she stopped abruptly on the threshold, her hand on her breast.

"Oh, dear! I've interrupted rehearsal," she drawled in a molasses-thick Southern accent.

"Not at all, not at all," Paul exclaimed, his arm around her shoulders, urging her forward. "Everyone, this is Camilla Nesbitt, our beautiful and mysterious Charmaine du Champs. We're a little late because we had to get her fitted for the gown."

"Come on in, Camilla," Doris said. "Glad to have you with us. Just take a seat next to Michael, there."

"Quite an entrance," Moira muttered softly. "Blanche DuBois couldn't do better."

"She doesn't look French to me," I whispered back.

How could they possibly hire a tall Southern blonde to play a Frenchwoman when they could have chosen Reine? I was flabbergasted, and not at all happy. Amid a flurry of greetings, Camilla made the rounds, shaking hands with each of us. Paul couldn't seem to pry his eyes off her, which was understandable. There was something spellbinding about her.

She grasped Moira's hand and exclaimed, "I am so thrilled to meet you, Miss Shaw. I'm so looking forward to working with you."

Moira dipped her head and said, "Thank you so much, my dear. We're so pleased to have you with us."

Then it was my turn. Her hand fell lightly on my shoulder, and she said, "You're Margie, the dear little governess. You're so cute on the show!" She laughed softly, her eyes twinkling at me. Her teeth were perfect, her nose exquisitely shaped. I knew there had to be something wrong with her, but so far it wasn't apparent.

I smiled. "Glad you're joining us, Camilla."

My eyes followed her as she slipped into the chair next to Michael and opened her script. "What page are we up to, Michael?" she whispered with a sidelong glance.

He put his arm across the back of her chair and leaned into her. "Scene three, page eleven. Does everyone tell you that you look like Grace Kelly?"

"Nooooo," she laughed. "And there's no prince in my life, either."

"That's good," he said. "I'm glad to hear the field's open."

Maxwell Faraby snorted and said, "Forgive the dear boy, Camilla. He doesn't get out much."

Danny made a rude kissing sound.

"That's enough, settle down everyone," Doris said. "Okay, let's take it from the top and give Camilla a chance to settle in."

This was not good. A terrible mistake had been made. She didn't look or sound the least bit French. Reine would've fit the bill perfectly, and she was my friend. While everyone flipped scripts back to the first page, I stared at Camilla. No one could possibly have a mouth as lush and prettily formed as hers, or cheekbones so perfectly sculpted. Compared to Camilla, Rebecca was just a pretty girl.

"You'll be speaking French in your scene, Camilla. I assume you can manage that?"

"Oh, *mais oui. Je parle Francais.*"

Great. The bitch could speak French, too.

We plowed through the reading, made some cuts and then took a five-minute break before starting to block the show. Camilla, whose character did not make her first appearance until the end of the episode, perched prettily on a corner of the rehearsal table, a sleek pussycat watching intently as Doris maneuvered the rest of us, scripts in hand, around the linoleum floor marked with yellow tape.

Horace could not have provided Charmaine du Champs with a more suspense-laden introduction. Speculation on the Mystery Woman, newly arrived in town, seeped into every scene, including the one in which Diana instructed me to deliver a ball gown to Mme. du Champs at the Stanhope Arms.

"But who is she, may I ask?"

"Never you mind, Margie," Diana said, as we made our way through the yellow-taped foyer. "I'm thrilled she's come back to us after all these years in Paris. I only hope she doesn't find us unspeakably provincial. Run along now, my dear."

I mimed opening the front door, my arms laden with imaginary props. Once I'd made my exit, I sank into a chair at the rehearsal table while Moira and Maxwell continued the scene.

"Quick as a bunny, aren't you?" Camilla whispered.

"What?" I mouthed the word because we were forbidden to speak during rehearsal.

Camilla smiled, her lips parting to show perfect white teeth. "A bunny. Scampering out the door like a cute little bunny. It's so adorable."

"Well, I'm the governess," I whispered, then pressed my finger to my lips as a warning to be quiet.

Camilla nodded. "Subservient, of course. Taking orders. But cute as a bunny."

I shrugged, glancing quickly at Doris. My stomach was churning, and not just because I feared a reprimand from the director. What was Camilla getting at?

"But Margie's probably got a secret life she's hiding behind that timid little pose, right? I'll bet she's not really a goody two shoes. Now that would be fun to play, don't you think?"

"Her dad's a drunk, and she's from the wrong side of the—"

"Meg, for chrissake! Show some common courtesy to the actors trying to work here, will you? Sorry, Camilla, but we have a rule here. Meg knows better than to talk to you during rehearsal."

"Sorry, Doris," I said. "Sorry, Moira, Maxwell—"

"I can't apologize enough," Camilla said. "I'm so sorry. I won't let it happen again. Forgive me."

"Fine, just take your jabbering out in the hall," Doris said, her voice dismissive. "Okay, folks, let's pick it up from Moira's speech at the top."

I crept quietly out the door into the hallway, my script tucked under my arm. I sensed Camilla making tracks behind me and headed toward my dressing room to avoid her.

"Hey, Meg, I'm really sorry." Camilla's hand brushed my shoulder as I reached for the doorknob. "Oh, dear. Your arm is so cold. It must be the air conditioning in here."

"I'm fine, really." The doorknob wouldn't turn. I tried again, but the knob wouldn't budge.

"What's the matter? Is your door locked? Here, let me try." In a quick movement, Camilla reached for the knob and turned it. The door swung open. "There you go. Must've been stuck."

My mouth fell open. I hadn't locked my door. But locked or stuck, opening any door should have been a snap for me. I looked at Camilla, dumbstruck. How did she do that?

"You're welcome," she said, smiling.

"Sorry. Thank you."

"Happy to be of service. Now, please, forgive me for getting you in trouble with the director. We'll be working together. I hate to start off on the wrong foot, especially with the series lead!"

"I'm not the—I mean, don't worry about it. I shouldn't have let it happen."

"No, really. It was stupid of me. I certainly know better."

"Well, I was trying to signal you—" I edged into my dressing room, my hand on the door.

"Oh, dear, you are angry with me, aren't you? You think it's my fault?"

"No, not at all. I just meant that I was trying to let you know."

Camilla leaned against the jamb, preventing me from closing my door. She crossed her arms and tipped her head. "And I was too dumb to pick up on it, is that what you mean? You shouldn't have answered me. That would've stopped it."

"You're right, Camilla. Let's drop it, okay?" Why didn't she leave? I wanted a few minutes on my own to figure out why my door hadn't opened. "Really, just go back in the rehearsal room. I'll be there myself in a jiffy."

"Jiffy. That's cute." She laughed. "Well, you probably want a few minutes on your own to figure out why your door wouldn't open." She patted me on the shoulder. "And put on a sweater. You're freezing!"

"I'm not. The door—I mean, I'm fine. I—" Yet I reached for my sweater and pushed my arms through the sleeves.

"Ahhh, that's better," she said, watching me, a smile on her lips. "Methinks the lady protests too much." She laughed, a tinkly little laugh that held no mirth. "You look very cross."

"I'm not!" I gave my blouse a yank under my Shetland sweater and smoothed my skirt. "Look, we better get back," I said, pushing past her. Again, I could feel her tracking my steps as I moved down the hall toward the rehearsal room. I threw my shoulders back and ran a hand through my hair, feeling oddly short-circuited. What was it about the door? Something was very wrong.

"Hey, pretty ladies," Michael said, as we rounded the corner into the reception area. He was leaning against the door to the rehearsal room, script in hand. "Your big entrance is coming up, Camilla. Our masked beauty finally makes her appearance. Ta da!"

"*Vous êtes trop gentil, mon cher.*"

"*Pas de tout!*"

"*Vous parlez français?*"

"*Un peu*, and that's just about it," Michael said, easing his hand onto the small of her back. "Hey, listen, Camilla, how about going up to Flinty's with me after rehearsal? It's sort of the hangout. I'll buy you a burger and fill you in on things around here."

"*Parfaitement!* I'd love it!" She smiled up at him, pressing her finger to her lips as he opened the door to the rehearsal room. He was beaming, his face ruddy with conquest as she brushed past him. I followed, slapping him on the butt with my script. He glanced at me, then mumbled, "You wanna come along, too, kid?"

"No, thanks. I have to wash my hair tonight," I said, bile rising in my throat.

Mr. Welcome Wagon had never invited me to supper. He'd had every chance, all those times when I'd dropped into Flinty's after work and bellied up to the bar next to him. We'd stood around with the other cast and crew members, our feet crunching on peanut shells, our bodies leaning and shifting within our convivial Happy Hour crowd—but never once had he invited me to join him afterward for supper at one of the blue-checkered tables with the red candles. Not once.

Instead of going to Flinty's, I hurried to catch a bus home after rehearsal. I propped my script in my lap to learn lines en route, but couldn't concentrate. I stared out the window, seeing nothing, my thoughts bobbing back and forth between Eric and Michael without dropping anchor anywhere.

It wasn't until late that night, lying awake and trying not to picture Michael holding hands with Camilla in one of the back booths at Flinty's, that it struck me: Why had she kept saying "bunny?" Even as the thought flashed in my mind, I knew the answer. My brain yanked an image of Camilla—black lacy dress, her hair in a sleek French twist—from the recesses of my memory.

Of course! She was the icy blonde I'd glimpsed sitting with Emmett Boardman in the Playmate Bar at the Club Saturday night. They were arriving as I ended my shift—that's how she knew I was a Bunny. How stupid of me not to have recognized her earlier. But my eyes had been on Boardman, a regular at the Club, who always showed up with a blonde. He was also the head of the theatrical agency that repped both Paul Abbott and Doris Franklin. Is that how she got the job? Wesley Truscott, my own agent, was good, but small potatoes next to Emmett Boardman. I'd give anything to be signed with his agency. I sank deeper into my pillow. I'd have to watch my step with her.

Almost everyone who worked at Playboy now knew I was in *Dark Passages*. The soap had become a favorite with the Lunch Bunnies, who watched the show in the employee lounge every afternoon. But I wondered if anyone at the studio, besides Camilla, knew I worked at Playboy. If so, no one had mentioned it. And did it really matter anymore? It was inevitable that my worlds would merge, and what difference did it make now? I was a bona fide working actress. I didn't mind at all when the wives and girlfriends of Playboy keyholders recognized me as an actress on *Dark Passages*. I'd even signed a few autographs after serving a round of drinks.

But I did mind that Camilla had made an issue of seeing me working as a Bunny. At least if *Dark Passages* went off the air, I had money in the bank and a backup job.

What was she doing having cocktails with Emmett Boardman, a married man old enough to be her father?

And how had she managed to open my dressing room door when I'd been unable to do it?

Nine

Camilla smiled. "Of course I know Elvis," she said, selecting the last jellyroll in the pastry box. "He took me out riding. My daddy about died when he heard—"

"Yeah? What was he driving?" Danny asked, trying to sound nonchalant.

"Oh, an El Dorado." Camilla glanced at Moira and Ginny, making a face. "With the top down, naturally, my hair blowing to bits. Men!"

"Wow. A convertible?" We were all impressed, and hoped Danny would keep asking Camilla questions. "What color?"

"Baby blue. But he had 'em in lots of colors. Sometimes he'd just take over a whole drive-in movie theatre and invite his friends. Everything free. We watched *Love Me Tender* once, with his arm around me."

Elvis! I remembered sneaking out of junior high with my friend Marilyn, taking the bus to downtown Minneapolis and screaming myself hoarse at a matinee of *Love Me Tender*. Wait until I told Marilyn that I knew someone who had gone to a drive-in with Elvis, eaten popcorn with Elvis—and what *else* with Elvis? I was dying to know.

I poured myself more coffee and hovered near the pastry table where Camilla was holding court. We still had a few minutes before morning rehearsal, time enough to hear more about growing up rich, pretty and popular in Memphis, Tennessee.

"So, you and Elvis, huh? Hot and heavy in the ol' blue Eldorado?" Ed McNabb was willing to tread where the rest of us wanted to go.

"Goodness, what are you saying! My mama would never have allowed that. I was a debutante, after all, and he—" Camilla dropped her chin and fluttered a sidelong glance up at Ed— "well, a girl has to watch her reputation."

What looked like drool bubbled on Ed's lower lip. "No smooching, eh?"

"Ed, you heard her," Ginny bleated, her face reddening. "Some things you don't ask a girl. I'm sure nothing like that went on."

Maxwell gave her a withering look. "Shush, child. Go on, Camilla, you and Elvis—"

"Tyrone Power once took me to Ciro's," Moira said. "It was in all the columns."

Camilla licked jelly off her lower lip. Savoring her rapt audience, she looked around, her eyes settling on me. "I can only tell you that when Elvis kisses you—"

I caught my breath. "You kissed Elvis? Really?"

"He kissed *me*," she corrected, "and that's a kiss you never forget."

I nodded, as though I knew what a kiss from Elvis was like.

Moira sighed, her voice throaty. "Ty was a good kisser, too. Quite unforgettable. And I was young, so very young."

Two things occurred to me at that moment. First: I was barely thirteen when I saw Elvis kiss Debra Paget in *Love Me Tender*. How old was Camilla? Second: Where were my Elvis and Tyrone Power? Eric turned out to be a good kisser, but he was not Elvis. I couldn't think of anything unforgettable that had ever come my way. No dark and dangerous man, no walk on the wild side. I hadn't even dated a Playboy keyholder, for God's sake. Nothing had happened to me that could compare to a kiss from Elvis. I'd barely even taken advantage of my special gifts out of what was beginning to seem like some misguided desire to be normal. The world was passing me by!

If I hadn't still been brooding about Camilla's Elvis kiss when I was zipping myself into my Bunny costume the following night, I probably wouldn't have taken Gloria up on her offer to go to an after-hours party. Gloria, a buxom blonde from Staten Island, who had no need of padding in her costume, was a regular at these parties. Her invitations to other Bunnies to accompany her held tremendous cachet. I knew that before Gloria had invited me, she had first cleared it with the host, a Playboy executive and C1 keyholder who was permitted to date any Bunny he fancied. Was I pretty enough? Sophisticated enough? Sexy enough? It was gratifying to know I'd been vetted and accepted.

Like me, most of the other Bunnies in the dressing room pretended not to care if they weren't invited. Only a few genuinely had no interest in going. While I was thrilled to get the invitation, I'd heard enough about these all-night parties to have my doubts about accepting.

"Do you know what goes on there?" one of the Bunnies asked me. "Believe me, these guys are sharks. They'll eat you alive!"

"You can always leave if you don't like it," Gloria said. "Besides, a limo will pick us up outside the Club. There'll be celebrities. Big shots. C'mon, don't be a dope. I've got a dress you can wear."

It was the lure of "celebrities" (Elvis?) and Gloria's assurance that she wouldn't object if I left early that convinced me. After all, it was Saturday night and I didn't have to worry about being on camera the following day. Besides, I was curious, and wearing one of the glitzy cocktail dresses Gloria had stashed in her locker appealed to me. I slipped out of my Bunny costume and stepped into the black crêpe de chine cocktail dress Gloria tossed my way. Fortunately I could wear the black satin stilettos that matched my Bunny costume.

Meanwhile Gloria, clad in a lacy merry widow corset, sat in front of the makeup mirror dispensing womanly wisdom while completely redoing her face for the party.

"Listen," she said, "nobody ever said you had to buy anything, retail or not. You just got to cultivate the garmentos in the showrooms. Guys love to see you looking good, and they'll give you stuff if you just treat 'em nice. That's how it works."

Gloria knew all about turning an eruption of teenage skin into a beauty mark, and lavishly spritzed perfume deep into her cleavage. "At a noisy party, the trick is to talk very quietly, because then the guy has to lean in and gets a whiff of your perfume. He feels like he's already being intimate, see?" she said in her kittenish voice. "That's exactly how Jackie attracted Jack Kennedy. Jackie always talks in a whispery voice. And that's Marilyn Monroe's secret, too."

Gloria piled her platinum blonde hair in a Kim Novak-styled twist and squeezed her bosomy body into a tight-fitting black satin dress with a plunging neckline. I waited by the door, tugging at my slinky dress. As Gloria reached into her locker for her mink stole, I saw her take a quick look around and then pull a long swig from a plastic Breck shampoo bottle she kept hidden on a shelf. I knew instinctively that she had replaced the amber-colored shampoo with Cutty Sark, her favorite Scotch. Then, as she was setting the bottle back on the shelf, she caught my eye. "One for the road," she whispered. "Can't walk into a party cold."

As promised, a limo was idling at the curb in front of the Playboy Club to ferry us to the party. Vince, the Club's doorman, held Gloria's hand as she stepped into the limo. When he saw me sliding in after her, he looked surprised. "You sure about this, cookie?"

"You think I'm not invited?"

"Nah, just be careful, okay. This stuff's not for everyone."

Did everyone think I was so unsophisticated that I couldn't handle myself at a party? Camilla had gone riding with Elvis Presley—he'd even kissed her! I'd like nothing better than to show up at the studio Monday with my own story to tell.

Minutes later the limo glided up to the entrance of the St. Pierre hotel. Gloria stepped out first, ruffling her mink stole around her shoulders to show off her cleavage. Like a movie star at a premiere, she swept through the lobby and headed for the elevator. I slunk behind her, my hands clutching the satin evening bag Gloria had loaned me. A brawny security man, wearing a shiny tuxedo and brandishing a guest list, stood sentry outside the entrance to the penthouse.

"Evening, Moe," Gloria cooed. "This is Meg. She's with me."

Without even checking his list, Moe nodded and opened the door. A noisy party was in full swing. We'd barely stepped inside when a man, slick in a sharkskin suit, wrapped his arms around Gloria. She giggled and leaned into him, her hand on his shoulder.

"Hey, Marty, not so fast. I got a friend with me who needs introducing."

"Your friend doesn't look like she's going to be lonely for long, kid." He winked.

"You go ahead. I'm fine," I said.

"See? Your friend's fine. And I'm not lettin' you get away from me again. C'mon." He tugged at Gloria. She shrugged helplessly.

"You see? I'm in demand. The bar's right around the corner, Meg. Have fun. Do everything I wouldn't!"

She giggled and disappeared into the throng with Marty. The lights were low, the music loud. I looked around, wondering if I'd actually see any celebrities. A pile of Polaroid pictures lay curling on a coffee table, each a candid tableau of naked body parts. I looked away quickly, then couldn't resist sneaking another glimpse. I'd recognized the face of another Bunny I knew.

A waiter passed with a tray of martinis. I took one of the glasses and edged warily into the crush of people. The room was clogged with bodies, some in committed stages of undress, a spectacle more distasteful than shocking. Even in the reflections of the windows and the smoked mirror behind the bar, there were images of couplings I'd never imagined and didn't actually want to see.

I maneuvered myself to the bar, perched on a stool and joined the only other fully clothed people at the party: a bartender and a guy wearing a seersucker jacket and light khaki pants. I set my empty martini glass on the bar and ordered the first thing that came to mind.

"Scotch and soda, please. With a twist."

"A twist. Doesn't that ruin the Scotch?" the man in the seersucker jacket asked.

"Not as much as the soda," I said flippantly. The bartender set the drink on the bar. I took a gulp.

"My name's Pete. Cigarette?"

I shook my head no, then took one anyway. Somewhere in the back of my mind, I remembered being warned not to accept a cigarette from a stranger because it could be a reefer. But then, what was the difference? I was already at what I figured was an orgy. Why not go for broke? I took another gulp of my Scotch and put the cigarette to my lips. Pete had already flicked his lighter. I leaned forward and tipped my head, looking into Pete's eyes the way Lauren Bacall looked up at Humphrey Bogart when he lit her cigarette. After a bit of fumbling, I managed to suck in a lungful of smoke.

"So. What do you do?" he asked.

"I'm a . . . actually, I work in fashion."

The Scotch tasted terrible. I caught the bartender's eye and ordered a cocktail I remembered serving in the Club. "Could I please have a Rusty Nail? On the rocks?"

I turned to Pete. He wasn't bad looking, and I liked that he was wearing seersucker like someone pictured in *Town & Country*, who might actually know his way around a yacht.

"Fashion. Sounds interesting. Retail? Editorial? A buyer?"

"Design. You?"

"Uh, sales. So you like Drambuie with Scotch better? "

"Yeah. I've never tried it before. Maybe I'll try a Stinger next."

I glanced over his shoulder and caught a reflected image in the mirror behind the bar. It was Gloria in her merry widow, splayed on the back of a couch. I quickly looked away and took another gulp of my drink. My experience with the grasshopper in Joe Allen had given me some inkling of my capacity for alcohol, but under the circumstances oblivion seemed like a welcome option. I tipped the glass to my lips with abandon.

"You should probably go easy, there. Tell me, uh—"

"Margaret."

"You a regular here?"

I shook my head, which made the room spin. I wasn't sure I could form the words, but I managed to say, "Came with a friend. You?"

"First time. I came with a buddy from Cleveland. He's a liquor distributor. To tell you the truth—"

"You're married."

Pete looked around and laughed uneasily, so I knew I was right. How could I have worked at the Playboy Club all this time and not know that a guy in sales from Cleveland wearing a home-ironed, button-down white shirt with a seersucker jacket was, of course, married? But I was also aware of something unpleasant happening to my foot.

I looked down and saw that a man crawling on all fours had slipped off one of my shoes and was licking my toes. I yanked my foot from his mouth, lost my balance and slipped backward off the stool on top of the guy who'd been sucking my toes.

Pete hauled me up off the floor and steadied me as I tried to wedge my damp foot back in my shoe. "I think I better get you out of here," he said.

Once on my feet and stabilized, Pete steered me directly into the crowd, probably a safer trajectory to the door than risking a tour through the tangled bodies at work in the shadowy fringes. With Pete's hands grasping my shoulders, I took leave of my body to get an overview of the room. The motion was momentarily liberating, but the sea of movement below made me queasy, to say nothing of the fug of cigarette smoke clouding the air. A threesome heaving away on a sectional sofa included Gloria in an act that required her full attention. It was not the time to bid her goodnight. Would anyone miss me if I dematerialized and took myself home?

I spiraled toward the door, glimpsing Moe checking in a blonde woman, her hair swept up in a smooth chignon. She was wearing a black silk suit with a shawl collar turned up, casting her face in shadow. There was something familiar about her movements and the tilt of her head that reminded me of Camilla. She was the last person I would want to cross paths with at this party—but then, what was she doing here? I swung around for a closer look, but felt resistance, something holding me back.

"Steady, steady," Pete said, as my body bumped into a dark-haired man making his way through the crowd holding two drinks aloft.

I zipped back into my body, shifting just enough to avoid a splashing cocktail.

"Nice work," the man said, his face inches from mine. "I almost ruined your sexy little dress."

"Thanks, no harm done." I recognized him. The Club? Was he a keyholder? I knew him from somewhere. Why couldn't I place him?

"You look familiar," he said.

"So do you—"

"You know each other," Pete said, sounding relieved. "Listen, nice talking to you. Take it easy."

He dropped his hands from my shoulders as though they were radioactive and pushed his way through the crowd. I suspected Pete hoped to make a furtive exit, too, without bidding goodnight to his buddy.

"Here, have a drink," the man said, shoving one of the cocktails into my hand. "I was delivering a daiquiri to someone, but I'll never find her in this mob."

I laughed. "Thanks, but I was just leaving—" I wished I could think of his name. He was nice looking, wearing a nice suit.

"Me, too. Drink that down and let's split. This isn't my scene."

"Nor mine." I took a sip. He smiled, grabbed my hand and pulled me behind him through the crowd. I was feeling light-headed, but no longer queasy.

"C'mon, bottoms up," he said, when we reached the door. I finished off the cocktail and set my glass next to his on a side table. "I've got my car outside. I can drop you, or —?" He smiled.

I smiled. "Great, let's go."

Moe, whose job was to see nothing, and everything, stood aside as we emerged into the brightly lit hallway. We headed toward the elevator, the man wrapping his arm around my shoulders. I remember telling him I lived near Gramercy Park as we stepped into the elevator. Things began to get murky as the elevator doors closed and we descended.

With his arm around my waist, we headed down the street, but I had the sensation of bouncing, almost springing in the air with each step. The man laughed and tugged at my hand. "Skipping is a little too exuberant for me," he said, "but go ahead."

Skipping? My inclination was to leave my body, soar high above and away, but I suddenly felt leaden, almost too heavy to lift my feet. The sidewalk seemed to ooze around my feet, like jelly.

"Come along, baby. You're fine," he said, maneuvering toward the curb. "Easy, I got you." We stopped and he fumbled for his car key. Moments later I sank back into plush leather and closed my eyes. "Good girl. Rest up, baby. We've got some fun in store."

Fun? The word rattled in my brain, raising an unpleasant memory. A sense of foreboding gripped me but I couldn't sort out my thoughts. I looked out the window through half-closed eyes at the blur of lights—white, green, red—melting together in a wavy stream. We were cruising downtown, the sway of the car both soothing and unsettling. We pulled up at a curb. The car stopped, but my body felt like it was still surging forward. I wanted to open the door, to run, but couldn't lift my hand, couldn't open the door. Then the door swung open and the man grasped my upper arms, hauling me to my feet and up some steps.

I kicked off my shoes, my feet sinking into spongy carpet that squished around my toes. We mounted stairs, his hands on my waist steering me upward toward pale golden light. We reached the landing and he turned me toward him, pressing his mouth on mine. "C'mon, baby, give." His hand pushed between my legs, his fingers roughly grasping my thigh and reaching up to my panties. "Playing hard to get, kid? Not with me, you don't."

A stinging slap sent me reeling to the floor. I landed heavily at the foot of the bed, bumping my head against the footboard. Then he was on top of me, his forearm pressed against my throat. His hand tore at my dress, pulling the slick fabric above my hips. Where was my strength? I couldn't lift my arms, move my hands to stop him grinding his body on mine. My mind drifted. I was losing consciousness and couldn't fight it. I heard myself whimper, then his voice, low and throaty as he pushed my legs apart, "That's it, baby, nice and easy."

Suddenly a fiery vision exploded in the blackness of my mind, flaring brilliantly like fireworks in the night sky. Shards of light swirled in my head, dancing like confetti, then congealed in a pixilated apparition floating above me, just beyond my reach. A face of breathtaking beauty, familiar yet otherworldly, emerged in the radiant light. It was Camilla, her crystalline blue eyes intense and mesmerizing.

Energy surged into my limbs, giving me strength to lift myself free of the man's weight. I flung his body off mine and rose to my feet, hypnotically moving across the bedroom, following the apparition floating just beyond my reach. I cried out as the vision disappeared in the depths of draperies. I lurched forward, ripping the drapes from the brass rods and threw aside the filmy curtains.

Through the window, in the inky blackness of the sky, Camilla floated barely an arm's length away, beckoning to me. I yanked the sash up with such force, the windowpane shattered. Unable to stop myself, I crawled through broken glass onto the sill.

Arms wrapped themselves around me, pulling me back. "Stop! What the hell's got into you!"

The man tried to wrest me off the sill, but I fought back. The apparition fluttered closer, as Camilla's hands reached out, enticing me to break free of the man's grip. His arm held me firmly at the waist, his other hand reaching up to pull me back. In the struggle, his hand slammed against the broken glass, a jagged edge slicing into his palm.

He screamed in pain, his hand spattering blood on my face. I grabbed his fingers, cupping his hand to my mouth.

At the first taste of his blood on my lips, my own energy burst forth. No longer in thrall to Camilla, I flew out the window, leaving my body clinging to the sill. Instead of falling to the courtyard below, I ascended high above the apparition. At once, its brilliance began to fade.

At its core, Camilla's face, no longer luminous, appeared frozen in shock, eyes fierce with anger. Her mouth opened wide, as though screaming her fury, then released a cloud of noxious vapor that enveloped me. With that, she vanished into the night sky, shrieking laughter echoing in her wake.

The vapor shaped itself around me, seizing me in its tight grip, robbing me of my own powers. Blackness enfolded me. I could feel myself falling back into my body, Camilla's mocking laughter ringing in my ears.

Ten

In what seemed a millennium later, I regained consciousness. My head felt like a bag filled with jagged rocks banging together. Cocktails were clearly not my friends. But I knew more than a prodigious mix of alcohol had incapacitated me. My life force was drained, my energy level so depleted I was practically sub-human. Questions roiled my brain. Some potent drug had to have caused the hallucinations. If so, how, when, where had I ingested it—and by whose hand? Was it jealousy on my part that caused the apparition to take the form of Camilla—or was the specter a warning of her destructive influence over me? Once again the worlds I tried to keep separate had come crashing together. I had to be more vigilant.

A telephone was ringing in another world, one far from my grasp. I cracked open an eye, not both, and saw a man's bare feet, with tufts of black hair on the toes, wading through orange shag carpet. Not a pretty sight. I closed my eye, deciding to play possum until I could get a grip on what was happening.

The terrible ringing ended. A male voice, no longer using the seductive, mellow tones I remembered from the night before, barked, "Yeah, that was me. I been leaving messages. Look, I don't know who she is. I found your number in her bag, so you must know her. Long, dark hair. Like I said, followed me home. Shouldn'a let her in, y' know? Yeah, you can talk to her. If you know her, you gotta come get her, okay?"

A foot nudged my ribs. "Hey, you. Wake up!" A hand gripped my arm and yanked me up to a sitting position. "I got someone wants to talk to you."

The telephone receiver was pressed to my ear. Possum-playing wasn't going to work. Still with my eyes closed, I wrapped my hand around the phone. "Hello?"

"Meg? Meg, for God's sake, is that you?" Ian Fletcher's voice, mellifluous even registering shock, wafted into my ear. I groaned. "It's you, isn't it?"

"'Fraid so, Ian. I don't know how he got your number."

"Doesn't matter, I'm coming for you. Are you hurt?"

"Don't think so. But I'm sort of a mess. Really, you don't need to come, Ian."

"Yes, he does!" the man barked, shoving me with his foot. "Who is he? Boyfriend? Hope for your sake it's not your husband."

"Who is that bastard?" Ian said. "Tell him I'm on my way!"

"Really, I can get a taxi, Ian." The thought of him seeing me in this condition was more than I could stomach. "I'm fine, really."

The man snatched the phone from my hand. "She's a wreck. And I want her out of here. Fast! Just get the hell over here or I'll dump her in the street, okay?"

He gave Ian an address in Murray Hill and slammed the phone onto the bedside table. "He's on his way, kid. Get yourself together."

"Coffee," I mumbled, opening my eyes a crack wider. The man was wearing a black silk dressing gown. One of his hands had white adhesive tape wound around a patch of gauze.

"Damn, you think I'm your butler?" he snarled. "I should make you clean up this mess!" The hairy-toed feet paced through the shag rug, stumbling over a tipped wastebasket. He reached down and set it upright, then stomped toward the landing. "Sure, why not? Coffee coming up. Just don't try jumping out the window again while I get it."

I sat up straighter and looked around, trying to get my bearings. I was wearing a wrinkled, sweaty version of Gloria's cocktail dress. My black satin stilettos were paired neatly next to the bedroom door, my apartment keys glinting from one shoe, my cocktail clutch wedged into the other. The decor registered as Guy's Deluxe Bachelor Pad—in addition to orange shag carpet, the room was fitted out with a black leather Eames chair, teak furnishings and a chrome wall unit with elaborate hi-fi equipment. Obviously my host was a *Playboy* magazine subscriber.

Otherwise, the bedroom was a wreck. No wonder the man was angry. Scattered debris, a broken lamp and drapes pulled loose from their rods littered the floor. Sheer curtains, stained with dark spots of blood, billowed in the breeze through a broken window. A newspaper lay open on the carpet piled with jagged shards of glass. Surely I hadn't caused this much damage all by myself. But then I recalled the struggle at the window. And Camilla.

I gradually became aware of other voices speaking softly somewhere in the room. I swiveled around and saw a handsome teak cabinet with a television screen flickering in shades of gray. The volume was turned low, but I could hear Hugh Downs and Barbara Walters chatting amiably about Jackie Kennedy's upcoming televised tour of the White House. I watched transfixed. I didn't even own a television set. I'd certainly never heard of having one in a bedroom. All this ran through my mind as I grabbed a corner of the bedspread and hoisted myself off the floor.

I waded through the sea of orange shag to the bathroom, my rubbery legs somehow supporting me. I flicked on the light switch, expecting a blast of harsh, incandescent glare. Instead, a wash of filtered light bathed the peach-tiled room in soothing tones. I ventured a look in the mirror. Even with the vanity lighting, I was not a thing of beauty. Tracks of mascara wound down the creases by my nose. Lipstick smeared my cheeks. The pins had come out of my hair and untidy lengths hung limply around my face. But my sorry appearance was entirely cosmetic. My scratches and bruises had already healed.

I turned on the taps and dunked a washcloth in a stream of hot water. I pressed the cloth to my face, burying myself in its damp warmth, trying to think. I should have a story prepared for Ian, but I couldn't come up with one that would cover all the bases. I realized, when the inevitable moment arrived, I would not be able to introduce Ian to the strange dark man in whose bedroom I had allegedly caused so much damage. I rinsed my face in cold water. I would like to have brushed my teeth, but there wasn't a chance I would put the man's toothbrush to use, or his water glass. Recalling the taste of his blood on my lips, I scooped water from the tap into my mouth and swished.

A door slammed. Loud voices. "Where is she? Meg? Are you up there?"

Feet pounded up the stairs. I ran my hands over the wrinkles of Gloria's black satin sheath and stepped out of the bathroom as Ian reached the landing. He stopped, his mouth falling open as he caught sight of me. "My God!"

That bad, I thought. And this is after I'd cleaned myself up. "Hi, Ian. Thanks for coming. I'm sorry about this."

"Don't be," he said quietly, his hand brushing my arm.

Morning stubble darkened his face. His sandy-brown hair had flopped over one eye; he shook it back as he looked around the room. He was wearing a white dress shirt, open at the neck, with the sleeves rolled up and the tails hanging loose over jeans. He'd obviously dressed in a hurry, jamming his bare feet into brown loafers.

The man pulled the cords tighter on his black silk dressing gown, his eyes narrowed on Ian. The two men were both of medium height, but had entirely different builds. Ian was slender with broad shoulders. The dark haired man carried his bulk in his chest, his head thrust forward. He cleared his throat and crossed his arms, sizing Ian up.

Ian, his face grim, turned to confront the man. "What did you do to her?"

"Don't look at me! This was strictly up to her. Her call. She couldn't handle it, know what I mean?"

"Handle what, for God's sake?" Ian's face was livid, his voice rising in fury. "What was she meant to handle?"

"Hey, I'm the injured party here," the man said, holding his hands palms up to show his bandage. "I try to keep her from jumping out a window and look what happens. Lucky I didn't end up in hospital with stitches. She trashes my place and comes off without a scratch. So just cool it, bub. I don't need this, okay?"

"Bub? You're calling me bub?" Ian's outrage, delivered in posh tones, almost made me laugh. But his face was fierce, his hands balled in tight fists. He was about to uncork. "Why would she be jumping out a window? What did you give her?"

"Me? Nothing. Just back off, okay? She got herself plastered, that's all."

"Wait, you did give me something," I said, the words springing from my mouth. "At the party. That drink."

"I was bringing it to someone else, sweetheart. You grabbed it. Gulped it down." He smirked, turning back to Ian, "Your friend here was all over me, you know?"

"And took advantage of you, is that it, bub? I think you drugged her."

"Yeah?" He laughed. "Try proving that one!"

"You bet. Let's call the police, shall we?" Ian sprang toward the telephone on the side table. The man managed to grab the phone first, hugging it to his chest.

"Ian, hang on. Maybe we should just go."

I could picture the fallout at the studio if Paul Abbott heard about a police report involving two of his actors. "Drunk and disorderly," wasn't a term I cared to have associated with my name, especially as there was probably already a police file on me, courtesy of Haddie's death. I assumed Ian had a green card, but there was no point in taking chances with Immigration.

"Yeah, listen to your girlfriend. I could'a put her out in the street, you know, with no one the wiser." He was still hugging the telephone, but smugness had crept into his voice. He clearly felt he had the upper hand. "This is what I get for showing compassion. I didn't need to call you, remember?"

Instead of backing off, Ian stepped forward. His voice calm, he asked, "May I have the telephone, please? She's got a brother on the Force. I think we might want to give him a ring."

Ian's audacious bluff had the desired effect. The man's shoulders slumped, but he tightened his grip on the telephone. He licked his lips, his voice a soft purr. "No need to get carried away here. Maybe I was a little rough, but—hey, you pick someone up at a party like that—believe me, it was no tea dance, know what I mean? What was I supposed to think?"

There was a brief silence, the man's words hanging in the air. I dug my toes into the shag and gazed up at the ceiling. Could this nightmare get any worse?

Finally Ian said, "Nothing. You are to think nothing. Say nothing. Clear?"

"Good. That's good. So let's just wrap this up. Jesus, I gotta get out to Nyack for lunch or my mother's gonna kill me."

It occurred to me then why the man was familiar. He was a creative director at one of the top ad agencies in town, a man I had seen on two occasions on callbacks for television commercials. I'd got one of the jobs. He'd shown up on the set during the shoot for the shampoo commercial, smooth in his two-button suit and slicked back hair. If I'd had trouble placing him, I could only hope he'd never remember me. I plucked my keys and the evening bag out of my shoes and stepped into them.

I was edging toward the stairs when the adman whispered to Ian, "Look, does she really have a brother who's a cop? I mean, there's no need to mention this, right?"

"Right," Ian said. "But we know where you live."

"Jesus. A good time is all I wanted, you know? Is that too much to ask?"

"Not at all," Ian said. I heard a heavy thump and looked back. Ian was standing over the ad man, who was sitting on the landing, his hand to his nose. "Having a good time now?"

I grabbed Ian's arm and hurried down the stairs, with him in tow. If a bloody brawl ensued, there'd be no way to avoid dealing with the police and there was far too much I didn't care to explain.

I pushed open the front door and blinked into the glare of morning sun striking the stoop. We bounded down the steps to the street, hand-in-hand, like two kids running from mischief, which was the case.

"I believe he and I reached an understanding," Ian said, as we hurried down the street, "but he won't be quite the prize package his mother is expecting at lunch."

"Serves him right," I said. "But let's hope he didn't keep your phone number."

"Blimey, hadn't thought of that," Ian said. We slowed up as we reached the corner and both drew deep breaths. "But I doubt he'll want to forge any lasting bonds with either of us."

"Hope not," I said, turning to Ian, who was still holding my hand. His white shirt gleamed in the bright morning light, and there was a sparkle in his eye. His face was flushed with exertion and, I suspected, pride in having bested the adman. “I don’t know what to say, Ian, but thank you.”

“Please, it perked up a dismal weekend. Anyway, no need to rush off. Looks like you can make it home under your own steam, but how about grabbing some breakfast first.”

“Thanks, but I look awful and feel worse. I really need to go home and put myself back together.”

“Come on, you look fine to me.” He was already steering me into the coffee shop on the corner. I didn’t resist. “Good girl. I’m famished.”

The cafe had just opened. The counterman, a young guy with a crew cut, was busy piling donuts and Danish under a glass dome. “Anywhere you like,” he said, without looking up. Mingling smells of brewing coffee and bacon sizzling on the grill permeated the air.

We walked past the stools at the lunch counter and slid into a red vinyl booth. Ian reached for two menus sheathed in plastic that were pressed between a napkin dispenser and a sugar jar. “Griddle cakes for me,” he said. “I’ve become addicted to your Yankee maple syrup. What do you fancy?”

I set my black clutch bag on the Formica table and stared blankly at the menu selections. Breakfast combos. Sandwiches. Fountain specialties. The thought of eating anything roiled my insides. My eyes were gritty, my tongue was sandpaper. Nothing appealed to me. “Not sure. Give me a minute.”

The counterman approached the table with a Silex of coffee. “You guys take milk?”

“Not for me,” I said, looking up.

“Or me,” Ian said.

“Holy smoke!” The counterman bumped the silex onto the table top, looked at me and then stared at Ian. “Oh, wow. I don’t believe it.”

“What’s the matter?” I asked. The counterman’s gaze swiveled back at me.

“He’s never served a vampire before,” Ian said calmly.

“What?” I gasped. For a terrible moment I thought I’d somehow given myself away. How could Ian know that I was a vampire? Why was the counterman staring? What had I done? I was about to bolt from the table when Ian started laughing.

"*Dark Passages*, right?" Ian smiled up at the boy, who nodded and continued staring at me. "He's a fan of the show, Meg."

"Could I just say it's a real pleasure serving you, Miss Harrison. You are so beautiful."

"Thank you, thank you very much," I said, sinking lower in the booth, grateful my wrinkled dress and untidy hair hadn't registered with him.

"There you go," Ian said, laughing. "Told you so, didn't I? You look absolutely blooming this morning, my dear."

"Mr. Fletcher, no one in the dorm is going to believe this. No one."

"Of course, they will. What's your name? We'll sign something."

"Oh, wow. That'd be great." The young man's angular face split into a grin. "William is my name. I mean, Bill. Actually, everyone calls me Billy."

"Just pour us some coffee, Billy. We'll order in a minute." Billy nodded, and poured coffee with a shaky hand.

"You looked like you'd seen a ghost," Ian said, after Billy went back behind the counter. "Get used to it. We're starting to get a following."

"I guess, but doesn't he wonder what the vampire is doing with the governess on a Sunday morning?"

"And she in a cocktail dress, no less." Ian laughed. "Can't be up to anything good. Come on, let's order. You want griddle cakes, too?"

"No," I said, glancing back at the menu. "Steamed vegetables. Side of spinach."

"Righto," Ian said, giving me an odd look. "Billy? You got that? The lady wants steamed veg, side of spinach. I'll have bacon with the griddle cakes."

"Coming right up," Billy said, his voice reverential.

"You want some pickles with that?" Ian asked, his voice low. "Strawberries, perhaps? Banana split with cheese whiz?"

"No!" I laughed. "I'm not pregnant. I just like vegetables. Honestly, I can't imagine what you're thinking."

"I'm thinking I haven't had this much fun in a long time. Is this your usual weekend prowl, or did I just hit it lucky?"

"Not usual," I said, firmly. It occurred to me that Ian had no idea that I worked weekends at the Playboy Club. What would he think if he knew I was moonlighting as a Bunny—or that I'd gone to the party because Elvis kissed Camilla? How could I explain ending up in the adman's bedroom? Or what made me climb out on a window ledge when I didn't know myself? Didn't he wonder why I showed no signs of having cut myself on all that broken glass? Ian's question hovered in the air and required a response.

"One thing just led to another," I said.

"I know." Ian put his hand on mine, his face growing serious. "You're cold as ice. You're pale. I think you've had a terrible shock and I don't mean to make light of it."

My hands were always cold, my face perpetually pale, but that wasn't something I cared to explain, either. I was still feeling a bit queasy, especially with the smell of fried bacon, but more than anything I was embarrassed. At the very least, Ian was someone I would be working with, and this crazy incident was not something I wanted to have stand between us. "I made a mistake in judgment. I'm sorry."

"Someone took advantage of you, Meg. The more I think about it, I'm sure that man slipped you LSD at the party. You're probably still coming down."

"LSD? You think so?" It would explain the hallucinations with Camilla, but how could LSD incapacitate my powers so completely?

Billy appeared with his Silex and refilled our cups. "Did I hear LSD? A little weed helps," he mumbled. "Smoothes ya out."

"Thanks," Ian said. "We got a handle on it, Billy."

Billy nodded, filled our cups and retreated to the grill. If I could blame this on LSD instead of Elvis and Camilla, I was fine with it.

"You might be right, Ian. But it was still my mistake. I don't think I want to talk about it anymore."

"Okay, but don't think I'm making any judgments. Lord knows I've been involved in a few scrapes of my own that I'd rather not reveal. I'm just glad you had my telephone number with you. Odd, y'know, but I don't actually remember when I gave it to you. Do you?"

"Uh, no," I said, choking on a swallow of coffee. That was a question I hadn't expected. "I don't even remember having your number." I snapped open the satin clutch and spilled its contents on the tabletop.

Lipstick. Powder compact. Comb. Handkerchief. Coin purse. Keys. I unzipped an interior pocket in which I'd stuffed my tip money.

"Very impressive," Ian said, eyeing the roll of bills spilling out of the unzipped lining of the bag. "At some point last night you obviously worked in a bank raid. We should be expecting sirens and guns drawn any minute."

"No, really—" I shrugged, knowing where an explanation would lead. "Look, breakfast is on me, okay?"

"You bet. And leave a big tip." He smiled. "Look, you don't have to justify anything to me. Lucky thing that SOB didn't relieve you of your money. He seems to have kept the phone number."

"But I don't think I ever had it." I opened the coin purse. Inside were a few folded bills, some small change and a curled bit of notepaper. I knew even as I smoothed out the scrap of paper what I would find written on it. "Recognize the numbers?"

"My phone number," Ian said with a sigh. "My handwriting. Mystery solved."

"I guess," I said. "Mystery solved." But it didn't explain how I happened to have it in my possession. I stuffed everything back into the evening bag, except the piece of paper.

Billy delivered our food, depositing a heaping plate of steamed vegetables in front of me. "It's everything the cook could find back there. We don't get a lot of calls for that stuff," Billy said, a note of distaste in his voice. "You want me to get you a side of fries?"

"No, thanks. This is perfect. Just a glass of tomato juice."

"Coming up," Billy said, hurrying off.

"No wonder your skin is smooth as marble," Ian said, pouring a river of maple syrup on pancakes slathered in melting butter. "Aside from a penchant for masses of steamed plant life for breakfast, anything else I should know about you?"

"Not really."

"Because you are sort of an odd duck, you know. A rather beautiful duck, but odd." Ian unsnapped the clasp of my evening bag and tucked the piece of paper with his phone number back inside. "There you go. I want you to keep my number and promise to ring me in advance of your next wild escapade. I'd hate to miss out."

An image popped into my mind of Ian tagging along with me on my next midnight foray to the Cloisters or zooming to the top of the Empire State Building for a view of the city that didn't sleep any more than I did. A companion on these excursions would be nice, and Ian seemed game for adventure. But the thought lasted the blink of an eye. I could never reveal myself to Ian. It was out of the question.

"There won't be a next time, if I can help it," I said, wondering once again how I'd happened to have Ian's phone number in the first place.

Eleven

Fortified with spinach, steamed broccoli, beans and carrots, I decided to walk home. In view of my disheveled appearance, I chose to make short work of it. I said goodbye to Ian outside the restaurant, waited for him to round the corner in the opposite direction and then streaked downtown. At the speed I was traveling, I was little more than a blur to early risers walking the streets on a Sunday morning. Breezing down Lexington Avenue, streams of cool, fresh air stroked my skin and ruffled my hair. I was feeling so good I whizzed down as far as Union Square before heading back up to Gramercy Park.

Once inside my apartment I shed Gloria's cocktail dress and left it in a heap by my front door. A good dry cleaner could rehabilitate it for another night on the town. How many other racy parties had that dress attended? I didn't dare think. Besides, dwelling on it reminded me of my own misdeeds. It also made me wonder how I could have allowed myself to be so dangerously vulnerable. Why had I become so pathetically weak and powerless that I couldn't even defend myself against mere mortal harm?

I stepped into the shower and turned on the faucet. Blasts of cold water struck my skin and ricocheted off my shoulders. Still pondering the events of the night before, I turned my face into the rush of icy water to clear my head. Something beyond my control or knowledge was at work. What was I missing? I switched on hot water and lathered up with soap and shampoo, glad to have the day to myself to think things through.

Viewed one way, the night hadn't been a complete loss. I had empirical proof that martinis and Rusty Nails didn't agree with me any more than grasshoppers. I could at least claim I'd been to an orgy; no celebrities, but a memorable encounter with a dark and dangerous man. It added up to an adventure of sorts, but not something I cared to talk about around the coffee urn at the studio or write home to Marilyn about.

My telephone started ringing just as I turned off the taps. Only my mother would call this early on a Sunday morning and she'd be suspicious if I wasn't home. She'd probably called even earlier when I was still at breakfast with Ian. I reached for a towel and made a dash to the kitchen, leaving a track of wet footprints. I grabbed the phone and said, "Morning, Mom."

"Sorry, Meg, it's Elke here." She sighed deeply as though she'd been holding her breath. "I'm so glad you're home. Audrey just called. I have to work a private party in the Penthouse today. I've got so many demerits I can't turn her down. Besides, I have need of the money," she said in her soft German accent.

"And you want me to babysit Elle?"

"Could you? It's a big favor, I know, but everyone else is working, too."

"Happy to help. I can be there in an hour or so, okay?"

"An hour? Sooner, if you can. Is good?"

Not so good, but I agreed. There goes my Sunday, I thought, as I hung up the phone. I stood for a moment, water pooling at my feet on the kitchen floor. I was suddenly feeling dizzy and not at all well. It was a strange sensation for me, probably a residual reaction to the LSD. But I couldn't call Elke back and break my word. I dried myself off and started getting dressed.

Minutes later I was on the street, my hair still damp, taking a moment to contemplate whether even little Elle might object to my odd choice of wardrobe—clogs, a faded Twin Lakes Swim Team tee shirt, peasant skirt and black satin evening bag. I had thrown on clothes without much thought, and not even bothered to properly dry my hair. But rather than take the time to go back in and change, I decided to wing my way to Savannah's house. I figured no one would see me but a grateful mother, her toddler and Savannah.

As I neared the house I slowed down and walked up the cobblestone street, smelling the tang of the Hudson River. Savannah, wearing jeans and a flannel shirt, was sweeping the steps. She looked up as I approached the stoop.

"You made it in record time," she said, setting aside her broom. "Noni and Allie have already left for the Club. Elke and I were just waiting for you. How come you didn't get called in to work this event?"

"Just lucky, I guess. I was probably next on Audrey's list."

"So how was the party last night?" We walked up the steps together and she shoved the door open. "Any celebs?"

"Not a one. Really, just tired old guys. Sedate and boring. I left early." Telling Savannah about the party was about as appealing as recapping it for my mother. And if I told her about the adman and his LSD, she'd want to pistol-whip him. Did everyone lie to Savannah?

"I figured as much. Of course, I've never even been invited to one of those parties. I have to say I'm curious."

"Don't bother. You're not missing a thing."

"Do me a favor and tell Elke to hurry up," Savannah said. "I'll grab a jacket and meet her outside. We should get going."

I hurried down the hallway and found Elke in the kitchen, looking glamorous even first thing in the morning. She was wearing white boots with a short skirt, her long blonde hair a wavy cascade on her shoulders. "Hey, you made it fast! I'm almost ready to go."

She was pouring milk for Elle, who was banging her hands on the tray of her highchair, only a breath away from squalling. As soon as she saw me, she squealed and kicked her feet against the chair legs, her chubby arms wind-milling above her curly blonde head.

"Hey, punkin! How'ya doin'?" I kissed Elle's forehead and put my satin evening bag on the table. "So, who are you subbing for, Elke?"

"Gloria. Who do you think? She's probably still partying. Thanks so much for doing this."

"It's a pleasure." Elle was clamoring to be picked up. I scooped her out of the high chair and kissed her chubby cheeks. "Do you mind if I take Elle back home with me? You could pick her up on your way home from work."

"That's fine with me. She loves being with you."

"Good, then you run off and I'll feed her." The explosive sound of a motorcycle revving up made us both jump. "Hear that? Better hurry, Savannah's raring to go."

"*Ach*, no! My hair!" Elke rolled her eyes. "I'd rather take the subway. She's crazy on that machine!"

In a flurry of movement, she pulled a scarf from her shoulder bag, tied it on her head, kissed Elle and rushed down the hallway. I followed Elke to the front door. She nuzzled Elle again and then ran down the steps to climb on the back of the motorcycle. Savannah gunned the throttle and waved.

"I'll lock up when I go," I said, waving back. Elle waved, too, bouncing in my arms and burbling, "Byebyebyebye."

Less than an hour later, I set off walking to my apartment, pushing Elle in her stroller. I was in no particular hurry and stopped often to look in shop windows. There was a smoky aroma of autumn in the air, and trees blazed bronze and gold. The neighborhoods improved as we headed east, and the streets began filling with people walking and sitting in sidewalk cafés. I turned uptown, walking past the Flatiron Building, then east toward Gramercy Park.

I found myself thinking of Eric. Back home, on a sunny afternoon like this, Eric and I would be flying high in the sky looking down on haystacks and cornstalks. Where was he flying now? I wondered what the chances were that Eric might turn up in New York on leave, surprising me once again. I ached to see him.

"Well, well, look who's here!" A voice, dripping in honeyed tones, sent a chill down my spine. I glanced up to see Camilla standing in the canopied entrance of the Player's Club, wearing a sleek blue shantung silk suit with a matching pillbox hat. Emmett Boardman was at her side lighting a cigarette. "My goodness," she said, "is this little one yours? You are so full of surprises."

"Hi, Camilla. This is Elle. I'm just looking after her for a friend."

"Babysitting. How sweet. So this is how you spend your weekends. No partying for you, I guess." She laughed and wiggled her white-gloved fingers at Elle. "I see you were on your school swim team."

"Yeah, you know, it was that or softball." Partying? I could feel egg slithering down my face, congealing on my cheeks. If she'd taken in my Twin Lakes swim team tee shirt, she'd also noticed my clogs, satin evening bag and drip-dry hairdo. "You look terrific, Camilla."

"Thanks," she said, adjusting her handbag on her arm. "We're going to a reception for Sir John Gielgud. Such a dear, funny man. Oh, do you know Emmett Boardman? Emmett this is Meg Harrison. She's in *Dark Passages* with me, playing the sweet little governess."

"Nice to meet you," I said. He glanced at me through a puff of cigarette smoke, nodded and pulled at Camilla's arm. I hoped he wouldn't recognize me from the Playboy Club and felt pretty sure I could count on it.

"We have to be going in," Camilla said, smiling radiantly. "Bye, see you next week."

"Have a good time." Instead of turning away, I lingered for a moment watching Camilla and Emmett Boardman glide through the entrance of the Player's Club, the hallowed actor's club founded by Edwin Booth in 1888. The Club was just down the street from my apartment, but I'd never been inside. I'd passed the famous townhouse many times, dreaming of the day when I might be invited to become a member.

Life had just become wildly unfair. I imagined Camilla, a glass of Champagne in hand, chatting with Sir John Gielgud. He would, of course, be entranced with her. Envy reared up and slugged me between the eyes. Once again an image appeared to me of Camilla, wild-eyed and demonic, beckoning me to step off the window ledge. Was I becoming so jealous of Camilla that I was having dangerous hallucinations about her?

I headed back down the street, another matter occupying my mind, one that I'd put off dealing with for some time. Instead of going directly to my apartment, I pushed the stroller into the park. Afternoon sun splashed puddles of golden light through tree branches, dappling the leaf-strewn paths. I lifted Elle from the stroller and set her down on the grass. Her hand gripped my fingers, her plump legs skewing around until she'd found her balance. Then, laughing and waving her arms, she toddled through a scruff of newly fallen leaves. I stood back and watched her before settling myself on a bench.

Dancing her baby jig through the leaves, she toppled backward onto her well-padded rump and looked up at me. Her cornflower blue eyes registered surprise, dismay and delight in quick succession. She rolled over, bits of grass and crunchy leaves sticking to her yellow corduroy overalls, and climbed back onto her feet. The game was on. Again and again Elle would present me with a leaf, then toddle back to pick up another for me to add to my autumn bouquet. Then she hugged my knees while I held the clutch of leaves high above her head and let them flutter down on her upturned face. She giggled and clapped her hands, then climbed onto my lap and squirmed around until she'd made herself comfortable.

I leaned down and breathed warm breath on her ear. She giggled again, and I whispered, "Can you keep a secret? How would you like it if I had a little one just like you? What do you think of that?"

Elle squirmed in my lap, looking up at me in puzzlement. "I know, how about that? I'm as surprised as you are." She put her hand on my mouth and patted it. "No? You don't like the idea? Well, I don't know what we can do about it now." She gazed at me, her blue eyes serious. "You're right, I should've been more careful. But it's done. Can't be undone. What am I going to do?"

She frowned and sighed so deeply I laughed, wondering if somehow she really understood what I was saying. But with the laughter came tears, my own, not Elle's. She clapped her hand on my cheeks, her fingers sliding in my streaming tears, making me smile again.

"It's okay. I'll work it out. But keep this to yourself, punkin'. Everyone'll know soon enough."

I cradled her on my lap, feeling her growing heavier in my arms as she fell asleep. My fingers ticked off the weeks since I'd seen Eric. I think I'd known for some time that I was probably pregnant but hadn't wanted to admit it. My letters to Eric had become shorter, less frequent. I just couldn't deal with the consequences for either of us.

Now, oddly enough, it wasn't Eric who came to mind, but Bonnie, our Twin Lakes homecoming queen. The story of Bonnie and her boyfriend Roy remained a cautionary tale for both Eric and me, one that we intended to avoid at all costs.

On the Monday morning following the big game, the news that the football captain had knocked up the homecoming queen spread like wildfire through our school's corridors. But while Bonnie and Roy were in Iowa getting married, Bonnie's mother hosted a tea (lemonade and cookies) for the Top Girls in school. Marilyn and I were invited, along with the cheerleaders, homecoming queen's court of honor, the student council vice-president and secretary, female merit scholarship students and Miss Ericksen, the home-ec teacher who taught personal hygiene.

Most of us knew the score, but to the credit of my fellow Top Girls, there was no snickering whatsoever when the homecoming queen's mother told us, in a small, tremulous voice, that "our doctor can find no explanation for Bonnie's virgin conception, but our hearts now must reach out to the young life created."

The words spoken by this pious sparrow in her pin-neat living room were both jarring and curiously erotic because one was forced to imagine what might have been going on with Roy, Bonnie and the Holy Spirit in Roy's blue Dodge parked at the edge of my dad's cornfield. A private religious ceremony was in the offing, we were told, but in the meantime, "Roy was doing the right thing" because he and Bonnie had been going steady. His signet ring had hung heavily on a cord around Bonnie's neck for nearly a year.

I'd glanced at Miss Ericksen, who was staring in some wonderment at Bonnie's mother's astonishing performance. I could see that an emergency hygiene class was forming in her mind, with more explicit information forthcoming. None of us (except, presumably, Bonnie) had a clear picture of what was actually involved in the coupling that led up to conception. Also, our homecoming queen was revered and it was obvious where this virgin-conception line of thinking would lead. For Marilyn and me, it led to a heated debate on our walk home.

"Marilyn!" I shouted with some exasperation, "If they own up to fooling around, get married and have a kid, it's over. She has more kids, he runs his dad's gas station, and who cares? But virgin conception? We will expect big things down the road!"

"How do we know that God's grace doesn't manifest itself in these miracles frequently because this troubled world needs divine saviors . . ."

"Fine! Let's call it a biological phenomenon, a miracle, if you will, but, believe me, it still wasn't *immaculate*!"

Although I had to acknowledge that if one were selecting the perfect vessel for a virgin birth, one couldn't do better than Bonnie. And if anyone could handle the upheaval of a teen preganancy with grace, even enthusiasm, it would be Bonnie. But I didn't want to emulate her.

The last time I saw Bonnie, she was pushing her grocery cart into my checkout line in the Red Owl. She looked like she'd swallowed a football and was suffering massive indigestion. Her skin was doughy, her hair stringy and she looked nothing like our homecoming queen in her gleaming satin gown with tiny glass beads sparkling on the bodice, a red velvet cape with an ermine collar draped on her shoulders and a sparkling tiara on her upswept hair. Nor was her white-gloved hand tucked under the arm of the football captain, who was probably pumping gas instead of playing varsity ball on a scholarship at the U. Still, her eyes were smiling and she appeared not at all self-conscious.

"Hi, Margaret," she said brightly. "I hear you were terrific in the school play."

"Thanks, Bonnie. How's it going?"

"Great," she said, her smile broad. We're about to move out of my folk's basement into a little apartment. Roy's sister is giving me a shower. Will you come?"

"You bet," I said, my brain fixed on the awful intimacy of ringing up Roy and Bonnie's lunchmeat, Velveeta cheese, toilet tissue and Drano. How could Bonnie, who had danced in satin and ermine, reconcile living with her husband in her parents' rumpus room, and keep smiling?

I certainly didn't feel like smiling. How could I tell Eric what had happened? "Do I have to be careful?" he'd asked me. What was I thinking? Just because we'd both escaped Twin Lakes didn't mean we shouldn't take precautions!

My shoulders slumped around the weight of Elle in my lap, panic lapping in my throat. With a bun in the oven, it was unthinkable that I'd last long playing virginal Margie, the Stanhope governess. I could be replaced as quickly as Rebecca had been. I couldn't bear the thought of losing my dream job, of no longer going to the studio. How could I tell Wesley Truscott?

I'd also have to forfeit my Bunny job when I could no longer fit in the costume. I had known for a while that I'd eventually want to turn in my Bunny ears for keeps. Every weekend I was signing more and more autographs for wives of Playboy keyholders, who invariably asked why Margie, the governess, was moonlighting as a Bunny. But the choice of whether to continue working at the Club would not be mine to make. As soon as my condition became apparent, I'd be stripped of my satin Bunny costume. I'd soon have no income at all. For now, it was better to keep working at the Club and save as much money as possible until I was forced to quit. How long did I have? Two months? Longer if I cut out a few calories?

Although I was banking almost my entire *Dark Passages* paycheck and living off my tips from the Club, I'd saved nowhere near enough to see me through more than a few months without working. At some point, I'd have to come clean with my folks, but wouldn't have to face it for a while. And I could put off telling Eric as long as he remained in Vietnam. The one thing I knew was that I had no intention of ending up like Bonnie, living back in Twin Lakes with Eric in the Blatch rumpus room.

My mother would know, unlike Bonnie's mother, that there had been no virgin conception—and she would be fearful in ways Bonnie's mother would find unimaginable. The biggest issue, the one I couldn't bear to think about, was the nature of the being growing in my womb. I shuddered at the thought—and at my mother's warning that childbirth for our kind was difficult, often deadly.

Elle awakened and squirmed in my arms. She was hungry, fretful and had no intention of allowing me to put her back in the stroller. She wound her legs around my waist and gripped my neck as I walked to my apartment pushing the empty stroller.

Fortunately I'd remembered to pack up baby food before leaving Savannah's house as there was no suitable food in my own cupboards. I opened a jar of applesauce and settled Elle in my arms, about to feed her, when the telephone rang. I didn't want to talk with my parents, or Marilyn, or anyone else I could think of who might call me on a Sunday afternoon. But, on the fifth ring, realizing it might be Elke calling, I answered the phone.

"Meg? Ian here. When you didn't answer I was afraid you'd gone out on the town without me again."

"Nope, Entertaining at home this evening. I was just serving dinner."

"Well, I envy your dinner guests their string beans and cabbage. Listen, I remembered that I wrote out my telephone number for Camilla the other day. She must have given it to you."

"Really." It was the only response I could think of, yet questions flooded my brain. Why would Camilla ask for Ian's phone number? When did she give it to me? Why? How did it find its way into Gloria's evening bag? I delivered a spoonful of applesauce into Elle's mouth and said, "Thanks for letting me know, Ian. Mystery solved yet again, I guess."

"I guess. Thanks for breakfast this morning. I wouldn't have missed it."

I laughed. "Imagine Billy showing off his autographed menu to everyone in his dorm! And again, Ian, thanks for everything."

"Don't give it another thought. It's just between us. See you tomorrow."

After hanging up, I sat for a moment completely still, my mind racing. Camilla, again. Was I losing my marbles?

"No, my dear," Haddie said, materializing in my crowded little kitchen, "your brain is quite intact, but you are not seeing what should be so clear to you by now."

I glanced down at Elle, to see if she had noticed Haddie joining us. She looked up at me, her lips smacking open for more applesauce. I gave her another teaspoonful.

"What's going on, Haddie? Everywhere I turn, it's Camilla."

"Forewarned is forearmed," he said sternly. "I told you there is a malicious force that wants to cause you great harm. You must be vigilant."

"Are you telling me to watch out for Camilla?"

"Of course, and it shouldn't come as such a surprise. She could be very dangerous if you fall under her spell. She has her own powers and she knows how to use them. She's well practiced in sorcery."

I laughed. "Like a witch?"

"Exactly. You mock her at your own risk. She's testing you. Locking your dressing room door was irksome. Drugging you and luring you to jump out a window more serious. And there's more to come. You must take heed."

"I have my own powers. And I have you." I slipped the last spoonful of applesauce into Elle's mouth. "I'm sorry, Haddie, but I have something more serious to deal with than Camilla. I'm in a real mess, and I can assure you Camilla had nothing to do with it!"

"Understood. And that little concern is not something I can do much about," he said primly. His voice became little more than a sigh as he began to fade. "You must stay vigilant, my dear. It's a warning you must heed."

Twelve

Propinquity had done its job. Over the weekend, Ginny and Ed had run off to Elkins, Maryland, to tie the knot. Neither of them had been scheduled to work in Monday's episode, but turned up in time for the afternoon rehearsal for Tuesday's show. The two arrived hand-in-hand, and Ed had a bottle of Piper-Heidsieck cradled in his arm. Michael, Moira, Danny, Maxwell and I were already seated at the table marking up our scripts when they made their entrance.

"Say hello to the missus!" Ed boomed in his put-on brogue. "I say, who's a lucky man?"

There was a moment of stunned silence. Doris, stopwatch in hand, looked stricken. "Married? You didn't!" She clamped her script to her chest. "You're serious? But . . . well, congratulations, of course." Her voice trailed off.

"Well, you old cradle robber," Michael said. "Congratulations you two!"

"Congratulations, Pop!" I said, "and you, too, Ginny!" Everyone laughed and bounded up from the rehearsal table. Paul and Horace appeared in the doorway and joined the crush. Nigel set out Styrofoam cups. Ed popped the cork.

I wasn't the only one whose eyes flew to Ginny's belly, wondering if the hasty nuptials had taken place because Ed had knocked her up. Considering my own condition, misery welcomed company. I picked up two cups of Champagne and passed them to Moira and Maxwell, who were whispering near the pastry table.

"Looks preggers to me," Moira said, her eyes on Ginny.

"Can't imagine the old fart had it in him," Maxwell whispered back.

"In her, dear boy," Moira said. "That's the way it works, darling."

"You don't say!" Maxwell fluttered his eyelids at me, his hand on his heart. "I'd got it so wrong all these years!"

I laughed and went back to the table to pour myself Champagne. I saw Doris, Paul and Horace edge into the hallway and knew they were speculating about Ginny as well. It didn't help that Ginny was wearing a loose shift and looked pale. There were shadows under her eyes and she wasn't her usual ebullient self. Marriage to Ed would have its challenges, but shouldn't they still be in honeymoon mode? I glanced at the newlyweds and raised my cup. Ed caught my eye and winked.

I sank into a chair next to Danny at the rehearsal table. He'd pushed his script aside and was catching up on his homework. I glanced at a page in his algebra workbook and knew it would be pointless to offer assistance.

"Poor Ginny," I said, knocking back my Champagne.

"I give it six weeks before she's off to Reno," Danny said, not lifting his eyes from his equations. "Even my mother wouldn't marry a perv like him, and that's saying something." Remembering Ed's wink, I shared Danny's foreboding.

The bombshell news pretty much occupied the week. I remained especially attentive to developments, figuring I was getting a preview of what I'd be facing. There was much discussion about whether we should give individual wedding gifts or chip in on a more elaborate gift from all of us. In the end we pooled our money and assigned Maxwell the task of selecting a gift because his current squeeze worked in Macy's housewares and could give us an employee discount. It came down to bedding, a fancy fondue set with serving dishes and a burner, or a Waterford crystal punch bowl with cups. We went with the Waterford, although I didn't see Ed as the punch-drinking type.

By Thursday, Ginny was looking very wan and none too happy. Ed wasn't working that day. "He went to the track to bet on the ponies," she said. "I went to Aqueduct with him once," she added, without much enthusiasm, "but I think he'd rather be there with his friends."

During a break in camera blocking, Ginny nodded off on a couch in the Stanhope living room set. "She's limp from overuse," Moira declared. "Someone should tell Ed she needs a night off."

"Not my area of expertise," Maxwell said. "Talk to the poor dear yourself."

Moira took him up on it. After the air show, I saw Ginny in Moira's dressing room, across from mine, crying her eyes out. "It's not what I thought it would be," I heard her sob.

"It never is," Moira said. "But they soon tire of it, if that's any comfort."

Deftly, Moira maneuvered the conversation around to The Question no one had had the nerve to ask. I hovered near my dressing room door, eavesdropping on the murmur of voices across the hall. There was a fresh spate of tears from Ginny, then her choked voice crying out, "No, of course not! He doesn't even want children! Ever! He makes sure I take my pill."

"That's a blessing. You keep right on taking it," Moira said consolingly. "If only we'd had such a thing in my day."

So there it was, The Answer. Ginny was not with child, nor would she be. I was, and no one had guessed. How long could I hold out? I envied Ginny's nap that afternoon, and wished I could do the same. Fatigue was an entirely new experience for me. But I couldn't take chances that anyone would wonder why I was so tired. Aside from fatigue and some queasy early mornings, I was holding up quite well. I'd taken to eating spinach for breakfast and nibbling on sticks of carrots and celery for lunch. But I ached with fatigue.

I wasn't in Friday's episode, but walked to the studio in the afternoon to pick up the following week's scripts to study over the weekend. The cast was in the rehearsal room getting notes on the run-through when I arrived, so I took the back route through the studio to get to the production office.

In the rear of the studio, home to the ubiquitous bramble-and-rock set, I came across Nigel and Lucy, the wardrobe mistress, clothing a bald dress dummy in shrouds of muslin. A veil with blood stains concealed the mannequin's face. A prop man had arranged a pail of dry ice at the foot of the dummy and set up a fan. Gaffers were rigging lights with green gels and a revolving kaleidoscope attachment that cast randomly moving shadows on the dummy. Nigel signaled the prop man and clouds of fog billowed up around the shrouded figure.

The fan rattled noisily, then blew a sudden blast of air that whipped the veil off the mannequin, revealing a ceramic face with a chipped nose and no eyeballs.

"What's that supposed to be?" I asked.

"Can't you tell?" Nigel sounded exasperated. "It's the ghost of the vampire's long-lost love."

"So now he's got a girlfriend? Looks like he didn't treat her very well."

"She jumped off a cliff into surf crashing on the rocks. You wouldn't look so hot yourself. What do you think of the effect?"

"Were you going for bald and blind with a bad nose job?"

"For your little comments, my plum, you've earned yourself a role as stand-in. You up for it?"

"To stand in for a dress dummy? I don't think so."

"You could be animate. Move your head and arms around a bit. Seriously, get me off the hook here. Doris is coming down after dress rehearsal to have a look. We have to squeeze this in before the air show while we have the crew. You game?"

"For you, Nigel, anything. You want me to put on the veil?"

"Sprint up to hairdressing first, pet. We'll have to get a wig on you. And ask Claude to paint you white. Or puce. Something ghosty."

I climbed the stairs to the makeup and hairdressing department, wondering if I'd made a terrible mistake agreeing to step in for the dummy. Madge was busy finger-combing Camilla's hair into long ringlets when I walked in.

"Well, you're here early. Are you lonely for us?" Camilla asked. "No one to baby sit today?"

"Just can't get enough of you all, Camilla," I said, ducking through the archway into the makeup room. What sadistic band of witches concocted her? By the time I plopped into Claude's makeup chair, I was fuming.

"Nigel just called up," Claude said, resting his hands on my shoulders. "I'm to make you look like the drowned and rotting apparition of Gwyneth Fairfax, may her soul rest in peace."

"That's her name? Where did she come from?"

"Other than Horace's fertile little imagination? I don't know. She's mentioned in one of next week's scripts. English, well-bred, 1770s. Sailed over with Thomas Jefferson, according to her back story."

"She had a fling with Jefferson? I thought she was supposed to be Sebastian Stanhope's girlfriend."

"A shipboard romance isn't alluded to," he said, applying a thick milky foundation. "But, who knows? It was a long voyage in those days. In any case, she ended up with the vampire, not a great choice. No wonder she jumped to her death. Not a nice way to go. Messy," Claude said, sucking his teeth.

I flinched. There was no need to get carried away. My father and grandfather seemed perfectly happy with their choice of vampiric mates. But what did Claude know? I decided not to take it personally. "So the dummy was supposed to look like a long-dead corpse?"

"Ridiculous! I told everyone the dummy wouldn't work. You need prosthetics. A gash or two, and I couldn't do that properly on the dummy."

"Of course not. But she'll need false eyelashes," I teased. "They were big in the 1770s."

Claude grinned, then looked at me in the mirror and shook his finger. "Strict orders from above, young lady. No false eyelashes on you or I'm out of a job!" He smoothed his own unruffled eyebrow with his little finger, then went back to stippling a dark bruise over my brow. "Besides," he said, "you have no idea how lovely you are. A little blush, a little gloss is gilding the lily."

"Thanks, Claude. I need the boost."

"Oh, everyone's quite taken with you, darlin'. And you'll look scrumptious in an antique frock."

This was all good news. There had been talk about exploring the Stanhope ancestral line as soon as Angela had discovered the trunks in the attic. Preparations for the Stanhope Costume Ball had become the central drama for weeks. While Claude puttered away, attaching a grotesque ping-pong ball, cut in half and painted like an eyeball, to my cheekbone, I contemplated what this development might mean for me. I could only hope there was room in the storyline for an eighteenth-century governess. Of course, I'd be relegated to a woolen dress with a stiff white collar instead of the lace and brocades the Stanhope women would wear, but I would put up with anything to stay on the show as long as I could.

Claude wrapped up his gruesome work, leaving me mercifully unrecognizable. Madge piled a heap of tangled hair on my head, greased it with baby oil and dusted it with talc. I headed back downstairs, running into Ian on the way.

"My God, is that you? What are you doing?"

"Playing a corpse. I'm just glad no one will recognize me."

"But why?"

"It was Nigel's bright idea. Besides, I practically volunteered. Come on over and watch. It shouldn't take more than a few minutes. I think I'm supposed to be your girlfriend, at least her ghost."

"Of course, Lady Fairfax. Have you read ahead? I'm the reason you jump off the cliff."

"Nigel mentioned it. Don't take it to heart, Ian."

Ian helped me climb up the riser to the bramble set. Lucy set the dummy aside and draped me in ragged muslin with some tattered lace hanging off my shoulders. Nigel aimed the fan in my direction and instructed me to raise my arms as though appealing for help. I stretched my arms out toward Ian, who was standing to the side of the camera.

Doris rushed over to take a look. I lifted my arms up and down, letting the muslin flutter in the breeze. Doris frowned, squinted, cocked her head sideways, looked back and forth between me and the clothes dummy, and finally said, "Yeah, okay. Better."

"Thanks," I said. "So I'm an improvement on the dummy?"

"Don't talk," Doris snapped. "Ghosts don't talk."

Paul and Horace had come down from the production office to take a look, too. "Works for me," Paul said. "How about a stronger wind."

The fan was turned on high, just below cyclone velocity. I struggled to keep my eyes open with gale-force wind slapping tattered lace and greasy hair in my face. My eyes watered and tears streamed down my cheeks.

"Great!" Horace yelled above the noise of the fan. "Look like you're screaming!"

"Don't blink!" Doris hollered. "Ghosts don't blink!"

"Let's shoot this sucker," Paul said. "We got a winner."

The commotion attracted the rest of the cast and crew, who gathered to watch. I heard laughter, and felt even more foolish standing amid fake foliage and fog wearing ghoulish makeup and shrouds. As instructed by Horace, I opened my mouth in a silent, tortured scream and raised my arms.

Since we were shooting without sound, there were plenty of comments from the cast. I heard Ed say, "That's what my first wife looked like getting out of bed."

"You are so mean, Ed!" Ginny said, punching Ed in the arm.

"Quite heroically pathetic," Ian said. "She's got Edvard Munch's scream down to perfection, really."

"Can you belt "Melancholy Baby?" Michael called out.

Maxwell began singing the lyrics to "I Don't Stand a Ghost of a Chance," and everyone laughed.

"Cut it out, you guys," Paul said. "Give her a break. You're looking at our new Lady Gwyneth Fairfax!"

"A star is born!" Maxwell crowed, fanning his hands by his face like Judy Garland. "Go for top billing, Megs!"

My eyes were bleary from not blinking in the gale-force wind, but I saw surprise register on various faces, with no one looking particularly pleased by Paul's announcement.

"Did you just decide that?" Doris demanded. "We ought to think this through, Paul."

Ginny looked stunned. "She gets to play two roles? How come?"

Ed's face stiffened as he worked out how this would affect him. Michael slowly shook his head, and Moira murmured, "top billing?" Camilla gazed unblinking, her expression inscrutable. Then another face appeared. I stared, recognizing Haddie, who rose and hovered above camera, beckoning to me. I lifted my arms up to him.

"Eyes down, eyes down," Doris hollered. "Lower your hands!"

I lowered my eyes, but only for an instant. Haddie rose higher above camera, beckoning to me. I leaned forward, teetering on the edge of the pedestal.

"Stand still, Meg!" Doris hollered again. "Okay, got it. Cut! Places for the air show, everyone. Paul, let's talk."

As I lowered my arms I sensed a heavy mass streaking down above me. I leaped off the riser as a bulky object just missed striking me. It thudded into the pedestal behind me as I bounded onto the stage floor and into Ian's arms. Cracking sounds reverberated amid gasps and screams.

"The light!" Maxwell shouted. "I saw it fall!"

"Stand back, everyone! Stand back!" Paul yelled.

Cast members closest to the set scrambled away from the dust and debris even as crew rushed forward to assist. There was a collective cry of shock, then a moment of stillness as everyone took in the near disaster. In the eerie green light, dust motes danced crazily above the demolished pedestal where I'd stood only seconds before. The clothes dummy, set aside in foliage just off camera, had been struck by the falling lamp and knocked face down into a pit of debris. The porcelain head was shattered, the smashed face lying in broken pieces.

I clung to Ian, my fingers digging into the folds of his cape. Looking up over his shoulder, I saw Haddie fading into the cavernous far reaches of the studio.

"Sorry, so sorry, love," Ian murmured in my ear. "You're safe now."

"That was a terrible accident. Thank God, you're okay," Paul said, touching my face. "You're pale and cold as ice, though. You had a horrible shock."

It was a shock, but I knew by Haddie's presence that it hadn't been an accident. In a flash, my arms still clinging to Ian, I left my body and soared above the stage for a quick check of the light grid. I needed no special expertise to see that there was an empty space and markings where a lamp should have hung.

The hubbub below had become louder and noisier. I looked down to see Nigel herding everyone away from the debris. "Let's clear, folks. Move back. We need to close off the area."

Several crew members, including the gaffer and grips, were inspecting the damage, their faces turned up to the rigging on the light grid. Only one cast member, Camilla, was looking up, her gaze startling me with its intensity. Her eyes, blazing with anger, seemed to follow me as I hovered above the grid. Haddie's words echoed in my ears: She has her own powers—and she knows how to use them.

With a shock of recognition, I looked down into Camilla's eyes and realized she could see me hovering above the light grid as clearly as I could see her flesh-and-blood figure below me. Her penetrating stare was frightening. She was indeed the malevolent force that Haddie had warned would harm me. But why? What did she want?

Thirteen

I heard Doris say, "Better get a doctor. No sense in taking chances."

"No! I'm fine," I said, instantly returning to my body. The sharp tip of a broken branch had pierced my arm, leaving a deep gash, but there was no pain, no blood flow. The wound wasn't visible under the ragged shreds of muslin, but I couldn't risk having it exposed. The last thing I wanted was anyone examining me for injuries. "I don't need a doctor," I said, pulling away from Ian, my hand clamped over the gash in my arm. "See? I'm just fine."

"You're sure about that?" Doris looked doubtful. "You want to lie down?"

"I'll just go up to my dressing room and rest for a while."

"I'll walk her up," Ian said.

"You can't," Doris said. "You're in the first shot. We have to go to air before we lose our time slot."

"I'll go up with her," Camilla said, taking my elbow. "Come on, Meg. I'm sure you want to get out of these rags, don't you?"

"No need," I said quickly. "Lucy can help me."

"Yes, go with her, Camilla," Paul said. "I'll be up shortly, Meg. I want to check out what happened here."

"My goodness, you're terribly cold! Your skin is like ice," Camilla exclaimed loudly. "Maybe you do need a doctor."

"It was the fan blowing cold air," I said, just as loudly, my hand still covering the gash on my other arm. "Really, I'm fine on my own."

"So eager to please," Camilla said, not releasing her hold.

"Yes, thanks for stepping in, Meg," Paul said, "I'm so sorry this happened. You did a great job."

"Thanks, Paul. I'm happy I could help out."

"You see? It was all worth it," Camilla said. Her voice was soft and soothing, but her grip remained firm as she steered me toward the studio door. "You brought her to life, Meg, and managed to get this lovely new role to play. Lady Fairfax. Young and beautiful, but so very tragic. All too soon, she's a ghost in rags, her beauty destroyed."

"Don't get too carried away, Camilla. Perhaps that's not her fate at all. Maybe it's just a sign of what could happen."

"Such an optimist!" Camilla's laugh was light and tinkly. "Just between us, I wasn't sure working as an extra was such a bright idea. But it turns out, you were in the right place at the right time, weren't you?"

"Hardly the right place and right time with that lamp falling. I could have been killed."

"But you weren't. And you wouldn't really have come to any harm anyway, would you?" Her grip on my elbow tightened. I turned to look at her. There was a small smile on her lips, but as her hand brushed across my sleeve, her eyes took on a look of alarm. "Oh, dear, have you injured yourself? Let me see—"

"I'm not hurt," I said, but as I pulled my arm free, the muslin fell away. With relief, I saw the gash had almost healed. "Look. Just a scratch."

Behind us I heard Doris holler, "Places everyone. Let's get a move on!"

"Lucky girl," Camilla said. "No need for a doctor, I guess. But I'd better get you upstairs."

Sensing Haddie's presence again, I focused on the thickly padded studio door only a few feet ahead. Before Camilla could reach for the lever, I caused the heavy door to swing open with such force that Camilla gasped and jumped back.

"Please, after you," I said.

She whipped around, staring at me, but didn't move. In the stillness of the sound stage, Nigel began his countdown. "Five . . . four . . . Three . . . ."

I quickly stepped out of the studio. Behind me, the thick metal door swung shut with a heavy thud just as Nigel finished his countdown. Camilla would have to remain in the studio until the first commercial break, leaving me alone to assess what had taken place. Camilla was indeed testing me. We'd revealed ourselves now, and enmity between us would only escalate.

Claude met me in the upstairs hallway and led me into the makeup room. "Thank God, you're okay. Saw it on the monitor, Meg. Honestly, you did us proud. Such a pro. Let me get the prosthetics off and you can take a shower."

Madge scurried in and said, "I put extra towels out for you in your dressing room." I thanked her as she peeled the greasy hairpieces and nylon skullcap off my head. My own hair stuck to my scalp in oily tendrils. I looked like a plucked duck. "I'll fix your hair after you shower, if you like," Madge offered.

Back in my dressing room, Lucy unwrapped the bloody lace and muslin shrouds, carefully hanging the garment on a padded hanger. "I have a feeling we'll be getting quite a lot of use out of this," she said, easing a plastic bag over the torn lace shroud as though she was covering a designer gown. I made a face and she said, "You never know what's down the road, dearie."

After she left, I stepped into the shower, letting hot water melt waxy, greasy sediment out of my hair. I scrubbed, then pulled bits of adhesive off my cheek and neck. As I slathered shampoo on my head, I thought about Paul's announcement that I would be playing Lady Gwyneth Fairfax. If the ghost became a full-blown character, I was beginning to regret that I'd looked so completely unrecognizable.

Later, picking up scripts in the production office, I lingered to check the schedule posted on the bulletin board. A character named Gwyneth Fairfax did not appear on any cast sheets, but there were references to "ghost" on the prop list. What did the production staff know that the actors hadn't yet been told?

"There you are," Paul said, stepping out of his office. "We're still looking into what could have caused that light to fall. You're okay?"

"Not a scratch."

"Good girl. Sure glad you came by today. That was a big help."

"Happy to do it. Do I get paid for it?"

He laughed. "Nope. You didn't speak."

"Right. Ghosts don't talk."

"But it was very effective. Horace said it made him want to cry."

Paul squeezed my shoulder. "You're a good little actress, Meg. We'll have you do the ghost again."

"Still for no extra pay?" I laughed.

He laughed, too. "We'll see. Have a good weekend."

On my way out of the studio, I passed the rehearsal room. Camilla and Michael were sitting together, his arm around her shoulders, she looked up, catching my eye. "Feeling better, I hope. How's your arm?"

"Just fine. Thanks for asking. Have a good weekend."

"We will," Michael said. "You, too."

They would probably end up at Flinty's later. Despite my resolve not to care, I cared. I caught the cross-town bus to the Playboy Club, imagining Paul Abbott's reaction if he knew his "good little actress" was pregnant and spending the weekend working as a Bunny. At least I'd earned a few good points with Paul for playing the ghost—and who knew where that would lead?

I'd also managed to work off my demerits at the Club. I couldn't afford to take chances. Therefore, I erred on the side of caution during the cocktail shift when Noni rushed into the service area and said to me, "Hey, Meg, that guy at the piano bar drinking the Seven and Seven? He just offered me two tickets to *Oliver!* It's the hottest ticket on Broadway. You want to go?"

"Are you kidding me," I laughed. I was perching on a corner of the ice machine waiting for the switchboard operator to verify a keyholder's membership. "Attention Bunnies: Wilmark detective skulking in piano bar. Proceed with caution," I said in a deep announcer's voice.

"Shut up, Meg," Noni snapped. "Free tickets? C'mon, it's completely sold out." She turned to Gloria and said, "You want to go? He told me I could bring a friend."

"Honey, that's a Wilmark guy. You show up to claim a seat and you're fired," Gloria said.

Allie, who was calling out a drink order to Mikey, the bartender, said, "I spotted him, too. Definitely Wilmark."

Cheri chimed in. "Did he give you the tickets, or do you have to meet him to get them?"

"He doesn't have the tickets on him, but he'll meet us at the theatre. He said he'd take me and a friend, okay?"

"No!" Savannah said. "It's the surest way to get yourself fired."

"You're all trying to spoil things! That's no Wilmark," Noni insisted.

"Look at his shoes," Gloria said. "The soles are an inch thick. Brown suit. Has he ordered more than one drink?"

"No. I'm just bringing him his check."

"Bring it. Accept the tickets."

"What is this?" Allie asked. "Suicide by Wilmark?"

Cheri rolled her eyes. "You guys are going to get caught!"

Wilmark detectives, hired by the Club to pose as customers, used every ruse to entice Bunnies into breaking the Bunny Manual rules. No matter how trivial the infraction, Wilmark detectives reported it to management. But the most serious offense a Bunny could commit was being caught "dating" a Playboy keyholder. It was considered instant grounds for dismissal. The Club was already under heavy scrutiny by the State Liquor Authority. With any evidence of Bunnies procuring or behaving like "B" girls, the SLA would slam the doors of the key club in a New York minute. Nevertheless, Gloria offered to go with Noni if only to prove that her customer was with Wilmark.

"You'll both get fired," Allie told her.

"Safety in numbers," Gloria said. "We'll all go. He can't wipe out the entire cocktail Bunny crew."

Feeling reckless, I joined Noni, Gloria, Allie, Cheri and Savannah after work, all of us changing clothes in record time and piling into a taxi for the short ride to the theatre. Once in the lobby, four of us hovered on the sidelines while Noni and Gloria greeted the customer, who was easily spotted in the crowd wearing his brown suit and thick-soled shoes.

"Enjoy the show," he said. "You two are both on report."

"Okay, here's the deal," Gloria told him. "We've brought backup. You promise not to file a disciplinary report, or we make a scene."

Holding up his notebook, he said, "Hey, I got your names, you know? This is my job. You break the rules, you pay for it."

Theatre patrons around us stared as Savannah bolted from our ranks, threw her arms around the detective's neck, and shouted, "But you told me you loved me! Now I catch you cheating on me!"

Allie hollered, "You son-of-a-bitch! What about the kids! You're walking out on me and the kids?"

"How dare you two-time me?" I shouted, grabbing his arm.

Everyone in the lobby laughed. The detective tried to push his way to the door, mumbling, "Hey! Cut it out! I'm just doing my job." We clung to him even as he reached the street. With her long reach, Savannah snatched his notebook and said, "So get another job!"

Rather than scuffle with a pack of women, the man retreated and disappeared down Shubert Alley. Gloria kissed the theatre tickets and waved them above her head. "Told you so!" she crowed.

"You, guys! I don't believe you pulled that off!" Cheri said. "Are you staying for the show?"

"Of course," Noni said. "Wouldn't miss it."

While Gloria and Noni stayed to see *Oliver!* the other Bunnies went to Sardi's to celebrate. I opted to go home, but decided to swoop up to the Chrysler Building on my way home. I settled on my favorite perch atop a radiator cap gargoyle and looked up Park Avenue. The moon was low and full, bathing Manhattan in an elegant gleam.

"Quite a day," Haddie said, settling himself next to me. "I see you gals didn't need my help."

"You know what Savannah's like!" I laughed. "That was fun. Besides, you were there for me when I really needed you. Thank you for that."

"Not at all. Happy to be of service."

"And I appreciate the warning. You were right. Camilla has powers, but she's nothing more than a witch, Haddie." I yawned and leaned back, my eyes zooming in on a glittering star. "Her sorcery isn't potent enough to really harm me. She's irritating, but her gifts are meager compared to mine."

"Beware of hubris, Meg! I'm an Army man, don't forget. The enemy is testing you, searching out your weakness."

"Camilla's seen me at barely more than human strength. She's gotten the best of me a few times, but only because I wasn't paying attention. Stick with me, Haddie, and I'll be fine."

I looked up at the buttery moon in the star-filled sky, thinking of the lush harvest moons I remembered hanging over the cornfields back home. "I know you have your hands full with me, Haddie, but keep an eye on Eric, too."

Fourteen

My front door buzzed, then buzzed again. I was awake and reading. I glanced at my alarm clock. Who could be dropping by at almost two o'clock on a Monday morning? The door buzzed again, with someone repeatedly stabbing the buzzer. I jumped out of bed and grabbed my robe. Eric? Maybe it was Eric!

I raced to the entryway and heard something thump against the door. "Who's there?" I called out.

There was no answer. I looked through the peephole and caught a fish-eye glimpse of the burly building superintendent waving his arms, his work shirt flapping over his massive belly. I released the chain, unlocked the door and pulled it open.

"We got bum here!" the superintendent said, kicking at an inert body curled tightly on the threshold. "Wake up! Wake up!"

"Stop! Not his face!" I shrieked. It was Michael. I could tell by the khaki bush jacket, the same one he was wearing at Friday afternoon's rehearsal. "I know him. Please, don't kick him!"

The superintendent looked at me dumbfounded. "A drunk? You know this drunk?"

"Unfortunately, yes," I said. "Let me get him inside."

"He stink! You don't want him. Shut door. I call police."

"No! No! You can't do that. Were you buzzing my door, or was he?"

"I no buzz. He buzz. I see him, then he fall down."

"I don't know how he knew I lived here. I'm sorry, Mr. Spichal. He's a friend. I have to get him inside. Can you give me a hand?" If the superintendent hadn't been standing there, I could have carried

Michael in by myself, but Mr. Spichal was already looking at me suspiciously.

"You crazy. You don't know what he could do." Mr. Spichal backed away, waving his hands. "You pretty girl. Gotta be careful."

"I know. But he's not going to do anything. I know him."

"No responsible," Mr. Spichal said, looking resolute.

I knelt down and gripped Michael's upper arm, gagging at the fumes exuding from his stained jacket. I pulled the collar of my robe across my nose and yanked his shoulder over the threshold. He was dead weight. I couldn't be seen to just pick him up in my arms. I looked at Mr. Spichal, who had backed several feet down the hallway.

"Thanks very much, Mr. Spichal. I can manage. You just go back to bed."

"He no stay in hallway," the superintendent said. "I call police now?"

"No, please don't. He'll lose his job."

Mr. Spichal shook his head. "He no work like this."

"He has to. Don't worry. I'll get him out of the hallway."

I stared down at Michael, sprawled on his back, a grim scenario unfolding in my brain. He'd thrown up, probably more than once. His cheek was scraped, and there was a bruise on his forehead. His script was rolled up and stuffed in his jacket pocket. He'd most likely been on a bender since taking Camilla to Flinty's Friday afternoon after rehearsal. It was now well after 2 A.M. Monday morning. He was due at the studio within six hours. If he didn't turn up, the show couldn't be done. He'd be fired. Who knew what the long-term effect would be on *Dark Passages*, and with it my future. That was the clincher. I had no choice.

I looked back at the superintendent, his arms folded across his chest, his stance unyielding. He was not going to move.

"He has to work," I said, speaking in low, careful tones. "This poor man is a famous actor, Mr. Spichal. Very, very famous, but he's fallen off the wagon. It will be a tragedy if he doesn't go to work in the morning. His career will be destroyed. Many people will lose their jobs. The world will lose a great actor. Won't you please help me?"

Mr. Spichal stared at me. I stared back.

"Out of deep gratitude, I could give you ten dollars. How about it?" I asked.

With some speed, Mr. Spichal rushed forward, seized Michael by the armpits and dragged him into my kitchen. As part of the bargain, I persuaded him to remove Michael's jacket, shirt and blue jeans. For another five bucks, he agreed to remove underwear and socks, but insisted I turn my back until he'd finished wrapping Michael's naked body in the quilt I provided.

While the superintendent stood watch in my kitchen, I sprinted down to the basement laundry room. I'd removed the script from the pocket of the bush jacket and left it on the kitchen table. But I had not found a wallet anywhere in his clothing. This did not bode well for the repayment of my fifteen dollars.

By the time I returned to my apartment with Michael's clean clothes, Mr. Spichal had made himself comfortable on my kitchen chair and was reading my newspaper. I forked over the cash. He shoved the bills in his pocket without looking at them and opened the door. "You no need me no more?"

"I hope not," I said, looking down at Michael curled up in the quilt. "Thanks for everything."

I closed and locked the door. For a moment I stood listening to the quiet of the night, deciding what to do. It occurred to me that Michael might need medical attention. He hadn't moved. I knelt next to his head to check more closely. His breathing was even. The scrape on his cheek looked superficial, but needed cleaning with antiseptic. The bruise on his forehead was grimy with oil and asphalt. I leaned closer to examine it, but his breath was so sour I pulled back. His skin was splotchy and the three-day stubble aged him. Claude would have his work cut out for him at the studio, but I didn't think Michael required a doctor. I decided to let him sleep it off on the kitchen floor.

I folded the sheets and blanket on my daybed and tucked them with my pillow in the rattan chest that doubled as a coffee table. Feeling less than fresh after grappling with Michael and handling his reeking clothes, I opted for a hot bath. I lit a candle, poured bath salts in the tub and was about to disrobe when a thought occurred to me. I went back into the kitchen to make sure Michael was still sleeping soundly. Then, as a precaution, I took my bottle of J&B with me back into the bathroom and locked the door.

By the time gray light began filtering through the French windows, I was bathed and dressed for the day. I'd also ironed Michael's clothes and made myself a cup of tea. At some point, probably while I was soaking in the bathtub, Michael had rolled over on his back, with the quilt wedged underneath him. At first it was a shock to see him naked, lying entirely exposed in the harsh fluorescent light of my kitchen. He looked like a lab specimen, a dingy-colored dead frog splayed out on the black and white checkered tiles. I averted my eyes, swallowed hard, and managed to step over him to put the kettle on. But by the time I'd made my tea and perched on a kitchen stool, a grim fascination had taken hold. I couldn't take my eyes off him.

Of all the ways in which I might have fantasized Michael lying naked on my kitchen floor, this was not one I could have imagined. While sipping my tea, I examined his entire awkwardly displayed frame, becoming serially fixated on one body part after another. I would not otherwise have known that his second toe on each foot was longer than his big toe. That there were little drifts of dark hair on each of his toes and fingers. Or that his calves were skinny, but hairy; his knees bony and his upper arms spindly.

There was a concave recess below his bloated belly, and quite a lot of hair that extended in dark, furry patches clear up his chest. His nipples were hard and dark as shriveled berries. There was also a thin scar on his lower belly—an appendectomy?—on which no hair grew. Overall, I determined he was best seen fully clothed and began to lose interest.

But then, rising from the hairy thicket of his groin, and trembling ever so slightly as it grew in size, was a distinctive body part that had been virtually hidden in short, curly brush. I recognized it immediately for what it was. I'd seen only one other penis in this state, and that was Eric's, but it was shaped entirely differently than this one. I watched it writhe and lift itself off Michael's thigh, a puckered shaft with a bold, shiny globe on top. My brain rummaged through its limited knowledge of male anatomy and came up with an answer almost immediately: circumcision! The whole top had been whacked off.

"You getting yourself a good gander?"

I jumped off the stool, tea sloshing onto the floor. My eyes flew to Michael's face, expecting to see his sly grin. He wasn't smiling. His eyes locked on mine, assessing me through a tired squint. I did not look away.

"Sorry, Michael. I should've covered you again."

"Doesn't matter. What time is it?" He rolled to his side and started to sit up, still watching me.

"Around six. If you want to shower, I'll make some coffee for you."

"Thanks." He pulled the quilt up around his shoulders, his eyes never leaving mine. "You okay? I mean, I didn't . . . you know, do anything, right?"

"Everything's fine. Don't worry. The super found you outside my door. How'd you know where I lived?"

"The phone book." He shook his head. "You should be unlisted, you know. Anyone could find you."

"I guess so. You never know who's going to turn up on the doorstep." I was momentarily relieved to know Camilla hadn't planted another phone number.

Then he made a noise that could have been a grunt or a laugh. "Camilla said you lived in Gramercy Park. Turns out I found myself in your neighborhood and looked you up. How's that for lucky?"

"Pretty lucky," I agreed. So Camilla had her hand in this after all. But why? I turned away so he could get to his feet without me watching. I knew it would be a slow, cumbersome process. "I'll make some coffee. How about a bran muffin? I'll get it together while you're in the bathroom. I put a towel out for you. And your clothes are hanging on a hook behind the door."

"Fine, fine," he mumbled.

"I've got some peroxide if you want me to clean up your face." Out of the corner of my eye, I watched him lumber slowly toward the bathroom, the quilt fanning like a cape on his shoulders. I held my breath, waiting for him to topple over. "Can you manage? You need help?" The only answer I got was the bathroom door closing.

I'd hidden the Scotch decanter and the lone bottle of beer from the refrigerator in the utility cupboard behind the detergent. I'd stashed the rubbing alcohol and cough syrup from the medicine cabinet in a shoebox. What had I overlooked? I busied myself sponging every surface in my kitchen, positioning the single bran muffin on a plate and brewing a small pot of coffee. For once, the smell didn't turn my stomach, but I didn't take any chances by pouring myself a cup. Instead, I made more tea and stopped myself from picking at the muffin. Otherwise there wasn't much to do but wait for Michael to leave. I huddled at the kitchen table, irritation building.

Why would Camilla send him to me? And in this condition? Had she caused him to go on a bender? I could not see how any of this played to her advantage.

Meanwhile I'd begun to feel like a hostage in my own apartment, thoroughly uncomfortable that he'd imposed himself on me—Michael, in whom I'd invested such longing! I was surprised at how much I resented his intrusion. The man who'd never bought me a burger at Flinty's had seen fit to show up on my doorstep drunk. Why hadn't he dumped himself on Camilla? What was I doing washing his filthy clothing? Ironing his shirt? Giving him my muffin! The longer he remained in my bathroom, the more enraged I became.

By the time he finally emerged from the bathroom, fully dressed, his damp hair combed low over his bruised forehead, I'd eaten the muffin. I had to admit he cleaned up nicely, the damage to his face barely apparent. How had he managed to look even more rugged and handsome with stubble and tired eyes? I suspected he'd looked in the bathroom mirror and come to the same conclusion himself. There was a swagger to his gait, although he might have been compensating for some residual unsteadiness. He'd left several buttons undone and turned up the collar of his shirt to good effect. He smiled and winked. I loathed him.

"I ate your muffin," I said. "Sorry."

"That's okay. Just coffee. Black and lots of it." He ran his hand over my hair and sat across from me, rolling up the sleeves of his bush jacket. "Thanks a lot for everything, Meg. I really appreciate it."

"That's okay. Happy to help." I poured him a cup of coffee and slid it across the table. "How are you feeling?"

"Pretty good. I'll live." He took a sip, then put his hand on mine and leaned across the table. "Really, Meg, you were there for me and

I won't ever forget it. Thank you." His voice was low, its huskiness lending sincerity to his words. I believed him and was beginning to remember why I'd had the crush on him.

"You know, I think you lost your wallet."

"Yeah, someone lifted it. Pretty lousy, huh? That's when I looked you up. I guess I knew I could count on you. Maybe you could spare me a few bucks?"

"Sure. By the way, I looked through your script. You've got two scenes with Camilla and one with Moira and Maxwell. You want to run lines?"

"Yeah, right. Good idea."

A shadow had crossed his eyes, the barest flicker, but I'd caught it. I picked up the script and turned to his first scene, mulling a suspicion building in my mind. "I could give you bus fare. Would that be enough?"

"Not cab fare? A couple bucks more sure would be appreciated."

I agreed, and we ran lines. His scenes with Camilla hinted at a budding romance. I wondered if Horace had picked up on their forays to Flinty's and was incorporating their mutual attraction into a storyline. I poured Michael more coffee and excused myself to go to the bathroom.

I found towels and hangers on the floor. My toothbrush was wet and a bar of soap was lying in a puddle on the sink. I could clean up the mess later. My mind was on the medicine cabinet. I examined every container, and then checked the wastebasket. Nothing was missing. Then my eyes fell on a bottle of mouthwash, pale in color and full to the top. I unscrewed the cap and knew immediately the bottle contained tap water. After reading the list of ingredients on the label, I realized that if Michael had polished off a bottle of Listerine, his bender wasn't over. I had no intention of giving him money or letting him make his own way to the studio.

By the time I returned to the kitchen, Michael had finished off the coffee. "I changed my mind, Michael. I need to pick up some scripts, so we can share a taxi."

"Really appreciate this, Meg." There was a glitter in his eye and I wondered what else he'd managed to find in my cupboard. Then both eyes filled and I realized they were awash in tears. "Camilla kind'a blew me off and I took it hard. This shouldn't have happened, you know?"

"Did you call her last night?"

"Yeah. Just before I lost my wallet." He looked sheepish, brushed his eyes and turned away.

"And she mentioned where I lived?"

"Sort'a. Like I said, I really appreciate this, Meg."

"That's okay. Anyway, let's get going."

Had we spoken a truthful word to each other all morning? I also realized this episode was yet another adventure I wouldn't be writing home to Marilyn about. A block from the studio, I paid the cab driver and got out. Michael rode the rest of the way, and I watched him enter the building. There was no reason to let anyone see us arriving together. As it was, only a minute later, Paul saw me walking down the street as he was getting out of a taxi in front of the studio. He waited for me, a smile on his face.

"You're an eager beaver. What're you doing here so early?"

"Picking up scripts. And Lucy mentioned working in a fitting today."

"I'm glad you're here. I got a little surprise for you."

Paul led me around to the side entrance where a crew was loading in the Stanford mausoleum set, a crypt with gargoyles on the walls and several dusty coffins. Young Danny would discover its secret entrance and I'd find him lurking in the bushes outside of it in Thursday's episode. Paul and I walked through the Living Room set that was used almost daily, and into Moira's boudoir, which the prop men were dressing. On the far side of the loading dock, Paul stopped in front of an easel supporting a large canvas draped in muslin.

"We had the prop shop do this up over the weekend. I wanted to have a look before it was finished." He lifted a corner of the muslin sheet and flipped it over the canvas. "What do you think?"

I gasped. "That's me!" At least it was a portrait of someone who strongly resembled me, but wearing an elaborate hairdo and eighteenth-century finery. The facial features were mine, and the pose had been copied from one of my headshots.

"A little brainstorm Horace and I had." Paul positioned me next to the canvas and looked back and forth comparing me with the portrait. "A good likeness, I have to say. Maybe a little too rosy in the cheeks. We don't want you looking like a milkmaid."

"So that's Gwyneth Fairfax?"

"Lady Gwyneth Fairfax," he said, arms spread wide. "Who else? Came to me Friday. Why not do a flashback and see her in the flesh?" He smiled slyly. "Hope you won't mind standing in for the ghost a few more times."

"For no pay!" I laughed. "I won't mind at all." The thought that it all might lead to silk gowns and fancy hairdos was very appealing.

"Keep this to yourself for a while," Paul said. "I'm not sure how we're going to work out the story line yet."

I had no problem keeping secrets. I had my own to keep, and I could handle another. Besides, I'd already noticed the empire design of Gwyneth Fairfax's gown and figured the high-waist fashion would suit my purposes nicely.

I walked with Paul up to the production office, where I picked up more copies of the same scripts I'd taken home on Friday. I was about to go to the wardrobe room to see if Lucy had time to do fittings when I saw Doris and Nigel hurry toward Paul's office. Ian, Camilla and Moira were hovering outside the rehearsal room, all of them looking concerned.

"A little problem's come up," I heard Doris say. "We're about to start blocking and Michael's gone missing."

"He borrowed a couple bucks from me to get some breakfast," Nigel added, "and he isn't back yet."

Without thinking of the consequences, I walked up to Paul's office door and said quietly, "You should probably give Flinty's a call. Maybe check out the liquor store on the corner."

Paul looked at me and nodded. "Right. Nigel, you and Claude better walk the neighborhood. I'll see if Flinty's is open yet." No one asked me for an explanation, and I didn't offer one.

But Camilla stepped forward and said, "This is awful! Meg, what happened to him? He mentioned to me that he'd spent the night at your place. You know he shouldn't be drinking."

The world stopped and there was silence. In a flash, everyone's expression changed and all eyes turned on me. Moira's face took on a cunning look. Ian looked hurt, and Paul, Doris and Nigel appeared stunned. Only Camilla registered deep, if feigned, concern.

"Your place? Drinking? What's going on?" Doris demanded.

"Nothing! It wasn't the whole night," I said, in lame defense. "I mean, he lost his wallet. He needed cab fare. I didn't give him anything to drink. Just coffee. I wanted to make sure he got here."

"You might've said something sooner," Paul said, his voice icy. "I would've called his sponsor if I'd known he was off the wagon."

"Oh, dear! Have I spoken out of turn? I'm so sorry." Camilla said.

"Never mind." Paul said. "Let's just find him."

"John Barrymore always used to turn up on my doorstep," Moira said. "Poor dear. What can one do but take them in?"

"Okay, everyone. Run lines. Eat. We'll try to round up our boy," Nigel said, as he hurried off.

My eyes were on Ian. He shook his head and turned toward his dressing room. I followed him down the hallway. "Ian, seriously, I found him on my doorstep, snockered. Nothing happened."

"Of course not. But you don't owe me any explanation, you know." He stepped into his dressing room, his hand on the door.

"I just don't want you to think—"

"What?"

"Nothing."

"That's precisely what I think. Anyway, I'm going to study my lines on the off chance we actually do a show today." He closed the door, gently, but firmly.

Camilla had entered her dressing room across the hall and left the door open. She stood in plain view, her script tucked under her arm, making no pretense of not having listened to Ian and me. "Boyfriend trouble?" she said, making a sad face.

"Ian isn't my boyfriend. Nor is Michael. Why did you do that?"

"I did apologize, you know. I was just thinking of the good of the show. I can't imagine why Michael was at your apartment. Drunk, as you say."

"Really? You told him where I lived. You set me up."

"Me?" she laughed. "You're being way too sensitive. Maybe you do need a boyfriend."

"I have one!" I regretted the words as soon as I blurted them out.

"That's wonderful, Meg. I had no idea. Who is he?"

"No one you know. Forget it."

"But how sweet. A secret boyfriend!"

I heard her tinkly laugh again as I hurried down the hallway to the wardrobe room. I wished I'd said nothing to her, but it was too late to take back my words.

Lucy had set aside a rack of outfits for me to try on. With her eagle eye, she caught me folding over the waistband on one of the skirts to make it shorter. My idea of a perfect length was a hem that met my fingertips. After some parrying, we managed a compromise. I was standing on a chair with Lucy pinning the hem, when Nigel appeared in the doorway of the wardrobe room.

"Lucy, we need to come up with some headgear for Michael. You want to come down to the makeup room and have a look?"

Nigel waited until Lucy was down the hall before turning back to me. "Thanks for the tip, Meg. Found the dear boy half-soused in a Puerto Rican barbershop down the street. He was giving himself a Mohawk. I suspect he'll be wearing a deerstalker with his Burberry for the next few weeks."

"Nigel, believe me. I didn't give him any alcohol. Nothing happened."

He winked. "Of course not."

Fifteen

I spent the entire night sitting atop the Chrysler Building. Feeling variously mortified, angry, sad, bewildered and very lonely, I gazed at the constellation of stars sparkling in the blackened sky that mirrored lights dotting Park Avenue. Haddie joined me for a while, trying in his own fashion to buck me up.

"You've got to soldier on, girl! Never complain and never explain," he exhorted. "The more you deny, the more you'll confirm." And finally, "Never surrender, never retreat!"

"Stop it, Haddie! No more, please!"

He faded for a moment, then returned, looking hurt. "Just trying to help," he said. "It's not all that bleak. In my experience, people are so concerned about themselves, they soon forget. The point is, put your best foot forward—"

"Please, Haddie. I've spoiled any goodwill I had with Paul. Doris, Moira, Nigel and everyone else think I'm responsible for Michael's getting drunk. And Ian—I don't know what he's thinking. Now, when they find out I'm pregnant—I really can't face it."

"You've done nothing wrong! When it comes to Camilla, you've got to take the bull by the horns. Fight fire with fire! Don't give her any ammunition!"

"Enough!"

I spent the rest of the night alone. Why couldn't Camilla just fade away? I didn't want to have to deal with her, but it seemed inevitable. I was letting myself down, and everyone around me, including Ian, by remaining so passive. But what threat was I to Camilla? What did she want? I indulged myself thinking that if only Eric would return, everything might sort itself out. I didn't see how, but at least I felt I could confide in him and have an ally I could trust.

With the first cold streaks of light, I headed home to get ready for work. Nigel had informed everyone that the afternoon rehearsal would be cancelled while the situation with Michael was being resolved. Certainly he was in no condition to work that day, even with a hat covering his Mohawk. We were still two weeks ahead with shows, and it appeared Paul was taking advantage of the downtime to tinker with the story line. Horace was working overnight on some rewrites and the schedule would be readjusted to accommodate an extra day of taping. In any case, we were to come in for a table read and rehearsal that morning. "You'll be learning your lines during lunch," Nigel said, cheerfully.

I wasn't feeling at all cheerful. I dreaded facing everyone that morning as much as I was sure Michael did. As it turned out, the first person I saw when I got to the studio was Ian. He looked gloomy. He was sitting all by himself at the rehearsal table and seemed utterly bereft. I poured myself coffee and sat down next to him.

"Ian, I'm really sorry."

"For what?" He looked surprised, then grimaced. "Oh, you mean Michael? I must say, you do get around."

"It's not what you think." Never complain and never explain, I reminded myself. "Anyway, can we just forget about it?"

"Sure. Frankly, your odd entanglements aren't uppermost in my mind at the moment."

"What is?"

"Well, the fat's in the fire now," he said, looking even more morose. "I've been fitted for teeth."

"Oh, I'm so sorry, Ian. You need dentures?" I'd heard British dentistry wasn't wonderful. Poor Nigel, who'd grown up in London, was always complaining about having to replace an entire mouthful of gnashers, as he called them.

"Fangs! Let's call them what they are, bloody fangs. They sent me to an orthodontist yesterday afternoon. There I sat in a waiting room full of schoolchildren getting braces. I was there to get fitted for fangs, these silly clip-ons that I'm supposed to attach to my canines.

off camera, one hopes. The idea I should be caught nationwide adjusting bridgework is too horrendous to contemplate. It'll come to that, believe me! I'll be the absolute laughingstock fumbling around when they slip off mid-bite."

It was the wrong time to laugh, but I did. It didn't go down well with Ian. He shot me a contemptuous look. "Sorry, Ian. It is funny. Maybe not to you now, but one day you'll laugh about this."

"I don't see it as a laughing matter, and I'm not just speaking of dentistry. The whole point of these rapacious cuspids is to tear and rip apart flesh. In this case, human flesh. Specifically a person's throat for the single purpose of consuming the blood of the victim. It's just so wrong!"

"I know, Ian. I understand." I put my hand on his shoulder to calm him, but I was beginning to feel anxious about my own plight. Yet how could I set him straight about vampire blood lust without incriminating myself?

"It's horrible!" He spoke with such vehemence he almost jumped in his chair. I had to somehow settle him down. Other cast members would arrive shortly to begin rehearsal. If Ian got too carried away in the presence of Doris or Paul, he could end up talking himself straight out of the role. I couldn't let that happen.

"Hey, pirates aren't so nice, either," I said, jostling his shoulder. "You didn't mind playing a pirate."

"Raping and pillaging is one thing. But sucking blood . . . do you know what these vile creatures do? They create living dead from innocent victims, their evil striking at the very moral fiber of humanity. It's hellacious! What does this teach children watching our show?"

"Take it easy. Children bite anyway. It's just a stage they go through. They don't turn into vampires."

"They'll have nightmares!"

"All children have nightmares. I had them after reading *Rapunzel* and *Red Riding Hood*. And I turned out just fine!" What was I saying!

"Fairy tales hardly count!"

"Relax, Ian." I could hear Camilla's voice in the hallway as she approached the rehearsal room. "Look," I whispered, "if you don't play Sebastian Stanhope, someone else will. And not as well you would. And the paycheck won't be in your pocket."

He nodded, his eyes beseeching. "I'm sorry. I know I get carried away, but—"

"Shhhh. All you can do is be the very best vampire you can be. You're a victim, too, you know."

"I hadn't thought of it that way," he said. "Thanks, Meg."

"What do you two have your heads together about?" Camilla asked, sliding her script onto the rehearsal table. "Plotting something clever?"

"On the button, Camilla. Ian and I see ourselves as star-crossed lovers."

"Sweet," she said. "The perfect couple, like Annette Funicello and Frankie Avalon. I see you've been pressed into service as the ghost again today, Meg. That can't be fun."

I didn't bother responding. Anything I said would sound defensive. Michael, Moira and Maxwell Faraby were approaching the rehearsal table with coffee and pastry. Doris, Paul and Nigel were huddling at the door and would soon join us. I didn't want to provide Camilla with more ammunition.

Besides, Camilla had given me an idea that was sweet, indeed. There was no reason why Ian and I had to think of our characters as the evil vampire and his pathetic victim. Given the chance to resurrect these characters in the flesh, we could play Sebastian Stanhope and Gwyneth Fairfax as lovesick and jealous as Annette Funicello and Frankie Avalon in *Beach Party*—becoming the perfect couple an audience wanted to see fall in love and stay together.

It was a huge stretch, given that our characters were a century or two removed from Malibu, and we were trading in bikinis and surfboards for windswept moors, but we could still play the romance rather than the gloom and doom. Maybe Horace and Paul would even find a way to "cure" the vampire— wouldn't that please Ian!

Moreover, ours would be a nice vampire story, one that would even appeal to my mother. Wouldn't that make her day!

I was so lost in fantasy, I almost missed my first speech. Ian ran his finger across my script, pointing to the opening line of the scene where I greet Sebastian Stanhope as he arrives at the mansion for the costume ball. He's dressed in satin breeches, a crimson waistcoat and brocade jacket, all said to be garments belonging to his namesake, Sebastian Stanhope, whose portrait hangs in the front hall. As Margie, the governess, I've been relegated to one of the lesser frocks found in the Stanhope attic, but Sebastian compliments me lavishly. I thank him and offer him a cup of punch.

As I read the last line in the scene, I laid my hand lightly on Ian's. If only I could make this work! If I were to portray Gwyneth Fairfax in the flashback sequence, I would be as perky and flirtatious as Annette bouncing a beach ball in the sand. Head over heels in love with Sebastian, Gwyneth would be the playful, spirited, lovesick reincarnation of the tragic ghost figure before she fell to her death.

I smiled even more warmly at Ian, who looked a bit startled and pulled his hand away. In view of my recent blunders, I realized I had some patching up to do with Ian if we were to have the right sort of rapport to play star-crossed lovers.

Meanwhile, a glance across the table told me the bloom had completely gone off whatever romance had been blossoming between Camilla and Michael. I'd avoided catching his eye when he arrived in the rehearsal room, and suspected Michael had made a point of not looking my way, either. It had been easier to look at him naked on my kitchen floor than face him fully clothed in public.

I turned my head, and without directly looking at him, watched him out of the corner of my eye. He looked dreadful. His face was ashen, his eyelids droopy. I'd done a nice job pressing his shirt in the middle of the night, but he'd obviously slept in it again. It was wrinkled and bunched up around the collar. I couldn't see his hair, but imagined the worst. Lucy had come up with a gray felt hat of the sort my grandpa Egstrom had worn when he was raking leaves in the backyard. At least while we were doing the costume ball sequences, Michael's hair would be covered by a powdered wig. But otherwise, he would be confined to doing nothing but exterior scenes where he could wear a hat until his hair grew back.

His arm was slung loosely across the back of Camilla's chair, but she was sitting forward, her back arched. The body language told the story: there would be no more forays to Flinty's for them after rehearsal. If Paul Abbott had any brains, he would make sure Michael's sponsor was available to take him to the nearest AA meeting whenever he wasn't working. Clearly some sort of deal had been struck, or Michael would not be rehearsing another episode.

Again, I looked upon this as a preview of my own future with *Dark Passages*: if they could put up with a drunk going off the wagon, would they make allowances for a pregnant ingénue? It was up to me to make myself as indispensable as possible. If it meant playing a ghost in rags for no pay, I was up for it, as long as it might lead to playing a living incarnation of Gwyneth Fairfax. The painting of Gwyneth looked like me. Once the portrait was established in the series, how could they replace me?

I'd thought it best not mention this extracurricular ghost role to Wesley Truscott in case he raised a stink with Paul Abbott about the no-pay issue. I needed to row through untroubled waters for as long as possible. In fact, I'd decided not to confide in Wesley Truscott about my pregnancy, either. I had no idea how he'd react, probably with some combination of shock and embarrassment. There was also the chance he'd be so disappointed in me that he'd drop me as a client. I didn't want to risk it until I had no other choice but to inform him. What would he be able to do now, anyway? Ethically, he'd probably feel obligated to tell Paul Harris and that would put a quick end to my role on *Dark Passages*.

I couldn't imagine Paul, Doris or the writers trying to accommodate my pregnancy. It would be one thing if I—or Margie—were married, and even then I was pretty sure I'd be let go. Having an illegitimately pregnant actress playing a virginal governess on a daytime show catering to an audience of housewives and schoolchildren didn't seem likely. Even if I spent all my on-camera time in close-up or standing behind a sofa, the audience would soon figure out something was fishy. My best course of action was to keep mum and take things a day at a time.

It also meant maintaining a neutral stance with Camilla. I couldn't afford a confrontation that would draw any more attention to me. As Haddie had predicted, everybody had their own concerns and no one seemed inclined to allude to the events of the day before involving Michael and me.

We took a break after the table read before beginning the blocking. As I was packing up my script, Nigel handed me a note. "You got a call during rehearsal. Your friend said it was urgent."

"Thanks, Nigel." I flipped open the note and read: *Dinner tonight. Savannah.* I smiled. Of course, Savannah would consider a meal an urgent occasion. I used the receptionist's telephone to call her back.

As soon as Savannah heard my voice, she said, "You're coming, aren't you? Everyone will be here, so you have to come."

"I'm working all day and again tomorrow. I don't know if I can manage it."

"No excuses! You can leave early," she said, and hung up.

Obviously this was a command performance and there was no way out. But I also found myself looking forward to an evening with my Bunny friends and a welcome escape from the studio. In the meantime, the cast spent the day in a race against time, all of us trying to learn lines and adjust to the new direction of the story line. One benefit of the time crunch is that we were all too consumed with our own work to spend any time socializing. I managed to avoid both Michael and Camilla most of the day since my scenes were with Ian or Moira.

Following the air show and afternoon rehearsal, I hurried down the stairs on my way out, only to encounter Michael near the lobby door. A scrawny-looking man with sandy hair and solemn eyes stood next to him in the narrow entryway. The two exchanged a look, then the sandy-haired man shifted closer to the wall and turned his back. I figured he was the AA sponsor assigned to force-march Michael to a meeting.

Michael stuffed his hands in his pocket and cleared his throat. "Hey, listen, Meg. About the other night, I'm really sorry. Thanks for taking me in and, you know, everything. I really appreciate it. I'll make it up to you. I think I owe you some money?"

"That's okay." I made myself look him squarely in the eye and lowered my voice. "Whenever you can. I gave the super fifteen bucks."

"Fine, fine. Tomorrow okay?"

"You bet." I could hear voices on the stairs. I wondered if Michael was going to apologize to everyone in turn. I was sure it had been an uneasy day on the set for him, especially in his scenes with Camilla.

I found myself feeling sorry for him. I smiled to show there were no hard feelings. "Take it easy. I have to run."

"Sure thing. I mean it, thanks." He stepped aside and opened the door. I hurried out into the fading twilight, sucking in a lungful of cool, fresh air. I was glad he'd said something, and that we could put it behind us. I also knew that every time I looked at him, I would remember. He had to know that, too.

I caught the subway on Eighth Avenue and got out five stops later, a ten-minute ride that took me from a shabby neighborhood to a derelict one. I pulled my jacket tightly around me and hugged my shoulder bag to my chest against a sharp wind coming off the river. I hurried toward Savannah's house at the end of a cobble street lit by old street lamps. Garbage was already piled high in front of the various meat-packing establishments, ready for early-morning pickup.

The restaurant supply shop on the ground floor of Savannah's building was shuttered. I hurried up the steps of the front stoop and found the door ajar. I pushed it open and breathed in the smells of beef stew and baking bread. A burble of female voices and laughter rose in the kitchen. Also greeting me was a bulky male figure standing on a low stepladder in the hallway screwing a light fixture in place.

"Hey, there. Nick Westry here. You gotta be Meg." His voice was warm, deep and flavored with Brooklynese. He brushed his hand on his pants and held it out. "Everyone's in there waitin' for you."

"Hi, Nick. Nice to meet you finally." I reached up and shook his hand, a meaty paw that enclosed my fingers in a firm grip. He was a teddy bear of a man, with dark brown eyes, bushy brows and a ruddy, cheerful face. I liked him immediately. Savannah had made a good choice, and cozying up to a neighborhood fireman couldn't hurt when you were living in a decrepit woodframe building in need of serious repair. The fact that he could fix things must have sealed the deal.

"Likewise. Go on in. I'm just finishing up here."

"Thanks for putting in a new hall light."

He made a face. "What needs replacing is all the wiring in this place."

I was sure that was on Savannah's wish list, along with plumbing repairs, plastering and painting. I made my way down the crooked hallway to the kitchen, following the rich aroma of Savannah's home cooking. A chorus of voices greeted me. Noni, Gloria, Elke and Allie were already seated at the long table. Elle, bathed and ready for bed, snuggled in Allie's lap.

"That's one cute handyman you've got," I whispered. "I could go for him."

"Hands off!" Savannah laughed and poured me some wine.

"Is this it?" I looked at the table set for ten. "Who else is coming?"

"That's it for dinner. Jolly and Liz are coming down after work. I tried to reach Cheri, but she didn't get back to me."

"She quit," Gloria said. "No one's heard from her. Audrey said she hadn't even come in to pick up her last check."

"That's odd. I hope she's all right," Noni said. "But then we'll all be checking out soon enough."

"What! Who else is leaving the Club?" I asked.

"Sooner or later we all will," Allie said. "I'm out by Thanksgiving. We can't stay Bunnies forever."

"That's for sure," I agreed. "So who's next?"

"We figured you'd be the one long gone by now," Noni said. "You've got a steady gig."

"I'm hanging in until the show gets picked up for the next cycle," I said. "Gloria? Noni? What about the rest of you?"

Elke looked at Savannah, who shrugged her shoulders. "We'll see," Elke said, "maybe soon, if all goes well."

"Shut up! You're going to spoil it!" Savannah said. "Anyway, I feel another purge coming on, although Audrey hasn't said anything. I think we're all safe, but the barracudas smell blood in the water."

We all laughed because it was true. We were safe, but the older Bunnies, the ones we called "barracudas," always felt their jobs were on the line. Many of them were years older than they claimed, and had come to Playboy from stints in Las Vegas and the Mississippi showboat casinos. They were voracious and predatory, a fearsome crew that knew how to work every angle to advantage. It was rumored that Bunny Dolores, a redhead who had worked as a magician's assistant on cruise ships, was forty-two-years-old, the age of some of our mothers. She didn't look that old, but Gloria had claimed you could tell by her elbows and the skin between her breasts. Periodically, Playboy Clubs purged their ranks by firing the older women, who no longer had the fresh, wholesome "Bunny Image." These purges, or "weekend massacres," usually occurred when the weekly schedule was posted on Saturday nights—if your name wasn't on the roster, you could consider yourself fired. It was cruel, but quick.

Meanwhile, conversation came to an abrupt halt as Nick entered the kitchen. Every eye followed him as he went to the sink to wash his hands. Savannah was a stickler for hand-washing and always used a cuticle brush. We watched Nick soap up, use the cuticle brush and rinse his hands thoroughly, an indication he and Savannah had spent more than a little time together. She gave him a towel. He turned around and grinned at the rest of us while drying his hands.

"Sorry if I'm breaking up the party. I don't mean to be a weasel in the henhouse here."

"Are you kidding? It's great to have a guy at the table," Gloria said. We all laughed.

"It's a treat for me. The rest of the guys were all jealous when I told them I was dining with Playboy Bunnies tonight."

"So bring them next time," Noni said. "Okay, Savannah, what's the big secret? We're dying to know."

"Okay, okay," she said. Savannah set the stew pot on a breadboard at the head of the table next to a stack of large soup plates. She stood with her hands on her hips for a moment, looking around the table, then announced, "Elke and I are taking over the restaurant supply shop downstairs. Their lease is up. We're opening a bakery and café. Soups, sandwiches, home-baked bread and pastry—"

"*Strudel!*" Elke yelped, bouncing out of her chair. "*Stollen und baumkuchen*, like home—"

"But no hamburgers and French fries," Savannah said firmly, cutting her off. "Only good home-cooked food. Fresh, whole grains. No steam table. No grill."

"Here?" Noni said, her voice jumping an octave. "Nothing fried?"

"If that's what these morons around here want, they can line up at a roach coach parked on any street corner," Savannah said.

"But this is the meat-packing district," I said. "This place is too scary for people who eat fancy pastry."

Savannah gave me a withering look. "People eat what's put before them. We put good food out, people will eat it. Besides, we've already got regular orders. A lot of it will be take-out, with bread and pastry going to restaurants farther west. You think I'm an idiot? You have to build up a clientele."

"Talk to Playboy," Allie said. "Get them to serve cream puffs with martinis."

"Not a bad idea!" Savannah laughed. "The VIP Room could serve strudel!"

"The fire station is already top of the list," Nick said. "We'll get bread daily with a strudel on Fridays."

Savannah smiled at Nick and passed him a huge helping of stew. "You guys could eat a strudel a day. Maybe we'll send over apple cake or apricot torte on Wednesdays, just to give you a sample."

"But the thing is," Elke said, "we need money, you know—"

"Investors!" Savannah said. "Investors. We don't need much to get started. Elke and I are throwing in our savings. Our overhead is low. We got a good deal on equipment because the restaurant supply is going out of business. We can do the renovation ourselves, so—come on, guys, a few bucks in the pot and we're in business! Who wants to opt in?"

I looked down at my plate of stew and knew that as much as I was hoarding savings for my own purposes, I had to contribute. "I can throw in a hundred bucks," I said.

"You're a TV star!" Savannah said. "Come on!"

"I meant two hundred bucks!"

Everyone laughed. "That's it?" Savannah asked.

"That's a starter."

"A starter is all we need," Elke said. "Is everyone in for two hundred dollars? Because that gives us all we need to set up shop."

"That, and a lot of elbow grease," Savannah said. "We start renovating this weekend, so all hands on deck!"

That meant Nick and his buddies doing hard labor and any Bunnies with a few hours to spare wielding brooms and paint brushes. We'd all done it before when Savannah was renovating the upper floors.

"We'll end up with a full-fledged restaurant one day," Savannah said. "With lines around the corner."

"Like Playboy!" Elke said, and we all laughed. I somehow didn't doubt it.

Sixteen

Marilyn said, "I love the vampires! Everyone here does. My sorority sisters all want me to ask you what he's like in person."

It was Sunday afternoon, a cheap calling day. Even though it was a trunk call and not person-to-person through an operator, I knew Marilyn would want fast answers. Should I really tell her Ian was a morose, introverted oddball, deeply agonized over his role as a vampire?

"He's a sweetheart, Marilyn. Really fun to work with."

"Single?"

"Absolutely."

"But not—"

"Nope, not at all. Very sexy. A big flirt."

"God, lucky you! I love his eyes. They just bore into you like you're the most important person in the world. Gives me the chills. I gotta tell you, if there was room for two in that coffin, I'd want to jump in!" She laughed recklessly. There was a bit of static on the line and I wondered if a couple of her sorority sisters might be listening in on an extension line. "I think you two are going to have a fling. Am I right?" Marilyn asked.

"The writers never let us know in advance," I said, "but it looks like I remind him of a long lost love. We'll see."

"Of course, Gwyneth Fairfax. We figured it out straightaway. It's so lucky they found a painting that looks just like you. How'd they do that? But I guess it means you'll be playing love scenes with him before you know it. Omigosh, that is so neat! Listen, if you come home for Christmas, could you come to the sorority house again? Everyone would love to see you."

"You bet. I'll let you know when I'm back, Marilyn."

I heard more static and background sounds as I hung up. I had a feeling Marilyn's sorority sisters had chipped in to pay for the long distance call. A tandem thought was that Marilyn had become a bit silly since starting college. She'd been so serious-minded in high school, while considering me frivolous. But then Marilyn was living in a cocoon of sorority teas, football games and French lit, while I was earning a living, paying rent and trying to navigate a pregnancy. I very much doubted I would be home for Christmas, or in a suitable condition to visit Marilyn and her sorority sisters on campus anytime soon.

With that in mind, I was glad Marilyn was so taken with our vampire that she hadn't asked if I'd heard from Eric lately. He was on my mind constantly, but there was no one I could talk to about him. Anything I could say would give away my secret.

I even had to be careful about what I said in my letters to Eric. I wrote about the Club and my days at the studio, joking letters I knew he'd enjoy. But I never said anything that might give away my pregnancy. Instead, I spent my nights writing in a spiral-bound notebook with ruled paper in which I poured out everything I couldn't tell anyone else.

Since I hadn't been to a doctor, I could only guess at the strange changes in my body. If my baby was a non-human like myself, instead of a so-called normal human like my brother, Eddie, there was nothing I could do about it. Women had been having babies since the beginning of time, many without medical assistance. I decided to put my trust in nature and common sense. I took a daily multivitamin, drank a glass of milk each morning and tried to stick to a diet of vegetables that gave me maximum nourishment for the least amount of calories. I was sticking to my "human" regimen. No blood. No animal flesh. So far it was working. I just had to be careful so I could keep working for as long as possible.

Marilyn's sorority-girl reaction to Ian was a hopeful sign that at least the show would stay on the air. There were other indications, too, that *Dark Passages* had taken off since Sebastian Stanhope's arrival in town. His initial appearance as some sort of moody pirate lurking on the cliffs had been entirely forgotten, never to be referred to again. Instead, he was the Stanhope cousin newly arrived from England, a man of mystery, who bore an uncanny resemblance to a portrait of an ancestor hanging in the front entrance hall. The Stanhopes were completely oblivious to his sinister agenda, but the audience had sussed out his true identity almost from the beginning—a Vampire on the Prowl! And they liked the idea.

Within a week of Sebastian Stanhope's appearance at the costume ball, school kids had begun showing up at the studio entrance in the late afternoon hoping to get Ian's autograph. The fact that he treated his young fans brusquely, barely acknowledging them as he scribbled his name, only seemed to add to his allure. The moment he appeared in the doorway, his head down, a black muffler wound around his neck that covered his mouth, there was a rush of adolescents thrusting autograph books for him to sign. Many of them carried Brownie pocket cameras and begged to pose with him. Standing among his young admirers, Ian looked like a sinister wraith, dark eyes smoldering beneath bushy brows. He was fearsome, but in an oddly appealing, child-friendly way.

I knew he was generally uncomfortable with attention, but I suspected the adoration was beginning to appeal to him on some level. He still dressed entirely in black at the studio, and before leaving for the day, would check himself out in the lobby mirror. The rest of the cast members were asked to sign autographs, too, but it was Ian who commanded rapt worship.

He and I often left work together, and I saw first-hand the affect Ian had on his young fans. One afternoon, a schoolgirl shrieked his name and swooned against him. Her friend managed to snap a picture as Ian caught her by the shoulders, his muffler-covered mouth just inches from her neck. From then on, that was the pose everyone wanted—and the shrieking that accompanied the swoons only grew louder.

Someone, probably Paul Abbott, alerted the newspapers. The *Journal-American* published a photo of Ian with his fans. The following afternoon, the mob outside the studio doubled in size. The *Times Mirror* and *Herald Tribune* sent photographers later in the week. Ian and I were pictured, heads together, posing for fans waving autograph books at us, and the wire services quickly picked up the story. Even my folks saw the news photo in the *Minneapolis Star-Tribune*. My mother wrote that she'd stuck the clipping on the door of the Kelvinator. I'd also clipped the photo and sent it to Eric.

Overnight, it seemed, we became a daytime ratings hit after struggling for weeks to gain viewers. The network took notice. The head of daytime programming, who had initially scoffed at Horace Milton's Gothic suspense plot featuring a vampire, did a complete about-face. According to Horace's gleeful retelling, the network executive had demanded to know how soon this vampire could be seen biting his first victim.

"All in good tiiiiiime," Horace crooned.

Moreover, the costume ball, which played out over the course of many episodes, generated so much fan mail, it was decided to recap the highlights in a flashback sequence. The ratings boost inspired Horace and Paul to brainstorm a dream sequence in which the entire Stanhope clan time-traveled back to the 1790s. Indeed, Gwyneth Fairfax would be seen in the flesh. My worst fear had been that another actress would be cast for the role, despite Paul's assurances that the role was mine. It had been a close call. Doris had to be convinced that I could play the embodiment of Sebastian's unrequited love without confusing the audience. In my opinion, Doris was somewhat lacking in imagination when it came to seeing me playing a second role in the series, but her opinion carried some weight.

She'd launched her objection the day Paul unveiled the finished portrait of Gwyneth Fairfax, which was to be hung in the Great Hall of the Stanhope mansion. The Great Hall itself was a newly built set, representing a derelict wing of the mansion that was no longer in use. Young Danny would break in, get lost and Margie would find him. Then, holding sputtering candles aloft, we would gaze up at the portrait, both struck by Margie's resemblance to the Stanhope ancestor. That episode, needless to say, would air on a Friday with a mighty sting of dramatic music heralding Danny's closing line: "But Margie, what could this mean? You look just like her!"

"You can't do that, Paul!" Doris said. "Maybe they look alike, but that's it. It's a small town. Intermarriage, or something untoward back then, could account for a lot, but the two characters can't be played by the same actress. The audience won't know what's going on. It's one thing to have Meg stand in for the dummy and play a ghost. But this!"

"I don't see why. The audience accepted Meg going from waitress to governess. Why not have her play the ghost come alive. It's only a dream sequence."

"But how can you show her as a governess in the present and then, following a commercial break, see her walking and talking in a completely different role? It doesn't make sense. No one's going to buy it!"

I wanted to scream, "Yes they will! It's a dream! Don't spoil it!" But I knew interfering would be a mistake, especially as I had no business eavesdropping on a production meeting. But under the pretext of checking the schedule, I'd hovered near the closed door of Paul's office and listened to Doris and Paul argue. Paul and Horace had come up with the idea, and I prayed Doris wouldn't talk Paul out of it. I hadn't exactly been subtle in campaigning for the role, eagerly stepping in for the dummy in several more episodes without complaint. And I had that portrait on my side.

I wasn't the only one to see the possibilities in this new story line. Maxwell Faraby and Moira Shaw were both angling to play antique versions of their characters if we stepped back in time through the dream sequence device. "They couldn't just drop us," Maxwell said. "Our fans wouldn't permit it!"

"Besides," Moira added drily, "we have contracts."

Camilla, too, was deeply absorbed in the notion of playing a grander, even better-dressed version of Charmaine du Champs. "I could, of course, be a courtesan," she murmured in Paul's ear one afternoon before a table read. Her hand brushed his upper arm. "French, naturally, but in the Madame du Barry mold."

"Wasn't she beheaded?" I asked, leaning across the table. "I'm sure she was. She screamed and cried on her way to the execution. It was really pathetic."

"I didn't mean to be literally her," Camilla said heatedly. "I meant a noblewoman of means, with power and influence—"

"And beautiful dresses. But Madame du Barry was a liar and schemer, not a nice person. I saw the movie."

"Interesting," Paul said. "You've given me an idea."

Camilla and I looked at one another, not at all sure who had come out on top on this one. I had to watch my back with Camilla, but I couldn't resist taking a shot now and then to keep the playing field level. She'd been at pains to point out to Paul how plump my cheeks were compared to Gwyneth's in the portrait. She'd also expressed doubt that anyone would believe that a simple governess and former waitress could have been a woman of stature in the Stanhope family in an earlier time. "How could she become so diminished in the present time?" Camilla asked.

None of us was immune from wanting to secure a substantial role in the new story line. It was clear *Dark Passages* was on the upswing and we all wanted to consolidate our positions, even Danny. A junior teen magazine had done a picture spread on Danny celebrating his thirteenth birthday and managed to work in a photograph of him shirtless riding his bike through Central Park. It was a sweet picture, perhaps only fully appreciated by impressionable twelve-year-old girls nursing crushes on young Joey Stanhope, whose adolescent physique was more plucked chicken than Charles Atlas.

Meanwhile, cartons of fan mail, each labeled with an actor's name, began piling up in a corner of the rehearsal room. The stacks provided clear evidence of who was generating the greatest number of devoted fans. Ian stole the show hands down, but Danny had a sizable following. I came in next, with Michael and Camilla trailing close behind. The production office begged us to take the boxes home and answer the mail, but I liked seeing it pile up.

I wrote to Eric, telling him that under no circumstances should he send a letter to me in care of the studio, as I would never manage to find it in my flood of fan mail. Some of these fans, I wrote, demand photos and keepsakes— "what's a gal to do?"

Eric wrote back that he was facing the same problem:

I ask myself, who are all these people and how do they find me in the jungle? Autographs, autographs—I barely have time to fly my plane!

I promptly wrote back:

Dear Flyboy, I've admired you from afar (way too far!) for such a long time. Please send me a lock of your hair to press in a locket to wear over my heart. Your secret admirer.

A pinch of ginger hair, all he could spare from his crew cut, was enclosed with his next letter.

I guessed you might be my secret admirer. God, I hope I'm right!

Fame was a new and intoxicating experience for me—even winning the Miss Twin Lakes crown hadn't prepared me for it. I was recognized in the post office and on the bus. Sometimes I'd be asked for an autograph, but mostly people just wanted to tell me how much they enjoyed the show. I was almost always called "Margie," and told how much I resembled a sister, daughter, aunt or friend. Everyone had a story.

"My kids race home from school and we all watch together!"

"My son has nightmares but begs to see the show!"

"I just love Sebastian! What's he really, really like?"

"Watch out for that Charmaine. She's out to get you!"

"My dad's a drunk, too, so I know what you go through!"

But with regard to Ed McNabb, the worst thing I faced was dealing with his obsessive love of the TelePrompTer. He no longer bothered learning his lines at all. In fact, he'd commandeered the TelePrompTer operator one day and arranged to have his stage directions typed in parentheses. The parentheses were accidentally omitted one day and on the air show Ed said, "You're home early, Margie, cross right to door."

"Right you are, Pop. I will," I said, trying to cover.

Because Ed read all his lines off the scroll mounted above the camera, he was never seen in profile. He also appeared a bit bug-eyed, since he rarely blinked while reading. Horace came up with the idea that his character should go blind so he could wear dark glasses. The clever plot twist provided suitable drama since Ed was playing a portrait artist and would lose his livelihood once he lost his sight. Also, Ed, standing on the front porch, would be unaware of the vampire's approach only a few feet away from him. He wouldn't know that the vampire, fixated on his sleeping daughter, was lurking in the shadows outside Margie's bedroom window.

The dream sequence presented some problems for Ed, because he fancied himself appearing as a sea captain. He thought an eye patch would be nice, and would take the place of the dark glasses he'd been wearing once his artist character had gone blind. Horace wasn't so sure. He thought Ed should play a wealthy landowner with perfect vision—and learn his lines. There was a heated discussion between the two, in which Horace suggested that learning lines was part of an actor's job. I suspected that even if Ed got to wear his eye patch, Horace would win in the end. Ed would end up playing a blind deaf mute.

But the biggest battle raged between Ian and the entire production staff. Ian flatly refused to be seen climbing into—or out of—the coffin. The casket, a dusty black box wrapped in rusting chains and shrouded in thick cobwebs, rested on a plinth a good four feet off the floor. The first time it was seen, at the end of a Friday air show, eerie music accompanied the appearance of a bat swooping across knotted chains that broke apart, crashing to the stone floor of the mausoleum.

In episodes spaced out over the following week, leading up to Sebastian's appearance at the Stanhope mansion, Ian's hand was seen lifting the lid of the casket. In the final show that week, the lid was fully raised and Ian was seen, eyes closed, lying in the coffin wearing the clothes of his ancestor that he wore to the costume ball.

Once the ratings began to soar, Paul and Horace wanted to see Ian back in the coffin, with eerie music and a bat swooping while the lid was raised. During morning camera blocking, a prop man stood by with a plastic bat dangling on invisible line attached to a fishing pole, ready to swoop. Another prop man crouched beneath the coffin, waiting for his cue to winch the creaking lid up. Ian had already requested that more air holes be drilled in the coffin.

But as several of us stood around and watched, it was apparent that Ian was still not satisfied. "It's bloody stifling in here, you know!" he said, as the lid was lifted.

"Dear boy, we can't drill more holes or they'll be seen," Nigel said.

"Then you'll have a dead vampire on your hands," Ian replied ominously.

It was a funny remark, and we all laughed. However, Ian's tone of voice sent quite a different message. Ian was the one getting all the fan mail. It was Ian attracting crowds outside the studio. Newspapers and magazines were more interested in Ian than they were in *Dark Passages*, and the network had taken notice. None of this was lost on Ian.

"I might add," Ian said, "that if I'm meant to climb out of here, fully clothed with a cane and cape, I'm going to look rather peculiar—like some silly bride clambering about in her carriage adjusting her bouquet and veil. It won't do."

"Well, you can't just sit in there, like a man in a boat without oars," Nigel said. "That would look even more peculiar."

"If I have to get out, I'll need help."

"Do we have a bridesmaid handy?" Nigel asked, looking around.

By that time, Doris, Paul and Horace had left the control room and arrived on set. "You simply have to climb out of there, Ian. We can't have you just sitting there," Doris said.

"Off camera, then," Ian replied. "I will not be seen hoisting my legs over the side and jumping." He crossed his arms and glared at Doris. "I absolutely refuse."

Doris rolled her eyes and looked at Paul. The rest of us remained completely silent. We sensed Ian was going to win this one. "What should we do, Paul?"

"Well, like the man says, he can't just leap down with all the paraphernalia. Maybe his cape and cane are hanging on a hook on the back of the mausoleum door?"

"Hardly." Doris said. "Okay, here's what we do. Camera One, follow the bat. Ian, you climb out, adjust yourself. We pick up your shadow on the wall where the bat was and pan back to you. Got it?"

"Just one thing more," Ian said. "Could we pull some steps up to the coffin?"

Ian got what he wanted. Joe, the prop man, stood by with a short stepladder and leant his arm to help Ian climb out of the coffin while off camera.

"It's a better shot, anyway," Doris said, as she stalked back to the control room with Horace and Paul on her heels.

Appeasing the vampire had become the order of the day. To his credit, Ian hadn't begun throwing his new-found celebrity around with other cast members, but Maxwell hinted darkly that it was just a matter of time. "They'll be hanging a star on his dressing room door soon, then watch yourselves."

"Seen it happen before," Ed McNabb rumbled. "He'll be giving us acting notes soon and asking us to step aside when he passes by."

Only Danny struck an altruistic note that halted their grousing. "We've got Ian to thank for our jobs," he said matter-of-factly. "You guys would rather be out pounding the pavements?"

Ian, who appeared to be unaware of their carping, saw himself as a standard bearer for the rest of us now that the show was gaining in popularity. "One has to preserve one's artistic integrity," he announced as we assembled for the afternoon rehearsal. "Sebastian Stanhope cannot be seen as a bumbling fool, or all is lost."

And there it was—Ian had come to embrace his role as our resident vampire. I felt a surge of pride, but kept it to myself.

Seventeen

The call came early in the morning. When I heard my mother's voice, my stomach knotted. Our trunk calls were few and far between. She would never call long distance early on a weekday morning with good news. Bad news happens fast. Good news can be sent with a postage stamp.

"I thought I better call you instead of writing," she said. "I'm so sorry. I thought you better know. Such terrible news. I ran into Eric's father. He said Eric was killed . . . shot down. His body is being shipped home for burial. It's so awful. That sweet, young boy, so tragic. You two were such good friends. I'm sorry to have to tell you like this . . . Margaret? Are you there?"

I managed to find my voice. "It's okay, mom. I'm glad you called. How's his dad taking it?"

"Clarence is having a rough time, just shut himself down when he heard. He's in complete shock, doesn't know what he's doing. He kept saying, 'The best go first, the best go first.' It seems to be that way. Now the poor man's all on his own without his boy. It's just too bad you couldn't get back here last summer when Eric was home. You never got to see how handsome he looked in his uniform."

"Too bad," I said, my heart drumming loudly in my ears. "When is the funeral?"

"Tomorrow. Eleven o'clock. Poor Clarence has left everything to Pastor Odegaard to handle. The Women's Guild is calling around to let people know. I'm sure the whole town will turn out. I'm taking off work, bringing my tuna hot dish everyone likes so well. I don't suppose you could . . . I mean, on such short notice."

"I can't get away, Mom. I have to work tomorrow afternoon. There isn't time."

"No, I suppose not. Still . . . I know Marilyn and your other classmates will be there. And your father and me."

A mound swelled in my throat. "Sorry. Wish I could."

"I know, Margaret. I'm sorry, too. Don't forget to send a card."

I thanked my mother for calling and said goodbye. There was barely a click as the line disengaged. I held the receiver to my ear as though there was more to come. I heard a persistent beeping sound and settled the handset back in its cradle. In the eerie silence that followed, I almost snatched the telephone back, as though I could rewind to a time before the call, undo what had been said. I sat back down on the kitchen chair, keeping very still. Maybe I'd only imagined the call, and my mother's voice, but I knew that wasn't the case. Eric's name exploded in my chest. *Er-ic, Er-ic.*

I sat, stiff and unmoving, thinking and trying not to think. As often as thoughts of Eric had come to mind day after day, I found it hard to grab onto more than fleeting images of him. Quick snapshots raced by: Eric climbing into his Taylorcraft, walking into the Playboy Club, turning his head on my pillow and waving through the taxi window. The brief glimpses vanished too quickly. I wanted so badly to be in his arms.

Could I make it home and back in time for rehearsal? I ached to be there for Eric, for myself.

The thought that kept recurring, the one I couldn't shake, was how odd it was that Eric had died and I didn't know. Where was I at the time? What stupid thing was I doing while he was dying? How could that happen? How could I not somehow have known—even prevented it? I tried to picture Eric flying aircraft I'd never seen in a place I'd never been. Instead I saw myself with him in the Taylorcraft, scuttling up over a stand of trees, skimming below clouds and looking down at green fields and patches of water. Again and again I replayed those flashing moments when he walked up the stairs to the Piano Bar, looked at me and grinned. He couldn't be dead.

I methodically went through my morning routine. I showered, dressed, made coffee. Then I put on my jacket and left my apartment.

I walked to the newsagent on the corner and realized I'd done so in order to buy a card to send to Eric's father. I tucked the card in my pocket and kept walking. I had no sense of my feet hitting the pavement. I didn't have to be at the studio, and I wasn't scheduled to work at the Club until the cocktail shift, so I kept walking.

Eventually I found myself so far uptown that I decided to turn back toward the Club. Once Audrey saw me walk into the Bunny dressing room, I was pressed into service in the Playmate Bar to relieve another Bunny, who wasn't feeling well. I don't remember putting on my Bunny costume or serving customers. I remember nothing, certainly not passing out in the service bar sometime that afternoon.

With Allie and Jorge, one of the Puerto Rican busboys, supporting me, I found myself perching on the edge of an upturned crate, my head pressed between my knees. I could feel the closeness of other Bunnies crowding into the service area, hear their high-pitched voices calling out drink orders and asking if I was okay. I stared down at the scuff-marked linoleum, my eyes catching a swirling rainbow of satin high heels moving around me as I tried to get my bearings.

"I'm fine, I'm fine," I kept saying, as one after another put a hand on my back or smoothed my hair.

Above the din, Gloria's voice rang out. "You better not be preggers, Meg!"

I raised my head and laughed. "Fat chance."

Everyone laughed with me. With that, I hoisted myself up and looked around for my tray.

"You're not going back on the floor," Allie said. "Bunny Mother's orders."

"I'm already covering for you," Jolly said. "I'll close out your tabs after another round."

"Thanks a lot. Sell mugs and boost my tip average while you're at it!"

No one served more drinks in souvenir Bunny mugs than Jolly. When she couldn't sell a customer on having the rum punch normally served in the mug, she'd offer to substitute a martini or whisky sour —anything to double the price for the take-home souvenir.

"For you, anything." She laughed. "You crumpled like a champ. How'd you manage not to fall on your face?"

"You must be joking. I'm an actor!"

Allie maneuvered me into the service elevator and we rode up to the sixth-floor Bunny Dressing Room. Audrey checked me out. Her relief that I'd fainted out of sight of customers and hadn't spilled any blood on my costume was evident. I'd only snapped the heel on one of my shoes and that wasn't Playboy property. With a notable lack of maternal concern, the Bunny Mother said, "There you go, kid. No damage. Go home."

Allie insisted on seeing me back to my apartment. But once in the cab, Allie directed the driver to stop instead on Park Avenue at a medical office where her boyfriend, Dr. Ted Robinson, practiced.

"I don't need a doctor, Allie," I said, when I realized what she had in mind, "certainly not an orthopedist! Look at me, nothing broken."

"Well, it can't hurt. I know Teddy's in his office now because I talked to him earlier. Besides, it gives me a good excuse to see him."

"You don't need an excuse."

She gave me a look, and I realized she did. Obviously they'd had another falling out and, as usual, Allie was probably to blame. Her feelings about Teddy were ambivalent, but he was her bird in hand until someone more appealing turned up.

"I really don't want to drop in on him like this, Allie. He has patients to see."

"Forget it. I've already called him from the Club. He's expecting you."

"He'll tell me to eat a sandwich, that's all. I feel fine."

By that time we had already pulled up at the curb outside his office. Allie paid the driver and climbed out, reaching back for my hand as though I might escape if she didn't keep a firm grip on me. I can't say it didn't occur to me. I did not want to see a doctor, certainly not her boyfriend, and not with Allie hovering in the vicinity. But I slid across the vinyl seat and allowed her to shepherd me into Teddy's office. Allie was friendly with the receptionist, and the two traded pleasantries. The only other people in the waiting room were a young boy with his arm in a sling, and a woman sitting next to him on a settee, probably his mother.

Allie took the clipboard from the receptionist, and we sat down in the two matching green-leather club chairs by the window. She uncapped a Biro and said, "Okay, date of birth."

"Allie, please, my arm is fine. I can fill out the form myself." I had no intention of telling her my legal name was Margaret Blatch, or even telling her my birth date, although we were probably only months apart in age.

"Fine. No need to get touchy," she said. She handed me the clipboard and picked up a copy of *Cosmopolitan.*

Fortunately Allie knew better than to follow me into the examining room when the receptionist called my name. Teddy, tall and trim in his white coat, greeted me warmly, taking both my hands in his. "How are you feeling? I hear you took a little tumble this afternoon."

"Fine," I said. "I forgot to eat and felt a little faint. I'll have a bowl of soup as soon as I get home."

"Good girl," he said, "But let me have a look at you first. I'll be with you in a minute."

I followed a nurse to one of the examining rooms. "Just sit on the table and we'll check your temperature and blood pressure," she said briskly.

"No need," I said, just as briskly. "I'm fine."

She looked at me in some surprise, holding a thermometer in one hand, a blood pressure cuff in the other. "We really need to do this. Is there a problem?"

There was, of course, but I wasn't about to bring it up. I hesitated just long enough for the nurse to come up with her own explanation. "Something religious?"

I nodded.

"I'll tell the doctor," she said. "But there doesn't seem to be much point in being here then." She handed me a gown and left the room. I hung the gown on a hook and sat in a chair. Ted knocked on the door and entered a few minutes later, showing no surprise when he saw I wasn't sitting on the examining table wearing the cotton gown.

"I really just need a bowl of soup," I said.

He perched on the edge of a stool and folded his arms. He smelled vaguely of sandalwood. I was starting to feel light-headed again, and felt his hands on my shoulders, steadying me.

"I know what's wrong with me, Dr. Robinson," I said, fighting hard to swallow the lump tightening my throat. "It's nothing to worry about. I'm not sick. I just need to go home."

"How far along are you?"

I gaped at him, caught by surprise. I'd been thinking about Eric, not about being pregnant. Dr. Robinson nodded, his eyes warm. "A good guess, I take it. And you haven't told anyone? Not even . . .?"

"No! Nobody knows. Not Allie. I don't want anyone to know. And I'm not very pregnant. At least to look at."

"Well, there's no such thing as being a little bit pregnant, Meg. Have you thought about what you are going to do? Or talked to the baby's father about this?"

"No, no, I haven't," I said, holding back tears, not wanting to have to explain. I could imagine what Ted was thinking. I'd heard his change of tone.

"I see. You aren't going to tell him. Have you seen a doctor yet?" I shook my head because I had no voice. "You really can't hold off, Meg. I'm going to give you the name of someone . . ."

"Wait, you don't understand. I don't want to get rid of it! I can't do that!"

I regretted the words the moment they flew out of my mouth. Dr. Robinson looked startled, then the corners of his mouth turned down.

"I'm sorry. I'm so sorry. I know you wouldn't send me to someone like that. I don't know what I was thinking."

"You need to see a doctor," he repeated carefully, "I can give you the name of a colleague. It's up to you, but I think you should." Ted picked up a pad and wrote a name and number. He handed the paper to me. I folded it and stuffed it in my pocket without looking at it.

"Thank you," I said, standing up. "I really appreciate it."

"Of course, and you know this is entirely confidential. But promise me you'll take care of yourself. Call me if I can be of any help, Meg."

One other person now shared my secret, and it was Ted Robinson. Thankfully it wasn't Allie. I wished it had been Eric. And if I couldn't be with Eric, I just wanted to be alone. Ted walked me back to the reception area where Allie was waiting for me.

"She's fine, not even a bruise," Ted said. "I'll take you both to dinner tonight, if you'd like."

"Thanks, anyway," I said quickly. "I have food at home and I need an early night. In fact, I think I'll walk home and get some air. You two have dinner on your own."

"You're sure?" Allie asked, looking relieved.

"Absolutely. Thanks so much!" I smiled and headed for the door. Nothing good could come of spending an evening with them. The less opportunity I gave Dr. Robinson to observe me, the better, and Allie could use the time alone with him.

Back in my apartment, I sat at the kitchen table to write a card to Eric's father. I came up with a few words of sympathy that seemed appropriate, but once I'd written the card, I realized there was much more I needed to say. I reached for stationery to write a letter. I wanted to tell Clarence that Eric and I had corresponded over the past year, that our friendship had deepened with the exchange of letters and how much I would always cherish having had Eric in my life—I was unable to put any words to paper. What couldn't be said is that I was carrying his son's child.

That thought made me sit back and consider my choice not to have written Eric that I was pregnant when I had the chance. It occurred to me that in the past few weeks I'd been naively looking upon my pregnancy as some sort of personal adventure, an experience full of surprise and hazard that involved me alone. I'd had only a vague idea of when and how I would let Eric know. I imagined he'd come home on leave and that's when I'd tell him. Then what? I hadn't really thought beyond that. We'd both felt sorry for Bonnie and Roy, even laughed about the consequences, without ever imagining such a thing would happen to us.

Not telling Eric I was carrying his baby seemed to be the best decision under the circumstances, but I deeply regretted it. If he'd known, would it somehow have made a difference? How could I ever make it up to Eric? I made another try at writing to Clarence, but the words wouldn't come.

I put down my pen and looked up to see Haddie hovering at the far side of the room, his presence silhouetted in the late afternoon sun streaming through the French windows. My eyes narrowed to a squint as I took in his brush cut and stiff military bearing. His expression was solemn, the leathery creases in his skin weighted in sorrow. Just such a figure in Air Force blues must have knocked on Clarence's door. If Haddie was meant to be my own personal bearer of bad news, it was too late.

"You've been in short supply lately. Where've you been?"

"Sorry, Meg. I hate to see a good man go down, least of all Eric. I tried my best, but—"

"You did? Really? I thought that lighter saw you through D-Day-plus-one." My voice was harsh, my anger welling up along with more tears. "What happened? How could you fail me? You were supposed to keep an eye on him."

"I tried. There was nothing I could do. He fought hard, Meg. He was so brave, but he couldn't pull out—I am so sorry."

"Shut up! That's not what I want to hear! I want him back!"

"I know, I know," Haddie said. I could feel him close to me, caressing my hair as I sobbed. "He didn't stand a chance, I'm sorry to say. He wasn't even under enemy fire. A bird crashed through his cockpit on takeoff. Nothing he could do."

"A bird?" My head snapped up. "What kind of bird?"

"Honey buzzard. A variety indigenous to Southeast Asia. I'm so sorry, Meg, but I think you know—"

"Camilla," I breathed. Horror engulfed me as I recalled the bird that had struck Erik's Taylorcraft. "It's always been Camilla. You warned me." So had Grandpa Egstrom, and I didn't pay attention then, either.

Rage tore through me in a frenzy so violent I could barely contain the howl surging up my throat. Haddie enveloped me, smothering me in a thick cocoon that muffled my screams of pain, allowing me to vent my wrath. "She robbed me of Eric!" I roared, my body rocking with the force of my rage. "How could I let her do that!"

Haddie's voice, whisper soft, seeped through my terrible cries of anguish. "I'm here for you, Meg. What do you want to do?"

I knew at once. "Eric's funeral. I want to be there."

"It'll be hazardous, but we can do it. You up for it?"

"Let's go. Now."

"Then suit up, gal. That's what I wanted to hear," he said briskly. "You can tank up on the way."

Eighteen

Soaring on thermals, I swooped into Canada at speeds far greater than an ordinary red-tailed hawk, my chosen conveyance for the journey back to Twin Lakes. I could transport myself faster, and more safely, by other modes of travel, but winging my way home for Eric's funeral seemed fitting. The wind skimming my feathers and the exaltation of traveling under my own power restored my sense of purpose. Whatever the dangers ahead, I would not be defeated. I owed it to Eric.

Haddie, unseen but ever present, served as my beacon. He was vigilant and tough. His personal anguish over Eric's death was painfully evident; he was not going to fail me again. He took charge, choosing a direct northerly route that skirted the broad expanses of the Great Lakes. At his direction, I'd tanked up on a white-footed mouse just outside Buffalo. Soaring high, expending little energy while viewing a sizable territory of grassland and marsh, I'd spotted my quarry in brush less than a half-mile ahead. The mouse, plump and reddish-brown, with a white belly, was scuttling across birch bark chasing a beetle.

"Zero in!" Haddie instructed. "I've got your six!"

I swooped down, grasping the mouse in my needle-sharp talons and crushing it in my powerful claws. I ate quickly, holding a portion in my crop to digest later, when I could take a little into my stomach at a time. Even with Haddie on watch, I couldn't afford the luxury of remaining on the ground for long. With my eyes fixed downward to feed, I was too vulnerable to attack.

We headed northwest, chasing the last glimmer of twilight. Darkness was falling as I crossed into Ontario. "You need fuel!" Haddie barked, alerting me to my need to feed again.

I glided high, with the last lavender glow sinking on the horizon. My eyes scanned the marshy shoreline, sorting through reeds and cattails. A bullfrog, thick-necked and olive green, emerged from a hollow log to claim impending nightfall with a deep-throated call. I locked onto its pale bulbous gland, swelling with sound, and swept down into the thick reeds. Equipped with upper and lower eyelids like humans, my red-tailed hawk also had a clear membrane, a third eyelid, that slid in from the side to protect my eyes from injury while swooping into the thick pelt of long grass to grab my prey. The bullfrog, meaty and ripe with fluid, burst with flavor as my beak tore into its flesh.

"Pull up! Right flank!" Haddie warned. I heard the caw of crows and took off, pocketing a last morsel of bullfrog before soaring up and away. "Can't hurt you, but their dive-bombing is a damn nuisance. You good to go for another thousand miles or so?"

"Full up, Haddie. Let's push on."

Night fell. I cruised high over dark plains and vast bodies of smoky grey water reflected in moonlight. It was a long stretch to the Canadian border, but at the speeds I was traveling, exhilarating, too. I circled down along the shores of Lake Superior before turning west. Even in darkness the terrain became familiar to me. These were the skies Eric and I had flown in together not a year before. I looked down on the barren cornfields, the dry, withered stalks already turned over in the rough earth.

Eric. Dead. Once again the image replayed: the huge buzzard ramming into the wooden propeller of Eric's Taylorcraft, and its raptor eyes locking on mine as the blade shattered. Eric's deft handling of the aircraft had spared us then, without my help. But Eric's last earthly vision of a buzzard smashing into his cockpit had been foretold, and I hadn't heeded the warning. Eric's death was not an accident. I should have seen it coming. I could not forgive myself.

"You okay? Stay alert, Meg! You got Twin Lakes coming up."

"In sight, Haddie. Let me take it from here." A half-mile ahead, I spotted my father heading out to the barn for a last check before turning in. Ruth was in the kitchen crumbling saltines to sprinkle on her tuna hot dish. She looked up, dusting her fingers on her apron, sensing I was close to home.

I skimmed low over the mortuary, a converted wood frame farmhouse just down the street from the church. Hovering above the eaves, I watched Pastor Odegaard talking with Clarence on the veranda, with only a porch light illuminating the entrance. A VFW member stood at the door. As was the custom in Twin Lakes, vets from the Legion Hall would take turns keeping vigil throughout the night. The pastor embraced Clarence's shoulders, patted him on the back, and set off down the sidewalk towards the parsonage. Official visiting hours were over.

I perched on the windowsill of the parlor and peered inside as Clarence returned to the reception room and laid his hand on Eric's flag-draped casket. Slumped in grief, Clarence looked old and lost. As he bent his head and wept, a fireball of pain shuddered through me. I wished I could comfort him, but what comfort could there be for a man who was burying his only child? Clarence patted the casket and turned away. The VFW member accompanied him outside and waited while Clarence climbed into his pickup and drove away.

Shaping had its limitations. However much I wanted to be closer to Eric, I would have to keep vigil outside. He was human and in transition. I would not be able to summon him. If he were to appear to me, like Haddie did, it would be of his own volition, knowing me now for what I was. This much I somehow knew, but I also realized how woefully lacking I was in any real knowledge of how to use my gifts. I utilized my powers to the extent I needed them and didn't bother to explore their potential. Nor had I fully appreciated that as great as my own gifts might be, there were forces practiced in destructive powers that could cause harm not only to me, but those close to me.

I huddled on the windowsill, alert to the chorus of sounds in the night. Crickets, beetles, wasps and termites had taken up residence in the old wood frame mortuary. Infernal mosquitoes and black mites, pests I seldom encountered in New York, flicked in waves around the porch light. A murder of crows swarmed noisily in a sycamore tree, taunting me. I turned my back on them, my eyes fixed on Eric's casket in the dimly lit parlor of the mortuary.

After a noisy flutter of wings taking flight, the crows fell silent and there was a moment of stillness. But in that fragment of silence, beware the killing creature that makes no sound at all! With no warning, except the absence of sound, a winged tiger of the night was upon me. Camilla, shaped as a great horned owl, swooped out of nowhere, her venomous yellow eyes fixed on me, talons extended.

In that instant of doom, a snowy white owl of huge dimensions dived down, plunging its talons into the silent killer, ripping it off me and flinging it skyward. The enormous white owl lifted me whole in its talons and ascended at great speed, its broad wings slicing through the night air. In the distance I heard the staccato hoots of the wounded great horned owl crying with pain as my mother swept me away, high above the cornfields.

Moments later, I blinked through human eyes and found myself looking up at the cabbage rose wallpaper of my old bedroom. I breathed in the familiar rain-fresh smell of bed linens, sun-dried on a washline. My mother, reshaped, her dark hair loose on her shoulders, pushed up the sleeves of her white chenille robe and looked down at me. Her mouth was pursed in a thin line, but her eyes were anxious.

"It's good to have you home again, but not like this. You're hurt, you know. But at least this way you can heal." She cocked her head and looked at me with consternation. "It's a wonder you survived at all. What were you thinking?"

"Where's Haddie?"

"You are not his responsibility! Mr. Haddock shouldn't have to hang around on call to do your bidding. Cut him some slack, Margaret. You're not a kid anymore. You have to take charge of yourself!"

Ruth was growing more exasperated the more she spoke. With some effort she'd been trying to contain her irritation with me, but was losing the battle. Compassion wasn't her strong suit.

"Honestly, you cannot be so dependent and hope to survive. It's plain silly to think you need to shape to travel a couple thousand miles—all very romantic, but you don't choose a shape that leaves you prey! Do you know how close you came to being attacked by a peregrine on the north end of Lake Huron? It's lucky he saw a hare that he figured would be more tasty than you. And to top it off, you leave behind your only method of reshaping! If something happened to you, how did you plan to restore yourself? You had no defenses! Really, Margaret, you should be figuring these things out for yourself. I had to!"

I let her run out of steam. When Ruth was on a tear, it was best to lie low. Besides, I'd already realized I'd made a number of tactical errors. "How did you shape me back?"

"Hair ribbon," Ruth said. "You left hair ribbons in your dresser."

"Thanks, Mom. I'm sorry."

"I know." She sighed. "I'm sorry to scold you. How are you feeling?"

"Better." I looked down at my deeply sliced arms, both of them healing quickly from the razor-sharp talons of the owl. Camilla had been ruthless, but I could only imagine her own injuries.

"You know what I mean," Ruth said. "You're pregnant."

I nodded. "It's Eric's. When did you know?"

"Not until I saw you. I surmised it was Eric's. It's going to be hard, you know."

"Will it be like me?"

"We won't know until its birth. There are no signs. As it should be, or one would . . . take advantage of options."

"I see."

"Nevermind about that now," Ruth said hurriedly. "With you or Eddie, one pregnancy is no less difficult than the other for our sort. It's just that—anyway, I want you to know I'll be there for you. When the time comes, I'll do what I can to help, to make it easier. There's no medical help. And you will be particularly vulnerable."

"Camilla."

"Yes, that's what she calls herself now." Ruth sat on the edge of the bed, her eyes falling on the slivery cuts on my forearms, now almost healed. "You see what she's capable of. I didn't realize she would be a danger to you, or I would have said something sooner. Your grandmother fought her off years ago and that should have been the end of it, but she returned." Ruth twisted the coverlet in her fingers, her voice taking on an edge. "She's a wicked, jealous creature, never satisfied. She tried to kill your father in the fields one time, you may remember. I punished her severely, and should have done worse."

"And Grandma Egstrom?"

"As strong and skilled as she was, my mother, Sarabeth, died in childbirth. Justine, as Camilla was known then, was her sister-in-law for a time. From what I know, it was a side of the family Sarabeth had little time for. My uncle, her brother, was a fool and a human who had inherited considerable wealth through his first wife. He got mixed up with Justine, who was a witch. It was the family's undoing. Justine was jealous of Sarabeth, who was very beautiful, and far more powerful than she was. But Justine—or Camilla, as you know her now, is cunning and relentless, striking out to inflict as much pain as possible."

"Eric." His name fell from my lips almost soundlessly, and with it a wave of terrible sorrow.

"Yes, Eric."

I clamped my eyes shut, struggling to contain my anguish. Gently Ruth placed her hands on my shoulders, easing my pain with her touch. "You know what you have to do, Margaret. You are the embodiment of Sarabeth, as beautiful as your grandmother, but not as merciless—and you must be."

"I will be," I vowed. "For Eric."

"Yes." My mother nodded and sat back. "We'll talk more later. You're almost healed. You better clean yourself up. I'll send your father in before Eddie wakes up. No point in confusing the boy more than he is already."

"I want to attend the funeral."

"You will, of course, but you can't go as you are. Did it never occur to you to shape as another human being?"

"I can do that?"

"Of course. Leave it to me. Nothing glamorous. You'll want to fit in without a lot of fuss. You'll sit next to Grandpa Egstrom."

"He'll be there, too?"

"Yes, sort of. In his own way. After all, he knew Clarence and was very fond of Eric. And he wants to see you. I'm on Altar Guild rotation this month, so I'm going to the church early. I need to put out fresh linens and supervise the mortuary people. You'll go with me."

Shortly before daybreak, my father knocked on my bedroom door. I was fully healed and looking presentable. With my father, there was none of Ruth's holding back. He pulled me in his arms and rocked me back and forth in a bear hug that would've broken anyone else's bones. There was even a tear in his eye when he said, "Your mother tells me you have to leave right after the service. Sure wish we could have you around here longer."

"I'll be back, I promise. And I'll come back in a regular way," I laughed. "We don't want people talking," I said, mimicking my mother's voice.

Ruth packed up the Pyrex baking dish with the tuna fish casserole in foil and a thick towel to keep it warm and we set out for church in the Studebaker. Dad and Eddie would drive into town later in the pickup. Ruth determined that I would be best served appearing as Dottie Wilson, a fictional friend-of-a-friend, who happened to be passing through town. On the drive to church, I transformed into Dot, a matronly woman with thick ankles, rubbery arms and a big behind, distinguishing characteristics that would not set me apart from most of the middle-aged farm wives we'd run into. I wasn't pleased, but I knew better than to protest lest Ruth come up with something worse.

When we arrived, an honor guard from the Legion Post was just departing after accompanying Eric's casket from the mortuary to the church sanctuary. "No one will be here for a while," mother said. "Why don't you go on in for a few minutes on your own." I gave her a quick look and she nodded. "It's okay. I'll stay out here so no one bothers you."

I slipped inside and stood for a moment in the narthex looking down the aisle at Eric's flag-draped casket. The church was as familiar to me as our farmhouse, but I'd never seen it before in the hushed light of early morning, with the pews empty, the candles unlit, the organ silent. I tiptoed down the aisle, smelling the hothouse mums on the altar and the spray of roses near the pulpit. By the time I'd reached the casket, I'd transformed. I stood there as Meg, with my hand on Eric's coffin, silent and penitent.

With my heightened awareness, I heard the brush of dust balls on the stone floor, and the march of ants in the choir loft. I could see grains of sand left by someone's shoe near the pulpit, and smell the drop of communion wine on the altar. But there was only stillness in the casket. Eric, dressed in Air Force blues, lay solemn and silent, and I'd expected nothing more.

"I love you so much," I whispered, and realized I'd never said it before. And then, before turning away, I leaned down and pressed my lips to the casket.

Outside, I stood in the cool sunshine, at some distance from the church entrance, watching everyone arrive. Marilyn, wearing a polo coat, her hair cut short, showed up early, holding hands with a rangy young man in a tweed jacket. I watched her look around; she was probably wondering if I would turn up. Her eyes were red, and there was a balled-up handkerchief in her hand. Roy and Bonnie were early, too. She held a baby in her arms, and it was clear another was on the way. No one paid attention to me, a well-upholstered, doughy-looking stranger wearing sensible shoes.

Grandpa Egstrom hovered just over my shoulder throughout the service. Marilyn's mother sang a solo before the gospel reading. Pastor Odegaard spoke touchingly of the young man he'd known since boyhood: his love of flying and his devotion to his father, who had raised him alone since Eric's mother died when he was nine years old. Pastor Odegaard's words were all the more moving spoken in his spare, uncluttered manner, even as he employed scripture and homily to address the questions foremost in everyone's thinking: Why Eric? Why so soon?

I stopped listening then, my eyes on the flag-draped coffin. Vengeance was on my mind, as much as I tried to push it away. I tried to think about the good times with Eric, and not about the interment or anything else that lay ahead. I knew where Eric would be buried, in the plot next to his mother in the part of the churchyard that caught the afternoon sun. I'd been there with Eric, and it would be unbearable to see that soil broken for his burial. Then, as I had before, I thought about my last jokey letter to Eric, and wondered if he had got it.

My mother would have liked to stay for the lunch in the church basement. The casseroles, Jell-O molds and sheet cakes made a tempting smorgasbord, and my mother enjoyed lingering with the other ladies over coffee before they started the cleanup. But following the interment, my mother had asked, "When do you have to be back?"

"Rehearsal is at four o'clock, and I should change first," I said.

"That's cutting it close. We're an hour behind here, Central time." She sighed and put her handbag on her arm. "We'd better be off. Say goodbye to your father. I don't know where Eddie is."

"How are we getting back?"

"Well, we're not traveling all the way back to New York as humming birds!" my mother said irritably. "Leave it to me."

Her sarcasm had as much to do with missing the church social hour as her disgust that I couldn't figure out transport for myself. I trudged over to say goodbye to my father, who had to put up with a hug and kiss from his daughter in the matronly guise of Dottie Wilson. I couldn't wait to reshape.

At supersonic speed, traveling as sound waves, Ruth and I made it back to my Gramercy Park apartment in no time. I shaped back and showed my mother around my apartment, offering her some tea. My mother, however, had noticed the J&B and cut-glass tumblers on my kitchen counter.

"Sooo—" my mother said, letting the ominous sounding Minnesota vowel linger with an icy chill, "I assume that's the remains of the Scotch from our cupboard? Anyway, I'd better get back home and fix supper."

"I'm sorry you have to leave so soon, Mom. It would be fun to show you the studio, maybe even take you to the Club."

"Another time," she said. Her eyes slowly traveled around my studio apartment, taking in the daybed and tall French windows. "Nice," she said. "You have it very nice here. Small, but nice," words I knew meant high praise. "I'll be back whenever you need me, Margaret. You let me know. Remember to keep your human emotions in check. Don't let them get the best of you."

Nineteen

I tried to put Eric and my hasty return from his funeral out of my mind as I hurried to the studio. The air show was about to go live, so I was able to slip unnoticed up the back stairs to my dressing room.

I'd forgotten who was working that day, or what the episode was about. I rarely read scripts I wasn't in, and almost never watched the show whether I was in it or not. Few of the actors did. Once work for the day was finished, it was forgotten—bloopers, fluffed lines and all.

With no editing, and no retakes no matter how dire the flubs, there were bound to be shows we hoped everyone would soon forget. We imagined kids watching at home looking at each other and asking, "Did you see that picture fall off the wall?" "Who's that man with the earphones walking through the mausoleum?" "I think the doorknob just came off in her hand."

Occasionally we were able to cover a mishap with a quick ad lib. During a scene with my father, a flag on an overhead light broke loose and fell to the floor. Ed looked up and mumbled, "Margie, better call the roofer," and then went on reading his lines off the TelePrompTer.

On some days, when there were so many special effects we barely had time to run the dialogue, it was like doing summer stock on live TV. Microphones dangled in shots. Walls wobbled. Doors swung open after being firmly shut. But I learned to trust my instincts and deal with whatever spilled, broke, fell or wouldn't work. It was often just too painful to watch the air show while it was being done, or the broadcast episode. But with time to spare, I decided for once to watch the show on my dressing room monitor.

The test pattern flickered and images appeared. Moira was on set, checking her makeup in her compact mirror as she always did immediately before the air show. As I watched her shift her head, holding the compact at arm's length, I realized she was checking her key light, not her powder. No wonder she had such an uncanny ability to find her best camera angle, a trick she must have learned during her Hollywood studio contract days. Satisfied, she snapped the compact closed and slipped it behind a cushion on the settee. Shelby was exercising his facial muscles, grimacing as though he'd just swallowed strychnine. His warm-up gargling noises were always disconcerting when you were about to play a scene with him.

On impulse, I hurried out of my dressing room and raced down to the narrow screening room near Paul's office. The dressing room monitors had picture only, no sound, and I wanted to hear the dialogue. I plopped down in a corner of the two-seater couch and nodded to a plump woman occupying the armchair. She was from the network, a Standards and Practices representative. I knew her only as Lydia. She arrived every day to watch the air show and, according to Paul, was there to make sure the commercials fed properly without being cut at the top or bottom, and that no curse words were uttered. Although Lydia appeared friendly enough, somehow we'd got the notion we weren't permitted to speak to her, and no one ever did.

The music swelled as opening credits rolled over waves crashing on a bleak, rocky shore. A voice-over announced that "Stanhope's mysterious visitor proved to be a long-lost cousin, but the circumstances of his arrival only raise more mystery . . . !" A crescendo of theme music rose as the pounding waves dissolved into a closeup of brandy swirling in a large snifter. The camera panned up to find Shelby standing near the fireplace, glowering. "I think you know how I feel about this, Diana—"

"Of course I do, Shelby," Diana cooed, her face tilted into the light, a smile playing on her lips. "You're jealous of Sebastian. It's clear as day. If I may say so, it's most unbecoming."

"Nonsense!" Shelby's nostrils flared, his eyes flashed. Nobody chewed scenery like Shelby. You could almost see his teeth gnashing.

"Sebastian Stanhope may flaunt the family name, but by damn he's nothing more than a phony—and I shall prove it!"

The camera cut to Joey Stanhope skulking behind the drawing room door, eavesdropping on his father and aunt as Diana said, "Oh, stop it! You'll make a fool of yourself and humiliate the entire family. To what end, may I ask?"

"He's taken over our lives, don't you see it? Look at the effect he's having on Joey." Without uttering a word, Danny's face registered disgust, then a crafty determination.

The camera cut back to Moira, who executed a perfectly timed turn into closeup, her chin lifted to her key light. In that elegant transatlantic cadence peculiar to 1930s-era Hollywood drawing room comedies and murder mysteries, Diana trilled, "There you have it! Pure jealousy, as I've already said. Or is Joey only an excuse? I think you're even more concerned that Sebastian has offered to renovate the East Wing. Why are you so dead set against it?"

"You're under the blackguard's spell, too, Diana. Utterly blind to what he's doing! I won't have it! It's wrong, I tell you! Wrong!" Shelby smashed the empty snifter into the fireplace, crossed to the drawing room door, turned, and said in menacing tones, "You'll not get away this. I'll not let you!"

Joey scurried to hide in the recess under the stairs as Shelby stalked across the entrance foyer to his office, slamming the door. It shuddered closed and the camera moved in on Joey, but not fast enough to avoid catching the door swinging gently open again.

It was all hokum, but well executed, completely riveting hokum. As the screen shifted to a spokeswoman demonstrating no-smear Hazel Bishop lipstick, Lydia flashed me a quick smile, "They give as good as they get, I'll say that!"

My sentiments exactly, but I was thinking more in terms of the script they'd been given. Moira and Maxwell had played the scene to the hilt, with no hint of condescension, despite turgid dialogue and a story line that made little sense. Yet the intrigue brewing in the great house on the hill held a fascination—what course would the mystery of the long-lost cousin take? I suspected even Horace wasn't sure. But the actors, who had no more inkling than the audience of what was to come, were wringing every ounce of drama out of each moment. I curled my feet under me and settled deeper into the couch as the commercial break ended.

The second act opened on a closeup of Joey's fingers exploring a ridge of molding above a paneled wall in the library. The camera pulled back as Joey's hand brushed across a lever releasing a secret panel that slid open. He stepped back, a look of wonderment flickering across his face. A second camera picked up Joey in a reverse shot, gathering his courage to step through the narrow opening. As he did so, his foot tripped a mechanism that slid the panel closed behind him. He swung around, but failed to grab the panel before it shut. He looked back across his shoulder with fearful eyes, his face shrouded in shadow. My own heart started to race, as I knew his must, as his eyes took in the gloomy, cobwebbed interior of the secret room.

I knew the cobwebs were made of a gluey substance spun into filament by a machine, and the eerie shadows were created by a revolving disc attached to a light, but the effect was scary and creepy nonetheless, invoking every fear imaginable: Trapped in a dark, enclosed space with spiders and who knew what else! But Joey bravely moved forward, brushing aside cobwebs, treading carefully through a narrow passage lined with packing boxes and odd pieces of furniture. Then, a tinkling sound was heard, mechanical but oddly musical. Where was he? What was that sound? Who else might be there? He stopped. His eyes widened, his mouth fell open and he slowly knelt behind a dusty steamer trunk.

The camera swung around, panning slowly across the top of the trunk to the figure of a man, seen in profile, holding a gold-encrusted music box and gazing up at a portrait. With a shock of recognition, I uttered a tiny gasp—it was me! Even though I'd seen the portrait before, I'd been caught by surprise. The portrait of Gwyneth Fairfax was hung above a mantel, tall candlesticks thick with drippings set on either side, their flames flickering on the shiny canvas. The music tinkled its thin melody as the camera moved in on Sebastian's face, his eyes filled with longing and desire.

The shot switched to Joey, cowering behind the dusty trunk. He covered his mouth trying to stifle a sneeze, but made a tiny sound. He crouched lower, eyes wide with fear.

Sebastian, in a medium closeup, swung around and snapped the music box shut. His eyes, rimmed in kohl, flashed with laser sharpness. "You!" he roared, the sound reverberating loudly as it filtered through an echo device. The camera picked up the hapless Joey slowly rising from behind the trunk. A sting of music rose out of the echoing sound before the camera cut to station identification. My heart was pounding, a sensation I imagined viewers across the country would experience when the show was broadcast the following week.

"Powerful stuff," Lydia murmured. "No wonder kids have nightmares."

"But they're still watching," I said. "The ratings are up."

"You bet. Who can resist this stuff?" Stopwatch in hand, her eyes glued to the screen, Lydia added, "I'm hooked."

I laughed. "Good to hear." Perhaps, like the Queen of England, one could speak to Lydia if she addressed you first.

The most powerful scene of the day took place following the station break and commercial, the confrontation between Joey Stanhope and Sebastian, the cousin from England. The boy, whose cold, unloving father paid him little attention, was both awestruck and fearful of the magnetic new presence in the household. That his father resented Sebastian Stanhope intrigued young Joey, who had been spying on him since his arrival. Sebastian had shown the boy kindness, giving him a toy replica of an old schooner. The generosity of that gift had been betrayed, and Sebastian's wrath was evident.

But the boy had discovered the secret panel. He had seen the portrait, and was struck by the resemblance to his governess. Sebastian had to make an ally of the boy. It was tricky terrain. An eccentric older man, claiming to be a family member, had drawn a young boy into a secret chamber—for what sinister purpose? What dangerous web was Horace spinning?

The scene picked up with Joey cowering behind the steamer trunk, mesmerized by Sebastian limned in the glow of candlelight.

"You're a clever lad, Joey. I see you've found the secret panel," Sebastian said, his voice conversational. "Welcome to the East Wing of the Old House, the original Stanhope home built in pre-Revolutionary times. You know about George Washington, I take it? He was a visitor here. Careful of your footing, now. The place is in terrible repair."

"Why was it closed off?"

"Why, indeed. It's disgraceful, in view of its historical significance alone. The door should be unlocked, but your father won't hear of it. I've even offered to bear the cost of renovation. It's the very reason for my return to Stanhope."

"You've been here before? When?"

"Ah, that's a long story best left to another time. I consider it my mission to restore Stanhope to its former glory."

"Can I look around?"

"Of course you may, Joey. And you must tell your father you've seen the ruined splendor with your own eyes. You must help me convince your father the East Wing should be reopened."

"He'll punish me if he knows I sneaked in here!"

"All this will one day be yours, young man. Be brave. No secrets!"

"And that portrait? Who is she?"

Sebastian held the candelabra high, gazing up at the painting with a sad, wistful expression. "A woman of beauty and refinement, so dear to my heart, yet doomed to suffer a dreadful fate. She is the Lady Gwyneth Fairfax."

A mighty sting of music climaxed the show as the camera zoomed in on the painting. The credits rolled over the portrait of Gwyneth Fairfax, the "beauty shot" of the day, as the *Dark Passages* theme music closed out the episode. My character was titled and refined, quite an upgrade from family governess.

"Hey, Morg," Danny said, plopping next to me on the settee. "What did you think?"

"Call me Meg—and I thought you were terrific. Great scene with Sebastian."

"He's the best. Want to watch the broadcast show with me?"

"Sure. You watch every day?"

"Of course." He looked at me puzzled. "It's homework. How else are you going to learn?"

Lydia turned her head and smiled. "He's my pal. Keeps me company every day."

The opening theme for the broadcast show began. I made more room on the settee for Danny and watched the opening credits roll over waves crashing on a rocky shore. I was beginning to understand why our ratings were on the rise—and why kids were running home from school to watch with their mothers. It was an escape into another world, a parallel time where cataclysmic events happened to other people, who only seemed far removed from one's own daily life. For the better part of an hour, I hadn't consciously thought about Eric, though my cheeks had been moist. Sebastian, at his most tender, had conveyed the heartache of doomed love.

I joined Danny, Moira, Maxwell and Ian for the afternoon table read in the rehearsal room. It occurred to me, as I glanced at the boxes piled up in the corner, that I should take some of my fan letters home to read and answer. As Danny would have said, "It's homework."

For all my concern about returning home from Twin Lakes in time for afternoon rehearsal, it was Camilla who was late. Doris started the reading without her, while Nigel tried to call her at home. Some twenty minutes later, Camilla hobbled into the rehearsal room wearing dark glasses, a long-sleeved shirt, slacks and a scarf wound around her head. Her face was puffy and discolored, and she moved stiffly with a noticeable limp. Her appearance was so startling there was a communal gasp when we saw her enter the room.

"My God, what happened?" Doris said, jumping to her feet.

"You've been injured," Ian said, hurrying to her side. "Here, let me help you."

"Sorry," Camilla said, "just a little accident last night. I ran into something in the dark. So clumsy of me."

"You look like you were hit by a truck," Maxwell exclaimed. "Are you all right?"

"Your face, my dear!" Moira said, "Your beautiful, beautiful face!"

"I'll be fine," Camilla said, easing herself into a chair at the far end of the table from me. "A bit of makeup, and you won't even notice."

"Are you sure you should work?" Doris said. "You look like you're in pain."

"Not at all," Camilla said, opening her script. "My apologies for interrupting rehearsal."

"I'm so sorry, Camilla. What did you run into?" I asked. "When? Where? How did it happen?"

"So many questions," she said, not looking at me. "When it's dark it's hard to tell. It's of no consequence, in any case. Please, let's rehearse."

"Such a trouper!" Moira said. "I do so admire that!"

We settled ourselves back at the table and resumed the read from Camilla's first entrance. She seemed to favor one arm and her jaw looked tender and bruised. Unlike me, Camilla obviously lacked the ability to heal immediately—and my mother clearly packed quite a wallop. I only wished Ruth hadn't rushed back to Twin Lakes instead of visiting the studio with me. I would've taken such pleasure in introducing her to Camilla. But my glee in watching Camilla struggle through rehearsal was small comfort. I couldn't help thinking about Eric and what she had done to him.

There would be a day of reckoning, and I had to prepare for it. I could no longer indulge myself with a human diet, nor deny the necessity of fortifying my powers. It was foolhardy to pretend my adversary would fade away. Camilla would strike again.

Moira, in effusive maternal mode, insisted upon seeing Camilla home. It was evident to all of us that she hoped some shared intimacies might induce Camilla to reveal what really happened. Maxwell hinted it might actually become a "police inquiry" if "rough trade" were involved. "Let's face it, pretty girls like bad boys," he smirked. "Who doesn't?"

I could have told them it was nothing more than a brief encounter between a vampire and a witch, and the witch had taken her licks—but I didn't.

Instead, I stuffed a few fan letters in my pocket and slipped out of the studio as soon as rehearsal was over. I was walking up the street, considering whether to take a prowl through Central Park for a quick feed, when Ian trotted up behind me.

"Hey, not so fast. I wanted to apologize," he said, falling into step next to me. "I was an insufferable prude the other day and I'm sorry. If you want to harbor lascivious drunks in your flat, it's quite all right with me."

"Oh, thank you very much," I laughed. "If you want to know, Michael was too drunk to be lascivious. Honestly, I really did find him unconscious on my doorstep."

"I believe you, of course. And dear Camilla tripped over a doorstop. Happens all the time. Anyway, to make up for my pathetic little fit of bad temper, could I treat you to one of Flinty's fine burgers?"

"Sold. Rare, with fries. And an ale."

"You drive a hard bargain, Miss."

We settled ourselves in a corner booth and ordered up. Ian was in his playful puppy mood, showing no signs of the gloominess he displayed regularly at the studio. I'd begun to wonder if the melancholia he exhibited on the set wasn't some manufactured persona he thought suited his role. If so, I wasn't the only one finding it tiresome. But he was in such expansive form that when our drinks were being served, he accidentally knocked the waiter's tray over. The ale glass broke, sending suds and shards spilling onto the table. Too quick to grab the tumbling glass, Ian cut his finger. In a flash, I grabbed his hand, pressing the bloody finger to my lips, surprising us both.

"No, stop!" Ian said, pulling his hand from my mouth. "No need to do that." He quickly wrapped a cocktail napkin around his finger as the waiter tried to mop up.

I licked my lips, then wiped them with my napkin. "Sorry, Ian."

He smiled. "My mother used to do that. Kiss and make it well."

"Is it a bad cut?" I asked, my eyes on the blood soaking into the napkin.

He laughed. "Not anymore. You made it well."

"Good." I sat back, trying to calm my racing heart. It had never occurred to me that I, too, could be a danger to those close to me. While I converted to a stricter vampire regimen, it might be wise to curtail my human social contacts.

Twenty

Doris was furious. "What is this, an epidemic!" she snapped. "Camilla last week, now Ed. Doesn't anyone take a read-through seriously anymore? On your deathbed, I want you here! On time! No excuses!"

Ed McNabb wasn't reliable when it came to learning his lines, but he was generally punctual. Therefore it was surprising when, ten minutes into the afternoon rehearsal, Ed still hadn't shown up. Camilla, Michael, Ian and I had all taken our places at the rehearsal table, scripts open, coffee at hand, ready to read.

I sneaked a look at Camilla, who had been on exceptionally good behavior. She'd probably been waiting to fully heal before attempting another attack. Claude had exercised his brilliance in covering her cuts and bruises, but the puffiness around her chin had to be concealed by ringlets and a high collar. Seeing Camilla almost contrite was a revelation, and a bit unnerving.

By the end of the week, when it was announced that Emmett Boardman's body had been found in the elevator shaft of his office building, I knew that Camilla had fully recovered. Apparently one doesn't end a romance with a witch by giving her dinner and an expensive piece of jewelry—and then expect to go on living. The fact that Camilla was prepared to snuff the life of a top talent agent made her retaliation all the more impressive. I took note.

Meanwhile, Doris was fuming. "Better call Ed's apartment," Doris barked to Donna Cruickshank, the production assistant. "We'll start the table read anyway. Nigel, read Ed's lines with Meg."

Michael and Camilla were already in the midst of reading the second scene when Donna returned. She stood in the doorway, waiting patiently for the scene to end.

"Well? Where is he?" Doris bellowed at her. "Why isn't he here?"

"Oh, he won't be coming in today," Donna said, in her desultory manner. "Ginny said he's feeding pigeons and won't come down."

"Down? What do you mean, down? Down to the studio?"

"Down from a ledge. He's been up there a while, I guess," Donna said vaguely. "Anything else you want me to do?"

"Paul! Where's Paul, for God's sake?" Doris jumped to her feet and hurried out of the rehearsal room.

"Take a break, everyone," Nigel said, brushing past Donna on his way out.

"What else, Donna?" Michael asked. "Besides feeding pigeons, what's he doing?"

"That's about it," Donna said, playing with a strand of her limp hair. "Ginny seemed pretty upset." She shrugged and returned to her desk.

Camilla laughed. "That beats everything!"

"Poor sod," Ian said. "He's obviously gone bonkers."

"Poor Ginny." Michael said. "I think this pretty much wraps it for the day. I'm going over there."

"Let's all go. I wouldn't miss it!" Camilla said.

We shared a taxi to Ed's apartment on Riverside Drive, arriving minutes after Paul, Doris and Nigel. Paramedics and a fire truck were already on the scene, with police cordoning off the area and restricting entry to the building. Paul and Doris managed to persuade a policeman guarding the door to let them in. Nigel and the rest of us were directed to an area across the street. We clustered on a grassy slope with a direct view of the McNabb's fifth-floor apartment. Ed was easily visible, barefoot and sitting on a ledge between two open windows. He appeared to be wearing nothing more than boxer shorts and a tee shirt despite the frigid air and darkening sky. He was holding a bottle of Piper-Heidsieck on his knee.

A small crowd had gathered, but Ed readily spotted us. He waved. We waved back. He swung his feet and waved again, then held the bottle up with both hands and took a sip of Champagne.

"He's going to fall!" I yelped.

"He doesn't care," Michael said. "As long as he's got an audience."

"Completely blotto. Even the pigeons are keeping their distance," Ian said. "Look."

Ed appeared to have a bag of seeds or crumbs in his lap. He tossed a handful onto the ledge, where a pigeon had landed. The bird stepped daintily back, watching warily. Suddenly Doris poked her head out a window and flapped her hands. The pigeon flew away, circled back and perched on the far side of Ed. He looked annoyed and waved the Champagne bottle at Doris.

"Go away," Ed shouted. "You're scaring off Sidney."

"Doris Franklin is not the emissary I would've chosen," Ian said. "Something lacking there in the empathy department."

Ginny appeared in the other window, clearly distraught, her hands cupped around her mouth. Her voice was faint, but she seemed to be imploring Ed to sit still. He looked around, then down. Police were setting up some sort of trampoline affair in case he jumped or fell. Ed waved, then scattered the contents of the paper bag on the emergency workers below, causing a battalion of pigeons to swoop in.

Paul appeared in the window next to Doris, his hands palms up in a placating gesture. Doris withdrew from the window. The two men talked back and forth for a minute, before Ed turned away and started whistling the theme from *Dark Passages*.

"He doesn't look unhappy," Camilla said. "What do you think he wants?"

"Not a hike in pay, certainly," Nigel said. "Generally this isn't an effective way to go about it."

"They're talking again," Michael said. "Paul's got his attention. Looks like he's offering him something."

Ed nodded his head, took a swig of Champagne and passed the bottle to Paul. Suddenly Ed shouted, "No! Help! Help!" With arms flailing, he appeared about to slip off the ledge as though he was being pushed.

I glanced at Camilla, who was staring intently up at Ed. I swung around facing her, blocking her line of vision. My eyes bored into hers, sapping her power to harm Ed. He remained on the ledge, catatonic and frozen in place as Camilla and I played out our radical game of chicken. The burn was intense, neither of us backing off. Suddenly she flinched and turned away.

I left my body and streaked up to Ed, who was already gripping the ledge, attempting to maneuver himself toward the window. In a flash I slid him toward the fireman, who threw a sling around his torso. Ed, tethered in a safety harness, was hauled back into the apartment.

Everyone clustering on the street applauded, including Camilla. "Nice work," she said, as I slipped back into my body. "And so effortless."

"Not much of a challenge," I replied.

"What are you two talking about?" Michael said. "That fireman saved his life. You know what kind of training goes into that?"

"Yes, quite impressive," Camilla said absently. "And quite unexpected."

"By the way," I said, "I'm so sorry to hear about Emmett Boardman. An accident?"

"That's what I hear. But then he was very depressed, poor man. *Quel dommage.*"

"Well, thank God Ed didn't kill himself," Nigel said. "I'm going to suggest you all go home and I'll call you later about the show tomorrow. I'm not quite sure how the powers that be will deal with this."

"I'm going to offer to stay with Ginny," I said. "She shouldn't be alone. I'm sure Ed will spend the night in the hospital."

"Or in custody. They won't just tuck him in bed, I can tell you that! I'm going to stick around and see how they handle this," Michael said, his voice tight. "Poor guy could use a helping hand." I figured Michael's compassion probably stemmed from personal experience spending a night in a drunk tank or psych ward.

No one was permitted to cross the street until Ed, strapped to a gurney, was loaded into an ambulance. Ginny climbed into the vehicle with him. Minutes later, with the siren blaring, the ambulance weaved around the other emergency vehicles and headed up Riverside Drive. By the time the five of us entered the building, Doris and Paul were already in the lobby.

"Okay, Sunday morning we do tomorrow's show out of sequence," Paul said, as we clustered around him. "Eight o'clock call. Sorry, everyone, but it's the only air time the network can give us. We'll have rehearsal tomorrow afternoon for the following day's show, and we'll go ahead with any wardrobe fittings scheduled. Remember, we go back in time again, so lots of special effects."

"What about Ed?" I asked.

"We'll know more later on. Meanwhile, Ginny has a sister in New Haven, who's coming to stay with her. Ed's just . . . let's say, exhausted."

"So, how did you get him down?" Nigel asked.

"The eye patch," Paul said. "I promised he could play a sea captain with an eye patch." He shrugged. "Maybe he goes down with a ship, comes back as a ghost. Who knows? Anyway, Nigel's going to check on Ed and we'll give you an update tomorrow at rehearsal. That's it. Excuse me, we've got a lot to sort out." Paul abruptly turned to Doris, and the two went in a far corner of the lobby to talk.

Michael jumped into a cab with Nigel to go to the hospital. Camilla waved goodbye and hurried off to hail a taxi on the corner.

"How about an early dinner?" Ian asked. "In your neighborhood, if you'd like."

"Thanks, but I have to see someone on the way home."

"I can drop you somewhere, if you want to share a cab."

"It's not on the way," I said, starting to walk up the street. "Thanks anyway, but you go ahead. I'm going to walk for a bit."

"Then I'll walk with you," Ian said. "You realize you'll soon be an orphan unless they come up with a replacement for Ed. I think we've seen the last of him. Anyway, it's a rum deal we lose our weekend."

"Can't be helped," I said. "They'd have to hire an actor or rewrite the script before tomorrow morning. I'm sure Paul and Horace will be up all night as it is. Anyway, you had plans?"

"I was going to my place in Connecticut. It's on the shore. You'll have to come up with me sometime."

"Sure," I said, "sounds good."

"You don't mean it, do you? Look, I did apologize, you know. Are you avoiding me for any reason?"

"Of course not, Ian." I stopped and turned to him. His eyes were anxious and I gave him a reassuring smile. "Why would I?"

"Good. Glad to hear it." Looking relieved, he said, "Right, then, I'm off. See you tomorrow afternoon."

He hurried into the street and hailed a taxi, waving to me as he got in. I waved back and waited until the cab rounded the corner. I didn't want to hurt Ian's feelings, but it was safer for both of us if I kept my distance. I was on my guard because of Camilla, and I was also feeding again, building up my strength. I couldn't be sure I could restrain my hunger and didn't want to take chances.

I streaked home by way of Central Park, my best hunting ground. I fed on rabbit with a side of vole and made my way back to Gramercy Park. Before I'd even slipped out of my coat, I called my answering service. The operator on duty breathed relief when she heard my voice. "Glad you checked in," she said. "There are eight messages, most marked urgent."

Marilyn had called to say I had been missed at the funeral and that she'd included some news clippings about Eric in her letter. The other seven calls, all marked urgent, were from Savannah, Noni, Allie, Jolly, Elke, Gloria and Audrey, the Bunny Mother. I called Savannah.

The moment she heard my voice, Savannah asked, "Have you talked with anyone else yet?"

"No. What's up?"

"Sit down and hold your hat. We just found out why Cheri quit the Club on such short notice. By the way, that's not her name. Her real name is Leslie Chase, and she's a writer. She's written some sort of exposé in a magazine called *Show Biz* that—get this!—her new husband started up. He's some incredibly rich schmuck in the garment industry that Gloria went out with once—but that's another story—who launched this publication that just sort of rats out people. So guess who she ratted on?"

"Me," I said, weakly.

"Us," Savannah said. "She didn't miss one of us, and all of it written in some holier-than-thou way that makes me want to puke!"

"It's out? People can read it?"

"You bet. Playboy has already dispatched Allie to do damage control. She's on David Susskind's show tomorrow night. They might even get her on with Johnny Carson this week. We're all at my place, if you want to come down here. I've got a copy of the magazine. And a bottle of wine open."

"That's okay. I'll go to the newsstand up the street. It's bad?"

"You won't like it. Sorry, Meg, she even wrote about some guy slipping you LSD at a party. Why didn't you tell me about that?"

"No one knew! How did she find out?"

"So it's true! She doesn't name a source, but someone had to tell her. Leslie even mentions the guy's name and some ad agency, so maybe he'll lose his job and sue her. Serves them both right! Call me when you've read it, okay?"

"Sure," I said, and hung up the phone. I headed back out the door, dread engulfing me as I walked to the newsagent. No one knew about that LSD trip except Ian. He'd even tangled with the ad man and knew his name and address. How could Ian be so stupid as to tell anyone about it? For that matter, how did he know Leslie "Bunny Cheri" Chase?

The magazine, a large-format publication the size of *Life*, was on the rack and cost more than I cared to pay. My stomach took an elevator ride when I saw the cover headline: *Inside Playboy's Bunny Hutch.* To fortify myself for the ordeal ahead, I drained my wallet to buy a pack of red licorice.

The first thing that hit me after I sank back on my daybed and read the article was that Leslie Chase had known she was going to write this sort of story when she took the job as Bunny Cheri. She was always snapping pictures with her Brownie, always asking questions. The second thing that crossed my mind is that the folks back in Twin Lakes were hardly likely to come across a copy of *Show Biz.* But Marilyn would, and it was only a matter of time before my parents, and Eddie, heard about it.

Indeed, Cheri hadn't missed a thing. I covered my face with my hands and let it all sink in. The most personally damaging information about me was her allegation that I'd tripped on LSD at a wild party with a well-known advertising executive, and her disclosure that I was Bunny Meg, who invariably arrived late for work and left early because of a starring role on the afternoon soap *Dark Passages.*

Surely someone at the network, if not Paul Abbott or Horace Milton, would be reading *Inside Playboy's Bunny Hutch.* Even though I'd been identified only as Bunny Meg, it was easy to peg me as the actress on *Dark Passages*. Was I in violation of some moral's clause in my contract? There was a good chance taking drugs was prohibited, if not moonlighting in a job involving serving cocktails while practically naked. I wracked my brains trying to recall if the adman's agency represented Hazel Bishop lipstick, Dreft soap powder or any of our other sponsors—that would be the death knell.

I'd probably be hearing from Wesley Truscott soon enough, asking me why in the world I would gamble a promising acting career to work as a Playboy Bunny. *Oh, and by the way, Mr. Truscott, I'm also pregnant, unmarried and unlikely to be able to conceal my belly for more than a couple of weeks.* Was there any point in putting another bullet in the chamber? What she had written was bad enough, but at least Leslie Chase hadn't known about Eric, or that I was pregnant.

Much of what "Bunny Cheri" disclosed fell into categories of embarrassing and silly, portraying other Bunnies as ditzy dumbbells with nothing more on their minds than clothes and marrying a wealthy man. Leslie Chase, having secured both designer clothes and a rich husband in a single package, had used the forum she'd married into as a means of skewering the women she'd worked with at the Club, which all stank of hypocrisy in my book. That she did so, while at the same time touting her tip average and divulging that she had no need to pad her breasts in the Bunny costume, also indicated a case of rampant narcissism. To rub salt in the wounds, I realized some of the snapshots of Bunny Cheri illustrating the article had been taken by me using her Brownie flash camera.

Leslie wrote about our adventure with the Wilmark detective, which was amusing, but she'd also quoted Rocco Bennetti referring to Garrison Schuyler Haddock as my "sugar daddy," which was not funny. According to Leslie, I'd been replaced as her Training Bunny because of repeated instances of tardiness and such alleged offences as "mingling" and "fraternizing." Gloria had been a great source of quotes about the after-hours parties—and some of Leslie's most villainous allegations were that a few Bunnies (Gloria among them) relied on drugs and alcohol to get them through a shift, and that several "dated" customers after hours. We'd all been tarred by innuendo.

I was too tired to cry, too wound up to think straight. I reached into my bag for the handful of fan letters I'd taken home from the studio and read a few while eating my red licorice. A letter from a girl in Florida read:

Dear Miss Harrison, I really like you on Dark Passages *because you are so pretty and don't take guff. My dad drinks and gets mean and we have to move house a lot. I would like to come and live with you.*

A boy in Ohio wrote:

The school bus is always late so we always miss at least five minutes. Could you please start the show later at our house so my sister and me can see it? Please send a picture.

A schoolteacher in Iowa wrote:

While the kids race home to watch, we always tune the TV set in the teachers' lounge to Dark Passages *at 4 P.M. Perfect timing for a perfect escape—thank you! Your plot line is a direct steal from Jane Eyre and thoroughly enjoyable. Best regards.*

What would any of them think if they happened to read the current issue of *Show Biz*? Finally I shed a few tears. Everything that seemed to have a purpose in my life was on the line. Everything had consequence. I'd have to go to the studio in the morning to talk with Paul Abbott in person. I really had no choice but to meet with Wesley Truscott. I would also have to confront Ian. How could he have betrayed me like this?

I was just stuffing the last of the licorice in my mouth when I detected a hazy presence near the French doors. "Haddie? Is that you? Listen, I'm sorry, okay? My mother said I took advantage of you, and I apologize for that. Do you want to come in?"

"No need to apologize," he said, looking a little less hazy. "Just thought I'd drop by and check up on you. Everything okay?"

"You know it's not. Have you got more bad news?"

"Just a thought. Camilla—"

"I know. She tried to wipe out poor Ed, but I got the best of her. Really, Haddie, I don't think she's all that powerful up against me."

"Minor skirmishes designed to test you. She's reconnoitering, still sizing you up. Camilla is looking for your weaknesses."

"But I've beaten her every time! What weakness could I have?"

"Compassion."

"That's a weakness? How do I get rid of it?"

"I don't think you can," Haddie said with some regret. "Curb your hubris . . . and stay vigilant. Remember the consequences when Camilla learned about Eric. You, and anyone close to you, will be in danger. You must prepare for battle." Haddie began to fade away, his voice a whisper. "To destroy her, you must be ruthless."

Had Camilla used Leslie Chase as an instrument to destroy me, too? There was a chance that in the course of the following day, I would lose my role on *Dark Passages*, my Bunny job, my agent and my friendship with Ian.

Twenty-one

I meant to begin my day of atonement with a brisk walk to the studio and a stop in Central Park to tank up. I also promised myself that if Ian invited me for dinner, I would decline. But he telephoned, catching me off guard early that morning as I stepped out of the shower.

"Listen, I'm dropping by the National Arts Club this evening to see a friend's exhibit. I thought you might like to walk over and join me. Seven o'clock? It's just down the street from you."

"Oh, I know where it is, but—"

"You see? You are avoiding me, aren't you?"

"No, Ian, of course not, but I'm working tomorrow, and—"

"Say no more, Meg. See you tonight."

Where was my resolve? But at least I would have a chance to find out if Ian had spoken to Leslie Chase. I also intended to drop by the Club to tell Audrey I was turning in my resignation. After that, I'd see Wesley Truscott and casually mention I'd quit my Bunny job—as though my agent had always known I worked as a Playboy Bunny. I wasn't looking forward to any of it. But the meeting I most dreaded was the one with Paul Abbott, and I wanted to get it out of the way before I lost my nerve.

After a brisk walk and quick feed in the Park, I arrived at the studio and went straight to the production office. Paul's door was ajar. Donna was nowhere around. I knocked once and stuck my head around the door.

Paul was lying back at a dangerous angle in his swivel chair, his massive shoulders bulging against the black leather head rest. His mouth hung open, and his legs were splayed across his desk, with his pants legs crumpled above the tops of his socks. He was wearing the same clothes he'd worn the day before and looked terrible. I wished I hadn't knocked. I was about to retreat, but Paul's eyes had already popped open.

In one seismic movement, the seat back thundered forward, his legs swung to the floor and he sat bolt upright. He rubbed his face and made some smacking sounds with his mouth, then looked at me through bleary eyes. "A little early for rehearsal, aren't you? What's up?"

"Sorry, didn't mean to disturb you. I didn't see Donna around. Can I get you some coffee?"

"Yeah. See if there's some Danish out there."

I poured two mugs of coffee and set them on a tray with packets of sugar, creamers, stirrers, napkins and a couple of cheese Danish. Then I breathed slowly until my heart stopped pounding and carried the tray into Paul's office. He'd somewhat pulled himself together, but still looked like a heavyweight contender down for the count.

"What's happening with Ed?" I asked, assuming that's why Paul had been up all night.

"You worried about him? That's why you're here?" He scowled and hunched his shoulders. "Who knows? They're keeping him for observation. Horace and I did some rewrites last night. We're going back to the 1790s anyway, so we can lose him without much trouble." He stirred creamer into his coffee and took a sip. "Nothing's definite. Keep mum. Understood?"

"Got it. I won't say a word. Listen, there's something I wanted to mention. You know, when I was first hired—"

"Yeah, you were the waitress. Now you're the governess. A ghost sometimes, to help us out. You're Lady Fairfax starting tomorrow. You got a contract that pays by the show, not the role. No extra dough for extra roles, got it?" he asked gruffly. "You here to angle for a raise or something?"

"No! That's not what I was going to say."

"Glad to hear it. You know, you're a good little actress, and getting better. You got a long career ahead, if you want it. Meanwhile, this is a great launch pad, so don't get carried away, okay?" He grimaced, which I took for a smile. "You want to change your name again?"

I laughed. "No, that's not it, either. The thing is, I was working this other job before *Dark Passages*, and to be on the safe side, until I knew for sure the show would take off—."

"Whoa, the Bunny job? Listen, I flipped burgers at White Castle and sold encyclopedias until I got a job in the mailroom at the network. You do what you gotta do."

"You knew? You didn't say anything."

"My accountant's a key holder. He mentioned seeing you there a couple weeks ago. I have to hand it to you, kid, you got some class. A lot of girls would be bragging they were Playboy Bunnies, and getting by on their looks, but not you. Tell me, you ever meet Hef?"

"No. He lives in Chicago." I slid my copy of *Show Biz* across his desk. "What I wanted to say is that a lot of people are going to know about my Bunny job because of this article. Did you happen to see this?"

"No. Pretty impressive magazine. Can you leave it with me? Maybe the PR woman over at the network could make some hay out of this. We could use a little more press." He settled back in his chair, sipped his coffee and smacked his lips some more. "Good work, Meg. How's everything else? Anything I should know?"

"No, that's pretty much it. Nothing else."

"Good, because I don't need more crap, you know? I got a guy likes to sit on a ledge feeding pigeons in his underwear. Then I got another guy likes to get drunk and give himself a Mohawk haircut. Thanks to him, we gotta do today's show on Sunday. Expensive and a big pain in the butt. By the way, Michael told me you took him in the other night and got him to the studio. You deserve a lot of credit for that, Meg, but you gotta be more careful. You don't know what a guy's gonna do when he's in that condition." He gave me a fierce look, then yawned. "Hey, you going to drink your coffee?"

"No. You want it?" I slid my untouched mug of coffee and cheese Danish across the desk.

"Anything like that happens again, you call me. Got it?" Paul picked up the slab of pastry, shoved a chunk in his mouth and washed it down with a swallow of coffee. "I mean it. No more taking in drunks."

"Got it," I said. "See you at rehearsal."

"Tell Donna to let Lucy know you're here. You might as well get yourself into wardrobe so that's out of the way."

"Sure thing." I left Paul's office as fast as I could. Since I'd resolved to come clean about everything, I didn't trust myself not to say something about being pregnant. It was better to quit while I was ahead. On the other hand, maybe he'd decide my pregnancy was a boon to the show, too! Who knew what he'd think after reading *Inside the Bunny Hutch*. The LSD episode alone could send him around the bend.

Donna was back at her desk, engrossed in filing her nails, so I didn't bother her.

Lucy, wearing her customary bib apron with deep pockets over a baggy sweater and skirt, was shuffling through a rack of empire-waist frocks in the back of the wardrobe room. Her face brightened when she saw me. "Oh, good. I wish everyone was as conscientious as you. Mind if we do a fitting in here instead of your dressing room?"

"Fine with me."

It was fine with me as long as Lucy didn't see me in my underwear. For rehearsals I'd taken to wearing loose shirts and peasant blouses over my blue jeans. No one seemed to take notice of any change in my appearance, but it was only a matter of time. My shape was altering by the day. I could only hope the plot line would keep us in 1790s costumes as long as possible. The empire silhouette would not only conceal my thickening waist, but make the most of my swelling breasts.

I slipped in between the racks and quickly pulled one of the gowns over my head, praying my bosom wouldn't strain the thin batiste top. I yanked my blue jeans down around my ankles and glanced in the full-length mirror. With horror, I saw my worst fears realized. The narrow shoulders barely fit me, the bodice not at all. The back gaped open a good six inches.

"Oh, dear! Sorry!" Lucy laughed, looking at me in the mirror. "I gave you one of Ginny's dresses by mistake!"

I laughed, too, with a giddiness that bordered on hysteria. I quickly shed the sheer batiste daytime dress and donned a more substantial traveling ensemble in mauve crepe, the outfit Lady Gwyneth Fairfax would wear for her arrival at the Stanhope estate.

"Perfect!" Lucy said. "Don't gain an ounce. Just let me shorten the sleeves a bit."

I also tried on several flowing peignoir outfits, choosing the fullest, fluffiest, most beribboned for my scenes with Camilla. The peignoir was so voluminous, my swelling belly would be completely camouflaged by the masses of ruffles.

The best news about going back in time, apart from the glorious costumes, was the decision to have Camilla play Lady Gwyneth Fairfax's maid, the role of Didi Smythe. Horace and Paul had included an overview of the 1790s story line with the new script rewrites, and Camilla's role had changed drastically. I suspected the plan wouldn't go down well with Camilla, who still had her hopes pinned on playing a role more on the lines of Madame du Barry.

As soon as Lucy finished fitting my wardrobe, I hightailed it to the Playboy Club to tell Audrey I was quitting. The lunch shift Bunnies were already down on the floor working when I arrived. No one was in the dressing room, except Betty, the seamstress. "Look out," she whispered when she saw me. "Audrey's on the warpath. She's been screaming at everyone all morning."

I found the Bunny Mother in her office, her eyes red-rimmed and swollen. A copy of *Show Biz* lay open on her desk. Audrey gave me a sour look. "You gals got away with murder, you know that? Whaddya think the State Liquor Authority's gonna make of this? And whose job you think is on the line, here? You're the ones running amok, and I'm the one that gets blamed!" She slammed her hand on the desk. "I'm taking the fall because I hired Cheri! Why didn't one of you say something! You had to know!"

I shook my head. "No, Audrey, I didn't. I mean, look at what she wrote about me. I had no idea."

"You should all be fired, every damn one of you!"

"Then fire me, Audrey. I think you should. If you don't, I'm going to quit. I mean it. I'm turning in my ears for keeps. Today. Right now."

She stared at me in shock, then screamed, "The hell you will! Easy for you to say when you've got a TV show! Oh, no, you're not walking out on me."

"But I can't work Saturday night. We have to redo a show on Sunday and I have an early call. I think it's better if I just quit."

"You can't! Absolutely not!" She was coming unhinged, her voice cracking with strain. "Savannah and Elke are leaving—to open some bakery, for God's sake! And Jolly is leaving for grad school. Allie turned in her notice. What am I going to do? At least stay through Thanksgiving until I can get some new girls trained," she pleaded. "Please. Don't do this to me."

"Thanksgiving, okay. I'll stay through Thanksgiving."

"You're a doll, Meg. It's means a lot." She looked as if she might start to cry. She reached for a tissue and blew her nose. "One thing, though," she said, her voice steely again as I was leaving her office. "Better lay off the French fries and malts for a while. You're starting to pork up."

"Righto!" I said, and hurried toward the elevator. I was pretty sure Audrey was completely nuts. It was better to stay on good terms with her. The day might come when I had to ask if I could work the Club's switchboard just to make ends meet.

Next stop: Wesley Truscott's office. "Well, you're a sly one," he said when he saw me.

"You saw the article?"

"Not yet, but Paul Abbot called and told me about it. I see you didn't bring me a copy."

"Sorry. Is Paul upset?"

"Hardly." Wesley peered at me over his gold-framed bifocals and raised an eyebrow. "Amused, I'd say. A little notoriety never hurts. I believe our Mr. Abbott is more concerned that you might want to hit him up for a pay raise. You're becoming quite the darling, according to my mole at the network—and, clever girl, you did yourself a big favor latching on to this new role. Onward and upward, my dear!"

"Thanks, Wesley. I would've mentioned the Bunny job, but it didn't seem important—"

"I must say it comes as something of a surprise. A bit more risqué than I would have pegged you for, but it's quite the 'in' place, right? Second only to the Peppermint Lounge, I hear, where Greta Garbo goes and does the Twist!" Wesley shifted his shoulders back and forth and made a gleeful face to show me he knew what the Twist was all about.

I laughed. "Believe me, Greta Garbo has never been to the Playboy Club!"

"What a shame. So that's it?" Wesley asked. "No more news? I do love a good gossip!"

"That's it," I said. Once again I'd dodged the bullet.

I arrived at the studio to find the cast already assembled for the afternoon read-through. I could feel the tension the moment I walked in and took my place at the table.

Horace had been summoned, and he rarely showed up at rehearsals any more. Camilla wasn't the only one sulking about the twist in her role. Maxwell looked mutinous, and Moira was wearing her Joan-of-Arc-at-the-stake face. Doris was drumming her fingers, exasperated. No one appeared to like the direction the story line was taking, except me.

"Role reversal, don't you see?" Horace said to Camilla. "Didi is jealous and does everything to undermine Lady Fairfax. And, growing up in this remote English village, she's dabbled in the black arts, learned a bit of sorcery."

"Not what I'd expected," Camilla mumbled, her face stiff with fury. Camilla clearly resented playing my maid, and wearing a plain muslin dress with a mobcap covering her blonde hair. I also suspected she wasn't thrilled to be playing Horace's notion of a witch.

"Well, at least they aren't putting you in a peaked cap and giving you a broomstick," Moira said. "Honestly, this really is the limit, Horace."

"It was Paul's idea, and I think quite a good one. Witchcraft was a big thing back then. Folks were uneducated and superstitious."

I glanced at Camilla to see how Horace's comments about witchcraft were going down. Not well, by the furious look on her face.

"For God's sake, man. You'll be introducing werewolves next!"

"Thank you, Maxwell," Horace said. "Great idea. I'll tell Paul we should consider that for your character."

"I'm not dressing up in a fur suit with paws!" Maxwell sputtered. "Where is Paul, anyway?"

"Wiped out. Went home," Doris said. "Is there any chance we can get on with this rehearsal so we can all go home?"

"Wait a minute. Maybe Didi attracts the eye of some wealthy landowner?" Camilla suggested. "And marries well?"

"Could be, could be," Horace said. "It's an idea. Could we just read the script through? I think you'll see it works."

Despite all the carping, the script was well written. There was no time for drastic changes, anyway. As much as she hated the idea, Camilla, playing Didi, my lady's maid, would be entering three steps behind me, carrying my hatbox and vanity case when we made our first appearance at the Stanhope estate. But by the time we finished the reading, Camilla, against all odds, had done a complete about-face and taken a liking to playing Didi Symthe.

"A delicious role!" she exclaimed, beaming at Horace. "You're quite right. I see the potential." She flashed a smile at me. "We're going to have such fun!"

Alarm bells sounded. *Fun?* The word had an unpleasant ring to it. Fun to Camilla could only mean something totally unpleasant for me.

"Wonderful!" Horace exclaimed. "You see? I think we'll all have some fun with this."

"Ready for more fun?" Doris said. "I've got some cuts and then we can all go home."

By the time I reached Gramercy Park, it was already dark. As I turned the corner, I saw Ian standing outside the National Arts Club. He waved and started walking toward me.

"It's not much of an exhibit," Ian said. "How about joining me for a burger around the corner?"

"Wait, first I have to ask you something. Do you know anyone named Leslie Chase? Or did you ever tell anyone about me and that man in Murray Hill?"

"No, on both counts. I don't know anyone named Leslie Chase. And I would never dream of saying a word to anyone about that night. It's just between us. Why do you ask?"

It wasn't just the look of alarm on Ian's face that told me he was telling the truth. I was also swayed by his clear concern for me. I believed him. "Let's eat and I'll tell you. In fact, let's stop at the newsstand first."

My Day of Atonement had gone surprisingly well—but as far as my resolve was concerned, I was a complete washout. I also realized how happy I'd been to find Ian waiting for me.

Twenty-two

Even though *Dark Passages' Governess Moonlights As Bunny* appeared boldface in Earl Wilson's syndicated *New York Post* column, I doubted anyone in Twin Lakes would ever see it. For the most part, the fallout from *Inside the Bunny Hutch* turned out to be more positive than negative, especially among my cast mates. Camilla, who'd taunted me about working as a Bunny, seethed with jealousy at my unexpected notoriety. I suspected she was somehow responsible for supplying Leslie Chase with information about the adman. If so, her meddling had backfired. Meanwhile, I basked in my new celebrity, happily responding to everyone's curiosity about the Playboy Club.

My "It Girl" status at the studio was all too brief, quickly overshadowed by news that Moira Shaw had flown with Ginny to Juárez, Mexico. Moira, who had had some experience in this area, had offered to shepherd Ginny through a quickie divorce from Ed McNabb. The one-day divorce proceedings culminated in a celebratory meal of enchiladas and margaritas before an overnight flight back to New York. Unfortunately, the feast took its toll. Ginny managed to shed a husband and catch Montezuma's Revenge almost simultaneously.

"Not a good trip home," Moira said, looking a bit under the weather herself. "I was more nursemaid than hand-holder. But at least Ed out of the picture."

In fact, as Ian had predicted, Ed was finito in terms of his presence in the new story line. His demise was so abrupt that he didn't so much die as vanish. There was no sign of him in the revised 1790s plot overview. Michael, witnessing just how effectively a troublesome actor could be dispatched from the show, quickly cleaned up his act. His sponsor appeared at the studio door after rehearsals each day and the two trudged off together to the nearest church hall AA meeting. I took notice, too, and was glad I'd had the sense not to mention my own predicament.

The only people who knew I was pregnant were my mother, Haddie and Dr. Ted Robinson; a vampire, a ghost and Allie's boyfriend. I felt my secret was safe until anyone with a pair of eyes could plainly see the truth.

I also knew I was traveling two parallel courses: preparing for the birth of my baby, and readying myself for the inevitable battle with Camilla. Oddly enough, she'd become a joy to work with, a skilled actress who electrified every scene we played together. We'd had a few brief scenes together when she first joined the show, but the characters we played in the present time had never really engaged with each other. In our 1790s roles, Camilla's displeasure at playing my lady's maid colored her portrayal of DiDi Smythe and mirrored the undercurrents in our own relationship.

Horace had sensed the dynamic between us and created a powerful story line: Lady Fairfax and her maid, a witch, had become rivals for the affection of vampire Sebastian Stanhope. The witch's curse had condemned Sebastian to an undead existence of perfidy and unrequited love. The warped eternal triangle presented a grim irony that was apparent to Camilla and me, but entirely lost on Ian.

For his part, Ian had become a matinee idol in the truest sense; he ruled afternoon television viewing. Lovesick women across the country swooned over vampire Sebastian Stanhope, and our ratings soared. To her sorority sisters, Marilyn had become a celebrity in her own right just because she knew me and could procure personally signed eight-by-ten glossies of Sebastian. As the fiancée of the vampire, I had my own devoted following, as did Camilla, the evil sorceress, but Ian was hands-down the breakout star of the show. He'd also accomplished this feat on his own terms. He had indeed become the "best vampire he could be," one who reluctantly fed on the blood of innocent victims and felt guilt.

Ian had pretty much got used to playing a vampire, but there were still things that made him queasy. Most of those bits seemed to involve me. Looking fearsome, swinging his cape across his shoulders on his midnight prowls, came easily to him. He'd done his stint in British rep, wearing tights and shirts with billowing sleeves, so flourishing his wolf's head cane and speaking in a thundering voice came naturally to him. But biting me seemed to bring on panic attacks.

Even in rehearsal, when we were only marking the moves, he'd invariably ask, his voice husky with concern, "Did I hurt you? Please, you must tell me."

"No! Stop asking," I'd hiss. "Just bite with conviction. If you don't scrape your fangs on my cheek, I'm fine."

"You're getting upset with me."

"I'm not! Sorry, but we're supposed to be acting."

Actually, the biggest problem was coordinating the camera work. Ian had to duck his head and slip the fangs on while the camera remained on me, sleeping Hollywood-style in full makeup and towering hairpieces. Once his fangs were in place, a second camera would cut to Ian in close up, his head drawn back so his incisors caught the key light before he buried his face in my neck. So far, it had all been a big tease. Lady Fairfax hadn't actually been bitten because Sebastian couldn't bring himself to condemn the love of his life to an eternity as damned as his own.

The scene itself was the very essence of dramatic bodice-ripping romance. Lady Fairfax, her skin alabaster in the moonlight, sleeps serenely in her massive four-poster bed. The camera picks up the gauzy flutter of draperies as French doors slowly swing open to reveal a caped figure standing in a wash of blue-tinged moonlight. In close up, Sebastian gazes longingly at Lady Fairfax.

Slowly he crosses to her bed, flinging his cape over his shoulder. He brushes her cheek lightly with his fingertips. She's aroused by his touch. Her eyelids flicker and her lips gently quiver. He curls a ringlet of her hair on his finger, his massive signet ring glittering against her naked shoulder. He draws his hand under her chin, turning her face to expose her neck. She moves restlessly on the pillow, a troubled look creasing her brow. Her head begins to lift, her lips parting as though yearning to be kissed. At that moment, the camera cuts to the terrible gleaming teeth before Sebastian's head plunges to her neck and the music swells.

The sexual implications were none too subtle. Schoolchildren saw the scary specter of blood and gore, but their mothers could fantasize about dark, brooding strangers with bloodlust in their hearts and redemption in their souls. It was a powerful combination, and the ambiguity in Ian's portrayal practically begged a woman's sympathetic understanding—and at a decent time of day. The show broadcast in late afternoon when the house was cleaned, the children were home from school, the dinner was in the oven and a husband was still a commuter-journey away. A half-hour of time travel to a place of forbidden love and intrigue was a welcome diversion. *Dark Passages* had found its audience base.

For me, there was considerably less romance and intrigue on the set. During a commercial break, Ian would remove his fangs, apologize profusely for spittle that had dripped on my neck and extravagantly mop it up with his handkerchief. I would assure him saliva forming on his fangs was perfectly natural and ask him not to muss my hair. Back on camera after the commercial break, I would make small whimpering sounds as Sebastian lifted his head, his fangs now fully retracted. He'd gaze mournfully into camera with the eyes of a man condemned to yearn for eternal love that could only come at a terrible price. Lady Fairfax, still asleep on her lacy pillow, had been spared once again.

We'd had only one major mishap during an on-air show when Ian's fangs had snagged on my ringlets. During the commercial break, he couldn't manage to tug the bridgework loose and had to abandon his fangs in my wig. He piled several ringlets on top of the teeth just before the commercial break ended, and by the time we were back on camera again the fangs were completely hidden from view. Madge, the hairdresser, had to be called on set with scissors to cut them loose after the air show was completed.

But mishaps aside, the scene was so effective that we played versions of it in three separate episodes, two of them as flashbacks. Soap opera magazines, and even a few big-city television critics, had picked up the story of the First Reluctant Vampire, Sebastian Stanhope of *Dark Passages*. Thanks to the network's publicity division, the fact that the aristocratic Lady Fairfax, the lovelorn vampire's fiancée, was played by Meg Harrison, moonlighting as a Playboy Bunny, always managed to find its way into these articles—as did the intriguing tidbit that Camilla Nesbitt, the conniving lady's maid, had once dated Elvis Presley. Our ratings soared after the launch of the 1790s story line, and the network was ecstatic.

So was Paul Abbott. It seemed he'd always harbored a yen to direct. On several occasions, Paul had taken the reins, with Doris standing by as his mentor. It was soon clear that Paul had found his true calling; he quickly mastered the rudimentary skills and jargon, and was fearless in uncorking his creative juices. Working with Paul was wonderful. He was inventive, encouraging and knew instinctively how to bring out the best in each actor. Doris, who was one of the first women television directors and had won prestigious awards in the heyday of live broadcast, doted on Paul as though he were her prize puppy. He, in turn, lapped up her lavish praise.

One afternoon, following the read-through of another episode he was directing, Paul announced that he and Horace had collaborated on a feature-length version of *Dark Passages* that he intended to direct. Like a kid with a new kite, he bubbled with enthusiasm. "If I can get a budget together, we'll go into production in the spring," he said. "We've got a great story, a great platform. Can't miss!"

There was a moment of stunned silence at the rehearsal table before Moira drawled, "Well, that's marvelous, Paul, but your cast will be busy doing the series. Tell me, who do you imagine will be playing me?"

"You!" Paul said. "Who else would play your role, Moira?"

"And me?" Maxwell asked.

"You'll all be in the movie!" Paul said. "We'll all be doing double duty. It'll be a logistics nightmare, but the only way it'll work is if we continue to do the series while shooting the film. We're a ratings bonanza for the network, so there's no chance they'd let us shut down for two seconds. We gotta work around the daily show." Paul swung his arm around my shoulders and squeezed. "Of course Meg and Ian, our star-crossed lovers, will carry the full brunt of this production, but they're certainly up to it. Right, Meg?"

"Absolutely. I can't wait," I said, finding just enough breath to speak. Squeezed in Paul's vise-like grip, I was caught between rapture and desperation. I was being offered a lead role in my first feature film, while at the same time knowing I couldn't do it. I'd be giving birth about the time production would begin. I'd have no choice now but to tell both Paul and Wesley Truscott that I was pregnant.

"And am I in it, too?" Camilla asked, a pout clouding her face.

"Of course! We need our beautiful vixen, Charmaine. Couldn't do this without you, Camilla."

"Well, I must say this comes as quite a surprise," Moira said, looking perplexed. "I assume our agents will be approached? Surely this won't be an extension of our soap contracts."

"All in good time," Paul said, an edge to his voice. "I should also tell you, and you may want to pass this along to your representatives, that this is a strictly low-budget production, scale-plus-ten percent. You want to come on board, you're welcome, but we're not going Hollywood with a big studio backing us. At least not this time around."

"And the story line," Ian said, his face stony. "Blood, gore and a stake through the heart, I presume."

Paul laughed. "Look, it's a horror film with a vampire. Sure, blood and gore, but I promise, no stake in the heart. Not if we're looking to do a sequel!"

Everyone laughed, except Ian. "What sort of message is that," Ian asked quietly. "A hero with blood lust. A killer with token remorse, who goes on to kill again."

"I'm not Western Union," Paul bellowed, still trying to sound jovial. "No message. Just entertainment. People eat it up. It's written that you feel bad about it, okay? You hate chomping on people's necks, but you can't help it because the witch, here, cursed you. You can't spend the whole movie moping around about it because that's boring. So maybe we undo the curse in a sequel, but in this one there's blood. Lots of it. And teeth!"

Maxwell laughed and Moira rolled her eyes. "So it's come to this," she sighed. "Back on the silver screen in a horror movie. But I'm absolutely drawing the line at anything featuring dinosaurs or Martians."

"Exactly," Maxwell echoed. "Togas and sandals, okay. Space suits or anything scaly is out."

"What's with all of you? We're not doing *War and Peace* here, folks. That's not what gets kids running home from school to watch. And no housewife is going to turn off her vacuum cleaner to watch some boring high-hat crap, either. We got a hit on our hands, folks, so let's make the most of it!"

Throughout Paul's rant, I'd stared hard at Ian, hoping he'd come to his senses. He was about to talk himself out of a lead role, a hugely popular one that he'd created and made his own. I couldn't let him do it. "Ian, just be the best vampire you can be. That's the message. You're the reluctant vampire and everyone sympathizes with you."

"There!" Paul exclaimed, giving my shoulders another squeeze. "Couldn't have said it better myself! Okay, let's get down to work here."

Paul loosened his grip on my shoulder and I reached for Ian's hand. "It's a great opportunity, Ian," I whispered. "You'll be super!"

"As long as I'm working with you," he said under his breath. "But I still don't like it."

Somehow it was entirely lost on Ian that people empathized with the unique character he'd created because they had their own demons and weaknesses to overcome. If there was a message he was sending, it was one of courage in the face of insurmountable odds.

I glanced at Camilla and caught her staring at Ian holding my hand. She looked up at me, her eyes venomous, then turned away. Also lost on Ian was Camilla's growing jealousy of his affection for me. Ian was unfailingly warm and friendly toward Camilla, but his fondness for me was becoming increasingly apparent. I knew it was a volatile situation, but despite my resolve to keep Ian at a distance for his own safety, we continued to see each other. We had fun together. When I was with him I relaxed, but I also recognized how dangerous that was for both of us.

I had to be more cautious. I let go of his hand.

Twenty-three

Despite a schedule of up to four shows a week at the studio, I was still working at the Club. I'd promised Audrey I would help her out at least until Thanksgiving and I kept my word. When she called on a Friday morning to ask if I could work the lunch shift, I agreed, since I wasn't working at the studio that day.

Before leaving for the Club, I checked my mailbox and found two plump envelopes, one from my mother, the other from Marilyn. There was also a long-delayed letter from Eric, surely the last he'd written to me before his death. It was a cold November morning, but I walked across the street and sat on a bench in the park before opening the envelope and removing the single sheet of familiar blue paper.

My eyes dropped to his signature, "Love, E." Below it he had scrawled, "Miss you, need you." It was the shortest letter I'd received from him, its very brevity on the flimsy onionskin paper making me ache with longing. He was tired and needed sack time, he wrote. Eric and a buddy from Ohio were looking forward to seeing Saigon on the weekend.

I wish sometimes that you could be with me, flying low over the treetops in this Garden Spot, but I wouldn't want you to see what we have to do. We don't leave it as pretty as we found it. I think of you a whole lot, so you take care of yourself. Love, E.

I read the words again and again. Eric's voice was in my ears, his name on my lips. I could not let him go. At odd times, I'd feel the sharp pain of longing and a penetrating sadness, then hold myself very still, hanging on to that feeling of loss. I feared the day when those terrible feelings would no longer visit me. That's when I really would lose Eric.

I folded the letter back in its envelope and tucked it in my bag with the thick packets from Marilyn and my mother. Reading about the funeral and looking at the news clippings could wait until I was back home, alone in my apartment.

When I arrived at the Club, the dressing room was buzzing with the news that Noni had been hired for a weekend gig at a downtown jazz club. Allie and Elke were organizing a group of Bunnies to attend. Allie tacked a notice on the bulletin board with a sign-up sheet for the first and second shows on Saturday night. Savannah had used Playboy's mimeograph machine to print flyers that Bunnies could pass out to the lunch customers. I signed up and took the handful of folded flyers Savannah gave me and we all headed for the elevator.

"You've been a stranger lately," Savannah said. "You don't like my cooking anymore?"

"Sorry, I've been working at the studio a lot. But I'll try to come down and help out. How's the bakery coming along?"

"Great," Elke said. "The grand opening is the weekend after Thanksgiving."

"We want to get a lot of Christmas cookie and strudel orders," Savannah said. "If you can pitch in, we could sure use help painting."

The elevator doors opened at the Living Room level, where the buffet lunch featured meatballs, spareribs and London broil. We checked in with Mikey, the elderly ruddy-faced Irish bartender, and set up our trays. Rocco Bennetti was on duty as Room Director and assigned our stations. I was his least favorite Bunny, and therefore wasn't surprised to be consigned to the Cartoon Corner, which was Siberia in terms of distance to the service bar. Savannah and Allie locked in the best tables.

I perched on the back of a chair in the Cartoon Corner and waved to Gloria, who was working the Gift Shop. Bunnies didn't make tip money working in concessions, but Gloria had a knack for selling jewelry and other trinkets with the Playboy logo, so management made it worth her while. Elke was working as Door Bunny, wearing a skimpy white fur bolero jacket over her Bunny costume to ward off the chill draft at the entrance. At precisely eleven o'clock, Bennetti unlocked the front door. The long line of key holders waiting outside in the frigid winter weather surged inside. Fridays were always busy.

Almost two hours later, I was calling out a drink order in the service bar at the height of the lunch crush and looked up to see Mikey standing frozen, the service phone clamped between his shoulder and ear. He'd stopped mid-pour, fifths of Johnny Walker Red and Wild Turkey poised in each hammy fist. He looked at me, his face sagging. Tears spilled from his pale eyes.

"The President," Mikey said. "Shot. They think he's dead." Tears coursed down his face.

"What?" I stared at him. "You mean President Kennedy? What happened?"

Allie, standing next to me, smoking a cigarette and checking her tabs, swung around. "Mikey? What did you say?"

"Our Jack. Someone shot him," he said, "in Dallas."

Allie stubbed out her cigarette, dipped under the partition and lifted the telephone from Mikey's ear. I leaned across the service bar and took the bottles from his hands. He slumped against the back bar and crossed himself.

I turned to Allie, who still had the phone to her ear. "It's true?"

Allie nodded, then turned to Savannah, who had just stepped up to the bar. "It was just confirmed. President Kennedy's dead. Shot in Dallas."

I felt as much as heard Savannah's gasp, and saw her hands tighten on the bar. I looked out across the crowded Living Room and Piano Bar. Bunnies in jewel-colored costumes, carrying trays of drinks, dipped and strutted among the tables, still unaware of the tragic events unfolding in Dallas. Customers, laughing and shaking off the November chill, were pouring through the front door and climbing the brass staircase. Rocco Bennetti was signaling busboys in orange jackets to hurry up and clear plates and cutlery. But here and there I saw a worried look, a shocked face as the staggering news spread from people arriving at the door to others checking their coats, to groups near the circular staircase waiting for tables.

"The President's been shot . . . Kennedy's dead, killed." The room seemed to grow quieter even as a buzz of shock ripped through the

Club. Moments later, the sounds of sobbing and horrified cries broke through the hush. I saw Bennetti's shoulders slump, his hands cover his face.

"I can't believe it," Allie said, touching my arm. "Somebody fired shots at his motorcade and killed him."

"Jackie? What about her?"

With tears in her eyes, Allie shook her head. "That's all I know."

I looked down at my tray, at ice melting in the tumblers. Who had killed him? Why? What next? Would Cuban missiles now fall out of the sky at last? I felt as though everything had been on hold for a long time, awaiting this final blow. Eric dead. Jack Kennedy killed. Could anything worse happen?

I looked up to see Allie standing next to Mikey, her arm across his shoulders. Dazed and red-eyed, Mikey began ringing up tabs and closing out checks. All around me there was movement, the clinking of ice dropping into tumblers. I stepped away from the bar, automatically emptying the watery ice from the glasses on my tray and refilling them with fresh cubes. The Bunnies around me spoke in quiet tones, in disbelief and shock. I called out my drink order and headed back out on the floor. Throughout the Club, Bunnies with tear-streaked faces served drinks, closed out checks.

Eventually the Club cleared and I made my way to the dressing room. With my costume unzipped, my shoes kicked off, I sat with other Bunnies watching a small, black-and-white television screen in the Bunny Mother's office as news unfolded from Love Field, Parkland Memorial Hospital and Air Force One.

It was dark by the time I left the Club and headed home. I crossed Madison Avenue to Park and turned south. The streets were quiet. The few people I did pass wore somber faces, their eyes downcast. I soared up to the Chrysler building and perched for a few minutes, watching people gather outside St. Patrick's Cathedral. Then I made my way home. I slowed to a brisk walk as I turned the corner onto my street.

Ian was standing outside my apartment building, his collar turned up, his face ruddy with cold. He reached for my hand as I approached. "I knew you'd eventually return." He pulled me into his arms and we held each other tightly. "Dreadful news. Dreadful. Are you all right? I had to see you."

His voice was warm breath in my ear. He stroked my hair and I pressed my face against his cheek. "I'm fine. And I'm glad you're here. Come inside. It's freezing cold."

I unlocked the door to the entryway and we walked across the small lobby to my apartment. "I have to warn you, there's nothing to eat. But I do have some Scotch."

"Perfect. A wee drop of whisky will go down quite nicely, thank you. And I'll order out for pizza, if you'd like."

I flipped on the light switch and held the door for Ian. "This is it. What you see is all there is. Let me take your coat because there is actually a closet."

"Charming, and very European." Ian smiled and made a show of spreading his arms, his fingertips almost touching opposite walls of the entryway. "But I wouldn't try moving a piano in here."

Ian took off his coat and muffler. I tossed my shoulder bag on the kitchen table, but it slid off, scattering the contents across the floor. Ian kneeled on the floor next to me, retrieving lipstick, pens and loose change rolling across the tiles. Eric's letter fluttered under the chair. I reached for it, my eyes fastening on the blue airmail envelope. Suddenly Eric came to mind with such force I could barely breathe. I picked up his letter, tears spilling from my eyes.

Ian moved closer, sliding his arm across my shoulders. "It's okay, Meg. Just cry your heart out. This is certainly the time for it." He brushed his fingers across my wet cheeks, then reached into his pocket for a handkerchief. "It's a terrible thing that's happened. The whole world is weeping."

"I know," I said, my voice choked. He mopped my face so tenderly that I smiled even as tears coursed down my face. "Thank you, Ian. Come on, I promised you some whisky. I may even join you." I scooped the remaining items on the floor into my bag and put the thick envelope from Marilyn, containing snapshots and news clippings, on the table with Eric's letter. "No television set, but I can put on some music."

"Excellent. How about giving me a tour and showing me where you keep your coat closet?"

"Right this way. We'll take the scenic route and you can admire the view. Don't blink." I hung our coats in the closet. As I did so, I was suddenly swamped by the memory of that intimate moment when I hung Eric's jacket next to mine. Once again, tears rolled down my face.

"How are you doing? Do you want to be on your own?" Ian's voice was gentle, comforting. He brushed his lips lightly on my cheek and held my shoulders.

"Sorry, Ian. Everything is catching up with me."

"Understood. Let's have a whisky, and I'll be on my way."

"Understood." I smiled. "On the rocks or straight up?"

"Neat, please."

"Good, because I think I forgot to fill the ice cube trays."

Ian sat at the kitchen table while I put my Dinah Washington LP on the turntable. He watched me light a candle, set out napkins and pour Scotch into the cut-glass tumblers.

"First class service, I must say. And I'm expecting a Bunny Dip."

"There you are, sir," I said, setting the glass on a napkin with an elaborate dip. "Always happy to show off."

"Well done. There'll be a big tip in this for you."

"Better be." We clinked glasses and sipped our whisky, listening to "What a Difference a Day Makes" playing softly. "Just twenty-four little hours . . ." The earthy voice and haunting lyrics lingered as the song finished and another began. Then, in the quiet of my kitchen, I began telling Ian about Eric. I hadn't expected to, or meant to, but felt no regret as I spoke. Ian listened without comment, his eyes steady even as I told him I was carrying Eric's baby.

I opened the plump envelopes from home that had arrived in the mail that morning. Both contained newspaper clippings. I spread them out on the kitchen table.

The *Minneapolis Star-Tribune* had run a long piece on Eric, with photographs of Eric's father standing outside his barn, wearing overalls and a bulky jacket; Eric's high school graduation picture; and a snapshot of Eric in his flight gear standing beside a T-28. Only then did Ian reach across and cover my hand with his. I gazed into his smoky gray eyes, at the flecks of golden brown glinting in the candlelight and knew my human emotions were gaining control of me.

"I'm so sorry, Meg. And I'm glad you felt safe confiding in me. When are you due?"

"In the spring. Early May." I heard the soft exhale and knew it had registered that we would not be doing the film together. "In fact, I don't know how much longer I can hold off telling Paul and my agent. It's not going to go down well."

"We'll see. Something will work out. They won't want to lose both of us." His voice grew even softer. "Besides, your baby is more important. There'll be other roles, other films."

I nodded. "I know. It's not the way I wanted things to go, but that's the way it is. I hate letting everyone down."

Ian leaned closer, taking both my hands. "You're not letting me down. And you know I'll always be here for you." He kissed my fingertips, then my lips. "I hope you'll let me. I don't want you to be alone." He cupped my face in his hands and kissed me again.

I pulled back and looked into his warm, kind eyes. He'd let me see how much he cared for me. I was drawn to him, too, but I couldn't encourage his affection. I grieved for Eric, and felt responsible for his death. He would still be alive were it not for me—and Camilla's vengeance. There was nothing more I could say to Ian without revealing what I was—and what I knew Camilla to be. Besides, if I were to tell him, he'd never believe it.

Ian sensed my withdrawal. His eyes clouded over and he pulled back, too. "Meg, I'm very sorry. I'm being frightfully insensitive in light of what you've told me. I don't mean to push myself on you."

"You're not. I wouldn't have confided in you if I didn't trust you." I smiled and jiggled his hand. "And I know I can count on you. You came to my aid in absolutely the worst circumstances. I'm completely in your debt."

"Good. I like the sound of that. But I have a sense there's more you haven't told me. Really, there's no need to hold back. I promise you I won't ever betray a confidence."

I shook my head. "That's it. I've actually told you quite a lot. It's your turn."

"Ah, that can wait until another time." He took a last sip of whisky and stood up. "I'm properly fortified and won't impose myself on you for another minute. I think you'd like some time on your own. I'll give you a ring over the weekend, if that's all right."

"Please do." I helped him on with his coat and walked him to the door. "Call me in the morning, if you'd like."

He leaned down and kissed me again on the lips. "Take care, Meg."

"You, too."

I closed the door, feeling oddly forlorn. I thought I'd feel relieved to be on my own. I looked around my darkened apartment, lit only by the candle on the kitchen table. Dinah Washington had finished her last number. The turntable was still, the room quiet. I gazed at the news clippings, aching somewhere deep beyond reach—for Eric, for John Kennedy and for all the unknowns lying ahead for my baby and me. I thought longingly of Eric, remembering our night together. We'd been like puppies at play, neither of us letting on what we were beginning to feel for each other. If only I'd had a presentiment of what Camilla would do to destroy his life. I could've saved him.

I picked up the whisky glasses to rinse in the sink and saw Ian's muffler looped over the back of the chair. In a rush, I grabbed the scarf and hurried out of my apartment, hoping to catch him before he'd hailed a cab.

I spotted Ian down the street, a dark figure a half-block away, his hands stuffed in his pockets. He was cutting behind a parked car to cross the street near Park Avenue. Suddenly, propelled by intense foreboding, I streaked toward him. Even as I flew down the street, the earth trembled, buckling the pavement. With a splintering crash and terrible thud, the parked car plunged into the depths of a gaping hole and disappeared. I slammed hard into Ian, scooping him back before he, too, could vanish into the crater. Clouds of dust and smoke billowed up. An acrid smell of sewer gas poisoned the air. I felt Ian go limp in my arms. I hoisted him onto my shoulder and retreated a safe distance from the cracked pavement.

I lowered Ian onto a bench outside the apartment building adjacent to mine. He started coming to, coughing, gasping for air. Above us, windows were opening and people were looking out. A siren sounded in the distance. I glanced toward the canopied entrance of my own building and saw Mr. Spichal gaping at me. I realized he'd seen me carrying Ian slumped over my shoulder.

"There's a sinkhole up the street, Mr. Spichal. You better call the fire department. I smelled gas."

"Who's he?"

"A friend. He's okay. Better call emergency."

"You carry man? How you do that?"

"Sometimes you don't know your own strength," I said. "I'll get the paramedics to take a look at him." Ian was leaning forward, his elbows on his knees, catching his breath. "Sorry, Ian, I sort of body-slammed you. Are you okay? You fainted for a moment."

"Just winded, I think. What happened?"

"Take a look." I helped him to his feet and we both peered down the street. Sirens screamed and red lights flashed as emergency vehicles pulled up on Park Avenue. Police were blocking traffic around Gramercy Park, and pushing back residents congregating outside their apartment buildings. "The street collapsed just as you were crossing it. I was trying to catch up to you because you left your muffler behind. I got to you just in time."

"And spared me a nasty fall into oblivion. Thank you very much."

"Just returning a favor. Are you okay? Do you want to see a medic?"

"No need. I suspect I have some bruises. Where did you learn to tackle like that?"

I shrugged. "Years of ballet."

Ian laughed and slipped his arm around my waist. "Remind me not to get on the wrong side of you."

I heard a noise overhead and looked up at a lamppost where a bird, a crow by the size of it, was fanning its broad wings. It cocked its head, looking at me. I knew it was Camilla. This had been her handiwork, of course. I did not shift my gaze, but focused my energy on the streetlight beneath her perch. Within moments the light flared brilliantly, then shattered in an explosion of sparks and glittering fragments. The crow flapped its wings, flew into the air and vanished into the night sky.

Startled by the fireworks, Ian grasped my waist more firmly. "I think that's quite enough for one night. Let me walk you home and I'll find a cab."

"You're sure you're all right?"

"Of course. And whatever befalls me, I can always count on you to come to my rescue, right?"

"Right." If only I could have been there for Eric, too.

Twenty-three

In the weeks since Savannah and Elke announced their joint venture, the former restaurant supply store on the ground floor had been completely transformed. What to call the café had never been an issue. Savannah's one extravagance had been a deep blue awning with bright yellow lettering: SAVANNAH'S HOMESICK CAFÉ. When I arrived early Saturday afternoon, Savannah was supervising Nick and one of his buddies from the fire station, who were installing the awning and a lighting fixture above the entrance.

"Why *homesick*?" I asked.

"It seemed right," she said. "Nick agreed. Haven't you noticed everyone in New York seems homesick for something? Even New Yorkers."

I nodded. "Especially today."

"Nothing will ever be the same. The news just gets more awful. You heard about Jack Ruby? It was on television."

"I saw it." I'd stopped in the café near my apartment and watched a replay of the shots popping, the scuffle among men in hats. The video footage, stark and senseless, had been repeated again and again, making the events of the past few days already seem distant and unreal.

"C'mon inside," Savannah said, squeezing my shoulder. "I'll show you around." She pushed the door open. "Everyone's back in the kitchen working. We got our first orders, so we're trying to get everything set up."

"I don't believe it!" I said, stopping in the entranceway to look at the bright, gleaming dining area. The grim, musty shop interior had been thoroughly remodeled. Nick Westry had pressed a couple of his firefighting buddies into service, removing the cracked linoleum and display cabinets. Wide plank oak flooring had been exposed, and vintage wainscoting was uncovered behind plywood showcases.

"Tearing out the improvements," Savannah crowed, "that's all it took!"

In fact, it had clearly taken long hours of brute strength and painstaking sanding and refinishing to restore the woodwork. Savannah would be feeding the crew from the fire station for years to come to make up for their "volunteer" work on plumbing, electrical and carpentry repairs. Cloth-covered wiring, corroded pipes and worn fixtures had all been replaced. The walls above the wainscoting were painted pale buttermilk. Globe lights hung from the stamped-tin ceiling. A long glass case, a vintage piece acquired from the restaurant supply firm, had been refurbished and installed in front of the kitchen entrance. A hand-painted sign was hung on the wall behind the glass counter: ELKE'S BREADS & PASTRY.

While the kitchen was fitted out with equipment Savannah bought cheaply from the restaurant supply firm, the chairs and tables for the front room were street finds.

There was almost nothing Savannah scavenged that she couldn't somehow rehabilitate. No two chairs matched. The dining tables ranged from a mahogany drop leaf to a pine trestle table. Nothing had been discarded that could be put to use. Jugs, pots and copper kettles that were no longer serviceable in the kitchen became décor. Savannah had lovingly collected vintage knobs, rusty ironwork and handmade square nails and pegs from the renovation debris and stored her finds in an old wooden crate. "Someday I'll make a collage," she said, "and hang it over the bar."

"I thought this was a café," I said. "You're serving drinks?"

"Not in the beginning. You need a liquor license, but someday—why not? For now, just soup, sandwiches and baked goods. We'll only be open during the day."

Since the neighborhood virtually shut down once the wholesale meatpacking establishments closed in the afternoon, it made little sense to stay open past five o'clock. Besides, Elke and Savannah planned to run the place entirely on their own. I was pretty sure that meant the rest of us would be "volunteering" on a regular basis.

In the kitchen, Allie and Elke, both with their hair tied up in scarves, were busy cleaning off newly installed storage cabinets. "Hey, glad you could make it," Allie said, "Grab some rubber gloves. We can use the help."

"Where's Elle?"

"Napping," Elke said. "I'll bring her down soon. How long can you stay?"

I shrugged. "As long as you need me. What about tonight?"

"Noni's show was canceled, of course. I don't think anyone feels like going out for a good time. She's hoping they'll have her on next weekend," Allie said.

"Stay for dinner," Savannah urged. "I've got stew simmering. Nick and a couple of guys from the fire station will be here." She handed me rubber gloves and a sponge. "I'll be back as soon as we get the awning up."

I thought back to my first week in New York, little more than a year earlier, when I'd rushed along the street to the Bunny auditions even as the sky held a threat of missiles striking the city. People around me had walked with their eyes cast down, fearful, not looking at anyone around them. But the day after President Kennedy was assassinated, a pervasive feeling of sadness and shared grief seemed to affect everyone. I could think of no place I would rather be than at Savannah's eating stew with my closest friends.

The week of Thanksgiving, the news that continued to dominate our lives was the death of President Kennedy. *Dark Passages,* along with most regular programming, was preempted by network coverage from Friday afternoon through the funeral in Washington D.C. and interment at Arlington Cemetery.

Following the air show on Wednesday, Paul Abbott was heard on the loudspeaker from the control booth requesting all cast and crew members to immediately assemble in the rehearsal room. Ian and I were both still in costume and sitting on a divan in Lady Fairfax's boudoir when we heard Paul's announcement. Ian tucked his fangs in the breast pocket of his suit and heaved a sigh. "It'll be Henry the Fifth exhorting the troops to take heart and battle on, I should imagine. Everyone's still pretty glum."

Given the events of the past several days, it was a somber group that gathered in the upstairs rehearsal room. An extra coffee urn and platters of cookies had been added to the pastry table for the larger-than-usual crowd. Camilla, who hadn't been in the show that day, arrived for the afternoon read-through wearing a stylish black suit and dark glasses. She brushed past me without a word.

Paul Abbott, in contrast to everyone else, appeared oddly ebullient. If he intended to address the tragic events of Friday he was hardly wearing an appropriate expression. When the room had filled to near capacity, Paul put down his cup of coffee and stepped up on a carton of fan mail so we could all see him. Nigel banged a spoon against the coffee urn and everyone stopped talking.

"Okay, everyone, I know we're all grieving and it's been a tough few days for all of us. Maybe sounding a word of optimism isn't such a bad idea right now, especially when it involves all of us. You know I've been trying to pull together the funding for a *Dark Passages* feature film, and it looks like—well, hey, great news! I just got the word! We'll be going into production late March, early April!" Paul broke into a grin and gripped his hands over his head like a prizefighter.

"Yeah, Paul!" Michael shouted, then gave an ear-shattering whistle. It was a signal for all of us to cheer, applaud, laugh, hug ourselves and each other.

"Hey, okay, everybody!" Paul hollered. "We're all in on this. Can't go ahead without everyone pulling together. It's a five-week shoot on a bone-dry budget, and we gotta churn out five shows a week or the network'll kill us. I'm counting on all of you to pitch in. You with me?" More cheers, whistles, applause. "Great! I got Doris covering my back, and Nigel running the home team here in the studio. Once we go into production, there'll be a lot of traffic between the studio and location. You guys all with me?"

I clapped my hands, along with everyone else. So did Ian, who caught my eye and gave me an encouraging look. I felt terrible, and Ian knew it. I should've told Paul a week ago that his leading lady would be out of commission. What a blow to find out now after he'd raised his budget and announced production. I glanced at Camilla, standing against the far wall, inscrutable behind her dark glasses. How much did she know?

"Anyway," Paul said, "I figured I better let you all in on this because you'll be reading about it in the Trades. Also, we're going to be doing some advance location work soon as we get a big snowfall. Several of you will be involved in those scenes, including Meg, Ian and Camilla. In the meantime, because of preemptions, two episodes will be repeated this week. We have enough shows stockpiled on kinescope to suspend work not only for Thanksgiving, but Friday, as well. I just want to say have a happy Thanksgiving holiday, everyone, and a good weekend. I think we all need to spend time with family and friends. See you Monday."

Ian whispered in my ear, "Jolly good. We can all use a break. Got plans for tomorrow?"

"Dinner with friends. You?"

"My place in Connecticut. On my own, unless you come with me. You're very welcome." I shook my head. "Too bad, but at least join me for a drink at Flinty's. Meet me in the lobby as soon as you've changed."

I knew I could take my time. Ian generally showered after shedding his vampire rig. The cape, worsted suit with vest and high-collared shirt easily brought on a sweat under the studio lights. Ian was mindful of the fans crowding around him when he left for the day. "No sense in putting them off with a pong," he'd say. "A smelly vampire wouldn't do at all."

I slowly climbed the stairs to my dressing room, regretting that I'd agreed to meet Ian for a drink. I doubted we would bump into Camilla, who rarely went to Flinty's anymore since breaking off with Michael, but there was no point in taking chances. The less she saw us together, the better. I changed out of the lacy peignoir and piled my mountain of ringlets on the vanity table for Madge to sort out. I brushed my hair and washed my face before putting on a loose wool shirt and jeans.

I wasn't feeling at all well. I sank back in my chair and looked out the frost-encrusted window at the darkening sky, my head swirling with conflicting emotions. I couldn't stop thinking about Eric. I knew I had to deal with Camilla—but when? How? She'd struck too many times. I couldn't give her another opportunity, one that could be lethal to Ian, or me. I'd cut back on my feeding, and shouldn't have. I couldn't afford to be weak. My human emotions—to say nothing of hormones!—were getting the best of me. And Paul—he had to be told soon. Should I tell him now, before the long weekend? But how could I spoil his moment of triumph? I hadn't the will to face him.

I closed my eyes, trying to concentrate, and instead drifted off. I awoke to a gentle rapping on my dressing room door and wondered for a moment where I was.

"There you are," Ian said, his face peering at me in the doorway. "Having a kip?"

"Sorry!" I bounded to my feet and grabbed my coat. "Did you wait long?"

"Not at all, but I didn't want to brave the gauntlet on my own. Ready to face the mob?"

I pulled my woolly cap on before we stepped out into the cold. A fierce wind whipped up the street, but didn't seem to deter the fans. Ian and I signed autograph books and posed together for several minutes before leaving for Flinty's. A few fans tagged along as we headed up the street to our watering hole, but most remained behind. They knew where we were going, of course, but some unspoken fan decorum stopped them from entering Flinty's with us.

The bar was crowded. The long holiday weekend had lured more of the cast and crew than usual for a Wednesday evening. Ian and I tried to squeeze in, but gave up and settled at a table off the entrance. Ian ordered a lager. I had a ginger ale.

"I hope you're not coming down with something," Ian said, "because I'm bound to catch it!"

"Don't worry. I think I'm just feeling drained after the last few days."

I looked around, glancing across the brass railing into the crowded restaurant area. My eyes stopped at a corner booth in the back. Camilla, striking in her black suit and blond chignon, was sitting with Paul Abbott. Both were drinking martinis and leaning into each other. Camilla was weaving her spell, and Paul looked captivated. I felt a heaviness in my chest, a deep sense of foreboding.

Ian reached for my hand. "You haven't touched your ginger ale. Are you really feeling bad?"

"I'm not good company, Ian. I should go home."

"Then I'll drop you off. I insist."

Ian finished his lager while waiting for the check. We caught a Checker cab on the corner just as the first snowflakes danced in the crisp air. By the time the taxi hurtled across town to Fifth Avenue and turned south, I was gripping the seat, feeling not at all well. When we reached Gramercy Park, I was barely able to slide out of the cab.

"Meg, are you sure you're all right? Let me see you to the door." Without waiting for an answer, Ian stepped out of the cab with me and took my arm. "Driver, wait please—I won't be a moment."

I leaned against Ian, feeling dizzy as I fumbled for my keys. He took them from my hand and opened the door, then walked me to my apartment. "Can you manage? I don't think I should leave you. I'll stay for a bit, if you'd like."

"No, please. I'll be fine. If it's a stomach virus, I've got the whole weekend to get over it."

"You're sure?" His eyes looked worried but he handed me my keys after opening the apartment door.

"Absolutely," I assured him. "Thanks. Have a good weekend."

I closed the door and leaned against it, listening to Ian's footsteps cross the marble entryway. Slowly I sank to the kitchen floor, gritting my teeth, holding my stomach. I gasped at the wrenching pain clawing through my belly and felt a sticky wetness on my thigh. I knew what was happening, had known since I'd felt the first sharp twinges in Flinty's.

I lay on the floor, lifting myself only enough to pull my arms out of my coat and cover myself with it. Curled in a tight ball, I clenched my teeth and strained against the hot, sickening waves of cramps ripping me apart. "No, please no," I whimpered, but I knew it was over. My baby was flowing out of me.

I rested my head on my woolly cap and strained against another spasm as the realization sank in: I'd lost Eric. Now I was losing our baby. I'd let this happen, or made it happen. What had I done wrong? Guilt washed over me in waves, worse than the spasms in my stomach.

I wanted to die. I knew it was possible. According to my mother, childbearing could be lethal for our kind.

Shivering on the cold tile floor, my coat draped over me, I strained against the pain and longed for oblivion. How much blood had I lost? Would it ever stop? My mind roiled as I lay in the semi-dark, gazing at light from a street lamp slicing through the panes of the French windows. The agonizing cramps tore through me with less regularity and I began breathing more evenly. Eventually, with my coat wrapped around me, I made my way to the bathroom.

Later, after I'd cleaned up, I poured J&B into a cut-glass tumbler and sat on my daybed looking out the windows. Snow was falling, a sprinkling of powdery flakes that as I watched grew into thick, wet puffs that stuck to the trees. I drained my glass and set it on the floor, then fell back into my bed and drifted asleep. Again and again, throughout the long night, I would awaken, my mind swarming with fragments of dreams, all of them about Eric, and then drift off again.

When I did fully wake up, my apartment was flooded with morning light. I also realized the door buzzer was sounding. I did not want to see anyone, but crept quietly to the door to look through the peephole. A deliveryman holding a long florist box was impatiently stabbing the buzzer. I unlocked the door and opened it.

"Sorry, Miss. The party insisted on delivery first thing this morning."

"That's okay. Happy Thanksgiving."

I shut the door and carried the long white carton to the kitchen table. Inside the box were two-dozen deep scarlet roses with a card:

Happy Thanksgiving! Feel Better, Love, Ian.

I breathed in the sweet fragrance and smiled.

I'd never received a bouquet of flowers before. I had no vase. I looked around for a suitable container and finally settled on the yellow plastic bucket I used for washing the floor. Arranging the red roses in the yellow bucket somehow cheered me, as did my relief that I had four days entirely to myself. I had already decided not to go to Savannah's for Thanksgiving dinner. I wanted time alone. And I wanted to walk in the snow.

I showered and then dressed in a thick sweater, trousers and snow boots. Just as I was putting on my heavy jacket, the door buzzed. Without even looking through the peephole, I opened the door.

"Happy Thanksgiving," Ian said, smiling warmly.

"Happy Thanksgiving, yourself. I thought you were going to the country."

"I am, but not before making sure you're okay. How are you feeling?"

"Good. I'm fine."

"Excellent, because I'm risking deadly contagion if you're not."

I smiled. "Don't worry. And thank you very much for the roses. They just arrived. Want to see them?"

"I take it I'm being invited inside," he said, stepping into the narrow entryway. "Ah, look at that. Nice vase."

"Serves double-duty. And I wasn't expecting flowers this morning, thank you very much."

"Next time I'll have them include a vase. You're sure you're all right? Because I don't think you are," he said, looking at me closely. "Very pale. More pale than usual."

"No makeup."

"I've seen you without makeup before, you know. Come on. I'm taking you to the country with me. Fresh air. Long walks. Wintry vistas and salt air. It'll do you good. My motor's outside, warm and rarin' to go. You won't need to take a thing."

"Thank you, anyway. But I need a bit of solitude."

"I can provide that, too. Loads of it. It's a huge house, made for hiding from the world. You'll barely see me."

"It's more than that, I'm afraid."

"I see." He looked at me carefully, then wrapped his arms around me. "Meg, I'm so sorry. How are you feeling? Do you need to see a doctor?"

"No, I'm okay, but not really up to seeing anyone."

"But I don't think you should be on your own, either. If you're up to the drive, a change of scene would do you good. I promise you all the solitude you want."

"You're right. How can I say 'no' to that? Give me a minute to make a call and pack a toothbrush."

I rang Savannah and told her I wouldn't be coming for Thanksgiving dinner. I could hear the noisy preparations in the background, and knew I'd hardly be missed at the table. Besides, as much as being alone had appealed to me, so did the idea of getting away from my apartment and all its memories of Eric. A change of scene probably would do me good.

Twenty-four

When Ian said his "motor" was warm, strictly speaking it was. His automobile, a two-seater open to the elements, was not. Parked at the curb directly in front of my building was a dark green sports car with a thick leather strap belting its hood, a steering wheel mounted on the wrong side and doors opening backwards.

"It looks like a toy! Where's the top?"

"Isn't one," Ian said, holding the door for me. "Now that I think about it, maybe this wasn't such a good idea. Will you be all right, do you think? The ride will be a bit rough and windy."

"I'll be fine. No turning back now."

"Excellent. Then hop into me mog and let's be off. The sooner we start out the better. The weather is not in our favor and I left the top, such as it is, in the garage." He dropped my overnight bag in a space behind my seat and tossed a thick muffler in my lap. "Afraid you'll need this," he said, sliding in next to me. "No heater, either. We'll just hope we're not in for a blizzard."

The car, he explained above the noisy growl of the engine, was a 1956 Morgan roadster that belonged to his uncle and "could get a little breezy once we hit the motorway." In fact, a damp chill seeped through my jacket before we reached the corner, but the cold didn't bother me in the least. I settled low in my seat, wound the muffler around my neck and pulled my wooly hat low on my ears so it wouldn't blow off. The Morgan was certainly a novelty, as was the sight of two people riding in an open-topped car on a snowy, frigid winter morning. People stared out their car windows, a few smiling and waving at us.

I pulled the muffler aside and shouted, "They think we're nuts!"

"Jealous!" He grinned. "You okay?"

"Doing just fine."

It was certainly better than sitting alone in my apartment with too much time to think, or roaming empty city streets on a cold, gloomy day. I was feeling well enough, but not up to spending a long afternoon sitting around Savannah's dinner table, keeping up with noisy conversation. I sat back and looked out the window, my eyes half closed against snow flurries flying around my face. The sky was leaden. There was little traffic, and the landscape, largely urban and industrial, flashed past.

An hour or so later, Ian pulled off the throughway and stopped at a gas station.

"Almost there. Want to use the facilities?"

I shook my head and stretched my arms. A blue Dodge pulled up at the gas pump next to us. A middle-aged woman wearing a felt hat looked across at me, then took in the Morgan. She said something to two children rough-housing in the back seat.

They pressed their faces against the window and peered at the car. The woman looked across at Ian, cocked her head and stared. A shock of recognition spread across her face as her eyes traveled back to me. She slapped her hand on her mouth.

She rolled down her window, pointing first at me, then Ian, who was handing cash to the attendant. "I know you! You're—wait, wait, who are you? The vampire, right?" The children froze, fear in their eyes. The man in the driver's seat leaned across the steering wheel and looked blankly at Ian, then at me. Ian jumped back in the car.

"I don't believe it!" the woman said, her voice a near shriek. "It's Sebastian!"

"Happy Thanksgiving," Ian called out, shifting into gear. We pulled away as pandemonium broke out in the Dodge.

"She thinks I've spirited you away," Ian said, pulling out of the service station.

"Well, you have," I laughed. "Those kids will expect to see us on TV Monday in a toy roadster."

"Worse, they'll have nightmares thinking I'm prowling their neighborhood. And they'd be right." Ian had turned down a narrow lane that bordered a rocky shoreline. Ahead, a village with houses and small shops hugged the roadside. A boatyard and several small vessels nestled along the shore. "The house is just up ahead. That body of water is Long Island Sound, and those bulky outcroppings you see in the water are known as the Thimble Islands."

"Perfect name," I said, looking at the rocky bits of land. "I see some of them are inhabited. Are we rowing out to one of them?"

"No, thank God! My uncle had the good sense to occupy a house on the point. The islands are certainly stable enough to build on, but one wouldn't want to be holed up out there during a storm. A hurricane blasted through in 1938 flattening almost everything. And, as a point of interest, the islands are named for the thimbleberry, said to be a sort of black raspberry. Having never seen one, I couldn't swear to it."

Ian made a sharp turn onto a promontory curving at an angle into the Sound. A sharp wind blew off the water as he navigated a narrow gravel road leading to a weathered gate. Light snow flurries had turned into icy flecks that stung my face and clouded visibility.

"There, you can just about see the pile I call home, and none too soon, either! Hang on," Ian said, and jumped out of the car to open the gate.

Looming above a stand of trees, almost blending in with the sullen, darkening sky, was a gray shingle house with a chimney and railed widow's walk on its roof. Ian jumped back in the car and drove down a slope, coming to a stop under a portico. "Just go inside and warm up. The door's unlocked."

I hurried up the steps and looked back to see Ian setting the bags on the veranda. He climbed into the Morgan and headed toward a shingle garage at the foot of the gravel driveway. I grabbed the bags, just making it to the door before an onslaught of icy rain slashed across the veranda. I shook off the sleet clinging to my jacket and pushed open the front door. It was warm inside, and smelled of roast turkey and spice. I pulled off my jacket and hovered in the darkened entranceway, waiting for Ian and breathing in the smells of Thanksgiving.

"That was cutting it close," Ian said, bounding through the door and shaking himself like a wet puppy. "Time for a whisky, I'd say." He flicked on lights and hung up our jackets. I saw we were standing in a roomy wood-paneled entryway. Framed watercolors of Stony Creek Harbor hung on a wall above a long trestle table. A tray piled with mail occupied a corner of the table next to an earthenware bowl of apples. A large enamel jug overflowed with an autumn bouquet: golden chrysanthemums, cattails and field grasses.

"You must've had elves at work. How did you manage to get dinner in the oven and arrange fresh flowers?"

"I'm a clever sod, aren't I? I rang the neighbor woman who cleans for me. That's actually part of her own family dinner we'll be eating. Very gracious of her."

I followed him down a hallway into a big farmhouse kitchen with high ceilings, vanilla-colored walls and well-worn wood plank floors. A drop-leaf kitchen table and two chairs occupied a nook in front of casement windows with brass latches. A pine sideboard, scuffed and sagging with an odd assortment of plates, cups and bowls, took up almost an entire wall. A rugged-looking stove, with pots on the back hobs, stood next to the pantry. Ian reached into a cupboard above the stone sink, took out two glasses and set them on a butcher-block side table.

"Now don't expect a lot. This place is ridiculously run down, but I rather like it that way."

"So do I. Don't change a thing," I said, peering out the casement window at a broad expanse of rough, rain-pocked ocean. "It reminds me of home, except we look out on fields instead of water. But we have a veranda running around the house, and a sun porch. I bet you don't have a storm cellar, though."

"Actually, yes, there is something of the sort. My uncle used it as a wine cellar." Ian took a bottle from the sideboard and inspected the label. "Bless him for leaving behind quite a nice store of decent plonk."

"Plonk? That's what you call wine?" I started to laugh, imagining my father wrestling a cork out of a bottle before we sat down to dinner. "We never drank anything fancy back home. Iced tea. Water. The first time I went out to dinner in New York with my agent, Wesley Truscott, I ordered milk. He was horrified. He told me I must never, ever drink milk except on breakfast cereal. He ordered a glass of rosé for me instead. I don't think I would have drunk it if it hadn't been pink. It was a bit sweet and looked so harmless I had a second glass and almost slept through the play he took me to. Sorry, I'm babbling."

"Not at all. Don't mind me." Ian had opened the bottle of wine and was carefully pouring it down the inside of a glass container. "Are you going to join me for whisky, or would you like a glass of wine? We might even have a spot of milk in the fridge, if you want to indulge yourself."

"Tempting, but I'll have wine."

"Excellent. While I get drinks organized and a fire going, why don't you settle in. Your room is at the top of the stairs, first to the right. I'll show you around the rest of the house later. Feel free to take a nap, if you'd like."

I left Ian puttering in the kitchen and returned to the entryway to pick up my bag. The house was eerily quiet, the only sound a muffled creaking of the carpeted treads beneath my feet as I hurried up the stairs. I turned right on the landing and pushed open the first door I came to. A chill draft swept across the darkened room as I entered. I heard a faint rustling. Mice? Could I resist? I'd eaten nothing all day.

But then I realized the rustling sounds were drapes billowing at an open window. I pulled the fabric aside and breathed in the chill, pungent smell of the sea before pulling the sash down. Stormy winds twisted tree branches and flattened wet leaves on the windowpanes before gusts ripped them away again.

I turned on a brass bedside lamp and looked around. Framed color plates of herbs hung on walls papered in a faded cornflower pattern. A rocking chair with a chintz pad sat on a braid rug between a walnut bureau and matching dresser with a mirror. I flipped my bag open on the bedspread, wondering how long Ian had occupied his uncle's house. I grabbed my sponge kit, and a towel and washcloth that was set out on the dresser, and went in search of a bathroom.

At the end of the hallway I found an airy black-and-white tiled bath that served all three bedrooms on the floor. I washed my face and brushed my hair, but didn't bother with makeup. I glanced in the mirror and saw that Ian had been right. Although I was feeling better, I looked more pale than usual.

Following the smell of burning logs, I went downstairs into a wide, cozy living room. A fire crackled in a massive fieldstone fireplace, its mantel lined with framed photographs. A large threadbare rug, faded and patched, covered the stone floor in front of the fireplace. A couch and several armchairs were grouped around a long driftwood coffee table on which Ian had set out a plate of cheddar, sliced apple, walnuts and crackers.

At the far end of the room, windows looked out on the Sound. Off to the left, glass doors opened onto what appeared to be an atrium with a glass-topped table and wire chairs. Ferns hung in baskets from the ceiling, and an assortment of plants stood on open metal stands. I stood for a moment breathing the musky, fragrant scents.

"We could sit in here, but it's better on a day when light streams in," Ian said, entering with a glass of whisky for himself, red wine for me. "Welcome and cheers!"

"Cheers to you." We touched glasses. I took a sip of the wine, its flavor bursting in my mouth. "It's wonderful! I know I'm being spoiled."

"It's the whole idea. There's a cellar full of good stuff waiting to be drunk. My uncle Joe, Communist that he was, saw no reason not to drink well. I think he intended the cellar to see him through old age, but instead it may have hastened his demise."

"Communist? Really? Are you one?"

"No," he laughed, "and my father was a diplomat. I come from a rather odd family. My father and uncle never got on. Opposites, really. Now both are dead. Let me show you something."

I followed Ian out of the atrium to a door off the living room that opened into a library. Books lined three walls, floor to ceiling. A mullioned casement window above an upholstered seat looked out on a rock garden. An oval table with two leather club chairs took up much of the room. Ian opened a drawer in the mahogany table and took out a cigar box.

"My uncle Joe, the younger brother, left home to fight Franco in the Spanish Civil War and joined up with the Lincoln Brigade. Eventually he landed in the Colonies, as my father referred to these American shores. This place in Stony Creek became a safe house for fellow travelers." Ian opened the cigar box and ran his finger through a thick pile of coins, military medals and small mementos. "All souvenirs from my uncle's 1937 excursion in Spain, the highlight of his life, he would tell you."

"He never returned to England?"

"Ah, this is the tricky bit. The family's not actually English, although my father was briefly an ambassador to the Court of St. James. I went to boarding school outside London." Ian took my glass from my hand. "Let me pour you some more. I see you like the *Pétrus*. And, why not? It's about as good as one could drink. I'll join you."

We went back into the living room. Ian poured wine from the decanter and we settled into armchairs in front of the fire. I realized there was something Ian wanted me to know about him, and that he was carefully setting up his story.

"The thing is, this will all come out eventually. Perhaps quite soon, with *Dark Passages* taking off the way it has. One's background always comes up when the press starts sniffing around. The English tabloids can be quite ferocious once they get wind of something. One wouldn't want to have one's livelihood destroyed over something one really had no control over. Know what I mean?"

"I do." I sat up and put my glass on the table, wary that Ian somehow knew more about my own situation than I'd thought.

"I know you have your own secrets. At least, I've guessed you do. I'd like to see what you make of this, as there could be significant ramifications."

"You mean the blacklist? Being a Communist?"

"Oh, God, no! Not me. I think I'm well clear of anything like that. No, it has to do with my family." He stood up and took a framed photograph from the mantel. "My father and his brother were Rumanian. This is the only picture I have of them together. You can see my father is taller and quite a few years older than my uncle. Because of that difference in age, they really belonged to two different generations. My uncle had nothing but contempt for the world of my father and grandfather. You see them here, standing in front of what was then the family home. A fortress, really. One of many, I might add, on the border of Transylvania. Upon my grandfather's death, my father became a baron."

"And now you're a baron? Baron what?"

"Well, it's all meaningless now. As a title, I mean. The communists took over in 1948 or so. Broke my father's heart. My uncle's, too, since he considered himself to be a communist in good standing, while the regime looked upon him as exiled aristocracy, a danger to the state. They wanted no part of Baron von Dracul's family."

"Dracula? That's your family name?" I almost laughed, but the look on Ian's face sobered me. "I'm sorry, I got it wrong. Your name is Fletcher, of course."

"My mother's name. She was South African. They lived in Switzerland after the communist takeover of Rumania. Both were killed in a car crash in the Gotthard Pass when I was away at school."

"I'm so sorry. And Joe, your uncle?"

"Josef by birth. He went by the name Joe Smith most of his life. He died two years ago. I spent a few weeks every summer with him, but he was very much a loner. He felt duped and abandoned by the Cause. Lived very much like a hermit. Collected butterflies. Ran his lobster pots. Drank."

"Is it the Count Dracula part that worries you?"

"That, and my bad luck to be cast in the role of a pirate who turns into some sort of Bela Lugosi character. All that Count Dracula rot was made up. Clever fiction, of course, but there are no vampires in the family closet, I can assure you. Imagine such a legacy! My father was the last Baron von Dracul, not a count. And no, we didn't live in Dracula's Castle. I'm rather proud of the old man. I would hate to see all of that dragged up and ridiculed because I'm playing an idiotic vampire in a soap opera. This whole vampire nonsense is complete myth! I hoped to avoid any sort of association like that by taking the name Fletcher."

"I completely understand." This was not the time to come clean with Ian and tell him that his houseguest was, in reality, a vampire. "I mean, I changed my name, too, though not because of any sort of family history. I come from a long line of Blatches. My real name is Margaret Blatch."

"So that's your secret? Your family name is Blatch? Not so bad."

"Bad enough." I polished off my wine and was grateful to see Ian refill my glass and his own. We lifted our glasses in a silent salute and drank.

"Do you mind eating in the kitchen, Miss Blatch?"

"Not at all, Your Excellency. I'd like it. My family in Twin Lakes is probably finishing up dinner in their kitchen about now."

"Would you like to call them? Please do. You can call them while I put everything on the table."

"You're sure you wouldn't mind? It's a trunk call."

"The telephone is on the table in the hallway. Call them. Talk as long as you want."

While Ian went to the kitchen, I walked down the hall to call home. It occurred to me that my mother would have invited Eric's father to join them for Thanksgiving dinner. Clarence lived just down the road. I suddenly missed home and wished I could have been at the dinner table with them.

My mother answered. I could hear the clatter of dishes in the sink and knew she was washing up. "You just missed your father and Clarence. They're out in the barn putting chains on the truck. We've got a blizzard coming in tonight. How are you?"

"Not so good. I lost the baby. Last night."

"I'm so sorry," she said. The clattering stopped and I heard her deep sigh. "If you need me, I'll come out. I can be there right away."

"I think I'm okay. Thanks, Mom."

"Have you fed? Because you need to do that. You're vulnerable now, and there are things you should know. It was a human child you carried. A nonhuman would not have expelled easily. You would have needed my help. Are you alone now?"

I cupped my hand around the receiver, muffling my voice. "No, I'm with a friend. But go on. I'm listening."

I could hear Ian in the kitchen, opening cupboards, preparing our dinner. What would my mother think if I told her Ian's family secret? If Ruth had a sense of humor, I'd be tempted to tell her. But then, what would Ian say if he knew the truth about my mother and me? Baron von Dracul and Uncle Joe, the Communist, were quaint relics compared to the family history I could relate.

Twenty-five

The moon was almost full, a great silver sphere illuminating the night sky and splashing Long Island Sound with a milky sheen. The snow had stopped falling, the winds calmed. I pulled the sash down farther and breathed in the fresh sea air from my guestroom window.

Ian and I had sat up very late, cracking open walnuts and polishing off a second bottle of red wine in front of the fire. Even if I could remember the names of the wines and vintages in Uncle Joe's cellar, I doubted my bank account could afford such indulgence. I smiled, recalling Ian's pleasure in serving me dinner. The neighbor lady had done the cooking, but it was clear Ian knew his way around a kitchen.

"I learned to fend for myself early on," he'd said. "I figured there had to be something better than school food. Cabbage, mutton and tapioca with treacle is pretty grim fare."

He'd set the old pine table with good china and heavy silver, and cleared the sideboard for serving. We'd eaten slowly, serving ourselves seconds, then thirds, talking, laughing and looking out the casement windows. The storm had already begun to ease by early evening. Gently falling snow powdered the landscape.

After stuffing ourselves, we'd cleared the table and washed up, enjoying each other's company. Now that I'd got to know Ian better, he was anything but a grim soul, certainly not the cheerless person I'd taken him for in the beginning. To his fans, he was the embodiment of the tortured wraith he played on *Dark Passages*, the gloomy vampire with the penetrating eyes, who skulked in the shadows. They would never have recognized the goofy clown who danced me into the living room in a giddy Strauss waltz. Nor could they have imagined his brilliant impersonations of George Harrison, his favorite Beatle, or Elvis Presley. But the most appealing discovery was the depth of Ian's compassion. Settled in front of the fireplace, with glasses of red wine, he'd gently led me into talking about Eric. I did so, and with joy, recalling the good times we'd had together.

"You know, I've dealt with a certain amount of painful loss in my own life," Ian said, "beginning with my parents when I was just a lad. It was a beloved headmaster who said to me, 'Young man, we come into this world alone, and we leave it alone, whatever our attachments may be during our lifetime. There is a certain majesty in accepting that and making the very best of things.' Anyway, his words have served me well when I needed bucking up."

"Thank you, Ian. I'll try to remember. But I deeply regret how short my time with Eric was. And I can't help feeling responsible for his death."

"But you're not! You can't allow yourself to think that." Ian leaned forward, resting his elbows on his knees and looked at me intently. "The survivor always suffers guilt. My parents were on their way to pick me up at a small airstrip for a winter holiday when they perished. Of course I felt responsible. But there's nothing I could have done to prevent the accident. There's nothing you could have done, either."

I listened and nodded. The admission had slipped out of my mouth, and I had no way of explaining to Ian that I was, indeed, responsible for Eric's death. I also realized, with great sadness, that with Ian there would always be this gulf between us. I tried to think of something to divert the conversation.

"Are there any attachments in your life now?"

"Any attachments?" He laughed and rocked back in his chair. "Oh, that is such a girly thing to ask!"

"No! Ian, I didn't mean it like that!"

"You didn't? I'm sorry to hear that. I was hoping you were burning to know."

"Sorry, it was the wrong thing to ask."

"I do love seeing you flustered. Anyway, *no* is the clear answer. There was someone a while back. She upped and married someone else, a university mate of mine. Broke my heart. But, *c'est la vie*, and all that. Besides, I've had quite a lot on my plate dealing with my uncle's estate, which is the primary reason I returned here. *Dark Passages* came along at a good time, the perfect sort of diversion."

"Diversion! We're a hit, in case you hadn't noticed. You're locked in for some time, Ian."

"Suits me," he laughed. "Who would have guessed?"

It was in that lighter moment that our eyes caught for that inevitable flash of assessment. Friendship had been firmly established, and perhaps something more. But later. Another time. I took the last sip of my wine and stood up. "By the way, do you like strudel?"

"Of course," he said, looking surprised. "Sorry I can't offer you any."

"That's okay. I'd love you to meet some friends of mine. They're about to open a bakery. Why don't you come with me to the grand opening next week?"

"I believe that's a roundabout way of asking me out on a date. You are being girly." He smiled and took my glass. "Of course, I'll come." He leaned over and kissed me on both cheeks, then on my lips. "Goodnight, Margaret Blatch. Sleep well."

"I will, Baron. Thanks for everything." I kissed him back and went upstairs, feeling as good as I had in months. But I would not be going off to sleep.

I was glad Ian had urged me to call home, and grateful I'd been able to speak with my mother privately. Her instructions were precise. I knew what I had to do.

I stood at the bedroom window a few more minutes, breathing in the brisk sea air and collecting my thoughts. Despite all the turkey, sweet potato and good red wine, I would have to remain alert, stay focused. I pulled the sash halfway up and left the bedroom, slipping quietly across the hallway to the landing. Ian's bedroom was downstairs off the library, so there was little chance we'd bump into each other, or that he'd even hear me moving about. I didn't want to have to explain my nocturnal ramblings.

Ian had told me to explore the house on my own, and I had. Earlier in the evening, as I climbed the stairs, I'd noticed a narrow door at the top of the landing that had an old brass latch instead of a knob. I'd pulled it open, expecting to see shelves stacked with towels and linens. Instead, I was greeted by a blast of cold air. I was about to push the door back on its latch when I saw that there was a spiral staircase. I knew instinctively that the iron steps must lead up to the railed widow's walk I'd glimpsed on the rooftop when we arrived that afternoon.

Now, in the silence of the night, I pulled the cupboard door open and climbed the short flight of steps. At the top, I pushed up a hinged lid and scrambled onto a small, square landing. I hunched over the railing for a long while, looking at the sheen of moonlight on the ocean meeting inky sky on the horizon.

The longer I gazed ahead, the more I focused on the stillness inside me, welcoming the calm after such turmoil. So much had happened so fast, been too significant and life changing. I'd worked hard to keep my worlds separate and orderly. All I'd really accomplished was scrambling to keep up with everything unforeseen. Now, the touchstones that had guided me in the past few months were no longer relevant. Eric would not be coming back. I was no longer carrying our baby. Suddenly there was nothing governing my life. My future was as opaque as the haze of moonlight on the water.

I'd let my human emotions overtake me. My life was in disarray. It was up to me to chart a course, one that would be sustainable for me as a nonhuman living in a human world, just as my mother had done. Ruth fully embraced her human life, but also exercised her superhuman gifts. She had found a balance, and a human mate. I had squandered a chance at such an existence by not recognizing the relentless power of a vengeful adversary: a rival not of my making, who was intent on destroying me and those close to me. I had human gifts, too, but in order to realize my potential and bring order to my life, I would first have to vanquish the powerful enemy stalking me. To do that, I would have to hone my warrior skills.

My immediate need was to feed. I had to restore my depleted energy and supplant the human hormones that had weakened me. As Ruth had coached me to do, I shed my corporeal state and assumed a vaporous form. I drifted along the shoreline, then followed a stream into a thick wooded area near a granite quarry. I wafted above the rock, a wispy cloud in the treetops. Below, a white-tailed deer stepped through the pebble-strewn creek bed, paused and raised its head, sensing danger. Above it, a mountain lion crouched on a granite ledge, its tawny pelt and black-tipped ears blending with the stone. Flexing imperceptibly, the cat rose on its haunches poised to strike.

I reconstituted shape and streaked down even as the beast, claws extended, leapt toward its prey. In a blinding flash I snatched the deer before the mountain lion could plunge its teeth into the animal's neck. I slammed my hand into the lion's snout. Its head snapped back with a terrible crack, the muscular body twisting midair, then landing on its back paws in the creek bed. I unhinged my jaw, breaking the neck of the stunned deer and fed greedily. The cat shook its head, wobbling drunkenly, then steadied itself, fixing its murderous eyes on me. With a soft hissing sound and low growl, the cat lowered its head, straining back on its haunches.

I thrust the deer aside, crouching to encourage attack. The cat sprang, as did I, our weights matching pound-for-pound. Its claws tore into me as the cat tried to thrust its teeth into my neck. I gripped its throat, twisting the neck back until it snapped, then sank my teeth into its sinewy flesh. Bloodied, my own naked flesh torn, I flexed my muscles and held the cat's torso in my arms as I drank. When I finished, I left my prey, dead and still warm, on the creek bank.

Fed and revitalized, I sprang high into the treetops, leaping through the thick canopy of branches until I reached the end of the forest. I flew high into the clouds, streaking through the skies as far north as Maine, before circling back to the waters of Long Island Sound. Dawn glistened on the horizon as I plunged into the deep ocean waters. The salt cleansed my wounds, healing the deep rips in my flesh. I swam among sharks, cutting through the depths in dazzling twists and switchbacks before surfacing, refreshed and energized.

Morning sun had risen in a crystalline sky and sparkled gem-like on the vivid blue ocean. Sunshine glinted off the rooftops of the village and danced across the glassy mounds of snow on the rocky shore. I swam on the ocean's surface, long laps back and forth from the pier to a buoy, concentrating on my long, clean strokes.

Looking toward land, I saw Ian emerge from the back door of the kitchen and stroll onto the veranda, a steaming mug cupped in his hands. He sipped, then tipped his head back, looking up at the clear sky and out across the water. Suddenly, in an almost comical gesture, his jaw dropped and he jerked forward, sloshing coffee out of the mug.

"Meg! For God's sake, what are you doing out there?" he shouted.

Startled, I began dog-paddling in the water, my head bobbing in the waves. How had it not occurred to me that if I could see him so plainly on shore, he could see my naked flesh plowing through the water? I raised my arm and waved. "Hi, Ian."

Ian gaped at me, then shouted, "Get in here! It's too cold! You'll freeze to death!"

"Coming. Can you get me a towel?"

"You're crazy!" Ian set his coffee mug on the veranda railing and raced inside.

I speed-paddled to shore, glancing down at my arms and torso to make sure I'd healed. I could only blame any lingering gouges on a shark attack, and that would entail more medical attention than I could risk. Fortunately the ocean had washed me clean of any blood, and there were no visible signs of my battle with the mountain lion.

Ian raced down to the rocky shore with a pile of towels as I emerged from the water. He tossed a towel to me, managing to look both angry and astonished. "You're mad! Completely off your rocker! What would possess you to go skinny-dipping in sub-zero water? How long were you out there?"

"Good morning to you, too. You know, once you're in, it's not that cold." I wrapped the towel around myself, and took another for my hair. "But I should have remembered to take a towel."

"Very funny, aren't you?" Ian was apoplectic. "Is this what the natives do in Minnesota? Unless you're part polar bear, you'll have hypothermia! For God's sake, let's get you inside. Go!"

He grabbed my arm and hauled me up the steps to the veranda and the back door of the house. Once inside, Ian hurried to his bedroom. "Dry yourself off! I'm getting you slippers and a bathrobe."

I wound a towel around my hair and patted my legs dry. I wasn't at all cold, but I shivered appropriately when Ian returned with a thick terrycloth robe and felt slippers.

"In my wildest dreams it would not have occurred to me that you'd go for a swim." He held the robe and I slipped my arms through the sleeves. "You cannot be in any sort of condition to do something so idiotic. You've just miscarried. I mean, you did, didn't you? Because I believed you." Genuine doubt crept into his eyes. His face looked pinched.

"Yes. I did. I'm sorry, Ian. It was a stupid idea."

"Granted." He looked at me a moment, assessing my sincerity. I had to let him make up his own mind because there was no explanation I could give for my confounding behavior. The divide between us was once again evident. How had Ruth ever come clean with my father? Or had she?

"Okay," Ian said at last. "Let's go to the kitchen. It's warm in there and I've got coffee brewing."

I followed him, my feet swimming in the slippers. I knew better than to kick them off. I climbed up on a kitchen stool and patted my hair dry as Ian poured coffee.

"You know, I'm deeply sorry for all you've gone through, Meg. If you are feeling despondent, I couldn't blame you. But had you set out to drown yourself, I don't know that I could handle it. You must tell me the truth. What made you go out in the ocean?"

"It's nothing like that. It was just a whim. I'm really sorry I worried you. Please forgive me."

"Forgiven. But, here's the thing. We both thought you couldn't do the film. Now, given the circumstances, you can. We're both committed and Paul is counting on us. Let's try to concentrate on something positive, all right?"

"Yes. I promise." I sipped my coffee, realizing just how difficult it was to manage balance and order, especially getting human emotions right. It hadn't occurred to me how much I had distressed Ian.

"Good, because the reason I was up so frigging early is that Paul called my answering service and left an urgent message. You probably got a call, too, but your service doesn't know where to reach you. Anyway, I got the message and rang him back. The gist of it is that heavy snow is forecast for next week. Paul is setting up a shoot to take advantage of the weather. He needs snow for a pivotal sequence."

"Amazing." I shook my head. "What a difference a day makes."

"Yes. You're back in play." Ian ruffled my damp hair. "Just try not to catch pneumonia for Paul's sake. He'd be very unhappy. And, by the way, so would I. How about some breakfast? An English breakfast, mind you, not your vegetable patch on a plate."

"Serve it up!"

I'd already had my breakfast. But all things considered, I could hardly turn Ian down. While he cooked, I hurried upstairs to retrieve my clothing from the widow's walk and got dressed. While I was at it, I packed up my few belongings in my overnight bag and set it by the front door.

Ian's idea of an English-style breakfast turned out to be sausage, eggs, thick-slab bacon, sautéed mushrooms, grilled tomato, toast and strong tea with milk. We settled at the kitchen table near the window and ate slowly.

"By the way, you know who's bankrolling this shoot?" I shook my head. "Camilla, believe it or not. Paul confided in me this morning. I don't know that she's funding the whole budget, but she's kicked in enough for next week."

I put my toast down and stared. "Where'd she come up with the money?"

"She's a witch."

"I know that, but where did she get the money?"

"No, I really mean it. The lady has to be a witch. She somehow got Emmett Boardman to bequeath her his millions."

"He was married."

"Maybe it will be contested, but Paul claims she's rolling in Boardman's fortune. I suspect her role gets sweetened. Lord knows what she's exacted from Paul in exchange for the dough. By the way, I think Paul regretted blurting all this out and asked me to keep it to myself. We should probably not say anything."

"Of course. Not a word." The news gave me pause. Camilla didn't do things out of the goodness of her heart, assuming she had one. There was an ulterior motive.

When we finished our breakfast, I told Ian I'd like to take the train back to the city that morning. "If we're filming next week, I'm sure Paul is sending over a script. I'd like the time to read and prepare."

"It's up to you, of course, but you're welcome to stay the whole weekend. You'll be skipping out on my roast pork and crackling tonight. Were you afraid we'd be having turkey hash?"

"Of course not! There were no leftovers, remember? But I'm sorry to miss the roast pork and more lovely wine."

Ian drove me to the New Haven train station before noon, and presented me with a bulky carton tied with cord. "Hope you can manage to carry this," he said. "A little souvenir of the weekend and something you desperately need."

I was back in my apartment by early afternoon. I set the box on the kitchen table and cut the cords. Inside was a tall pale green pottery vase with a relief of pink flowers on the side. A note was tucked in the mouth of the vase:

My darling polar bear, you are a delight! You are welcome in my home anytime. Love, Ian

I stood for a moment, turning the beautiful vase in my hands, then filled it with water and transferred Ian's roses from the yellow plastic bucket.

For weeks I'd been mentally rearranging my apartment, figuring out how to accommodate a bassinette and all the other things I would need for the baby. It would be a squeeze, but I would manage until Eric and I figured out what to do. I placed the vase with the bouquet of roses on the coffee table and sat on my daybed. I looked around the studio apartment, mentally erasing the changes I'd intended to make. There would be no changes. Except that I would no longer have to keep such a close eye on my bank account. Or work two jobs. I could also invest more money with Elke and Savannah now that I would soon have a movie contract, too.

I sat for quite a long time before I realized I was still wearing my heavy jacket. My overnight bag was propped against the door where I'd dropped it. I started to take off the jacket, then decided to walk down to the corner store for the newspaper. The air was crisp, the sun warm on my face as I stepped out of the building.

I started to cross the street to walk through the park when I saw a young man in an Air Force uniform turning the corner. He was tall like Eric, but stockier. His hair was dark, not ginger. My heart skipped a few beats imagining Eric in Air Force blue, striding along the street toward me. I watched the young man coming nearer, then realized his eyes were on me. He stopped.

"You're looking for me, aren't you? I'm Meg Harrison. Margaret."

"Yes, ma'am. First Lieutenant, Gary Metzer, ma'am. A friend of Eric's."

"From Ohio, I'll bet."

"Yes, ma'am. I came by a couple of times earlier, but you weren't in. I'm catching a train in a little while, but hoped I could see you."

"Of course. I'm glad you came by." I reached back in my pocket for keys, then changed my mind. "How would you like to sit in the park? It's a bit chilly. Do you mind?"

"I'd like that, ma'am. The park suits me fine."

We crossed the street and entered the park, neither of us speaking until we'd settled on a bench that caught some warmth from the sun.

"Call me Meg. I just got back from Connecticut. I'm really glad you came by again, Gary. I appreciate it. You were supposed to go to Saigon with Eric, right? He wrote me about that."

"We didn't go, ma'am." His eyes flicked down for only an instant, then looked back to mine with what seemed to be sheer force of will. When he spoke, his voice was strained. "We promised each other, and that's why I'm here. Eric would do the same for me. I couldn't let him down."

"I understand. What happened to him? Are you allowed to say?"

"He was flying Close Air Support, low and slow, when a bird struck the craft. Sounds crazy, ma'am, but it happens. His 'chute deployed but he didn't stand a chance. A medevac chopper brought him in, and—sorry, ma'am. I promised him if anything happened, I'd get this to you. Like I said, he'd do the same for me." He reached inside his jacket. I saw that his arm was stiff and he was missing a thumb. He produced a small packet tied in brown paper. "These things were in his pocket. And he'd given me a letter."

"Thank you. Thank you so much." He handed me the packet. It felt warm, almost alive, in my hands. "Gary, what about you? Tell me, how are you doing?"

"I'm fine. Good. My girl is meeting me at the station and we're going up to see her folks." Realizing the significance of what he was saying, he shook his head and looked down. "I'm so sorry. Eric talked about you all the time. He couldn't wait to get back. I'm sorry he didn't make it home."

I nodded, realizing that Eric would have been home now, too. He would have come back at the same time as Gary. "I understand. But you take care of yourself, okay? I know how hard this has to be. It means a lot to me."

"Thank you, ma'am." He stood. "I have to go, but I'm glad you were home. I owed it to Eric. I owe him a whole lot." He turned and walked away quickly, his shoulders slumping only slightly at the park entrance as he disappeared from sight.

I loosened the string and the soft brown paper fell open. Inside, nestled in a pale blue handkerchief, was Haddie's Zippo lighter with its distinctive camouflage markings. I'd felt the shape and weight of it in the packet, and knew I would find it. I wrapped my hand around it, not wanting to see it. If only it had done its job! Or perhaps it did—as much as it could.

I drew a thin square of blue onionskin from a small, narrow envelope and read:

My dearest Meg. If you should get this letter, please know that I am telling you now what I should have written to you many times over. I love you. I carry you in my heart every moment and dream of the day when you are again in my arms. I pray I'll soon be at your side, that we can be together always—and that this letter will never be in your hands. I kiss your eyes, your lips, your body and soul. Yours forever, Eric.

I read the letter again, then carefully refolded it and tucked it back in its envelope. With the lighter warming in my hand, I sat back and imagined seeing Eric flying high over the treetops, skimming across cornfields and dazzling me with his freckle-faced, lop-sided grin.

A breeze ruffled my hair and I heard a soft, familiar voice in my ear. "Sorry to intrude, Meg. I think you know what's ahead. We need to be prepared."

"Camilla, I know. You'll be with me, Haddie?"

"Of course. I won't ever let you down again. That was nice work with the mountain lion. You're taking possession of your gifts. You'll need them. She's set the stage. It's just a matter of time."

"But why? Why did she have to take Eric? Or go after Ian?"

"Or attack your father and grandfather, for that matter? It's a settling of scores, the origins of which are of little consequence. Nothing will appease her thirst for vengeance. It's warfare, one battle following another until you stop her once and for all. You must vanquish her, as Ruth and Sarabeth failed to do."

I nodded and closed my hand around the lighter. Again, the soft voice whispered in my ear. "Keep it close to you at all times, my dear," Haddie said. "D-Day is upon us."

Twenty-six

Paul Abbott's rise as a television producer wasn't so much meteoric as instantaneous. It was the ideal medium for him: he was a born pitchman and knew how to close a deal. He'd worked his way through college selling vacuum cleaners, insurance policies and encyclopedias door-to-door, coming face-to-face with the most sales-resistant customers on the planet. By the time he took a job selling television commercial airtime, he was a skilled operator. He hadn't been at the network more than a couple weeks before he set his sights on becoming a producer.

He began by scouting his best entry into the ranks and settled on daytime television. He button-holed the network executive in charge of daytime programming and boldly asserted that afternoon viewing was stale fare: tired game shows and dull soap operas that were little more than animated radio scripts.

"You got something better?" the executive barked.

"You bet," Paul said, and took the opportunity to spin a tale based on a dream he had that he thought would make great daytime drama. "Something mysterious, a girl on a train going to a place she's never been to work as a governess for people she's never met. We throw in a ghost, 'cause the place is haunted, sort of a twist on *Jane Eyre* and *The Turn of the Screw*. And get this," Paul said, "I hire a real movie star to play the *grande dame*, someone classy who'll pull in the housewives."

"We can do three game shows on that kind of budget, and pull in housewives by giving away cars and refrigerators. Sponsors donate the stuff and we can do it on the cheap. All we need is a front guy and a model demonstrating the merch."

"Give me the same budget and I'll give you first-class drama."

Within months, after jumping over some ratings hurdles, Paul had the hottest show in daytime. That, in a nutshell, was the story Paul told in every media interview he gave. Among the major contributors to his success, he acknowledged, were Horace Milton and Doris Franklin. Together they facilitated Paul's every whim. It could be argued that with their mentoring, Paul was also on his way to becoming their equals in both writing and directing. His film script, with some tinkering from Horace, was gripping, and no one doubted his ability to direct it.

And his salesman's instincts were still intact. He'd cut deals on equipment, signed cast and crew on the cheap and found bargains on props and wardrobe that would allow him to film a thirty-day schedule on a miniscule budget. Incredibly, he'd managed to secure permission to shoot on location at an old robber baron's estate on the Hudson River, a landmark operated by the National Trust—and got consent to build additional sets on the grounds. A dilapidated barn, scheduled to be demolished, had been quickly converted into the exterior of Sebastian's Old House guest quarters on the Stanhope estate.

By pushing to shoot the wintry exterior sequence by week's end to take advantage of a heavy snowfall that was forecast, pre-production work was carried out at breakneck speed. Paul rallied his troops with such fervor that everyone leaped on board at dirt-cheap pay with little negotiation.

Moira Shaw, who hoped to command her former Hollywood salary, signed on for union scale, plus ten percent for her agent. Since Ian got top billing, Moira demanded an "And Moira Shaw" end credit, which she considered some sort of victory. Camilla was given an "Introducing Camilla Nesbitt" separate card despite the fact that more than half the cast members were newcomers— including me! But then I hadn't bankrolled film production.

That Camilla had put up the money was apparently not generally known. Paul hadn't officially announced the source of his financing, and Ian and I agreed we should say nothing about it. A rewritten script was circulated on Wednesday, in which Camilla's role had been substantially expanded. The plot now centered on the great love affair between the witch and the vampire. Poor Lady Fairfax, suffering unrequited love, leaped to her hasty demise less than halfway through the script.

But was getting a larger role Camilla's sole objective in providing financing? There had to be a reason for funding the shoot other than just satisfaction in playing Paul's Lady Bountiful. She was setting the stage, but for what? I was mindful of Haddie's warning that D-Day was near—and kept his lighter on me at all times.

The major exterior sequences requiring snow were shots of guests arriving for the costume ball, the prelude to Gwyneth Fairfax's deadly jump. Most of the regular cast was required for these scenes, but the network balked at forfeiting another day in the studio.

Therefore, we would be shooting on Saturday. Once again, Paul was lucky all around. The heavy snowfall began early Friday and continued until late evening, allowing snowplows time to clear streets and highways during the night.

Moira, Ian and I, all living on the East Side in relative proximity, were to have a studio car pick us up between 4:45 and 5:00 in the morning for the drive to the location. I stood outside my building in pre-dawn gloom waiting for the car that was picking up Ian first. Moira had insisted upon being last. I wasn't at all prepared for the stretch limo with tinted windows that turned the corner and cruised to a stop at the curb in front of me. The driver, wearing a natty uniform and cap, clapped his hands with cold as he hurried to open the door for me.

I stepped in and saw Ian lounging on a plush leather seat in the rear of the cavernous limo. He grinned. "Camilla must've thrown in some loose change at the last minute. Paul spared no expense. If you want a highball, there's even a wet bar."

I laughed and plopped next to him. "Terrific! I could get used to this movie star stuff."

"You want to run lines?"

"Sure. Sebastian! Sebastian, where are you?"

"Gwyneth, Gwyneth!"

"No! Help! Aaaaaargh! You want to run them again?"

"I think we've got 'em down. Ah, the movie star life. I didn't even mind getting up this early."

Moira, bundled in a sable coat, matching hat and dark glasses the size of hubcaps, strolled out of her Park Avenue building carrying a dainty Tiffany shopping bag that no doubt contained her daily ration of homemade soup. Her doorman and the limo driver vied for the privilege of escorting her to the car. She stepped in and eased herself into a seat, wafting a cloud of Chanel N°5.

"I must say, this is more like it," Moira said. "I was imagining an out-of commission school bus with bald tires. Of course, dear Louis B. Mayer always sent a car for me."

"Well, it's another first for me," I said. "What's it like acting in a movie, Moira? Any tips?"

"As lovely Spencer would say, 'don't act'—quite good advice, really. Otherwise, don't move your face around too much, or shift your look from one eye to the other. Hit your marks and mind your posture. That's about it." She unbuttoned her sable and peered at us over her dark glasses. "Rather generous of Camilla to finance this little snowbound shoot, *n'est-ce pas*? Paul desperately needed a sample reel to snag investors."

I glanced at Ian. "Some secret."

"I think he's told everyone. In confidence, of course," Moira said. "So exuberant, like a puppy chasing his tail. Paul so reminds me of darling young Orson Welles in our Mercury Theatre days. Orson loved bamboozling people."

"So Paul doesn't have financing for the whole film?" Ian asked.

"Apparently not. But this is a good ploy. The Trades will be full of it." Moira rummaged around in her voluminous handbag and took out a folded newspaper and ballpoint pen. "Anyway, an hour should give me just enough time to finish the morning crossword."

As we approached the gated entrance to the estate, Nigel, wearing a hooded parka and boots, waved a walkie-talkie to flag us down. The limo driver lowered his window and Nigel stuck his head in.

"Morning, kiddies. Everybody bright as buttons? Paul's already got cameras set up under the portico, shooting dawn for dusk. We have another limo pulling up behind yours, forming a procession."

"We're filming without wardrobe and makeup?" Moira asked, her throaty voice sounding panicked.

"You won't be seen inside the car. It will just look like party guests arriving. Paul doesn't want tracks in the snow until he's got the shot. Then you'll go directly into makeup. Breakfast is already set up in the downstairs kitchen."

"My God, I hope Paul's filming right now," Ian said, lowering a back window. "It's a glorious study in black and white. Look!"

I looked over Ian's shoulder and caught my breath. The rolling grounds of the estate were covered in a smooth blanket of glittering white, with thick shelves of snow clinging to the trees and wrought iron fence. Looming in the distance was the dark hulk of the neo-Gothic mansion. The first smudges of pale dawn were creeping up over the peaked roof and towers, limning the massive structure in a ghostly sheen. As we watched, lights were switched on throughout the house, every window glimmering brightly to welcome guests attending the Stanhope costume ball.

"He's shooting even as we speak," Nigel said. "When you've got the Almighty serving as your set designer, you make the most of it. 'Scuse me." His walkie-talkie crackled and he stepped away.

I glanced out the rear window and saw we'd been joined by the other limo that had transported Maxwell, Camilla and Michael. Nigel hid himself in the shadows of the stone archway and gave a signal. The tall iron gates opened and our limo rolled forward toward the portico. Despite tinted windows obscuring us, Moira applied lipstick and slipped the tube back into her handbag before our car glided past the camera.

An assistant director waved our car around to the side of the building. The limos pulled up to a freshly shoveled walkway near a side door and we all piled out. I glimpsed Camilla emerging from the second limo, bundled in a hooded coat and dark glasses. Michael looked half asleep, but appeared to be sober. Maxwell, who had affected some sort of alpine look, wearing a loden coat and matching hat with a feather, waved jauntily.

Moira took the arm of the assistant director and led us up the walkway. "Your name, young man?"

"Brian, ma'am. Mind your step everyone."

We trooped through the side entrance, following Moira and Brian down a stone stairway.

"The servants' entrance, of course," Moira said, gripping a handrail. "No heat, alas, and breakfast in the cellar. One does long for the old days on the studio back lot with a decent commissary nearby."

"One more bit of bad news, Miss Shaw," Brian said reluctantly. "The pipes froze and the sewer backed up."

Moira stopped in her tracks. "Not at all nice. Are we meant to wear galoshes down here?"

"We should have it under control by now. You and Miss Harrison go into makeup first. Unfortunately our makeup and hairdressing people aren't quite here yet. Mr. Fletcher and Mr. Faraby into wardrobe. Everyone else can have breakfast until we call you. "

Moira and I were ushered into a whitewashed room fitted with zinc counters, tubs and vintage laundry equipment. An alcove had been set up with lights, two portable makeup tables and chairs. Still wearing her sable, Moira settled into one of the swivel chairs and removed her fur hat and dark glasses. From the depths of her bag, she produced a handsome crocodile makeup box and set to work.

"Always go on location fully equipped," she said. "Monty Westmore kitted me out with emergency supplies. Feel free to help yourself."

A swarthy plumber, packing up his tools, looked at her and asked, "Say, aren't you Moira Shaw?"

"I used to be," Moira sighed, sponging foundation on her forehead.

Amid considerable chaos, everybody somehow managed to be ready by the time Brian reappeared to hustle us up to the entrance foyer for a blocking rehearsal. The shot being set up was Sebastian's arrival at the costume party, cantering across the snowy landscape on a black stallion, his trademark cape billowing. Camilla would alight from a limousine and, as the camera pulled back, the rest of us would be revealed hovering in the grand foyer. Members of the Stanhope clan were costumed in lavish satin, velvet and brocade finery. As Margie, the governess, I wore one of the more modest frocks found in the attic trunks, an unadorned gray silk dress with long sleeves.

The camera crew was setting up the elaborate tracking shot as we arrived. Paul, rumpled and unshaven, looked as though he hadn't slept in a week, and probably hadn't. His voice was a tired croak as he made the rounds, greeting us and explaining the shot. "Gotta do this in one long take," he said. "It's MOS, so I'm gonna talk you through it. Let's get 'em marked, here!" he bellowed, his voice cracking.

"MOS?" I whispered to Moira.

"Mit out sound," Moira and Maxwell chorused.

"No boom mic," Michael explained. "No sound recorded."

"We've got one day to squeeze in a lot of setups," Paul rasped. "Let's walk it through. Rehearsal, please. Where's our lovely Camilla?"

"Here I am!" With a swish of silk, Camilla appeared in the doorway looking radiant in an ivory silk gown and embroidered velvet cape. Paul's glower transformed into a reverential gaze as he hurried to her side. "Such fun!" she beamed. "I've so been looking forward to this day."

"I understand we have you to thank for making it possible," Maxwell said.

"Oh, dear! Paul, did you tell everyone? I was meant to be a silent investor."

"Cat's out of the bag," Paul wheezed, taking her hands in his. "Without you, we wouldn't be here."

"Hear, hear!" Michael said, and began applauding. We all joined in as Camilla waved her hands in winsome dismay. "No, no, please! I'm just thrilled to be a part of this."

"Then let's do it," Paul said, speaking barely above a whisper. "Camilla, you're just outside the door, on your mark. We'll pick up a shot of you getting out of the limo later. Let's rehearse camera, everything except Ian on the horse. Action!"

We rehearsed the shot several times, before going for a take. Across the snowy field, in front of the newly constructed Old House façade of the barn, Ian appeared astride a black horse.

"Quite a dazzling spectacle," Maxwell murmured to Moira. "Now I see why the dear boy is arriving on horseback."

Ian did indeed look spectacular, a dark and romantic figure framed against the expanse of gleaming snow. But why had the scene been altered to have him arrive on horseback? While it was cinematic, there was hardly a need for him to work up a sweat getting to a party when he was a houseguest on the Stanhope estate.

I glanced at Camilla and caught her staring at me intently, her gaze fierce. The moment our eyes met, she looked toward Ian, her lips moving imperceptibly. What was she doing? Had she set the stage for another accident? Seized with alarm, I slipped my hand in my pocket, wrapping my fingers around Haddie's lighter.

Paul called "Action!" In the distance, Brian, with a walkie-talkie pressed to his ear, signaled Ian and slipped back behind the barn. I held my breath as the horse trotted out across the field. Then, without warning, the horse broke its canter and started galloping.

"Stay with it!" Paul barked.

The horse pounded through the snow toward camera, then reared up, wild-eyed and whinnying, its front hooves raking the air. Everyone gasped as Ian was almost thrown from the saddle. Miraculously he managed to hang on. The horse reared again, Ian's cape flaring as the animal bucked.

Vapor rose from the horse's forehead, encircling its neck. The horse began to calm and I knew Haddie was at work. Within moments, Ian regained control. The animal snorted and stamped, then trotted up to the portico. Ian dismounted and Camilla rushed into his arms.

Paul called, "Cut!" and there was pandemonium, everyone noisily surging toward Ian. "Brilliant!" Paul said. "My God, did we get it?"

"Got it," the cameraman said. "Beautiful!"

I caught sight of Haddie, a faint apparition in a curl of steam rising from the panting horse. He fixed me with a solemn look that I took as a warning of worse to come. I rushed to Ian. "Are you all right?"

He nodded, his face ashen.

"Of course he is," Maxwell said. "Magnificent, my boy! Dazzling!"

"Damn good," Michael said. "Where'd you learn to ride like that?"

"You see, Meg? You worry too much," Camilla said, with a faint smile. "What did you think would happen?" She turned abruptly and walked toward the makeup woman, who was waiting to touch her up. I followed.

"Seems to me I have something to worry about," I said quietly, aware that the makeup woman was only steps away, ears attuned. "Why did you do that to Ian?"

She turned and gave me an incredulous look. "Are you saying I'm responsible for that little mishap?"

"I know what you are. And I know what you did to Eric," I said, my voice barely a whisper.

"Eric? Now, who would that be? A friend of yours? In any case, I know what you are, too. Would you like everyone to know?" She glanced at the makeup woman, then back at me. "You're hardly in any position to threaten me, are you?"

"Why are you doing this?"

"Because I can. I want to. And you can't stop me."

Camilla turned and sauntered over to the makeup woman, who glanced at me with a look that indicated hissy fits between actresses were nothing new to her.

"Okay, everyone, let's move it along," Nigel said. "We're setting up for Camilla's arrival by limo. Ian, stand by. Everyone else take a break. We've got some bad weather rolling in, so let's try to wrap up early."

The limo driver hurried over to grasp Moira's hand. "It's been a privilege driving you, Miss Shaw. Sorry I won't have the pleasure of taking you home again."

"Why not? Where are you going?"

"After this take, it's back to town and off the clock. Sorry, ma'am."

"Quite all right. I knew it was too good to be true. You hear that, Maxwell? We'll be piled into an orange school bus for the trip home."

"Grim," Maxwell said. "But I'll share my flask."

I pulled Ian aside. "Typical, isn't it? Everybody's moving on without giving a thought to you. You're sure you're okay?"

"Just grateful to be alive. It's the nightmares that'll kill me. I still can't believe I got that horse to settle down."

"You were terrific!"

Ian shook his head. "I ride, but I don't do rodeos. I'm lucky to be alive."

True, and we had Haddie to thank for that. While Ian went back on the set, I threw a heavy shawl over my dress and went to investigate the building to be used for Lady Fairfax's leap into oblivion. The exterior of the old barn, which had been converted into the façade of the Old House, was the original Stanhope mansion and the home of Sebastian Stanhope in the late 1700s.

In the television series, Lady Fairfax fell off a cliff onto rocky shores. In the film, the venue had been changed to the roof of the Old House, the scene of a magnificent party hosted by Sebastian.

Charmaine du Champs, the witch, uses sorcery to enchant Sebastian Stanhope, destroying his betrothal to Lady Fairfax. During what was to have been their engagement party, Gwyneth Fairfax is lured to the roof, where she is trapped and accidentally plunges to her death in the snowy courtyard. Her death is deemed a suicide. Sebastian's guilt is intense and he enrages the witch with his grief. She curses him, condemning him to an undead eternity as a vampire in perpetual search of his lost love.

My mother would not be a fan of the movie version of *Dark Passages*, but there was nothing I could do about it.

I took the long way around to the rear of the barn so as not to make tracks in the snow. The set up for the shot would have to begin immediately after the lunch break. We would start losing light by mid-afternoon, with the sun setting before 4:30 P.M. Another snowfall was forecast, and the sky was already darkening. The barn itself was essentially open to the elements, with sagging walls and great gaps in the roof. According to Paul, the building was beyond restoration, and not worth the effort for landmark preservation purposes. It had little architectural significance and been constructed long after the mansion was built.

The sturdiest part of the set construction was a staircase built directly behind the two-story façade. I began climbing, occasionally glancing down at the debris-strewn interior. When I reached the platform at the top, I looked across the grounds to the portico, where filming was just wrapping up. The limos were turning in the circular drive, heading toward the gates. Paul was talking to Ian, Nigel and Camilla, all of them heading toward the main entrance. Ian happened to look up and stopped short when he saw me. I waved. Everyone looked across to the Old House and waved, except Camilla, who hurried inside the house. Paul gestured toward the barn, and the camera crew started packing up their gear. Nigel, Paul and Ian started walking across the field toward the Old House set.

Evidently, with the sky growing darker by the minute, Paul had decided to rehearse the scene with Lady Fairfax before the lunch break. I walked around the platform, getting my bearings, thinking about the scene. My Gwyneth Fairfax costume would have a velvet cape with a hood, and shoes with French heels. I lifted the shawl over my head and turned back toward the stairs when suddenly I lost my footing.

The attack, when it came, was swift and fierce. The shawl whipped out of my hands and I was pitched onto my back. I rolled across the walkway so fast I couldn't stop myself. Somehow I managed to grab onto the edge before tumbling off the platform. But I had no leverage. My head was dangling over the rough wooden ledge.

I glanced down at the figures striding across the snowy field and saw Ian break into a run. I struggled to maneuver myself back onto the platform. Where was my strength? Whatever power was forcing me off the platform was not visible, had no form. It had to be Camilla. But where was Haddie? I fumbled for the lighter, pressing my hand on the pocket of my silk dress. The lighter had no warmth. Something had happened to Haddie!

I managed to raise myself on one elbow and roll onto my stomach. I saw Ian racing toward the Old House and feared that he was somehow in more danger than I was.

"Get back!" I shouted. "Stay back!"

He heard me. He paused, then started running again.

"No!" I shouted again. "Stay there!" I was thrown back onto the platform, my arms pinned by some invisible force.

Before Camilla could completely incapacitate me, I streaked out of my body in search of her. At the speed of light I infiltrated the mansion, at once permeating every room. I instantly spied Camilla in a recess of the attic hunched over a wooden tabletop practicing her diabolical craft. In the frail light of a dormer window, I saw her twist the woolen sweater I'd left in the wardrobe room, stretching it over the edge of the table.

Ian's muffler was around her neck. In a bell jar, an undulating vapor spread itself against the glass. I knew it was Haddie trapped inside. Fierce as a gale-force wind, I shattered the dormer window and overturned the bell jar, freeing Haddie in a rush of vapor. In the same instant, I ripped my sweater from Camilla's hands.

She shrieked with demonic rage, clutching Ian's muffler. Dematerializing in a spectral haze, Camilla propelled herself through the window into the storm-darkened sky, trailing Ian's muffler. I whirled after her, an icy blast of wind that sent her spinning toward the Old House. Below, I saw Ian stumble in the frozen field of snow and fall to his knees, panting for air. Paul and Nigel raced to help him back to his feet, all three battling a sudden onslaught of snow and ice. Camilla snapped the muffler, then twisted it in the wind, even as she spun in the sky. Ian grabbed at his neck, fighting for breath.

With a thunderous clash that rent the sky in a storm of ice and flashing light, I walloped a cyclonic gust into Camilla's spinning dervish, thrusting her against the façade of the Old House. The impact sent a shudder through the wooden frame. Momentarily stunned, Camilla's ghostly presence hovered in a suspended state within the eye of the whirlwind. The muffler, whipped from her grasp, fluttered like a leaf to the snowy field, releasing Ian from its grip.

With Ian safe, I took no chance that Camilla could recharge. I spun icy shards into the column of air, whipping her spectral being high above the platform, then slamming her down on the rough wood. I regained my own form just as Camilla reshaped. Her ivory silk dress was in bloody tatters, her face lacerated by wind and ice. With a high-pitched shriek as fearsome as a howling wind, she lunged at me, her hands clawing at my face. I twisted away, striking her jaw with a heavy blow. She fell back and came at me again, punching at my eyes. Half obscured in a blizzard of snow and ice, we slipped, fell and fought each other on the narrow platform until I hurled her onto the stairs with such force the façade creaked and swayed.

Camilla tumbled backward, regained her footing and lunged, falling against the loose façade. With a terrible wrenching sound, the new construction separated from the stairs and crashed to the floor of the barn. Arms flailing, Camilla shrieked as she plunged backward off the steps into the wreckage below. I streaked down after her, landing on my feet next to her bloody, broken body impaled on splintered lumber. Her eyes were glassy, her mouth slack, oozing blood.

"Finish it!" Haddie said, his phantom presence materializing at my side. "You know what you have to do."

"She's dead, Haddie. It's done."

"She's returned before and will do so again. This is your chance, Meg. For Eric. For Sarabeth. Hurry!"

I heard the shouts in the field outside, heard Ian call my name. I pulled Haddie's lighter from my pocket and flicked the flint wheel. Flame burst forth in a great blue streak, incandescent in the gloom of debris and wreckage. The splintered wood caught fire immediately, fanned by the wind howling through the remains of the old barn. I turned away from the heat of the flames and walked out into the field, not looking back.

Epilogue

As Moira had predicted that morning, *Variety* and the other trade papers were full of stories about our snowbound shoot on the Hudson—but she could never have imagined the extent of the media coverage around the world by that evening.

Adhering to the old adage, "If it bleeds, it leads," even Walter Cronkite's news broadcast led with the tragic death of Camilla Nesbitt, whose body had been recovered in the fire-gutted wreckage of an old barn used as a set for a feature film based on *Dark Passages*, daytime's highest-rated show. According to authorities, the cause of the blaze was still under investigation, but initial indications were that the fire had been ignited by a freak winter lightning storm.

I was interviewed extensively as the "brave survivor of the catastrophic fire, who escaped from the burning building after courageous attempts to rescue her costar." One reporter referred to me as "plucky." There happened to be film on hand to support his contention. The camera crew, preparing to set up the shot of Lady Fairfax plunging to her death, witnessed the drama unfolding and filmed it.

Obscured by the blizzard, dim figures of Paul, Nigel and Ian are seen battling their way across the field, while Camilla and I are faintly visible on the platform, apparently struggling in fierce winds to assist each other to safety. I'm seen supporting poor Camilla, who then falls from my grasp. Moments later, I'm running from the burning building as it's consumed by wind-whipped flames.

The intense conflagration was seen for miles. In no time the estate was inundated with fire trucks, ambulances and news crews. My biggest struggle, after racing to stop Ian, Paul and Nigel from trying to rescue Camilla, was persuading everyone that I did not require medical attention. In fact, I adamantly refused it.

The first thing I did when I eventually got back to my apartment was to call my folks in Twin Lakes. They'd already watched the *Evening News with Walter Cronkite* and, according to my mother, their telephone had been ringing off the hook.

"Thank God, you're safe," my father said. I could hear the catch in his voice when he added, "You did your best to save your friend, but I can't bear to think it could've been you."

"Yes," my mother said. "I'm very proud of you. You're quite certain about Camilla?"

"I am. She perished in the fire."

"I see. You've been through quite a lot, Margaret. You've handled yourself very well. When will we see you again?"

Words of praise from my mother were so rare, it took me a moment to find my voice. "Thanks, Mom. Everything's sort of up in the air. I hope soon."

In fact, nothing was certain in the following weeks except that *Dark Passages* had become the most popular, talked-about series on television. The network took advantage of the show's newsworthiness by having all of the cast members appear on various talk shows. I was a mystery guest on *What's My Line*, Moira appeared on *Girl Talk*, and Michael flew to Hollywood to do *The Dating Game*. Ian appeared on *The Tonight Show with Johnny Carson*, securing its all-time highest ratings.

A single mention in Earl Wilson's *New York Post* column that Ian and I would be attending the grand opening of the Homesick Café was enough to pack the place to the rafters. Thanks to the feverish zeal of a young network PR woman, news crews showed up. The café was even featured in the food section of the Sunday edition of *The New York Times*. Savannah and Nick Westry took advantage of the grand opening to announce their engagement, with a wedding planned in the spring.

Elke and Savannah were only the first of my friends at Playboy to turn in their Bunny ears for keeps. Jolly, who'd attended NYU while working as a Bunny, left for grad school at Stanford. Allie got a job as a weathergirl on a local station in Cleveland, and Noni hooked up with a jazz combo that played clubs in Chicago.

"Who knows," she laughed, "I might end up playing the Playboy Club circuit!"

Gloria became a booker with a new modeling agency. We all agreed that Savannah's Homesick Café would be Bunny Central, our clearinghouse and mail drop so we wouldn't lose touch with each other.

Christmas day fell mid-week. Paul Abbott promised us a long holiday weekend, giving me five days for a trip home. The moment I heard, I called my folks.

"We hoped you'd be here," my mother said when she heard the news. "I so wanted a family Christmas!" There was a click on the line and I knew it was my father. I could hear him breathing, and knew he'd hurried from the dining table to pick up the extension phone.

"We can see what you look like on television, but it's not the same as a visit," my father said. "We sure miss you. Your brother wants to say something."

Eddie took the receiver, his voice cracking as he greeted me. "When you come at Christmas, could you bring me a Playboy Club key ring?"

I laughed. "You bet. Are you as tall as Dad yet?"

"Taller," he said, his voice going deep. "And some ashtrays, too."

"You better not be smoking!"

"He's not!" my mother said. "Here let me put Clarence on. He's having supper with us."

"Hey, Margaret, how ya doing? Sounds like we'll be seeing you pretty soon," he said, sounding so much like his son it could have been Eric speaking to me.

"Can't wait to see you," I said, trying to keep tears from seeping into my voice. "How're you doing? Okay?"

"Yup. Hard, though." His voice broke, and I could hear him swallow hard. "Got your nice letter. You come see me when you get back. You'll do that?"

"Sure will. See you at Christmas." I curled up on my daybed and hugged my pillow. It had been tough listening to Clarence's voice, its timbre and rolling vowels so much like Eric's. And I realized how much I missed everyone back home. I'd pack up Playboy Club swizzle sticks, ashtrays and a key ring for my brother, and a few *Dark Passages* scripts to dazzle Marilyn's sorority sisters. But I'd also spend some time with Clarence, and visit Eric's graveside.

Ian had invited me to come to the country with him for Christmas, promising me "roast goose with a good claret, a proper English plum pudding and loads of vintage Champagne."

"Save it for New Year's and I'm yours," I'd told him.

The evening before I left for Twin Lakes, Ian and I walked up to Flinty's to join Paul Abbott for a drink. "How about if I pick you up at the airport when you come back from Twin Lakes next week," Ian asked. "I'll even put the roof up on the Morgan."

"It's a deal. And so is New Year's in the country."

"Excellent!" Ian said, taking my hand. "We've got quite a lot to celebrate."

Including, it appeared, filming a feature of *Dark Passages* in the spring. Looming over everything in those frenetic weeks after Camilla's death was Paul's determination to raise financing for the film.

"I don't mean to be ghoulish," he confided to Ian and me over drinks at Flinty's, "but the kind of publicity we got can be a boon or turn everyone off. In this case, it worked. I've got a studio lined up at twice the budget and we're set to start shooting in May. Poor Camilla, so generous, so keen to see it happen, and now she won't be in it. Very sad." Paul raised his glass, "To Camilla, wherever you are, thank you."

I didn't like to think about Camilla, wherever she was, but I raised my glass anyway. "To Camilla. Rest in Peace."

"Yes, to the beautiful Camilla," Ian said, and we clinked glasses. "You know, Paul, you could honor her by dedicating the film to her."

"I was thinking about that," Paul said. "By the way, I had an odd call the other day. Did you know Camilla has a brother? A kid by the name of Damon. Turns out he's an actor, too. I told him to come in and see me after Christmas. Maybe we can find a role for him."

"How about that," I said, setting my glass back on the table. "Camilla has a brother."

Also by Kathryn Leigh Scott

The Bunny Years
Dark Shadows Memories
Dark Shadows Companion
Dark Shadows Almanac
Lobby Cards: The Classic Films
Lobby Cards: The Classic Comedies

Author/actress Kathryn Leigh Scott grew up in Robbinsdale, Minnesota, and now lives in Beverly Hills and New York City with husband Geoff Miller. She continues to work as an actress and has completed her second novel.

Please visit the author's website: **www.kathrynleighscott.com**.

Ms. Scott is available for Book Club chats on Skype.
Email: **pompressweb@gmail.com**